Roisin Meaney was born in Listowel, County Kerry. She has lived in the US, Canada, Africa and Europe and is now based in Limerick city. She is the author of numerous bestselling novels, including *The Restaurant*, *It's That Time of Year* and *The Anniversary*, and has also written several children's books, three of which have been published so far. One Saturday a month, she tells stories to toddlers and their teddies in her local library.

She is a fan of random acts of kindness and believes in the power of kindness to change mindsets. With a friend, she manages the Random Acts of Kindness Limerick page on Facebook, where RAKs are shared and celebrated.

www.roisinmeaney.com   @roisinmeaney

www.facebook.com/roisinmeaney

Life
Before Us

Roisin
MEANEY

HACHETTE
BOOKS
IRELAND

First published in Ireland in 2022 by HACHETTE BOOKS IRELAND

First published in paperback in 2023

1

Cataloguing in Publication Data is available from the British Library

ISBN 9781529355710

Typeset in Book Antiqua by Bookends Publishing Services
Printed and bound in Great Britain by Clays Ltd, Elcograf S.p.A.

Hachette Books Ireland policy is to use papers that are natural, renewable
and recyclable products and made from wood grown in sustainable forests.
The logging and manufacturing processes are expected to conform to the
environmental regulations of the country of origin.

Hachette Books Ireland
8 Castlecourt Centre
Castleknock
Dublin 15, Ireland

A division of Hachette UK Ltd
Carmelite House, 50 Victoria Embankment, London EC4Y 0DZ

www.hachettebooksireland.ie

Dedicated to the brave and passionate people of Ukraine

Alice

IT WAS GOOD NEWS. NO, IT WAS BETTER THAN THAT. It was great news, marvellous news. Liz and Emmet were thrilled. She'd never seen them looking so happy. Middle of September, they'd told her, and this was the middle of March, so Liz was just three months gone. Married ten years, probably time for them to start a family. All good.

Well, mostly good.

The only tiny thing, and it really was of no consequence, was that Alice would have to find someplace else to live. Not that they'd said anything, not yet, but a baby would make them a family, and a tenant would become surplus to requirements. They'd been glad of her when she'd moved in, glad of the help with the mortgage repayments on their newly acquired house, but now, ten years later, Emmet had his own company, and Liz's move to the bigger dental clinic would have helped too. They didn't need Alice any more.

At her lunch break she rang Tina and told her. 'I'll have to find a new place to live.'

'Or maybe you won't,' Tina said. 'When is she due?'

'September.'

'There you go. You and Chris will be moved in somewhere by then.'

'What?' She laughed. 'What are you on about?' Waiting for more. Lapping it up. Letting on it hadn't crossed her mind, despite the big obstacle.

'You'll be going out a year in September, won't you? More than a year. Of course you'll be living together. I'd say it'll happen in the summer.'

'You're forgetting about his mother.'

'Not for a second – but it's time he cut those apron strings, Alice. He needs to live his own life.'

'She can't be left on her own, though. Not full-time, I mean.'

'And that's why they invented nursing homes.'

'Ah, Tina, he couldn't do that to her. She's only in her sixties.'

'Alice, have you actually met the woman yet?'

'No …'

It was ridiculous. She knew it was. Six months without laying eyes on his mother or setting foot inside his family home. Give it another while, he'd say, anytime Alice hinted at a meeting. She's going through a rough patch – so he and Alice had never spent a night there.

The other option was to bring him back to Liz and Emmet's house, but Chris had vetoed that too. It would put you in an awkward position, he'd said, when Alice knew it wouldn't, but he'd stood firm. Instead he'd told her about a pal with an apartment in the docklands, so they met there whenever the pal was out of town. It was, Alice supposed, furtively exciting, even if the place was shabby, and not very romantic.

But Tina was right; something had to change. The more she thought about it, as Friday afternoon crawled by, the more she resolved to move things along. She wouldn't nag, she'd simply ask, firmly, to meet his mother, even if it was just briefly. She'd do it this weekend.

The thought of the weekend caused a happy leap inside her. Their first away together, Chris's first time to have Saturday and Sunday off work since they'd started going out. A neighbour coaxed to keep an eye on Mother, everything in place. They were only going as far as Courtown in Wexford, because he'd spent holidays there as a child. He'd booked them into a little hotel; she felt another flare of excitement at the thought. Their first time waking up together, in a bed they could stay in all day if they wanted. Twenty past two, the clock on the wall told her. A couple of hours and she'd be off home to get ready.

And then her phone rang, and she saw his name on the screen, and instantly she felt a clutch of alarm. He knew better than to ring her at work unless it was urgent, particularly when they were meeting later. Please let his mother not have taken a turn. Please let him not be calling to cancel the weekend.

She swept a quick glance about the silent waiting room. Three out of four heads were bent towards their devices, everyone engrossed, except for David Ryan, seventy-two and prone to mouth ulcers, who was gazing off into space, arms folded.

She lifted her phone and pressed answer. 'Hi,' she said, in the undertone she used when she took a personal call at work. 'All OK?'

'Are you in a relationship with Chris Delaney?'

Unexpected. Not Chris, a female voice, the question snapped

out, hostile-sounding. Was it his mother, using his phone to tell Alice to leave her son alone? No, the voice was surely too young, too healthy. And then another thought flashed into her head: something terrible had happened to Chris. This was a medic, or maybe one of his colleagues, ringing to break bad news to Chris's girlfriend. Not hostile, just stressed.

She swivelled her chair to block out the patients. 'Is something wrong?'

She heard a kind of snort, or maybe a throat clearing. 'Is something *wrong*?' Her question repeated, the voice now filled with what sounded like scornful incredulity. 'You could say that. You could put it that way.'

Alice's stomach clenched. This was no medic, or work colleague. This wasn't that. She gripped the arm of her chair. The waiting room was far too quiet. She imagined ears pricked behind her. 'What? What's happened?' And why the anger, from someone who must be a total stranger? What on earth had Alice done to deserve it?

And then it came.

'What's happened is Chris is *married*. He's married to me. I'm his *wife*.' Each final word snapped out, in that same tight, infuriated tone.

Alice frowned. What she was hearing made no sense. Of course it wasn't true, she knew that – and then she twigged, and breathed out.

'Tina – God, you had me fooled. Look, I have to go, there are people here. See you next week.'

'*Don't* hang up! Don't you *dare* hang up!'

Louder. Shriller. On the point of disconnecting, Alice tensed again. 'Tina? Seriously –' She darted a glance around the back of her chair. No change in the postures, but she sensed the listening ears. 'Cut it out, Tina,' she murmured. 'Joke over.'

But hang on – it couldn't be Tina, not on his phone. What was happening? Was this real, or some nightmare? She couldn't think straight.

'I'm not *Tina*. My name is Janice Delaney. I'm married to Chris Delaney.' Every word deliberate now, and all too clear. Every word causing Alice's heart to set up a sudden unpleasant thumping around the back of her throat. 'He's a guard stationed in Store Street. We've been married for eight years. We have three children, and we live in Newbridge. I just found a text to you. Looks like he was about to take you away for a dirty weekend, after telling me he was going to be working double shifts. He's in the shower right now, getting all clean for you.'

Not Tina. Not an ill-judged practical joke from her friend.

This was not happening. This could not be happening.

Alice ran a tongue over lips that had dried, searching for something, anything to say. Her fingers were cold, icy. Her shoulders ached. Behind her someone sneezed, making her start.

'Well? Do you believe me now? Any more you need to hear?'

'I –' She stopped, breathed, began again. 'I – I didn't know.'

'No, I dare say you didn't. None of the others knew either, until I broke the news to them.'

She closed her eyes. Others. She was one of others. He was married, and she wasn't even special enough to be the only one he'd been unfaithful with.

'His ... mother,' she said.

'What about her?'

'He told me she's sick. He – he said he lives with her.' What did it matter now? 'Look, forget it, I don't know why –'

'His mother is hale and hearty and living in Fermoy with his father. Anything else?'

His father, still alive. Chris had told Alice the man had died twenty years earlier of a heart attack, aged just forty-five. She didn't bother mentioning the brother and sister who were supposedly living in Australia. They probably didn't exist – or did, and lived in Galway.

All lies. Every single word a lie. Every 'I love you', every 'You're the one I've been waiting for.' Just a joke to him, just a diversion from his wife and three children, safely situated thirty miles away in Newbridge.

Wife. Three children. She felt a sudden unpleasant, nauseous lurch. She might be sick, might throw up right there. She took a breath, willed her stomach to behave.

'I'm sorry,' she said. 'I'm … I don't know what to say.' What a fool she'd been to believe him. What a fool he'd made of her.

'You just stay away from my husband! You hear me?'

'Well, I … of *course* I—'

'Right. Now go off and cry your eyes out, and find a single man for yourself.' And abruptly, the call was ended. Alice sat unmoving, stunned, trying to take it in, her mind reeling with the impossible information she'd just been given. He was married. He was a father of three children. He was a married man. She'd just spoken with his wife.

His *wife*. He had a wife. It wouldn't sink in. It couldn't be true.

But she'd never met his friends, his work colleagues, any members of his family. He'd kept her out of his world entirely. I want you all to myself, he'd say, and of course she loved that, and put up no objection.

She looked at her phone screen, at the two of them in the little

Greek restaurant he'd taken her to for her thirty-first birthday in October, six weeks after they'd met. For once she'd looked halfway decent in a snap – hair freshly cut and highlighted, blue dress she'd splashed out on, face bright with the excitement of a budding romance.

Next birthday I'll take you to Greece, he'd promised that night – but he'd known it wouldn't happen, couldn't happen. His flings, his … affairs – God, the word made her cringe – had by their nature to have a short shelf life, before the duped woman started asking questions he couldn't answer. By Alice's next birthday he'd have moved on, having found a way to dump her in the meantime. He'd be bringing someone else to that grotty apartment, spinning them the same lies about sick mothers and dead fathers, and love that didn't exist.

A door opened behind her. She dropped her phone onto her lap and swivelled to face the room as a patient emerged from one of the surgeries and made for her desk.

She greeted him with a voice whose forced jollity made her cringe. She felt as if she'd been picked up and shaken roughly, and set down again any old way. Her hands trembled as she called up his file and tapped her keyboard and handed over the card terminal, fake smile frozen in place. She doubted her legs would work if the need arose.

Dearbhla, assistant to Philip, appeared at the surgery door. 'Now David,' she said, and he got to his feet as Dearbhla threw a quick smile in Alice's direction – and inexplicably seemed to notice nothing amiss.

For the remainder of the afternoon, time played tricks. Minutes became elastic, stretching out endlessly, taunting her with their snail-slow progress. How could a day possibly be this long? She felt numb, and yet also perilously close to tears as her traitorous mind insisted on replaying the short, impossible phone conversation.

Somehow she got through it. Somehow she took calls and made appointments, and spoke with patients and filled forms. All the tasks she'd been carrying out at the clinic for over a decade, the routines she usually didn't have to think twice about, but which felt today like near-insurmountable challenges.

Each time she opened her mouth, she was afraid her voice would betray her. Every smile felt grotesque, pulling her mouth in a direction it didn't want to go. A few people looked at her in mild puzzlement – or maybe she imagined it. Nobody commented, nobody remarked on the distraction that she felt must be obvious to them all.

Above all else, she wanted to talk to him. She needed to hear his voice, needed him to reassure her that it had been a joke that had gone wrong, that he was terribly sorry. But she was too afraid to call his phone, in case he wasn't the one who answered.

Janice. My name is Janice Delaney. I'm married to Chris Delaney. How could it be, how could there be a wife when she, Alice, had imagined herself married to him, had planned their wedding and their honeymoon, had window-shopped for a going-away outfit, for Heaven's sake? Far too soon to be thinking about marriage, but they got on so well. Right from the start, from the rainy September evening he'd stopped to change her flat tyre, they'd clicked. They'd been so easy together. 'Driving around with a tyre like that is an arrestable offence,' he'd said. 'Lucky I'm a guard – hang on while I get the handcuffs out of the boot.' The first of many times he'd made her laugh. Finally, she'd thought, he'd shown up. The one she'd been waiting for, the one she'd almost given up on.

Fool. Such a gullible, trusting, stupid fool she'd been. All the lies she'd swallowed without question, all the last-minute phone calls he'd made to cancel a date, blaming work or his mother, when in all likelihood it had been a sick child, or another family issue needing his attention.

The owner of the grotty apartment would surely have known of Alice's existence, though. She imagined him and Chris sniggering about her, and she felt another stomach lurch.

She wondered how many women his wife had found out about, how many texts she'd intercepted. Shouldn't a garda be smarter than that? Wouldn't a man of any intelligence delete all incriminating texts? Unless – horrible thought – he wanted to be caught. Unless that was all part of the game for him. Maybe he got a kick out of the drama, the accusations, the apology, the promise never to do it again.

How could his wife still love him? How could she love someone she couldn't trust, someone whose phone she had constantly to check, waiting for the next betrayal? Stayed with him because of the children maybe, or out of habit, or fear of being alone.

Or maybe – a fresh, equally unsavoury thought rose up – they had the kind of marriage where affairs were permitted, on both sides. Maybe they each made these phone calls, whenever one of them grew tired of their current dupe. Maybe they laughed together afterwards, replaying the conversations, detailing the innocent party's shock and confusion. Alice's head buzzed as she searched for answers only he could give her.

By twenty past four the waiting area had finally emptied out, with just one patient left to emerge. She carried out the usual end of day tasks: tallied the cash takings for Philip to bank on his way home, added the card payments to the relevant file, straightened the chairs and bundled the magazines and leaflets neatly on the low tables. Organised Alice, dependable Alice. Hoodwinked, deceived Alice.

'Enjoy the weekend with lover boy,' Dearbhla said, a few minutes later. 'Don't do anything I wouldn't do.'

Alice thought of the small packed case that sat waiting at home, the weekend that wasn't going to happen, lover boy who was no more. She said nothing: no way could she trust herself to go there. 'Do you have any plans?'

Dearbhla made a face. 'We haven't a hope of getting out. Gary's teething, so I couldn't inflict him on a babysitter. Three nights of Netflix and popcorn, that'll be the height of it. Conor's offered to hold the fort if I want to go out with the girls, but I'd feel mean deserting him.' She zipped up her jacket. 'You OK, Alice? You look pale.'

'I'm fine, just a bit tired. Didn't sleep so well.' That much was true, too wound-up about going to Courtown. Too excited about their first break together.

'Oh dear. Make sure Chris pampers you all weekend.' And then she was gone, home to spend three nights in with a man who almost certainly didn't cheat on her, and a son who might be teething but who'd curled tiny fingers around Alice's thumb only last week. Lucky Dearbhla.

Her laptop shut down, her coat and bag retrieved, her indoor soft-soled shoes exchanged for boots, Alice left the building. A sharp wind snapped at her coat hem: she hurried to her car, fishing out keys. As she got in, her phone rang. Her heart leapt. What if it was Chris? What if it was all some horrible sick joke?

She pulled it from her bag. It wasn't him. She ignored the swoop of disappointment and pressed the answer key.

'I'm glad I caught you,' Kate said. 'Just wanted to wish you well for the weekend. Are you out of work? You finish early on Friday, don't you?'

Kate. She couldn't speak. She was literally struck dumb.

'Alice? Hello? Can you hear me?'

She thought again of her weekend case, packed with the clichéd lacy underwear and hold-up stockings, and the same blue dress she'd worn to the Greek restaurant, because he liked her in it. Matched her eyes, apparently.

'Alice? Are you there?'

'I'll pick you up at six,' he'd said, so her plan had been to hurry home and shower, scrub herself from top to toe, dress in specially washed jeans and new top. Make up her face, spray perfume.

'Alice, I don't know if you can hear me, but I'm getting nothing, so I'm going to hang up and—'

'He's married,' she said. Blurted it out, just like that. 'His wife phoned me at work today.' The words, spoken aloud, turning it into reality. Causing her to squeeze her eyes shut, tighten her grip on the phone.

And Kate, marvellous Kate, didn't miss a beat.

'Bastard,' she said calmly. 'Come to me for the weekend.'

'No, I can't. Thanks, but—'

'Why can't you? Don't think about it, just come.'

She couldn't. All she wanted to do was go to bed and curl

up in a ball, and stay there till Monday morning. The house blessedly empty, the other two gone for a weekend with Emmet's father. 'No, Kate.' She searched for excuses. 'You'll be working.'

'I can get cover. Come on, no point in staying at home and moping. You'll be better off here.'

And suddenly her defences crumpled. She felt a wave of exhaustion – from shock, she thought. She tipped forward and laid her head wearily on the steering wheel, eyes still closed. 'I can't think,' she said.

'Where are you now?'

'Just leaving work.'

'Go home,' Kate said. 'Make yourself a cuppa, or have a lie-down. Let the traffic ease off, leave around six, or half past. You'll be here in a couple of hours. I'll have dinner ready.'

It would be better, wouldn't it, to be with Kate? To be with anyone would be better than staying alone, with nothing to come between her and this horrible new situation.

'OK,' she said.

'Drive carefully,' Kate ordered. 'Doesn't matter if you're late. Mind yourself, Alice.'

'Thank you,' she whispered, and hung up before she could fall to pieces. She drove to Liz and Emmet's, car radio blaring. She let herself in and stood in the hall, thinking of how happy she'd been as she'd left for work, calling a cheery goodbye to the others, who'd just told her they were pregnant. It felt like a million years ago.

She imagined having to break the news to them – and she'd have to tell them the truth. She couldn't lie and say he'd simply broken up with her: they'd see through that, or Liz at least would. They'd be shocked and sympathetic – and pitying.

Their pity would be unbearable. She thought back to her conversation with Tina earlier, how both of them had assumed that she and Chris would be living together by the time Liz and Emmet's baby arrived.

Tina. She'd have to tell Tina too, and Dearbhla, and others. She imagined people asking how the weekend had gone. A fresh wave of misery hit her – and then, about to climb the stairs, she stopped, struck by a new thought.

Maybe it wasn't true. Maybe none of it was true. Why should she believe this woman, this complete stranger? Maybe she wasn't his wife at all, maybe she was an ex-girlfriend, and jealous of Alice. Maybe she worked with him, and had managed to get hold of his phone, and checked his texts and found Alice's, just like she'd claimed on the phone, but maybe she wasn't *married* to him. Maybe it was all lies.

Alice could ring him now, and ask him outright. She took her phone from her pocket and found his number. Call him, she commanded silently. Ask him. You deserve to know.

But she couldn't do it. She wasn't brave enough. What if he really was married, and he admitted it? She didn't think she could bear that. She'd wait till six, and see if he showed up.

She went upstairs, hope battling with despair. She opened the door of her room and saw her case, sitting by the window where she'd left it. She sank face down onto the bed and lay there, mind in turmoil. What to do, what to do, what to do.

Eventually she forced herself to sit up. She regarded the waiting clothes, folded neatly on her chair. She unzipped her boots and stepped out of them. She shed her work clothes quickly, letting them drop to the floor, her skin tightening as it met the unheated air of the room.

In the bathroom she stood beneath the hot water, shampooing, conditioning and soaping. Don't think, she ordered. Don't torture yourself with imaginings. All you have to do is wait.

By ten to six she was ready. Dressed, hair styled, face on, just as she'd planned. She sat huddled in her coat in the darkening sitting room, case at her feet, and watched the street through the half-closed venetian blinds.

Time passed. It occurred to her that he might have called while she was in the shower. She checked her phone and saw no missed call, no voicemail waiting to be heard, no unread text. She heard the chime of bells from the church on a nearby road announcing six o'clock, each peal seeming to mock her. Fool. Fool. Fool.

Five past six. A streetlight on the path outside flickered on. She watched passers-by move into and out of her field of vision. Ten past six. She flexed her calf muscles, pushed off her shoes to massage her feet. Again she found his name in her phone; again she ducked away from calling him. The dark shape of a car slowed outside, quickening her heartbeat, before the sweep of its headlights guided it into the driveway next door.

A quarter past six.

He wasn't coming.

She stemmed the wave of despair. Get going; don't think about it. She left the house and pulled the front door shut. She got into her car and turned the radio on again, loud. She drove out of the city, along with everyone else who was escaping for the weekend.

It began to rain as she approached the motorway exit for Naas, the first drops on the windscreen serving to release her tears. For the next ninety minutes the rain fell, as dusk turned to darkness and she cried all the way to Kate's town.

At last, at last, her motorway exit appeared. She changed lanes and drove up the ramp to the roundabout at the top. Her eyes burnt from crying, and still she couldn't stop. She dashed at the tears as she exited the roundabout and made for the town, whose streetlights she could see up ahead, putting out their orange rays.

And as she approached them, it happened.

A cyclist appeared suddenly, crossing right in front of her. She slammed on the brakes, heart leaping – and then time stopped, or seemed to stop as the car crawled towards him, second by excruciating second, and her foot pressed the brake to the floor, her whole leg rigid with the effort, but the car kept crawling, crawling, inching forward in slow motion, getting closer and closer to the cyclist, who turned his head slowly, slowly to look at her, and there was nothing at all she could do to avoid the impact, and when it happened she felt a thump, and heard a loud terrifying shout, and at the same instant there was what felt like an explosion as her airbag whooshed out from its compartment and slammed painfully into her chest, punching the breath from her and thrusting her back against the seat, her head slamming into the headrest. And still the car went on moving – how could it still be moving? How was it possible, with her foot pressed so hard to the floor? – and it took what felt like an eternity to come at last to a long, screeching halt, the cyclist left somewhere behind.

The radio blared on. She jabbed, fumbled for the off button, and when she found it the silence was immense. She sat there, rigid with shock. What had just happened? No cars passed, or came towards her. The air seemed hazy, cloudy – smoke? God, was it smoke? She sniffed, and smelt nothing but the rubbery deflating mass of the airbag. Why was there no sound from the cyclist? Had she killed him? She whimpered with fright. She had to move – she had to go back and see.

It took several attempts to release her seatbelt, her fingers clumsy and uncooperative, and to push the soft puddle of airbag out of her way. She wrenched the door open and half fell out, heart pounding, breath coming in short, loud, panicky bursts – and there on the road, fifty feet behind, more, a hundred feet, picking himself up slowly, thank God, thank God, thank God, was the cyclist.

She stumbled, lurched, wobbled her way back to him, barely able to remain upright in her fright. 'Oh God, oh God,' she gasped, as she approached, the words difficult to get out, so breathless with panic she felt. 'Are you alright? Did I hurt you? I'm so sorry—'

He got to his feet, glaring at her. He was taller than her, but then so was everyone. He had a cut on his cheek; the blood that trickled from it looked black in the sodium light. 'You idiot! You broke the lights!' he snapped – and only then did she see the traffic lights that she'd driven straight through in her distress.

'I'm sorry,' she repeated, fresh tears spurting. 'I didn't, I'm so— Are you OK?'

'Of course I'm bloody not OK! You could have killed me!' He half hopped, half hobbled across to his bicycle, lying at the far side of the road.

'Oh, please let – please let me help—'

'Stay away!' he commanded. 'You've done enough damage.' He righted it, groaning with the effort, and she saw that its front wheel had been badly buckled by the impact. He turned to fix her with another fierce stare. 'Just get lost, would you?'

'But – you should get to a hospital, I can take you—'

'I said get lost!'

'Well, at least let me pay for the—'

'Jesus!' he yelled. 'Do you want me to call the guards and have you arrested for dangerous driving?'

That silenced her. That would be all she'd need to make this the absolute worst day of her life. 'I'm so sorry,' she whimpered again, and he made no response to this. She stood where she was and watched as he limped away, keeping his left foot clear of the ground, using his damaged bicycle for support. She wanted to ask his name, get his number so she could sort out whatever damage she'd caused to him and the bike, but she didn't dare follow him.

She saw him pause, and lean against a garden wall. He must be weakening; he might have internal bleeding. He needed help. She must help him, whether he wanted it or not. As she took an uncertain step in his direction he pulled out a phone, and a few seconds later she heard the murmur of his voice. She held back, unsure of what to do: he hung up and spotted her, and immediately began limping off again.

She looked around to where she'd abandoned her car in the centre of the road, driver's door open, lights still on. She tottered back to it, feeling fragile as a convalescent, still in danger of imminent collapse. Was she in shock, could she even drive? Would she have to ring for help, like he had?

As she got in and pulled her door closed, another car came towards her, the horn honking sharply as it passed, making her start violently. She stuffed the airbag back into its compartment as best she could. She rummaged shakily on the floor and found the steering wheel cover that had burst off, and managed somehow to tap it back on. Her hands wouldn't stop trembling.

She started the car. She pulled in to the side of the road and turned off the engine. She rested her head on the steering wheel and forced herself to take deep, shuddering breaths until she felt a little steadier. The dashboard clock told her it was approaching half past eight. If she left it any longer, Kate would worry.

She clipped on her seatbelt, her movements slow and careful. She pulled out and drove slowly, knuckles white on the wheel, every sense on high alert, until she reached the road where Kate lived. She turned into the driveway and parked behind Kate's old red Volvo.

In the dark silence she sat, unable to move, her mind spooling between the twin catastrophes of the day. She'd been deceived by one man and had almost killed another. She felt empty, disoriented, broken. She got out and walked stiffly around to the boot, a hand keeping contact with the side of the car in case her legs failed her, and retrieved her case.

Before she had a chance to ring the bell, the door was opened. 'I saw you from the landing window,' Kate said, placing hands on Alice's shoulders. 'You're later than I expected – traffic must have been bad.' She took up Alice's case and brought it into the hall. 'Throw off that coat,' she said. 'I've the fire lit.'

No questions. The hall was warm, the cream walls looking darker in the soft light. Alice draped her coat on the end of the banister and followed Kate silently into the familiar cluttered sitting room, and sank into one of the twin giant chairs that flanked the fire.

'We'll eat in here,' Kate said, 'but first a drink.' Without asking Alice she took two glasses from a shelf and poured a measure of sherry into each from a waiting bottle. 'Now,' she said, 'tell me.'

So Alice told her, through more tears, of the phone call from Chris's wife, and also of the cyclist she'd just collided with.

'Are you hurt?'

'Not hurt, no. Just – shocked, I think. I can't – I'm shaking, I can't stop.'

'And you think he was OK?'

'Yes … at least, he left on his own. He was limping, but he wouldn't let me help.'

Kate nodded. 'Lucky,' she said. 'Let me throw on the pasta.' She topped up Alice's glass. 'Sit tight. Deep breaths.' She left the room, and Alice sat back wearily and listened to clattering from the kitchen. Kate's cooking was miraculous: she could take the simplest ingredients and make a feast of them. Cooking was what had brought her and Alice's uncle Aldo together; sadly, it hadn't managed to keep them there.

Alice sipped her drink. She couldn't remember the last time she'd had a sherry, but its sweetness and its burn were soothing. Gradually she calmed, and the tremors eased. The log fire crackled gently; she was rolling up the sleeves of her shirt as the door opened again.

And over bowls of bolognese, and accompanying crisp triangles of garlic flatbread, and glasses of oaky red wine, Kate spoke.

'I have a proposition for you.'

'What kind of proposition?'

'Just listen. I think it might be what you need right now. It would involve a lot of change for you, so I don't want you to say yes or no to it right away. I want you to give it serious thought. Will you do that?'

'… I will.'

And that was how it started.

George

'HOW DO I LOOK?' SHE ASKED, DOING A LITTLE TWIRL, and he took in the pink suit that washed her out a bit, and the grey shoes and bag that didn't quite match one another, and the rather odd purple feathery affair on her head, and the tentative smile underneath it.

'You look beautiful,' he said, and the smile wobbled, and she fished a pink lacy hanky from the grey bag and dabbed at her eyes.

'You'll have my mascara running,' she said, and he promised to run after it if that happened, which prompted the laugh he was after. 'You're a tonic, George Murphy,' she said. 'Is it time to go yet?'

She was like a hen on a griddle. 'Not unless you want to arrive before the groom,' he told her, so she resumed her seat at the table, and he emptied cold tea from her cup and replaced it with hot, even though he knew she wouldn't drink it in case she was short taken at the church.

She spoke then of her first wedding, thirty-eight years ago last month, and she looked beyond him, beyond the kitchen where they sat, as she described the rain that had fallen in sheets from early morning and stopped five minutes before she was due to leave for the church in her father's car. 'The sun came out,' she said, 'and shone like it had never shone before. The puddles were dry by the time we got to the church.'

George had heard it all before, more than once. He was well versed in the brightly shining sun that had followed the sheets of rain. He didn't mind. She'd always enjoyed dipping into the past, rummaging around and pulling out stories of her childhood and early adulthood, and where was the harm in it?

She'd asked him, the evening before, to come with her to the graveyard. 'I'd like a word with him,' she'd said, so George had driven her across town and walked with her past headstones until they'd got to his father's, and there they'd stood for a handful of minutes, until she'd finished saying whatever she needed to say.

George still missed him too. So many things could trigger a small stab of loss: the sound of piano notes drifting through an open window, or a certain burnt-toffee snatch of pipe tobacco caught on a breeze, or the sight of a tweed jacket with leather elbow patches, or a bald spot on a man's head in precisely the same location it had occupied on his father's. They could come at him without warning, these little prods of sorrow, and cause him to stop what he was at while he gave them room, and then nudged them away.

Five years since his father had left them without warning, his car veering off the road and hitting at speed a sycamore tree on the outskirts of town, not half a mile from the street where they lived. It had been sunny that day too, his father returning to work after lunch on an unseasonably beautiful February day, early spring sunlight washing from a pale blue sky onto houses and gardens and sprawled cats, shining on clothes lines full of gently billowing white sheets, picking out pinpricks of light on a crumpled black Volkswagen Passat.

George had been informed of the accident in a phone call to the school, the secretary appearing at his classroom door to summon him to the office. It was ten minutes before the end of the school day, and his twenty-three students were taking down their homework from the whiteboard. 'I'll stand in,' Irene had said, and George had hurried up the corridor, feeling uneasy. As he'd listened to the soft, careful, awful words delivered by a neighbour, he'd felt something dropping heavily through him, leaving him hollow and shaken.

The principal had driven him home, her eyes brimming with the tears George had yet to shed. His mother's face looked as emptied-out as he felt. George, she whispered, reaching up to him from the couch where she sat, surrounded by silent neighbours and friends, her hair salon abandoned in the light of this about-turn their lives had taken.

A major heart attack was the cause, they were told in due course. In all likelihood, the doctor said, he was gone before the collision occurred. George wasn't sure if this information was meant to console them. But of course life carried on, grief eventually blurring around its edges, and he and his mother went back to work and got on with things, and learnt how to manage without father and husband.

And today she was getting married again, and George, her only son, her only child, was walking her up the aisle. And the man who would be waiting at the top was John, a long-time family friend whose wife Miriam had died too, her death infinitely slower than George's father's, cancer attacking her repeatedly for over a decade before it had finally taken her.

And John had asked George, prior to his proposal, if George would be happy with that turn of events, which George had taken as a very good sign, and he'd said yes he would, and given John his blessing.

John was sixty-eight, George's mother Evelyn sixty-six. She and Miriam had grown up together, friends since early schooldays, staying in touch through the years, through marriages and children and the rest. George had known the other couple all his life, had met their offspring on several occasions in his younger days, not so much since they'd all moved into adulthood and gone their separate ways. But this new union felt fitting, even if he was also conscious of the tiny disquiet it engendered.

'I'm not replacing him,' his mother said now, reading his mind, as she often could. 'I'm just being practical, George. I'm thinking ahead.'

'I know.' But he didn't know really. He wondered if romantic love came into it, for either or both of them. It wasn't something you asked your mother. And was it so bad if it didn't, if she was marrying her friend for company, and security, and whatever else she felt was needed in the years to come?

'I wish you'd find someone though,' she said. 'I'd love you to be sorted, George.'

He *had* found someone, twelve years earlier. Her name was Claire, and she'd been twenty to his twenty-two, and right from the start he was consumed by her – and to his astonished delight, she saw beyond the shyness that normally crippled him when he fancied someone. She saw his attraction and coaxed him gently towards her, and made it plain that his feelings were returned. After painful years of missed chances and clumsy approaches that more often than not were rejected, she was his first proper girlfriend.

Within months, notwithstanding misgivings from both sets of parents, they found a tiny apartment whose rental they could just about afford, on his newly qualified teacher's salary and her earnings from the bookshop job she'd gone straight into after school.

They were careful, but not careful enough. Six weeks before their first Christmas together she told him she was pregnant. No matter: they loved one another, they'd have had children eventually. The first flush had eased; the excitement they'd fired in each other had calmed, which was to be expected. They were still happy together; the love was still there.

They broke the news to their families, who accepted it with varying degrees of understanding. Your life is ruined, his mother wept, and flapped away George's father when he attempted to comfort her. That woman has trapped him! she insisted, and both of them knew better than to argue, and George hoped silently that time would bring her around.

To his relief, Claire's parents received the news with more equilibrium. Her father avoided eye contact with George, which he understood, and which was preferable to a display of anger. Her mother said that she'd have preferred if they'd waited a while, that they were tying themselves down very young, but throughout the pregnancy she kept Claire supplied with iron and folic acid tablets, and she slipped her an envelope of money each time they met.

The tiny apartment seemed to shrink in direct proportion to the swelling of Claire's midsection. As the pregnancy advanced, irritations bloomed between her and George. Tempers frayed, rows grew more frequent. George began to dread returning home after work, wondering what new battle he'd have to fight. He still loved her, that hadn't changed, but by the time Suzi was born in June they were barely on speaking terms.

For a while, she brought them back together. They were united in their fascination for her. George happily changed nappies and wheeled her out in her buggy, even when every one of his muscles screamed for sleep, and he kept Claire supplied with tea and KitKats during the night feeds.

And eight months after becoming a father, when he was beginning to think they'd got over the hump, Claire told him she was ending it.

We're not right for each other, George, she said. I fell for you because you weren't like the other guys I'd dated. I thought I'd been going for the wrong type – but now I realise we're not a good fit either. We're shaped differently – there's too much space between us. All we have in common these days is Suzi.

It was a bombshell he hadn't seen coming. What? No. What are you saying?

It's over, George.

It's not over, he insisted. I love you. We love each other. We have a child.

She made no reply.

He didn't give up. He couldn't lose her. Claire, we have Suzi. We can work it out. I can change.

George, we can't work it out. She rubbed her eyes tiredly. I don't love you any more. I don't know how it happened, but it's true. I'm sorry, really I am.

Claire, that's just … Look, every relationship has its ups and downs. I know it was tough for a while, I'm not denying that, but now we're over the worst. He reached for her hands; she drew them away.

No, George. I'm really sorry, but I can't stay with you.

He had to ask. He couldn't ask. He had to. Is there someone else?

She sighed. No, there's nobody else. Look, my mind's made up, George. Please let's part as friends.

Part. He couldn't bear it, couldn't countenance it. He continued to protest, trying desperately to change her mind but she remained unmoving, until finally he had to accept the unthinkable. She and Suzi stayed on in the little apartment while he packed his bags and moved back home – and somehow he managed to struggle through the days and weeks that followed for Suzi's sake, and to make do with being her mother's friend instead of her lover. They shared parenting duties, he dropping by the apartment every other evening to see his daughter until they worked out an arrangement where Suzi spent every second weekend with her father and grandparents.

His parents rose to the occasion. They doted on Suzi, his mother in particular – but out of earshot of her little grand-daughter, she left him in no doubt about her feelings for his ex. I hate her for what she's done to you, she said. I hate her for breaking your heart, and for denying Suzi an upbringing with both parents.

George tried without success to convince her that Claire hadn't intentionally hurt him: she would have none of it.

How can you defend her, George? And how can you be happy with having Suzi only every second weekend? That's ridiculous – but it shows exactly what she's like.

She didn't relent, and Claire remained the wicked witch, and any occasion that forced them together – Suzi's first communion, her school concert appearances – reminded George of the bad old days when Claire was pregnant, so frosty was the air between the two women. An eruption, he felt, was always imminent – but so far, to his vast relief, they'd avoided it, presumably for Suzi's sake, or maybe for his.

And much to his surprise, Claire had been invited to the wedding. You won't have time to look after Suzi, his mother had said by way of explanation, so her inclusion was practical rather than a preference, but it didn't matter. After all these years, despite her rejection of him, George continued to enjoy the company of his ex. He was glad they'd had Suzi, glad there was that constant connection between them.

'Suzi's been practising her song,' he said, the thought of her reminding him.

'She's not nervous?'

'Not a bit of it. She can't wait.'

By special request from bride and groom, both long-time Leonard Cohen fans, eleven-year-old Suzi was going to sing an unaccompanied solo version of 'Hallelujah' right after the vows. From her paternal grandfather she'd inherited a musical flair that had bypassed George, along with more confidence and courage in her small toe than her father had in his entire six-foot-two bulk. George avoided confrontations whenever possible; Suzi met them head-on, and stared them down. This quality in his daughter both awed and terrified him: what trouble might it land her in, some fine day?

His mother got to her feet. 'Maybe we should go. I don't want to be too late.'

She'd barely be late as it was: hopefully John would be there on time. George took her cup and poured its untouched contents into the sink. 'By the way,' he said, 'I've had an idea.'

A week or so ago, on her insistence, they'd gone to the family solicitor and put the house into George's name. He was still trying to decide how he felt about that. It seemed very final for her to be handing it over now, instead of years into the future when she was gone. He wasn't entirely sure he was ready.

His mother's new marital home was in suburban Galway, roughly forty minutes in a car from her old one. It would be George's first time in his life to live alone, and he suspected it wouldn't appeal to him. 'I'm thinking,' he said, 'of taking in a tenant.'

'A tenant?' She stopped fussing with her headgear to stare at him. 'Here?'

'Of course here. Where else?'

'Don't be smart, George.' She tweaked the feathery thing some more. 'You're talking about bringing a complete stranger into your home.'

'Well, yes – but lots do it. And the place is too big for just me.'

'You and Suzi.'

He didn't respond to that. Any reminder that he saw too little of Suzi could send her off on another Claire tirade.

She pulled on the blue anorak she was wearing to get her to the church. 'If you must do it, be careful who you let in –

there are all sorts of weirdos out there. Make sure you get good references.'

'I will.'

'And start with a six-month lease – or even a shorter trial period, a month or two.'

He knew perfectly well why she was saying this. Whatever about her talk of weirdos, it wasn't really that she was afraid of him inadvertently giving accommodation to an axe-murderer. She didn't want him saddled with a tenant in case the woman of his dreams came along. She lit a candle every Thursday and prayed to some saint whose name George couldn't recall – and she'd never said, and George had never asked, but he was reasonably certain that she was praying for a daughter-in-law.

He could see her point. He was thirty-four, and he hadn't managed a proper relationship since Claire. A few dates here and there, a few women who'd lasted beyond the first date, but they'd all fizzled out within a month or two. It wasn't him, they each assured him in turn, it was that they needed space, or they were getting over someone else, or they weren't ready to commit – but he didn't believe them. He was reasonably sure that it *was* him, that he was to blame. However he'd managed it, he lacked what was needed to keep another person interested.

On the other hand, none of them attracted him like Claire had. None of them caused the fizz of excitement that the sight of her, even the mention of her name, had generated. He wondered if it only happened once, and if she had been his once.

Of course, his mother was having none of that. In her eyes he was a great catch. She'd list off his attractions: education, steady job, dependability, thoughtfulness, kindness. Look what a great father he was, she'd say, look how good a son – and while he liked to think he did indeed tick all of those boxes, he would have appreciated the sort of attributes that women in search of a mate might be more interested in.

Good-looking would be nice, but he was average at best in that department. Sexy he could live with, but instead he was possessed of a frame that was big and shambling, and he looked better in clothes than out of them. Charming would be good, but he sorely lacked the easy charisma that other men seemed to have been born with.

And even if he *had* all those qualities, where was he to display them? Work was a non-starter in terms of looking for love. He was one of just two males on a staff of twelve, but of the females, six were married, two were closer to his mother's age and the other two were as indifferent to George as he was to them.

There were a few single mothers among the parents of his present class. One or two might be open to an approach, but making any moves in that direction seemed fraught with risk. What if he was turned down – or, worse, what if he started something that didn't work out? They'd still have to meet regularly, until the end of the school year; how awkward would that be? Besides, any teacher–parent relationship outside the official one would most likely be frowned on by the principal.

His friends were all married, or in long-term situations. He was the spare, the misfit, the unaccompanied extra at their social gatherings. Most of the time it didn't bother him. He played five-a-side soccer with a gang every Wednesday evening in the community sports hall; he also lifted weights and ran on a treadmill three times a week in the gym across the road, and sometimes he plodded around the neighbourhood too, or did a few laps at the nearby GAA grounds.

He wasn't a natural athlete. He had to force himself across to the gym, or into the running gear, but the exercise kept him in shape for the soccer, which he enjoyed, and counteracted the Friday-morning cakes in the staffroom, and the rather large appetite he'd been blessed with.

He and Claire had a loose custody arrangement over the summer: Suzi was usually with her mother for the month of July and with George for August, unless holiday bookings necessitated some tweaking of dates on either side. He was happy, of course, to take his daughter whenever she was offered to him – and so far, she'd come willingly, but already he was bracing himself for a possible change in her teens.

He figured it could go either way: her father could turn into her biggest embarrassment, or become her closest confidant, or maybe they'd settle somewhere in between. Time would tell. In the meantime he was fairly content with his life as it was, even if it didn't include romance, or a hint of it.

'You OK?' he asked his mother in the car. She was uncharacteristically quiet, the bunch of big colourful flowers she'd bought in Aldi the day before – giant daisies, he'd call them – resting in her lap.

'I'm fine. Just …' She brushed something from a sleeve. 'Don't forget to water the flowers in the planters.'

'I won't.'

He probably would. There was no garden to the front of the house, just two rectangular containers flanking the door that she looked after, filling them with bulbs in the autumn and seedlings in the spring. What was growing in them these days? He couldn't say.

'And keep the lawn cut, won't you?'

'I will.'

The medium-sized back garden had always been his father's territory. He'd kept it neat, if a little lacking in imagination, with a row of shrubs marching down on the left side and a long narrow flowerbed running across the top. There was a shed halfway down on the right, with a small paved area outside it, home until last year to a slowly rusting metal table and four similarly deteriorating chairs, and a rotary clothes line beyond that. The rest was lawn, the grass patched, despite his father's efforts, with moss and clover.

Since his death, George had taken over the cutting of the lawn, but the shrubs, for want of pruning, had long since grown straggled and unruly. For a while his mother had kept the weeds at bay in the flowerbed, but eventually she'd lost interest and gone back to her more civilised front planters. She and George had also given up sitting out on the patio: she'd eventually asked him to pack up the furniture and bring it to the local recycling centre.

'You put my case in the boot, didn't you?'

'I did.'

Third time she'd asked him since breakfast. The newlyweds were going to Donegal for a five-day honeymoon. They'd booked into a small hotel that overlooked the sea. They were both walkers: he pictured them swaddled in coats and scarves, marching arm in arm along country roads, or across a windswept beach.

'I forgot to tell you – I've asked Kate to keep you in eggs.'

'Have you?'

Kate was one of her clients at the hair salon. She and George had never come face to face, but he knew of her because of the eggs. She ran a little Italian restaurant across town, close to his mother's salon, and she kept hens in her back garden. For years, she and his mother had had a barter arrangement – six-weekly haircuts in exchange for a dozen free range eggs a week, which Kate brought each Saturday morning to the salon.

And you'd have to say that those eggs were things of beauty. Big and brown, downy fluff still clinging to shells, yolks a creamy orange shade. George's usual Sunday breakfast was a couple of soft-boiled eggs, into whose gooey centres he'd push buttered strips of granary toast, and eggs featured during the week too – hard-boiled in his lunchtime sandwich, or whipped up into a dinnertime quiche, or fried to accompany a sausage.

But now that the salon was closing, and his mother was becoming a lady of leisure, George had assumed that Kate's eggs, as he always thought of them, would become a thing of the past, and he'd have to look elsewhere for his pale orange yolks. Seemed he was wrong.

'You needn't have done that.'

'I wanted to,' she said. 'And I've paid her too, so there.'

'Mam, you don't have to pay for my eggs.'

'I know I don't, but I *want* to.'

Something in her voice made him look at her – and he saw for the second time that morning the pink hanky coming to the rescue. He found her arm and squeezed it briefly.

'I'll just miss you,' she said. 'That's all. I'll miss having you near, George.'

'You won't have a chance to miss me. You'll be too busy putting your own shape on John's house – and Suzi and I will visit, as often as you want us. And you can come back anytime you have a row with John.'

She managed a smile. 'George Murphy, you're an awful joker.' And then the church came into view, and both of them set aside the subject of eggs, and focused on the main task of the day.

And later, much later, after the vows and Suzi's song and the confetti, after the prosecco and the buffet and the speeches – George's shorter than a minute, John's thankfully not much longer – after Suzi and her mother had departed, and the newly minted Mr and Mrs Stewart were waved off on their way to Donegal, George walked home alone through a light drizzle, having thought it more prudent to leave his car in the hotel grounds for the night.

He entered the house and closed the front door, and listened to the silence. He went into the kitchen and put the kettle on for tea, and turned it off again. He'd only ever had tea at night to keep his mother company.

She was Evelyn Stewart now, not Evelyn Murphy any more. He'd have to get used to it.

He climbed the stairs and entered the room that had been his since childhood, the second largest of the three bedrooms, his single bed exchanged for a double when he'd outgrown it in his teens. He supposed he should move into the room his parents had occupied, and offer this one to a tenant. Suzi would be content, he thought, to remain in the smallest bedroom on her visits. Last year, at her request, he'd painted over the magnolia walls with a sea-green shade, and the colour lent the room a fresh, open feel.

A few flakes of confetti – yellow, pink, white – drifted from his suit jacket as he took it off. In the bathroom he brushed his teeth. He washed his face and towelled it dry, and every small sound he made was magnified in the silence.

He got into bed and turned onto his side. He needed another person in the house. He needed to hear a cough, or a toilet flushing, or someone else's phone ringing. He wanted evidence that he was not alone. He reached out and turned on the radio, and listened to a weather forecaster telling of high winds in the morning.

He hadn't switched off the landing light. He imagined what his mother would say to that, but the rim of yellow around his bedroom door acted as a kind of detached sentinel, a vague reassurance, a comfort until he surrendered to sleep.

On Monday, Barb who taught third class announced in the staffroom at first break that her brother had been knocked off his bicycle on Friday night by a female driver who'd gone through a red light.

'Is he OK?' Vicky, Junior Infants.

'He is. He sprained his ankle, and got some cuts and bruises. He was lucky, could have been much worse. His bike needs a new front wheel – you should see it.'

'Isn't he getting ready to open up?'

'He is – or he was. Opening was this Friday, but he's been told to stay off the ankle for a few weeks, so he's had to postpone it. He's not happy.'

'I hope he got her insurance details.' Dermot, fifth class. 'She deserves a whopper of a bill.'

'He didn't. She did offer them, but he says he was too mad at her. He was probably in shock.'

George thought about the driver of the car who hadn't stopped for a red light. He imagined the fright of a collision. A memory surfaced of a boy in the school some years back who'd been knocked off his bike by a lorry. He remembered the blotched, destroyed face of the boy's mother at the funeral, the way she'd seemed not to see George when he'd taken her hand – cold, so cold – and offered his sympathies.

He wondered if the lorry driver had been at the funeral. How did you live with the knowledge that you'd cut another life short, however unintentionally? At least Barb's brother was still alive, and the woman responsible for his injuries had offered help.

'How was the wedding?'

Sheila from first class, cutting into his thoughts. 'Good. It went fine.'

'Any photos?'

He took out his phone and showed her the few he'd thought to snap: Suzi singing on the altar, the newlyweds emerging from the church, the cutting of the cake, the happy couple waving from the car as they left.

'You'll miss her,' Sheila said, her eyes on the screen. 'The house will be quiet.'

'I'm thinking of looking for a tenant,' he replied. 'I'm wondering how to go about it. You let your house, didn't you, when you got married?'

Not putting it out there to the room, just directing the question at Sheila – and still Dermot heard from across the table, and pounced. 'Ah George – there are easier ways of finding a girlfriend,' he said loudly. 'Go down to the local pub, man.'

Heads turned in George's direction. He felt himself getting hot. 'I'm just letting out a room, Dermot.'

'Ha – that's what they all say!'

'Shut up, Dermot,' Sheila said calmly. 'Ignore him, George. There are Facebook pages where you could advertise, or you could put it up on Daft – or just take out an ad in the local paper.'

'What do I need to look out for?'

'Well, make sure you have a lease. I googled something like "Irish tenancy lease" and picked the one that was written in the plainest English – some of them would need a barrister to translate them. I'll email it to you if you like.'

'Would you? That'd be great, thanks.'

'Make it for six months,' she said, and he was reminded of his mother's similar advice. 'You can always extend it if you're happy with your tenant. And just go with your gut, I suppose, when you meet applicants. You could look for character references, but I didn't bother – you'd have to be a bit of a Sherlock Holmes to find out if they're genuine, or just written by pals. Be on the alert when you meet them, see if they're acting a bit shifty, or too cocky. You'll know yourself.'

But he wasn't sure he'd know himself. He tended to take people he met on trust, and hope they didn't disappoint him – and inevitably, the world being the way it was, some did.

He'd been conned out of money on the street once by a man who'd fed him a sob story about being robbed of his wallet and needing two euro to get a bus somewhere – when George had obliged, the man had snatched the coin without a word of thanks and run off. Another time he paid an online subscription for a magazine that never arrived. Every so often his trust was abused – but still he persevered. More good folk than bad out there.

He'd have to be careful though, with his choice of tenant. Someone sharing his house, free to poke about when George wasn't home. He'd want to be as sure as he could that they were trustworthy. He'd just have to hope his instinct was up to it.

After school he went to the gym, where he worked his way doggedly through his weight-lifting routine and a twenty-minute treadmill run, his gaze fixed on the music videos that played non-stop and too loudly on several screens, his mind wandering about as it usually did in the gym, touching down on Suzi, and his mother, and Barb's brother with his sprained ankle.

That evening, after a cheese on toast dinner – why bother cooking a proper meal for one? – he drifted around online house rental sites for a while, then set about composing his ad.

Person wanted to share house. Double room available.
Must be non-smoker.

Could you specify a non-smoker? Were you infringing on someone's right to pollute your air?

Person wanted to share house. Double room available.
Non-smoker preferred.

Maybe he should give a bit more information.

Person wanted to share quiet house with owner. Double room
available. Reasonable rent. Non-smoker preferred.

Should he mention that Suzi would be staying every so often? No – time enough for that when he was face to face. He went online and found the local paper's website – and then he balked.

Maybe he was rushing into this. Maybe he should wait and see. Living alone might grow on him. Did he really want to share his home with a stranger?

He decided to sit on it for a while. He saved the ad and clicked out of it. As he was shutting down his computer, his phone pinged with a text.

Having a lovely time, his mother wrote. The hotel is beautiful. Hope you're eating sensibly.

Eating fine, he replied. Glad you're enjoying yourself. Hello to John.

It was still only eight o'clock. He flicked through the offerings on TV and found nothing of interest until the news at nine. On impulse, he phoned Suzi.

'Hey, George. What's up?'

'Nothing much, just wanted to say hello. Any news?'

'Nah … We went to see Bernie yesterday.'

'Who's Bernie?'

'Rob's sister. She lives in Tipperary, and she's an artist, and she's going to do a painting of me.'

'Is she?'

'Yeah. And she says I can call her Auntie Bernie if I want.'

Something coiled inside him. 'She's not your aunt though.'

'I *know* that, George.'

She wasn't Suzi's aunt. She was Rob's sister, and Rob was no relation. Rob was just the man who'd been seeing Claire for the past two years, and who'd moved her and Suzi into his house after Christmas. Rob was twenty-eight, six years younger than George, and four years younger than Claire, and a podiatrist. Rob was pleasant and polite when he and George encountered one another, and George was still working on not resenting him for being the man his daughter lived with most of the time.

At least there was no talk of her calling him Dad.

He switched direction. 'The wedding was good, wasn't it?'

'Yeah, it was really good. I loved that dessert so much. Mum gave me hers.'

'I just got a text from Gran. They're having a lovely time. We can visit them in John's house when they get back.'

'OK.'

He decided to run the tenant idea by her, see her reaction. 'Hey, how would you feel about me getting someone to share this house, now that Gran's moved out?'

Pause. 'To share for how long?'

'Probably six months to start with.'

'Would you get a man or a woman?'

'Hadn't really thought about that.' He hadn't. Hadn't thought it through at all, really. 'What do you think? Who would you like to move in?'

'Someone funny,' she said immediately. 'Wouldn't matter really if it was a he or a she. And someone who wouldn't steal stuff when you weren't there.'

He laughed. Two pretty important considerations. 'Well, I'm just thinking about it for now. See you Friday. Love you.'

'Love you too, George.'

She was in sixth class, but she didn't attend George's co-ed school. Claire had wanted her to go where she'd gone herself, so Suzi was a convent girl. The decision had disappointed

George – how much more he would have seen of her if she'd been just down the corridor from him every weekday; how much more contact he would have had if he'd taught her for a year – but characteristically, he hadn't argued. Things might change when she started secondary in September: the school she was booked into was a lot closer to his.

He decided to move into the main bedroom, just in case the other was needed. In the wardrobe he found a blue shirt of his father's, folded neatly on a shelf. He pressed it to his face, but any scent it might have had was gone from it. He hung it with his shirts, unable to contemplate anything else.

He lay in his parents' bed later, in sheets he'd just taken from the hotpress, and watched the outline of yellow light around the door. He should assert himself more. His mother had often said as much, and he knew she was right.

He taught sixth class every year because nobody else wanted it. He let Claire dictate how much contact he had with their daughter. He was goalie for the five-a-side games more often than any of the others, even though he was no better or worse than them at stopping the ball. He endured all of Dermot's digs at school, never seriously objecting.

You could say he was obliging and easy-going, but closer to the truth was that he was a pushover. He allowed people more leeway than they deserved; he didn't protest or speak up when he should. It was just easier that way.

He was a teacher, and he thought a fairly decent one, but he was less able to navigate the world than an eleven-year-old girl.

He turned on his other side and went to sleep.

Alice

A FEW DAYS AFTER KATE'S ASTONISHING PROPOSAL, Alice handed in her notice at the dental clinic. 'I'm moving back home,' she told them. 'I've had a job offer, and I'd like to take it up.'

She didn't add that the job was jack-of-all-trades in her aunt's restaurant. Kate hadn't called it that, but that was what it was. Helping in the kitchen, Kate had said, and filling in on the floor if anyone was out. Part time, she'd added, three or four shifts a week – which probably meant that Alice wasn't really needed, that a space was just being created for her. How humiliating was that?

But it wouldn't be for long – she'd keep an eye open and hopefully pick up similar receptionist work easily enough – and Kate was offering accommodation too. Not in her house, in the adjoining garage that she'd converted for her son, who lived most of the year in Italy. A converted garage – which in fairness she probably thought Alice would prefer, since it meant she'd have her own space, and which was being offered free of charge, and which was actually quite cute, if tiny.

I'll think about it, she'd told Kate, and think about it she had, all through the weekend and all the way back to Dublin. She'd thought about how kind her aunt was to offer her this option, and how leaving Dublin would take her away from all reminders of Chris, and would surely help her to forget about him – and by the time she arrived at Liz and Emmet's, she'd decided to do it.

And now she was doing it, or the first part of it at any rate.

To her slight dismay, her employers took the news of her resignation well. They knew about Chris, of course: she'd told Dearbhla on Monday, knowing it would be passed on to the others – and sure enough, she'd seen sympathy in faces on Tuesday, although none of them had commented.

'Will you stay till we find a replacement, Alice?' her immediate boss asked now.

'Of course.'

She told Liz and Emmet that evening, after dinner.

'You're moving home?' Liz looked genuinely confused. 'What are you talking about? You *are* home. Your home is here, with us.'

Alice smiled. 'You've both been so good to me—'

'Good nothing – you pay us rent, Alice. You help us every bit as much as we help you. It's that bastard, isn't it? He's why you're leaving.'

'He's part of it,' she admitted, 'but, Liz, you're having a baby. I'd have to find another place sooner or later, and I'm afraid I've been far too spoilt here to be happy with anywhere else, so I think I'm better off making a clean break. I'm staying until the clinic replaces me, and I'll have to train in the new person for a week or so. I'll let you know when I have a finish date.'

'But what about work?'

She told them about Kate's offer of shifts at the restaurant. 'Just a stopgap, until I find another job like mine.'

'And what if you can't? Good jobs aren't that easy to come by, Alice.'

'Oh, I'm sure I'll find something.'

'Well, we'll really miss you. You're like one of the family – and nobody makes a lunchtime sandwich like you. You have to swear you'll come back often.'

'I will,' she promised.

She told Tina, her oldest friend. This would be the first time for them not to live in the same town. Maybe not such a major deal since Tina had become a wife, and borne three children in fairly rapid succession – Lou and I are going for the hurling team, she'd told Alice – but leaving her would still be a wrench. They practically read one another's thoughts.

On hearing of the move, Tina was emphatic. 'A mistake, Alice. We left home for a reason – remember?'

'I do remember, but it's different for you now. You've put down roots here. You married a Dublin man, your kids were born here. I have none of that. I have no ties – and I just feel that maybe it's time to go home.'

'Rubbish. You're running away from your problems. Why should that man make you leave?'

'It's not just him' – but if she was totally honest, it *was* just him. Of course she could find new accommodation if she tried, other people managed it, but he'd taken away the joy of Dublin. She had no heart for it any more.

She tried to think of the change in direction as a fresh start – but was Tina right? Was she making a mistake? She'd drifted away from all her old friends at home; she hadn't meant it to happen, but it had. Some of them had moved away, further than Dublin; the rest had got married, their lives moving onto other tracks, and Alice, invited to weddings and christenings – was it out of duty, or pity? – had felt every inch of the distance between them.

But what did she have to show for her years in Dublin? No property, no man, no special achievement to brag about. She was thirty-one, older but not a scrap wiser than when she'd stepped off the train in Heuston Station with Tina, both of them eighteen and innocent, armed with nothing more than the address of the hostel that was to house them for a fortnight. Not a single job prospect between them, but at eighteen that didn't seem like a big deal. Dublin was full of jobs – they'd just have to find the ones that suited them.

Over the following weeks and months they'd found a lot of jobs that didn't suit them. Customer care operatives for a phone company, their time spent trying to reason with irate customers; shelf-stackers in small supermarkets that paid tuppence an hour; door-to-door leaflet distribution that brought them into plenty of dodgy areas; night-time office cleaning that involved journeys home in the small hours on buses full of dubious characters. The one job they'd both liked, working behind the counter in a sandwich shop, had lasted three weeks before the business folded. Eventually, Tina had ended up behind the bar of their local pub, a job she'd taken to immediately, and Alice had landed a temporary receptionist position that had eventually become permanent.

They'd stayed a month in the hostel, and gone from there to a shared house with two young chefs from Carlow, who brought different girls home every weekend and never cleaned the bathroom, but who kept the kitchen spotless and the fridge stocked with leftovers, and who cooked dinner on their nights off for Alice and Tina.

Eventually Tina had moved in with Lou, manager of the bar, and Alice had bade goodbye to the chefs and taken up an offer of lodgings with Liz, who'd also worked at the dental clinic, and her recently acquired husband Emmet.

And that last move had been over ten years ago.

Sometimes she wondered if there was something wrong with her. Why was she still alone at thirty-one? How had finding a mate come so easily to her friends, when for her it seemed impossible? He's out there, everyone told her. Searching for her, apparently. In the meantime, she'd met plenty of men who were searching for someone who wasn't her – or in Chris's case, a man who'd already searched for someone and married her, but who fancied a girlfriend on the side.

She'd grown up three streets from Kate's house, with an Italian mother who'd come to live in Ireland with her family at the age of sixteen, and an Irish father. When Alice, their youngest child, had moved to Dublin they'd wound up their respective jobs – he was a graphic designer, she managed her own little bakery – and put the family home on the market. They'd relocated to southern Italy, to the area in Puglia where Alice's mother had grown up, and now they owned a vineyard and operated a wine bar there, and were surrounded by her mother's relatives. They seemed, as far as Alice could see, to be perfectly content.

They'd done it. Pulled up the roots of their lives, packed away everything familiar and embarked on a new path when they were a lot older than Alice. She could do it too. She could make this work.

Of course Kate wasn't her aunt, not really. Her marriage to Alice's uncle Aldo, her mother's older brother, had lasted just seven years: after its ending, Aldo had been the first of his family to return to Italy, taking his by then widowed mother with him, and leaving Kate with the house they'd shared, and Borelli's, the restaurant he'd inherited on the death of his father, and term-time custody of their five-year-old son, Paolo.

The boy had shuttled between Ireland and Italy as he'd grown up, being educated in Ireland and holidaying in Italy until he left school at eighteen. During his Leaving Cert year Kate had converted the house's double garage into a self-contained apartment. She told Paolo she'd train him up as a chef in Borelli's, or fund his college expenses if he preferred to go in a different direction – but despite her efforts to keep him in Ireland, Italy won. Now he came to his mother for scattered weeks throughout the year, staying in the apartment she'd thought might keep him with her, and the rest of the time he spent working in the beachside *trattoria* his father had opened on his return to Italy.

Alice and Kate had always got on. Over the years Alice had been a regular visitor to her aunt's house, even after her move to Dublin, and her parents' relocation to Italy – and before the pandemic, Kate had taken regular day trips to Dublin, often meeting Alice for coffee or lunch. Now, when the country was finally emerging into something resembling normal life again, she was offering Alice a fresh start – and despite her misgivings, Alice was going for it.

Her parents were astonished when she rang to tell them. They'd known about Chris. She'd passed on all his lies to them – the sickly mother, the dead father. They'd been impressed that he was in the guards, and thought him very dutiful to care for his mother like he did. I think he might be special, Alice had confided to her mother when she'd gone to stay with them at Christmas. I think this might last.

They knew about the break-up too, but that was all. She'd left out the rest of it. It didn't work out was all she'd told them, and they'd offered their condolences and hoped she was OK – but now she heard concern in her mother's voice.

'You're moving home, after all these years? What's brought this about?'

'I feel like a change,' Alice said. 'I'm tired of Dublin.' She told them of Liz's pregnancy. 'I'd have had to move anyway, and I'd never find a place with anything like the rent I was paying Liz and Emmet. Not in Dublin.'

'But what about a job? You shouldn't have given up yours until you'd found another.'

'I know – but Kate's giving me work until I get sorted. It'll be fine.'

It would be fine. It had better be.

Within a month she was ready to leave, a replacement receptionist having been found for the clinic. On the eve of her departure, she packed her car with clothes and shoes and books and the rest of her thirteen-year paraphernalia, minus what she'd bundled into boxes and black bags and donated to charity, or deposited in Liz and Emmet's recycling bin.

And as she found space for her various belongings she had a thousand second thoughts, and she smothered them all.

She got into the car the following morning, glad her housemates had both left for work. She felt fragile, close to tears as she regarded the house that had been her home for more than a decade. But of course it wasn't just the thought of leaving here that was making her emotional. It was Chris too – because a month after the phone call that had ended everything, she wasn't over him. Far from it.

The memory of what he'd done lingered, sharp as a toothache. How could he have used her like that? The thought of him caused her to swing between anger and sadness, wanting one minute to storm into Store Street garda station and confront him, to create a scene in front of everyone, to expose him for the lying cheat he was – and the next minute wanting only for him to appear at the clinic door, full of remorse, offering a plausible reason for his actions and declaring his love for Alice, only for Alice.

She hadn't blocked his number. When it came down to it, she simply couldn't. In spite of his deceit, that gesture of cutting him out of her life so absolutely was beyond her. So many times she'd picked up the phone to ring him, so many times she'd stopped herself, unable to face the possible consequences. Wanting a call, if it happened, to come from him – but as the days had passed with no such call, her pain had increased rather than lessened. Was his silence prompted by cowardice, or just plain indifference? She wondered if he'd blocked *her* number, and simply moved on to the next unsuspecting woman. Around and around her thoughts spooled, torturing her.

Enough of this. She turned the key and started the car – and just then her phone, sitting face down on a box of books on the passenger seat, pinged with a text. She turned it over and saw Chris's name.

Oh God. Oh God. Oh God. She felt an inner rush, so strong it made her light-headed. She switched off the engine and took a breath, and another. In spite of wanting so badly to hear from him, she was completely thrown by this sudden communication. What was he doing, texting her now out of the blue?

She'd delete it. She wouldn't even read it – but of course she didn't delete it. Of course she read it.

Alice, I'm so sorry. Can you ever forgive me? Could we meet to talk about it? I'd love to explain everything to you – Chris xx

No denial. No insistence it wasn't true. Wanting to meet her, wanting to explain everything, after a month of silence. And even though she'd yearned for some communication, for anything at all from him, she was torn now. What was there to explain? He was married, and he'd lied repeatedly to her. The End.

She sat there as people walked past, as a tabby cat darted across the street, as cars drove by. She sat in her packed-up car, reading and re-reading his short message, head in turmoil. She was pulled back to the day in the clinic that had led to this about-turn in her life. She felt again the disbelief, the shock, the nausea that his wife's words had caused.

She should have blocked his number. She'd do it now – but instead she pressed *Reply*.

Leave me alone. Don't contact me again.

She sent it off before she could change her mind, and away it went. Now she would block him – but again she didn't.

He hadn't blocked her – had he? Surely you couldn't still make contact with someone you'd blocked?

She was torn in two.

She placed her phone back on the box and started the car again. She turned on the radio and set off, pushing him out of her head each time he entered it, which was roughly once every five minutes. Listening, despite herself, for another ping from her phone, tuning into it beneath the sound of the radio, but it didn't happen.

She would forget him. She *would*. Seven months ago, she hadn't known he existed. She'd rekindle her old friendships, or find new single friends. She'd hunt down a job once she'd settled in, and move out of the garage the minute she could.

Apartment. She must remember to call it that, like Kate did.

The miles sped by. She stopped for nothing, wanting only to arrive and unpack, and be done with the move. She exited the motorway and took the usual turn at the roundabout. She approached the traffic lights she'd missed a month earlier, and she thought of the cyclist she'd hit, as she had when she'd driven through them the opposite way on her return to Dublin that weekend. He'd probably always hop into her head at this spot. She hoped he was OK.

It was shortly after noon when she landed. She rang Kate's bell and her aunt appeared with a set of keys. 'Welcome,' she said. 'I'll help you unload, and then you can come back here for lunch.'

On the face of it, Alice couldn't fault the apartment, now that she was seeing it properly. The bedroom was a lot smaller than her old one, but the bed was a generous single, and her things fitted, just about, into the compact wardrobe and built-in drawers. A full-length mirror was fixed to the wall, next to the window. With no dressing table, the sill would have to do for her various bottles and jars.

The living space was furnished with a neat two-seater couch and accompanying armchair, glass-topped coffee table and television set. No bookshelves: she'd find wooden crates and copy something she'd seen on Instagram.

The kitchenette held the usual storage units and appliances, even if everything looked as if it had been reduced by a few sizes. The fridge was slotted in under the worktop, the only freezer space a little compartment within it, but she was pleased to see a washing machine, and the hob on the narrow cooker had four rings. There was even a miniature microwave.

A counter separated the area from the living room, and served as her dining table. Two stools would be plenty: it wasn't as if she was planning to host dinner parties while she was here.

No bath, of course, just a shower. She'd get used to it, although the little rubber duck Emmet had jokingly presented her with one Christmas, a nod to her love of baths, would have nowhere to float. She'd sit it on the windowsill, along with the pumice stone and scented candle that had always accompanied her soaks.

She wondered how it would be, living alone for the first time in her life.

'Thank you,' she said to Kate, as they sat in Kate's kitchen with bowls of potato and leek soup. 'I really appreciate all you're doing for me. I'd like to repay you in some way. Any ideas?'

Kate thought. 'How about looking after the hens? You'd have to feed them, collect the eggs, check that they were in for the night, clean out the run every now and again, that sort of thing.'

Kate owned fifty-four hens, located behind her house in a

large run. Alice had heard their soft clucking as she'd unpacked, but hadn't paid it too much heed.

'Sure. I'd be happy to.' Something new, to go with her new life. Why not?

'It's pretty straightforward. I'll take you through it tomorrow. How do you feel?' Kate asked then. 'About moving back here, I mean.'

Alice hesitated. 'To be honest, I'm not entirely sure – but I'll give it my best shot.'

'Did you ever hear from that man again?'

Alice hesitated. She couldn't lie to Kate. 'He texted, wanting to meet me. I told him to leave me alone.'

True, all true.

'I'm glad to hear it. Some chancers will try anything on: I'd block him if I were you. I know it'll be a big change for you here, but you're young, you'll get on fine. You have WiFi in the apartment, by the way – you can pick up my signal out there. I'll give you the password.'

'Great.' Another saving.

'And I have a fold-up bed you can have if you ever want to invite a pal for the weekend.'

'Thanks' – but she couldn't see that happening. Her Dublin friends, like her old gang here, were all married or coupled up, and most of them had at least one small child. Alice couldn't imagine any of them rushing away from their full Dublin lives for a night or two on a camp bed.

'One more thing – I have a gym membership that I'm not using. I signed up in a moment of weakness in January, and used it about three times. You're welcome to it, if you'd fancy. It's good till the end of June.'

'Really? Are you sure you don't want it?'

'Positive. I don't know what I was thinking. The gym is about ten minutes from here in the car, not far from the GAA field.'

'Do they have classes? I'm not into the machines, but I did yoga in Dublin.'

'They do run classes. I never investigated, wouldn't be bothered, but you can check them out.' She found her membership card and gave it to Alice. 'You'll have no problem being me – nobody has a clue what I look like. And if you do end up going there regularly, you could save me a trip. I deliver eggs once a week to a house directly across the road.'

'Do you? I didn't know you did that.'

'I generally don't – this was a special arrangement I had with my hairdresser, eggs in exchange for cuts.'

'That sounds great.'

'It was, worked fine for both of us. I used to deliver to her salon but she retired a month ago, got herself remarried and moved away. I thought that would be the end of the eggs, but she asked if I'd keep supplying George.'

'Who's George?'

'Her son. He still lives in the home place, and apparently he's a big fan of the eggs.'

He sounded like a proper Mummy's boy. 'Who's paying for them?'

'Evelyn. His mother.'

'Could he not buy his own eggs – or at least pick them up himself? I'm assuming he's a grown man.'

Kate laughed. 'I'm sure he wouldn't mind collecting them,

but I offered to deliver, because I've known Evelyn for years and she's a dote. And I imagine he'd happily pay for them too, if Evelyn hadn't organised that with me. Will you let me off a job, or not?'

'Of course I will – but it still seems like you're totally spoiling him.'

'Ah, poor George. Wait till you're a mother yourself, Alice – you'll do anything for them.'

She must miss Paolo, living away from her for most of the year – and with the pandemic, she'd seen even less of him in the last two years than she normally did. Unlike Alice, Kate never travelled to Italy. Alice could understand it: as the woman who'd divorced his father, she was bound to feel uncomfortable among her son's extended family. It meant though that she was completely dependent on Paolo's visits to Ireland. With Italy only a few hours away on a plane, Alice privately thought he should come more often. Aldo could surely spare him from the *trattoria*, even if it was only for a few days. Still, none of Alice's business.

'Take the weekend to settle in,' Kate said as they washed up. 'I'll add you to Borelli's roster next week. And come to dinner here on Monday night.'

'Thanks, I'd love that – but don't feel you have to feed me too.'

'I don't – this won't last. Have you enough money for now?'

'I have.'

She had her savings account, money she'd been putting by each month for a rainy day. She'd dipped into it for wedding gifts and christening gifts and the odd holiday, but it was still healthy enough. She hadn't imagined she'd need to live on it anytime soon, but it would have to supplement whatever Kate paid her until she found something permanent.

On her return to the garage – no, apartment – Alice stopped to regard the hens. She dimly remembered Kate's first clutch of chickens, half a dozen or so, which she'd acquired shortly after her marriage had ended, and Aldo had left for Italy. Since then she'd worked her way up to this number, learning along the way.

Pretty much all of her large rear garden was given over to them now, a safely enclosed space that housed a wooden coop and a generous run, part earth, part grass. Alice watched them wandering about, laying their caramel-coloured eggs wherever they chose, scratching and pecking happily, and occasionally making sudden darts at one another – purely, it seemed, for the fun of hearing the other's startled squawk.

She thought she'd enjoy living within earshot of them. Their clucking would remind her that she wasn't alone.

She put on her jacket and walked the ten minutes to the library, still located where she remembered it, although the faces behind the desk were unfamiliar. She checked out the situations vacant in the newspapers, but found no receptionist jobs on offer.

She went back for the car and stocked up at the nearest supermarket. She filled the apartment's fridge and bread bin, stacked tins and cartons in the empty press, radio on to break the silence. She went online and searched for jobs, and again no receptionist positions were listed anywhere in the region. Early days, no panic.

She put a frozen pizza into the oven for dinner, opened a bottle of wine, toasted her new life aloud to nobody at all. 'Here's to me,' she said. 'Here's to happiness.'

She slept fitfully, and woke with a dull headache. The small bedroom needed an air flow, but leaving a window open on the ground floor felt unsafe. Teething problems: tonight she'd leave the bedroom door open, see how that went. She'd check out the gym after breakfast, walk rather than drive, use up more time and get some fresh air.

The April day was chilly, causing her to quicken her steps as she rubbed her gloveless hands together. She was familiar with the general layout of the town, and the GAA grounds were a well-known landmark, but she passed quite a few places that were new to her. A big aqua centre – Kate had mentioned it, opened a few months ago. Two or three restaurants that definitely weren't there in her time.

An unfamiliar optician's across from the tennis courts caught her attention. It had the fresh appearance of a recently opened business, and looked altogether more contemporary than Fleming's in the town centre, where Alice had been brought as a pre-teen to get her first pair of glasses. Newman Optician's, she read above this window. She wondered if that was a joke, or actually the new man's name. She was overdue an eye test, having ignored her last two reminders. Might be worth checking this place out.

It took almost forty minutes to walk to the gym. It was new to her too, with plate glass windows and a rotating door, and plenty of cars parked outside at eleven on a Saturday morning. A welcome blast of warm air met her. She approached the reception desk, behind which sat a fair-haired young man. 'Hi there,' he said brightly.

'Hello.' She presented Kate's membership card warily, but as

Kate had predicted, no comment was made. 'I'd like to check out the classes,' she told him. 'Are they free to members?'

'Sure are.' He handed her a leaflet that listed circuit training and step aerobics and HIIT and spinning and Pilates, but no yoga.

'What's Pilates like?' she asked.

'Great for strengthening the core,' he told her. 'Not unrelated to yoga, a lot of similar exercises. You've just missed today's class' – and she saw it listed at half nine. Another on Tuesday evening: she'd be ready for it, if she wasn't working at Borelli's. She pocketed the leaflet and thanked him, and walked home a different route, reacquainting herself with more of her old surroundings. After Dublin, the town felt tiny.

The rest of the weekend passed with a lesson in hen husbandry from Kate, and lots of reading, and a few walks around the main park in town, which she'd always loved, and half a dozen texts to old friends, who all expressed delight at the news that she was back home, and declared that they *must* meet up, but didn't, any of them, suggest when exactly that was to happen. Never mind: she'd taken the first steps.

Monday came, and with it heavy, incessant rain. She spent the day indoors, reading and watching Netflix, apart from occasional dashes to the hens' enclosure for feeding and egg collection, and depositing the eggs as instructed by Kate's back door. She sent emails to Tina and Liz, attaching a few snaps of the apartment, telling them how adorable it was. *I'm as snug as a bug*, she wrote, *with everything I could possibly need. I'm so lucky to have it for nothing*. Told them about the hens, and the gym membership she'd been gifted, and the free WiFi.

She didn't tell either of them about Chris's text. He hadn't sent another; it looked like he'd got the message, and was leaving her alone. Better this way, she told herself: fresh start meant no room for lying exes.

But still. But still.

He hadn't blocked her. That insisted on going round in her head like a hamster wheel, bringing with it a traitorous hope.

Within minutes, Tina responded:

I might have sounded negative at the notion of you moving home, but I'm glad to hear it's starting off well. Keep me posted, say hello to everyone I know. Sorry for short reply – two waiting for nappy changes here, and Lou at work!

Liz's email came later:

Living alone seems to be suiting you – maybe you're relishing the peace after the noise of us! The gym sounds interesting – should contain plenty of toned males! Any new job on the horizon? Hope those hens don't keep you awake at night. All good here – I think I'm getting a bump, but Emmet says I'm imagining it. I suspect he's afraid to agree – he was so used to denying it anytime I'd moan about putting on weight before! Poor Emmet. He says hi and don't be a stranger. Your bed is here whenever you need a reminder of big city life.

As dinnertime approached she showered and changed and made her way to Kate's. Instead of entering by the back she decided to ring the front bell, like a real visitor – and was surprised to have it answered by a stranger. Kate hadn't mentioned another dinner guest.

'Hello there,' the woman said. 'You must be Alice.'

'That's right.'

'I'm Valerie – Val. Feel like I know you already. Thank goodness that rain has stopped.'

Almost as short in stature as Alice, and heavyset. Iron-grey hair with silver lights shot through, a choppy cut showing off its thickness. Full burgundy lips, grey-blue eyes fringed with dark lashes, a tiny uptilt to the nose. Skin flawless, or skilfully made up. A musky, heady scent; a wide-legged jade-green jumpsuit whose fabric draped and gathered and flattered. Age uncertain. Somewhere in her fifties, or maybe the far side of sixty. Maybe.

Alice followed her into the sitting room. No fire tonight, the rain accompanied by a softening in the air temperature, but a grouping of lit candles in the fireplace – and Bertha, perched in her usual spot to the left of the hearth. Bertha was a papier-mâché hen, black with white spots on thin wooden legs, that someone had presented to Kate when she'd bought her first lot of real ones.

'That was me,' Valerie, Val said.

'Sorry?'

'Bertha. She came from me.'

'Did she? She's very cute.' So she and Kate went back a long way, over twenty years.

They took seats, Val claiming one of the fireside chairs, so Alice positioned herself on the couch. Val crossed a leg, revealing flat black pumps on small feet. 'Kate tells me you worked in a dental clinic in Dublin.'

'I did. I was the receptionist.' Alice wondered what else she'd been told. Would Kate have spoken to her of Chris, and the wife whose existence Alice had been unaware of till she'd picked up the phone? She hoped not.

'It's a big change for you, moving back home.'

'It felt like the right time,' she replied, using the line she'd decided on. 'I'd been in Dublin long enough. And Kate made it easy, with the offer of the apartment, and the work in Borelli's.'

'She's had a rough couple of years, like everyone else in hospitality. For a while she wasn't sure the restaurant was going to make it.'

'Really?' Kate had never even intimated as much to Alice – but she'd clearly talked about it to a friend. 'I didn't realise things were that bad.'

'She wouldn't have wanted to worry you.'

'I'm worried now, though – maybe the last thing she needs is to be carrying me for a while.'

Val shook her head. 'Things are more settled now. Kate wouldn't have offered if she didn't think she could manage it. Anyway, you won't be with her long. Are you looking for another receptionist job?'

'Yes. I'm not really qualified to do much else, but so far I haven't seen any advertised.'

'Here we are.' Kate appeared, carrying three stemmed glasses already filled with something orange. 'Aperol and soda. I made an executive decision. Alice, there was no need for wine, and you on a budget.' She passed around the glasses and raised her own. '*Saluti*. Here's to happy Mondays.'

Val sipped, and smacked her lips. 'Do you see many changes in the town, Alice? How long since you've lived here?'

'Over twelve years – but I've been back every now and again. I noticed a few new businesses when I walked to the gym on Saturday.'

'The gym?' Val threw a look at Kate. 'You passed on your membership, didn't you?'

Kate laughed. 'You know me too well. If you say I told you so, I'll send you home without dinner. She never misses an opportunity, Alice.'

'Well, I did tell you. Those gyms have a good laugh at the January new members.'

'Well, I'm glad I helped with that. Everyone needs a laugh in January.'

Alice enjoyed the banter. Clearly, they knew one another well. 'I passed an optician's,' she said, 'near the tennis courts. I'm due an eye test, and I thought I might try there. Do either of you know anything about it?'

'I do,' Val told her. 'His sister lives next door to me – she was telling me about it. Only opened a short while. Later than planned, she said – he sprained his ankle or something.'

'You should give him a go,' Kate added. 'Fleming's is a bit old school.'

'I can't believe Fleming is still going,' Val said. 'He must be a hundred.'

'He is not a hundred – if he heard you! But I'd say he'll be retiring soon.'

'I should hope so.' Val uncrossed her ankles, crossed them the other way. 'Alice,' she said, 'I'm the editor of the *Bulletin*.'

'Are you really?' The *Bulletin* was the town's weekly newspaper. 'I worked there for a few months in my transition year. Frank Mulcahy was the editor.'

'He was. I took over from him when he retired, coming up for eight years ago. Kate tells me you wrote a weekly diary.'

'I did.' They'd clearly had a good chat about her.

'I showed her the clippings,' Kate said.

Alice looked at her in astonishment. 'You still have those?'

'Of course I do.'

She hadn't given her stint at the paper a thought for years. Her English teacher had suggested it, knowing Alice liked to write. The diary had been a suggestion of Frank, no doubt wondering what to do with this student who'd turned up on his doorstep looking for work experience.

A weekly account of teenage life in around three hundred words, he'd said. Light-hearted, nothing too dark. You could write under a pseudonym if you liked. It would allow you more freedom. Having expected to spend her time at the paper making coffee, and possibly proofreading other people's work, Alice had jumped at it. 'A Teen's Life', it was called, and she'd chosen Anna McCarthy as her pseudonym.

She'd had notions then of being a journalist. She'd gone back to Frank after her Leaving Cert, looking for more permanent work with him, but he'd told her he was fully staffed. I'm sorry, Alice, I simply don't have the budget to take on someone I don't need. Try Dublin – but she hadn't had the confidence to knock on bigger doors than his, suspecting they wouldn't look at her without some kind of qualification in journalism. The last thing she'd wanted was more study, so she'd packed away her writing ambitions and forgotten about them.

Almost.

And now Kate had told a newspaper editor about her teenage scribblings. She could feel the heat of her blush. 'I was sixteen. I thought I could write.'

'You *could* write,' Val said. 'You just needed a little more practice. Have you done any writing since?'

'Not really. I do keep a diary, and I scribble in it most nights, and I write the odd letter, but that's about it.'

'She writes a great letter,' Kate said, getting up. 'One of the few letter-writers I still know. Come on, dinner's all ready.'

In the kitchen, while Kate served up a blue cheese and spinach pie, Val took a bottle of white wine from the fridge and opened it. Knew her way around, didn't have to hunt for the corkscrew on a hook beneath the cookery book shelf. 'I hear she has you feeding the hens, Alice – and she's put you into that tiny place next door instead of making room here for you.'

Alice laughed. 'I can't say I feel hard done by. I'm thrilled to have the apartment, and the hens are sweet. I'm going to enjoy looking after them.'

'Have you met your charming neighbour yet?'

Before Alice could respond, Kate spoke. 'She won't meet him – he never comes out any more. I haven't seen him in months. Mr Costello,' she explained to Alice, 'across the road, the little bungalow. He's over eighty now, and cranky – he used to give out if anyone parked outside his house, although he cycled all his life, never owned a car.'

'Came out ranting at me once,' Val added. 'I had the audacity to reverse into his driveway when I was turning. He must have been behind the net curtains, waiting for his chance.'

'And woe betide anyone who kicked a football into his garden.'

'And the cat. Spare me the cat.'

'God, yes – I'd forgotten the cat. A scrawny little black thing, Alice – hissed at me anytime I saw it. I'd swear he trained it. Haven't seen it for ages either.'

'Does he live alone?' Alice enquired.

'Yes, for a long time. His wife died young, I never knew her, and they had one son who emigrated to— Where was it? Australia or Canada, can't remember which. He turns up every couple of years, stays a week or so and disappears again.'

'You tried, Kate,' Val said. 'You did your best.'

'I did. Everyone around here wanted to help him out, once he got to a certain age, but he made it perfectly clear that he'd rather be left alone, so what could we do? I think he has a home help now though – I've seen a young man going in with shopping bags.'

'Let's hope the old grouch has mellowed.' Val topped up glasses, again without waiting for an invitation. The wine was cold and sharp. Alice felt a small pleasant swimming in her head – had she skipped lunch today? She couldn't remember. Without a nine to five job, the hours muddled into one another.

Val set down her fork. 'Now Alice, I want to run something by you, a kind of proposition. There wouldn't be a lot of money going along with it, but Kate thinks it might interest you.'

Kate thinks. Another thing they'd been discussing. 'What kind of proposition? Something to do with the paper?'

'Yes. I've had this idea in my head for a while now. I want a column that focuses on local good news stories.'

A column. Alice felt a leap of excitement. 'But wouldn't you be reporting them anyway?'

Val shook her head. 'Not these ones. They wouldn't be major deals, nothing headline-grabbing, just some positive, feel-good happenings in the community. Sort of local notes, but with a bit more depth to them.'

'More depth? In what way?'

'More detail, more background, more fleshing out. Giving them more of an emotional pull, making the reader care about what they're reading. They might be tiny in themselves – an act of kindness that takes a second but has a big impact, or maybe a special anniversary that someone wants to flag up, or something found that was lost, that sort of thing. I want happy stuff, something to counteract all the bad news we have to print because tragically, that's what sells. I want a page that people will go to, knowing it'll put a smile on their faces.'

A page to make people smile. The more Alice heard, the more she liked. The long-ago diary hadn't always been happy. Alice had recounted her share of teenage angst – the heartbreak of unrequited love, the anguish of not getting a card on Valentine's Day, the embarrassment of your parents' interactions with your friends. How much nicer it would be to focus only on the positive, to deliver only good news.

'What do you think? Would it interest you? Remember, I couldn't pay much, say a hundred euro per column.'

A hundred euro sounded good. A hundred euro would easily cover a week's groceries, and petrol too. 'I'd love it,' she said. 'Are you actually offering me the gig?'

'I'm offering to let you try out for it,' Val replied. 'You'd have to show me you were capable – I have standards to uphold. But I did see potential in your earlier work, so I'm hopeful.'

'I'd love it,' Alice repeated. 'Thanks so much. I'd really love to try.'

'Good. It would give you something else to do until you got a fulltime job – and maybe, if it went well, you could keep it going even after that.'

Better and better. 'So what happens next?'

'What happens next is that you write me six hundred words by the end of the week.'

'Six hundred words … about what?'

'An imaginary account of something good. A practice run for the real thing. Create your characters, give them voices. Let me see an emotional pull.'

Six hundred words. The three hundred of 'A Teen's Life' had run to just a few paragraphs. Twice that wasn't too intimidating. 'You're on.'

'Good,' Val repeated. She lifted her glass. 'Here's to trying new things.'

They clinked. Alice caught Kate's eye. Kate winked. Piece of cake, the wink said. No bother to you, the wink said. Looking out for Alice again, showing Val the old diary clippings, just in case.

'If I like what I read,' Val went on, 'I'll open a dedicated email account. I'll invite readers to submit their good news experiences, and I guarantee they'll come in. People love to get into the paper, and this would be a relatively easy way. Oh, and you can be thinking about a title too. Something snappy. Something happy.'

Kate began to clear plates. 'This is all very exciting, Alice. You could be on your way to a whole new career.'

'Hold your horses,' Val protested. 'I have no openings for anything else. Don't give her any notions.'

'Not right now,' Kate said, bundling cutlery, 'but you never know.'

That night, Alice's head buzzed with more than wine. Six hundred words of a short, happy story. She searched her memory for Frank's advice. Keep it simple, he'd said. Write like you speak, write like you're telling it to a friend. Yes, that was what she must do. Now all she needed was to come up with a story.

Suddenly she sat up in bed. She already had the story. She reached for the diary she'd scribbled in an hour earlier, on her return from Kate's, and riffled back through its pages.

By morning she had six hundred and eight words, and a title for the column.

George

'WHAT KIND OF PEOPLE LIVE AROUND HERE?'

'Um … well, they're all pretty normal, really.' He wished she wouldn't stare so intently – made him feel like something under a microscope. And she hadn't smiled once since he'd let her in. Made no comment on the room either, just lifted the duvet and peered at the sheet, and pressed down on the mattress.

'I mean what age group? Young, old? Like, would they mind a bit of noise in the evenings?'

'Noise? In what sense?'

'I play the drums.' Still the solemn, unblinking stare. 'It's my therapy.'

'… Oh.' He imagined that bashing at a set of drums would probably do the trick if someone needed to blow off steam, but the sound might well have the opposite effect on anyone else within earshot. 'And how long would you be … drumming?'

'Not that long. An hour, hour and a half.'

Up to ninety minutes of drumming every evening, after a day in a classroom with its own share of noise. His students' chatter might not achieve the same decibel level as a vigorously attacked drum kit, but he did relish the peace of the house when he came home. He thought fast.

'I'm afraid that really wouldn't work here. You've seen that the house is terraced – and there's an old couple on one side, and a baby on the other. I don't think either household would take too kindly to loud noise every evening. I'm really sorry.'

A total exaggeration in both cases. The Mitchells, hale and hearty, were hardly out of their sixties, and both dedicated hill walkers, and the 'baby' was just a few years younger than Suzi – but George was reasonably sure that neither set of neighbours would be impressed if he took in a drummer.

Thankfully she put up no protest, just gave a resigned sigh and left, presumably to go and sit in front of her drum kit and belt out her frustrations. After he'd seen her off the premises, George changed into his workout clothes. He supposed lifting weights and pounding the treadmill was *his* therapy – shame it didn't feel more therapeutic at the time.

As he waited for a gap in the traffic to cross the street, he wondered if he'd made the right decision, after nearly a month of living alone, to go in search of a housemate. He needed the company, needed another voice in the house – but how many more prospective lodgers would he have to meet before he found one that suited?

The first respondent, a pinstripe-suited man who looked to be in his fifties, had asked to visit the bathroom immediately on his arrival, and had spent the best part of ten minutes there before revealing, on his eventual reappearance, that the house was a little old-fashioned for his liking, and that he wouldn't be taking up any more of George's time. He'd left a smell of toothpaste in his wake, and six Quality Street wrappers in the bathroom bin. The bristles on George's toothbrush had felt dry, but to be on the safe side he'd added it to the sweet wrappers and invested in a new one.

The second applicant had seemed more promising. Call me Ed, he'd said, grasping George's hand. Looks to be a nice settled neighbourhood. No rowdies, no parties.

It's quiet, George had agreed. The houses around here are mainly owner-occupied. Twenties, he guessed. Late twenties. Cufflinks at the ends of his shirtsleeves. Would you like a coffee?

Great. Coffee would be great.

He'd followed George into the kitchen, dropped into a chair. I like it, he'd said. I like the vintage feel. You live alone, George? You all by yourself here?

I am, for the moment. Well, my daughter comes every second weekend, but apart from that …

Right, right. Must be, what, three beds? Family home, George? You grow up here?

Yes, it's a three-bed family home. My father died, and my mother remarried recently, and moved in with her new husband. He'd spooned coffee into the cafetière as his visitor got up and crossed to the window.

And I take it you're an only child. I think you said in your ad that you're the owner of the house. Am I right?

That's right. Lots of questions, he'd thought. Bit probing.

Nice. And the garden is … fifty metres? Would it be that?

George had begun to wonder who was interviewing whom. I really couldn't say. You take sugar?

No sugar, George. The man had turned from the window. Yes, it's a great house. How old, would you know?

George had shrugged. Forties or fifties, I think.

Forties or fifties. He'd slid open a drawer, glanced at its contents – cutlery – and closed it again. George decided to say nothing. The man had probably done it without thinking.

Would you like to see the room while the coffee's brewing?

Sure, sure. Let's check it out.

He'd kept up the questions as George had shown him the bedroom for rent, and the bathroom. Wanting to know if the main room had an ensuite, if the third bedroom was much smaller, if the heating was gas or oil. He'd tapped a wall. He'd studied the trapdoor in the landing ceiling.

That go to the attic, George?

Yes. He'd felt a prod of impatience. For God's sake, where else could it go?

Attic not converted, no?

No.

But floored, yes?

George had had enough. You ask a lot of questions, he'd said, for someone looking to rent a room. He'd laughed then, wanting to take the sting out of it.

Ed had laughed too. You've cottoned on to me, George. You've exposed me. I'd better come clean.

Turned out he was an estate agent, there purely to persuade George to put the house on the market. They're crying out for old houses, he'd said. Seller's market right now. You'd make a packet, George – enough to buy a very nice apartment, with plenty left over for a nest egg or a little place in the sun. At least have a think about it. Will you think about it, George? Will you do that much?

George had regarded the little business card the other had

handed over. Cream, crinkly around the edges. *Properties bought and sold. Friendly professional service, realistic rates.* He'd lifted his gaze back to Ed.

So just to be clear, you're not looking to rent a room.

Sorry.

George had folded his arms, annoyance rising within him. Is this what you do? Go around pretending to be interested in renting, just so you can see what a house is like?

Not always, George – only when we're desperate for properties. Look, I can see you're a bit put out. I should probably have been straight from the start, but at least you know now that your house is very sellable, right?

Except that I'm not selling it, I'm just letting a room. He'd indicated the stairs, aware that his heart had begun to pump a little faster. I'd appreciate if you left.

For a few seconds Ed hadn't moved, just continued to regard George thoughtfully. What if he was the type to fly into a rage if he didn't get his way? Should George have played along, pretended to be interested in selling up until he'd got him safely back on the doorstep? Come to think of it, maybe he wasn't even an estate agent. Anyone could get business cards printed.

Then, to his relief, the man had given a genial shrug and thrown a hand on the banister. Right you are, George. No hard feelings, OK? I'll get out of your hair – but hang on to the card in case you change your mind. Okey doke?

George had not hung on to the card. Little pieces of it had drifted into the kitchen bin not a minute later, right after he'd poured himself a large solitary mug of coffee.

The next respondent was a woman who'd seemed less interested in the room than in telling George all about her bad break-up. He got the house! she'd said fiercely. I *know* he owned it before he met me, I *get* that – but I lived there too! I gave up a lovely house share to move in with him, and now I'm left homeless!

Oh dear, George had murmured.

And I have a cat, she'd added, glaring at George as if it was his fault. My mother is looking after it till I find a new place, but she has two of her own, so it's far from ideal. They don't get on at all.

Er –

You'd be alright with a cat, would you?

George had grown up in a pet-free house. He had yet to make the acquaintance of a specific cat. He was ambivalent about them at best. The Mitchells had a tom that limited its contact to perching on the dividing wall and regarding George with a lofty stare. He tucked hands into armpits, feeling under siege. Well, um, I've never actually –

It's house-trained, in case you're wondering.

Well, in that case ... and here's the bathroom.

She hadn't even looked in its direction. I may have people staying overnight, she'd stated, again daring George, it felt like, to challenge this. I'd be entitled to bring someone home – I know my rights.

A cat, and now a possible succession of strangers in the house. George felt he needed to take some kind of a stand. Well, technically ... but I do have lots of others to interview, so –

Oh, I get it, she'd said grimly, sweeping past him to march downstairs. You're another of those men – I don't know why I thought you'd understand.

George had had no idea what kind of man she'd imagined him to be, and why she'd thought he'd understand whatever it was she wanted understood. He also wondered what she meant by 'those men' – but he'd been happy to leave the issues unresolved as he'd followed her down. He'd stood on the bottom stair and waited for the slam of the front door, and it had come.

After that there had been the prank call from Dermot, in a silly high-pitched voice. Saying he lived life a little off the beaten track, if George followed. Saying, with a giggle, that there was room for everyone in the world, all that was needed was a little open-mindedness. Asking questions George should have seen through ages before he did: would George object if his mother stayed over every now and again – she could hop in beside me, no bother. You said it was a double bed, didn't you? And would George be comfortable if he hosted little dinner parties from time to time, all like-minded friends, and very discreet, if George got his drift.

George *should* have copped on, instead of stuttering and stammering his way through the conversation until Dermot had guffawed and confessed, and hung up before George could voice any objection, leaving him feeling angry and humiliated. The following day he'd heard laughter coming from the staffroom that had petered out upon his entrance. He'd caught Dermot's smirk, and had swallowed the rage that had bubbled up in him.

And now the latest, the drummer, had proved another non-runner. He entered the gym and began his workout, lifting and lowering weights with his usual lack of enthusiasm, and he thought with dread of the next interview, scheduled for ten in the morning. The person had sounded perfectly normal on the phone, but so had all the others, apart from bloody Dermot. If this one didn't work out he'd give it up, resign himself to living alone and get used to it.

As he was making his way out of the building some forty-five minutes later he encountered a female coming in through the rotating door. He stood back to allow her to pass, and she smiled her thanks. Short, fair hair, glasses, already dressed for a workout. She took an immediate left, in the direction of the studio where classes were held. He'd been meaning to try out the Pilates: maybe next week.

And the following day, Jack showed up.

'I'm gay,' he said by way of introduction. 'You should know that from the outset, so if it's something you'd object to, you can say it now and we won't waste each other's time.'

A careful expression on his face. George guessed he'd already encountered a few who weren't OK with a gay tenant. He wondered what it would be like to have doors shut in his face simply for being who he was. 'It's not something I'd object to,' he said – and then added, 'I'm straight myself, just so you know.' Might lighten the moment, might make the other feel better not to be the only one declaring his sexual identity.

It worked. The man's features relaxed into a wide smile. 'Well, that's that much out of the way.'

Like most people he was shorter than George, slight and as small-boned as a boy. Early to mid twenties, his head topped with a flop of auburn curls and shaved at the sides. The style suited his lean face. His teeth were perfect, his nose long and slender, his eyes hovering between green and brown. He wore a grey hooded sweater and skinny black jeans that didn't quite meet his black loafers. No socks, an inch of tanned skin. He smelt good. He was, George thought, someone who looked after himself.

He didn't enquire how many square feet the property was, or whether George had inherited it. He didn't mention drums, or exes, or cats. He didn't ask to use the bathroom. He expressed delight at the fact that the bedroom being offered overlooked the rear garden: 'I haven't lived in a place with its own garden since I moved out of home – I love it.'

'It's gone a bit wild,' George said. 'My father used to keep it up, before he died.'

'Any garden is great,' the newcomer insisted. Back downstairs he enthused over the old black and gold sewing machine that sat on its table by the sitting room window, precisely where George's mother had left it. 'That has to be an antique. It's amazing.'

'It belonged to my grandmother,' George told him, 'so yeah, possibly an antique. My mother never used it, just liked the look of it.'

'And you have a piano – do you play?'

'No, my father did. He was a piano tuner. He did his best to teach me, but I never got the hang of it. Do you play?'

'I plink a little. You wouldn't pay to hear me.'

He said yes please to coffee and no thanks to a biscuit. 'I'm not a fan of the sweet stuff in general – a direct consequence of having a grandfather who was a dentist – but I do cook a mean curry. How are you with Indian?'

George was fine with Indian – and once he'd converted his mother, the two of them had shared a takeaway biryani or a korma every so often. Suzi was still hovering around the edges of Indian cuisine, happy enough with an onion bhaji or a saag aloo, and fond of the poppadom, but circumspect about anything more ambitious. George was working on her.

He told Jack about Suzi. 'She stays over every second weekend, and random other times.'

'You've got a daughter – excellent. I love kids. I have two nieces, four and one. They live in England so I don't get to see them half often enough, but when I do I spoil them rotten. How old is yours?'

'Eleven, nearly twelve. She plays the piano, actually – my father started teaching her when she was very small, and she took to it straight away. I think she's pretty good.'

'That's brilliant. I love to see kids developing their talents.'

Over coffee, which he took black, he told George that he worked as a carer. 'I have my little gang, mostly over eighty, and I visit them in rotation. I pop in, do whatever needs doing. A couple of them wouldn't be the easiest to manage, which is fine – I reckon you've earned the right to a bit of awkwardness if you make it that far.'

The more he said, the more of himself he revealed, the more George could see them sharing the place comfortably. He wondered if there was a partner on the scene – and then Jack spoke again.

'Maybe I need to fill in a few gaps here,' he said. 'Just for the record. Full disclosure kind of thing.'

'Like what?'

Jack laced his fingers together – long and slender, nails clipped short – and gazed at them. 'I mean,' he said, 'I think I should tell you that the person I adored died in a motorbike accident over a year ago.' He lifted his head then, and George was alarmed to see the rims of the hazel eyes redden, and the eyes suddenly brim.

'Apologies, George – still can't talk about it without blubbing,' he said, giving a half-laugh as he dashed away the tears with the back of a hand. 'Anyway,' the smile fading, 'just thought you should know.'

George felt awkward in the face of such open grief. 'I'm very sorry.'

'Thanks.' Jack took a sip of coffee. 'I just prefer for people to know that. I'm not sure why.' Another short laugh. 'Don't worry, you won't be getting my life story. That's it, end of.'

He seemed on the level. He was clean and personable and friendly, and George had no appetite for interviewing more prospective tenants. What had Sheila said? See if they look shifty, or too cocky. Jack displayed no sign of being either.

'I'd be happy for you to move in,' George said. What was there to think about? Taking in a stranger was always going to be risky, but this particular stranger seemed like a good bet.

A beat passed. 'Are you sure? You can take a bit more time if you want. I wasn't expecting a yes right away.'

'I don't need more time,' George replied. 'The room is yours if you want it.'

A smile spread slowly across his face. 'In that case, I accept.' He extended his hand. 'Thanks, George. You won't regret it. I can't promise to be the perfect tenant, but I'll do my best.'

The lease was produced. George washed up while Jack read through it, and signed on the dotted line.

'How do I pay the deposit and first rent?'

'Online, if that's OK with you.'

'Sure.'

George gave him his bank details. 'When do you want to move in?'

'How's the end of the week, say Saturday afternoon, around four?'

'Fine.' It was Suzi's weekend. George had a feeling they'd get on. They'd bond over the piano.

Five minutes later his new tenant was gone, having lodged funds there and then via his phone to George's bank account, and having been furnished with a receipt and a door key, and leaving a drift of scent behind.

George rang his mother and told her.

'A carer,' she said. 'I like the sound of that.'

'He plays the piano.'

'That's nice, Suzi will like that. Has he a girlfriend, did he say?'

'No girlfriend, he's single. He's actually gay.'

'So what?'

'So nothing, I'm just letting you know.'

'Sally is gay.'

'Sally who?'

'John's younger daughter.'

'I didn't know that.'

Pause. 'Actually, I thought *you* might be gay, George.'

She could still astonish him. 'What?'

'I thought maybe that was why you and Claire didn't last. I kept waiting for you to come out. I wouldn't have disowned you.'

'... OK.'

'I still wouldn't, George.'

'Mam, I'm not gay.'

'Well, that's fine then.'

Did everyone wonder about him? He needed to find a girlfriend. 'How's everything else?'

She made a sound that could have been a sigh, or a yawn, or just an inhalation. 'Everything's fine, George. I'm fine, and John is fine. We're both perfectly fine.'

'And are you meeting people? Are you keeping busy?' She hated to have time on her hands.

'I'm doing the best I can. I hope you're watering my flowers.'

'What? Yes, of course.' They'd completely slipped his mind. He had no idea what state they were in. 'Look, say hi to John. Suzi and I will come and see you soon.'

'I'd like that, George. Come when you can. Come for lunch some Saturday.'

After hanging up, he wondered if she'd sounded a little off, or if he'd imagined it. He supposed some emotional stuff was inevitable, after having been uprooted from the town where she'd lived since moving there as a young bride. Now she had a new husband and a new home – and a whole new way of life, after giving up work. He'd deliberately held off on suggesting a visit, wanting to give the newlyweds space to ease into life together, but maybe he should plan one soon.

He rang Suzi and told her about Jack. 'He's moving in on Saturday, so you'll meet him.'

'Did you tell him about me?'

'Of course I did. He plays the piano too.'

'*Does* he?'

'Yes. He's looking forward to meeting you.'

'Cool.'

'Suzi, you know what being gay means, don't you?'

'Course I do.' Pause. 'Are *you* gay, George?'

His daughter too. 'No. Why would you think *I* was gay?'

'Well, because Ursula Tobin's parents got divorced, and now her father lives with another man.'

Roisin Meaney

'That doesn't mean he's gay. Men can share houses, and so can women, without being in a relationship.' Maybe the sex-education talk she'd had last year in school had left a few holes.

'George, they live in an apartment, and it's only got one bedroom. Ursula has to sleep on the couch when she stays.'

'Right. Well, that's—'

'And Yvonne Harney's brother is gay.'

'OK.' Clearly not an issue. He let it drop.

Later he regarded his collection of saucepans and other cooking utensils, and found it wanting. Everything was battered and tired. Lids were missing, handles were loose. His one and only wooden spoon was half a wooden spoon, having split down the middle sometime in the last twenty years.

He phoned Sheila from school. 'Where's the best place to get pots and pans?' he asked. 'And general kitchen stuff, sieves and wooden spoons and things.'

She told him. 'Have you found a tenant?'

'I have, finally. A guy who works as a carer.'

'I like the sound of that. He seems normal?'

'As far as I can tell. I suppose I won't know for sure till he's been here a while.'

'Good luck,' she said. 'Fingers crossed.'

Today was Wednesday. In three days, he'd have a housemate. Tomorrow he'd go shopping after school, kit out the kitchen properly. Do a bit of a clean on Friday too – Suzi would help if he promised a takeaway pizza for dinner.

And after that, time would tell.

Alice

SHE NEARLY WENT WITHOUT THE EGGS.

'The house is literally across the road from the gym,' Kate had said. 'It's number twenty-six, a blue front door. What time is your class?'

'Half nine.'

'In that case I'd say deliver the eggs before the class, in case he's an early riser, but don't ring the bell in case he's not. Just leave them by the door, they'll be fine.'

She'd given Alice the carton of eggs when they'd got home from Borelli's last evening, and Alice had set it on the counter of her kitchenette, and walked right past it on her way out in the morning. Luckily, she remembered them at the gate: God forbid poor George would have to do without the eggs Mummy paid for.

Turning onto the street, she glanced across at the bungalow opposite, and thought of the man living alone there who didn't come out any more. The old grouch, Val had called him. What name had Kate given him? Costello? Considine? Alice had noticed a red Mini parked outside the house a few times: might belong to the carer they'd mentioned. At least he had someone looking in on him: even old grouches deserved that. She scanned the raggy lawn in front, and saw no sign of a cat.

The town was quiet at nine on a Saturday. As she walked, she pondered. Just over a week into her new life, and she had yet to decide whether she'd done the right thing. Her first two shifts at Borelli's, five to midnight, had been spent in the kitchen, peeling and slicing vegetables, making sauces and grating cheese, topping pizza bases and assembling salads, while Kate and Danny, the sous chef, churned out fresh pasta, and kneaded and stretched dough for the pizzas, and cooked lasagnes and risottos and *arancini*, and Maggie, stout and silent, who'd worked for Aldo's father before Kate's arrival, scrubbed pots at the giant sink, and polished cutlery, and emptied and filled the dishwasher.

Alice will be helping out for a while, was how Kate had put it to the kitchen staff and the two waitresses, Claudia and Freya. She hadn't mentioned the family connection. If any of them were surprised at the boss suddenly producing a new employee, they didn't show it. They all seemed friendly enough.

Alice had found it ... what? Mildly interesting would probably be a fair description. She'd never worked in a restaurant kitchen before, so there was the novelty factor. Not really how she'd choose to earn her living, but she was grateful, of course she was, and it was only temporary. She'd just have to keep looking for the job that surely would materialise soon.

On a happier note, the new column in the paper was happening. The sample piece Alice had written involved a missing item that had found its way against the odds back to its owner. What she didn't tell Val was that it was based in reality. She'd mislaid her own watch a year or so ago during a day trip to Bray with friends. It had been found by a person who'd taken a snap and put it up on social media, where it was shared and re-shared, and eventually seen by one of Alice's friends. Alice had made contact with the finder, and within a week the watch had been returned to her.

She'd changed names and places in her retelling, and turned the watch into a bracelet, but she'd held on to the sequence of events that had led to the happy outcome, and she'd injected an emotional element by making the bracelet a gift from a beloved grandparent who'd since died.

Well done, Val had emailed. *Consider yourself hired*. It was a positive development, and Alice took it as a sign that things would work out. She just needed to give it time – and to stop checking her phone every day for a message from Chris, and swinging between disappointment and relief when none arrived.

Number twenty-six, directly across from the gym, as Kate had said, was terraced, and red-brick like its neighbours. Flanking the blue front door were two long terracotta planters, the flowers they contained – a mix of crocuses and dwarf tulips – drooping and sad. Small wonder, with their compost looking bone dry. Why plant them if he couldn't be bothered to water them?

She was setting down the egg box as instructed when the front door was opened. She looked up and saw a girl of around ten or eleven with a face full of freckles, and brown hair still tousled from sleep. Grey pyjamas with a blue check pattern, pink slippers. One cheek slightly rosier than the other: the pillow cheek, Alice guessed.

'I saw you coming,' the girl said, 'from my bedroom window.'

'Hi.' Alice stood and held out the eggs. 'These are for George, from Kate.' She'd assumed he lived alone.

'Thanks. He's having a shower. I'm in charge of breakfast, because he got the pizza last night.'

Alice smiled. 'Sounds like a fair exchange. Is he your dad?'

'Yeah.'

'So what's on the menu?'

'Tea and toast. And orange juice just for me – George gets hives if he drinks it.'

'Oh dear.' She called him George, not Dad. 'Well, have a good Saturday.' On impulse, she added, 'I'm Alice. Kate gave me the job of delivering the eggs.'

'I'm Suzi.'

'Pleased to meet you, Suzi. You could add eggs now to your breakfast menu.'

'Well, I don't really know how to cook them, but George does. He loves eggs.'

Lover of eggs, allergic to orange juice, father of a young girl. She was finding out all about George. She said goodbye and crossed to the gym, and set her mind to the business of Pilates.

An hour and a quarter later she was out again, hair still damp from her shower, face warm from the exercise. Fifteen minutes, just enough time to walk to Newman Optician's. William, the owner's name was. She liked the fact that the receptionist who'd made the booking had called him that, and not Mr Newman, or whatever his real name was. Maybe she was his wife, and used his first name automatically. 'William could fit you in at eleven,' she'd told Alice.

The front of the premises was painted olive green. Above the gleaming plate glass window the name was inscribed in fancy black lettering. A dozen or so spectacle frames were laid out on a single long glass shelf inside the window. Upmarket, it said. Expensive, it said.

She wondered if she should have gone to Fleming's: who cared if it was there a long time, and maybe a bit old-fashioned? She'd been hoping to get new frames if she needed a new prescription, her existing ones bought with her first pay packet in Dublin, but they might be too pricey at this place. Too late now. She pushed the door open.

The woman behind the pale wood reception desk looked to be in her sixties, older than she'd sounded on the phone. 'Have a seat,' she told Alice, after she'd completed a form. 'William's just finishing up with a client.'

'I might just have a look at the frames.'

'You could do that,' the woman agreed, so Alice wandered about, slipping off her wire-rimmed glasses to try on new styles – not as expensive as she'd feared – and peering into mirrors that were dotted about the walls. Of course, without the help of her glasses she couldn't really see the others properly. She selected a dark-rimmed pair and perched them on her nose, and impulsively stuck out her tongue at her blurry reflection.

'Alice O'Mahony?'

She whirled, grabbing the new frames to prevent them from flying off. Had he seen her silliness?

If he had, he hid it well. 'Sorry – I didn't mean to startle you.'

She fumbled on her old specs and saw fair hair with a kick at the front – a bull's lick, her father called it, insisting that it occurred predominantly on male heads – and glasses with narrow rectangular tortoiseshell frames. Good-looking enough. Presentable, you'd call him.

He wore a pristine white shirt, sleeves rolled to his elbows, and dark suit trousers. He looked about her own age. The receptionist, if she was related, was more likely to be his mother.

'William Newman,' he said. 'Pleased to meet you.'

She clattered the new frames back into place on their stand. 'Alice O'Mahony,' she said, forgetting in her fluster that he already knew it. Was there something familiar about him? Maybe she'd passed him in the gym, or stood behind him in a supermarket checkout queue.

He gave no sign that he recognised her. She was probably mistaken. 'Follow me, please,' he said, leading her into a small inner room. He sat her down before a machine she recognised – all the eye tests she'd had since primary school – and took the seat across from her.

'Chin here,' he told her. 'Look directly into the light, eyes wide open.' With the brightness of the beam that he shone into her right eye she sensed rather than saw his face draw closer, so close she could hear his breathing, and catch a faint whiff of coffee under another scent – aftershave? cologne? – that had a tang of the sea in it. 'A little puff now,' he said. 'As still as you can please, eyes wide' – and there it came, the tiny blast of air that never failed to make her blink.

'Sorry.'

'Don't be. Everyone blinks. Let's give it another shot.'

His voice was calm and low and soothing. Eventually he pushed aside the machine and dimmed the lights and listened as she made her way through the rows of letters on the lit screen that was fixed to the opposite wall. In the half-light he became a soft presence at her left shoulder as he slipped the test frames onto her face and slid the familiar series of glass discs into them and asked her to choose, again and again, between options.

Patient. Precise and measured and patient.

Afterwards, he raised the light he had dimmed. 'There's been a deterioration since your last prescription, more in the left eye than the right. Nothing major, but I'd still recommend new lenses. Are you happy to go with that?'

'Yes.'

'And keep your old frames, or get new ones?'

'I'd like new – I've had these ones for ages. I'll have a look.' Her savings could handle a small splash-out.

'Fine.' He jotted on a card. 'Ever worn contacts?'

'I tried them, but I couldn't get used to them. My eyes felt too dry.'

He nodded. 'Not for everyone. I prefer the specs myself, but I have contacts for when I'm out on my bike.'

His bike.

An image flashed into her head, a series of images, or sensations. Her foot slamming on the brake pedal, an airbag whooshing out of its compartment, a thump, a muffled shout. Fear. It made her stiffen, catch her breath.

God. It was him.

Was it him? Could it be him? Impossible to be sure, given that she'd been in a state of shock, and it had happened after dark, and lasted for such a short time. And what had she to go on but a few angry remarks, and the way he'd limped from the scene? And yet she felt strongly that they'd met before, and now something, some instinct, kept insisting that this was the man.

Wasn't it?

'You're a cyclist,' she said.

'When I get the chance.' He clicked his pen closed and slipped it back into his shirt pocket.

It *was* him. She was certain. Practically certain. The height, the build.

He dropped her card into a box on his desk, not appearing to notice her preoccupation. 'My secretary will put your information online later,' he told her, 'but I like the hard copy too, in case of system failure.'

Don't say it. Don't go there. It's clear he doesn't remember you. Let it be.

But she couldn't let it be.

'Were you – did someone … knock you off your bike, about six weeks ago?'

For a few seconds he didn't react, his polite smile remaining in place. She was acutely conscious of the small space between them, the little room that suddenly seemed much too little. She was right though, she was sure of it. What were the chances they'd come face to face again?

Finally, he spoke. 'It was you.' His tone remained perfectly civil. She heard no trace of the anger he'd shown that evening, but he might yet order her from the premises, refuse to have anything more to do with her. Tear up her card, maybe, just to drive home his point.

She got to her feet, gathered up her jacket and bag. Just in case. 'Yes, I was the driver. I'm so sorry.'

He shook his head. 'Small world.'

So calm. Not a hint of the furious man she'd seen that night. 'I'm really sorry,' she repeated. 'I'd had a –' No, don't make excuses. 'Did I – I mean, did you— Were you badly hurt?'

'A sprained ankle,' he replied mildly. 'A few cuts and bruises.'

'And your bike?'

He raised an arm. Instinctively, she tensed – but he was simply reaching past her to open the door of the little room. 'I'm lucky,' he said. 'I have a friend who sells and repairs them. He went easy on me.'

'Please let me pay whatever it cost,' she said quickly. 'I'd be happy to. I felt terrible afterwards.'

'Honestly, you're fine. I appreciate the offer, but it's not a big deal.' He gave a smile, a feeble enough one. 'As I remember, I was pretty angry with you at the time. I know you didn't do it deliberately – at least, I assume you didn't.'

She knew he was joking, but an answering smile was beyond her. He was being so calm and reasonable about it. 'Could I buy you lunch then, or coffee?' she blurted. 'Just to make amends. Not today, I mean – unless it suits you. I don't start work till four.'

What was she doing? She never did things like this. She'd never asked a man out in her life. Not that she was asking him out, obviously.

The colour in his face deepened slightly. He pushed his glasses higher on his nose. 'You really don't have to do that.'

'And you don't have to say yes – but it would make me feel better. I mean, I'd be happy to, if you wanted.'

He made no response. He looked hunted. Clearly he didn't want.

'Just a thought,' she said quickly. 'Forget it. I'm glad you're OK, and the bike.' She scuttled out of the room without giving him a chance to respond. She wanted to keep going, leave the shop and not show her face there again until she had to, but she'd already said she wanted new frames, so she spent the next few minutes agonising at what had just happened as she pretended to deliberate over the frames on display.

Why had she opened her mouth? She tried on a pink pair, pulled them off. What if he'd said yes? She took a gold-rimmed pair from their slot and checked the price, and put them back. What did they have in common, apart from the fact that she'd nearly killed him? Lunch, or even coffee, would probably have been excruciating, for both of them. She tried another pair in olive green. Just as well he hadn't felt the need to accept politely.

'Get those.'

The voice startled her. She turned to see a dark-haired woman observing her from the padded bench seating. 'They're perfect for you,' the woman said. 'The colour suits your skin tone, and the size is ideal for your small face.'

'Really?' She was glad of the distraction, glad to be pulled out of her thoughts. She took off the frames and slipped on her glasses to examine them properly. They were more compact than she'd worn before. She slipped them on again and squinted into the little mirror. Light and comfortable too.

'I hope you don't mind me butting in,' the woman added.

'Not at all, I'm grateful for the opinion. It's hard to tell when I'm so short-sighted.'

'You should have asked William to help you,' the woman said. 'He's got a brilliant eye – no pun intended. I'm probably biased though. He's my brother.'

His sister. Of all the women she might run into, it had to be his sister. Alice imagined telling her about the accident. I knocked your brother off his bike, she could say. I didn't mean to do it, but I ran a red light and drove straight into him. Bet that would go down well. 'Thank you,' she said instead.

'I'm Barb, by the way.'

'Alice,' she said. 'Nice to meet you. Thanks again for the advice.'

Without waiting for a reply she gave a ridiculous little finger-waggle wave and turned for the reception desk with the green frames, where she was asked for a deposit, and told to expect a text when her new glasses were ready for collection.

Collection. Already she was dreading it. She'd act as if nothing had happened, and make sure she found another optician for the next sight test. Had to be plenty in Galway, if Fleming's closed down in the meantime.

She put him out of her head and drove home to find an email waiting for her.

Alice –

Attaching the first five responses to my call-out for good news stories. Pick your favourite two, make contact, have the chats and give me six hundred words on each by end of Wednesday.

V

PS I'm also attaching the number of my photographer, Mike. Pass on contact details to him when you've picked your subjects, and he'll accompany you to the interviews and take snaps.

Alice set the embarrassment of her encounter with the optician to one side. She opened the attachment and scanned the items, then reread each one carefully. The return appearance of a long-lost cat, a baby born after years of waiting, a golden wedding anniversary, an all-clear after cancer treatment, and how a new pup was mending hearts that had broken from the death of the previous pet.

She read through them a third time, lingering over the phrases. *Tinkerbell padded in as if she'd only left an hour before ... We never thought the day would come when we would hold a child of our own ... I love her as much now as I did the day I waited for her at the top of the aisle, still unable to believe my luck ... The relief to be told the good news was overwhelming ... This little bundle of mischief is making a family out of us again.*

She became aware that she was smiling – and also that tears were dangerously close. There was nothing of major import in any of the messages. No big drama, no stop-the-presses stuff, but there was a genuine sweetness to each recounting. Val wanted an emotional pull in the column: it was already there.

The only problem was how on earth to choose two out of the five. Alice decided she needed help. She went next door to Kate.

'Read these,' she ordered. 'Pick your favourite two.'

Kate read them silently. 'The golden anniversary and the new pup,' she said. 'Or maybe the baby and the pup. But you can't leave out the cancer patient – that's a real feel-good one. And cat people would love the cat one.'

'Well, you're a big help. They're all feel-good. I hate the thought of leaving any of them out.'

Kate considered. 'How many words does Val want?'

'Twelve hundred in total, six hundred each.'

'How about this? Pick one of them to be your main story. Write five or six hundred words on it, and split the remaining words between the other four.'

'But Val said pick two.'

'Val loves a bit of initiative. Tell her it's too hard to choose, and you want to include them all, with snaps just for the main one. It's worth a try – and if she says no, you can put them into a hat and pull out two. How did you get on with your optician?'

Alice had almost forgotten him. 'Fine, new specs on order.' She'd leave out the bit about discovering she'd nearly killed him. She returned to the apartment and emailed Val with her alternative proposal – and waited in some trepidation for a response, wondering if Val would take offence at her newest recruit wanting to do it her way.

She didn't.

I'll leave it up to you, Alice. This is your baby, so it's your decision. I would say that once you set the format you'll have to stick to it. It'll mean more work for you, following up more stories – and bear in mind that a hundred and fifty words or so on each of the minor ones will only allow you a few sentences, so every word will have to count. Just make sure it's the way you want to go.

It was her baby, her decision – how wonderful that sounded. She had her very own newspaper column, and already she'd put her stamp on it before she'd written a word. Full of elation, she rang Mike the photographer to introduce herself.

'Hey, Val said you'd be getting in touch. Welcome to the paper.'

'Thank you.' She explained what she was planning, and that he'd only be needed for one of the chosen pieces. 'I'm wondering what time generally would suit you, morning or afternoon?'

'Anytime – I'm used to running around. Just give me as much notice as you can, and always make sure you get an Eircode when you take an address. I might not arrive when you do, but work away and I'll turn up.'

She thanked him and ended the call, and started making contact with the five respondents. Within an hour she'd got more than enough scribbled detail on the four minor stories – and everyone she spoke with was delighted to be featuring in her first article. So far, so good.

She dialled the final number, a landline.

'Hello?' Eight rings later, as she was about to hang up. A young child's voice. 'Who's speaking?'

'Hello, I'm Alice. Can I talk with your mum or dad please?'

The phone was dropped with a clatter. Alice heard '*Muuuum!*' and waited, and listened to the high-pitched staccato of other children's voices all colliding into each other, and something else, some music, beneath it – and was that the yipping of a pup, or did she imagine it? – before the phone was lifted again.

'Hello?'

Alice introduced herself, and explained. 'I'd love to come around with a photographer for a chat, some day early next week.'

'Oh, that would be wonderful – they'll be thrilled to be in the paper!'

Five children under ten, she told Alice, and a husband, and two cats and a rabbit, and now a new pup. 'It's mayhem, but we love it. The kids were so upset when we lost poor Sal – well, we all were – but Cookie has changed everything. We got him as a rescue, and he's a real handful, chews everything he gets hold of, and I mean *everything*, but we wouldn't be without him. Oh, I can't wait to tell everyone! You've made our day – Alice, was it?'

They settled on Tuesday for the visit, after school when everyone would be home. Alice hung up and texted Mike with the information and the address, and got an immediate thumbs-up in response.

It was happening. She was making it happen. She felt a fizzle of excitement. All she needed now was a new job – but with earnings from the column and the Borelli's shifts, she needn't be in as much of a rush with it.

On Tuesday, Mike – red-haired, bearded, older than his voice had suggested – was waiting by the gate with his camera when Alice showed up at the house. 'Early!' he said with a grin. 'Won't last!'

The children, aged from one to nine, crawled or clamoured about the kitchen, the younger ones with chocolate-smeared faces that their apologetic mother scrubbed in turn – 'They found a leftover Easter egg' – before assembling them for the photo.

The new pup, black patched with white, wriggling and waggy-tailed, attempted at every opportunity to eat Mike's camera strap, but the photographer seemed well-practised in coping with chaotic scenarios, and rescued the strap good-humouredly every time the little dog got his teeth into it.

The father, pale and dark-haired, considerably quieter than his children, was summoned from upstairs – he worked from home, Alice had been told – to stand in for one of the snaps, after which he immediately vanished again. Following a quick trip outside to be shown where an unsolicited hole had been dug in the flowerbed, Mike packed up his camera and left, and while their mother peeled potatoes for dinner, Alice sat at the table with the children.

'Tell me about Cookie,' she said.

'He did a wee on Helen's PE shoes. Helen cried.'

'I did not – you're a liar!'

'Helen,' her mother said warningly, without turning from the sink.

'He made a hole in Dad's leather jacket,' another child offered. 'Dad said a bad word.'

'He eats *dirt*.'

'He does not!'

'Does so, I saw him.'

Alice decided to steer the conversation in a more positive direction. 'What do you love most about Cookie?'

'His ears are really soft. He's good for cuddling.'

'He watches telly with us. He licks my face all over.'

'He likes it when I rub his belly. He growls, but Mum says it's a happy growl.'

'He's the fastest dog ever.'

Eventually their mother shooed them into the living room and told Alice about Sal, another rescue dog, who'd joined the household before any of the children were born, and who'd died a few months ago of heart failure. She spoke of the children's devastation at the loss of the pet they'd known all their lives, and the decision, with some reservations, to obtain another pup a few weeks later.

'I wondered if it might be too soon, but it wasn't. Cookie was the cure we all needed. We'd be lost without him now, even if he *is* a handful. He'll be grown up soon enough, and we'll probably miss his puppy ways. Will you have tea, Alice?'

'I won't. I'll get out of your hair. Thanks for this.'

'Oh, we're the ones who should be thanking you. I think it's a lovely idea, doing good news stories. There aren't half enough of them out there. Wait till we tell everyone we're going to be in the paper!'

That evening Alice opened a new file on her laptop and began to write up her first column. She faltered at first as she tried to find a foothold into each story – and she quickly discovered, once she did, that her only problem would be fitting what she wanted to say into the limited words at her disposal. She persevered, deleting and rewriting until she'd produced 1,017 words that she was cautiously satisfied with.

She read them and reread them, tweaking and tightening as she went. The third time, she read them aloud, and found nothing she wanted to change. Then, feeling a little nervous, she emailed the document to Val. The sample story she'd written was all very well, but that had never been destined for the paper. This, she felt, was the real test. Half an hour passed, during which she checked for a response roughly once a minute. When the ping finally came to announce a new message, her heart jumped.

Well done. This works very well, and Mike has sent me some good snaps. Tomorrow I'll hand the email account over to you, and you can monitor it yourself. Twelve hundred words by close of business every Wednesday. Good to have you on board!

And just like that, she was a writer – of sorts.

And on Friday morning Kate knocked on her door and handed her the local paper, open at page twelve. 'Congratulations,' she said, and Alice read Happy Talk in bold lettering at the top – her title, also approved by Val – and underneath, 'Accounts of everyday joy by Alice O'Mahony', which she hadn't known would be there, but which felt perfect. And while she was reading her words Val rang, and said lovely things about the piece.

She needed to hear them. In the two weeks since she'd made contact with them, not one of her old friends had got back to her about meeting up, which was disappointing. She'd been reluctant to make another move in that direction, not wanting to seem needy, so a lot of her free time was spent alone.

No more texts from Chris either, so it looked like that was finally over, and still no sign of a receptionist position that she could apply for. But she must focus on the positives. Happy Talk, of course, and the twice-weekly Pilates classes, which she was enjoying, along with the changing room chats afterwards – and even the shifts at Borelli's, which she was getting used to.

As she was getting into her restaurant clothes her phone rang. She took it from the counter and saw Chris's name on her screen, and her heart did a double flip before setting up a thumping in her chest.

She answered. Against every instinct, every sensible impulse, she pressed the answer key – and then she said nothing, because speech promptly deserted her.

'Alice?'

His voice.

'Please don't hang up.'

She closed her eyes, throat tight. Stopped breathing, in an effort to hear his.

'Alice, I know you're mad at me, and you have every right. I know I behaved despicably –'

He broke off. She waited.

'Look,' he said urgently, 'I've tried to leave you alone, I've tried to do what you asked, but I have to see you. I have to explain, because you don't understand. Please, Alice. I called to the clinic, but they told me you'd left.'

He'd called to the clinic. She couldn't believe it. She was clenched from head to toe. Everything tight, everything frozen. If the apartment suddenly burst into flames she doubted she'd be able to move.

Finally, she found her voice. 'No,' she said, and again, louder, 'No.'

'Please, Alice, please let me explain.'

She found her voice. 'You're married.'

'I know, I know. It was a mistake, Alice, we were too—'

'You're married, and you didn't tell me. You had an *affair* with me.' Her voice wobbling dangerously. She drew in air to steady it.

'That was never meant to happen. I'm not that kind of man, Alice – I swear I'm not.'

'Your wife told me you'd done it before.'

'She lied. She said that to keep you away from me. You were the only one. I tried to fight it, but I couldn't. I love you, Alice.'

Silence followed this. What could she say to that, apart from 'I love you too'? But that was not to be said.

'Please, Alice. Please listen to me. We married when she got pregnant, we were both eighteen, it was crazy. Our families were against it, but we went ahead. I made a mistake, we both did.'

'So why are you still married?'

'For the kids. Only for the kids, I swear.'

'Why did you have more children, if you knew you'd made a mistake?'

'It wasn't what I wanted, but she persuaded me, Alice. She knew how to get around me. And now that they're here, I love them, naturally I do – but I need you, Alice. I can't live without you. I know you feel the same. Please meet me again. Please let me come to you, wherever you are.'

He was saying everything she wanted to hear – apart from the most important thing.

'Will you leave her?'

'Alice, I can't. I have to think of the children. I would otherwise, I'd leave her in a heartbeat, but our eldest is doing Leaving Cert, and the next is going through a tough time at school. She's being bullied. It's not easy, Alice.'

'So what are you saying? You want us to keep having an affair?'

'Don't think of it like that. We love one another, don't we? We're just not able to be together, not now. But soon, Alice. I promise.'

What was she to do? Could he be believed, after his months of deceit? She thought of something else. 'You told me your father was dead.'

'He *is* dead.'

'Your wife said he's still alive. And she said your mother was healthy. She said they live in Fermoy.'

She heard him draw in his breath. 'Alice, I'm so sorry. I'm sorry she phoned you. I'm sorry she found your number. I should never have let that happen.'

'Is it true or isn't it?'

'No, it's not. I'm telling you, she was saying things to make you go away. She was so angry.'

'But you don't live with your mother, like you told me.'

'I do – she lives with us. She's not well. That's all true, Alice.'

Suddenly it was too much. She couldn't take it in, couldn't sift through what he was saying and pull out the truth. 'I can't,' she said. 'I can't do this, not when you're married.'

'Can we just stay in touch then? Can I call you now and again? Please. Let me do that much.'

She closed her eyes.

'Can I, Alice? Please?'

'… Yes.' What was she doing? What was she doing? 'I have to go,' she said, and hung up without waiting for a response.

And for the rest of the day she alternated between regret and tremulous hope.

George

HE CRACKED FIVE EGGS ONE AFTER ANOTHER INTO A bowl as he listened to the goings-on in the next room.

A sequence of piano notes, repeated. A new sequence, again repeated. A snappy, ragtime tune that George had heard enough times by now to be able to hum along with it. The music continued until a bum note brought it to a sudden halt.

'I *keep* getting that bit wrong!' Suzi, exasperated.

'Girl, you're doing brilliantly.' Jack. 'This is a tricky tune, and you've almost got it after just a few practices. Let's take it from the top, one more time.'

He'd lied to George. He didn't just plink on the piano, he played quirky, tap-along jazzy tunes with such ease that he made them sound effortless. He didn't read music: he played by ear. I'm hopeless, he'd protest, when George praised his performances. I make mistakes all the time, so that's why I go for this stuff – it lets you away with them.

Suzi didn't think he was hopeless. Suzi, as far as her father could see, was experiencing her first crush, or the first he'd witnessed.

She and Jack had hit it off from the start. Jack had bowed solemnly on meeting her, and told her that he was delighted to make her acquaintance, and Suzi had replied in her direct way that he smelt really nice, which had made him laugh, and that had set their tone with one another.

He'd complimented her freckles, told her he knew guys who got them tattooed on their faces. I hear you play the piano, he'd said, whereupon she'd sat and given him a demonstration, always happy to perform. He'd clapped loudly afterwards, declaring her much too good for an eleven-year-old, and it wasn't long before they were trading tunes.

On his first night in the house he'd cooked a chicken korma that she'd devoured, her usual caution around Indian food nowhere to be found. After dinner he'd produced a Scrabble board, proclaiming himself to be a bit of a champion, and he and Suzi had wrestled happily with words until her bedtime.

George grated cheese and added it to the eggs. He tipped the mixture into the new omelette pan and squeezed oranges into a jug. He toasted crumpets that Jack had got in especially for Suzi when she told him that she'd never tasted them.

He looked out at the back garden as he waited for the eggs to cook. A month after Jack's arrival, the view was beginning to change.

Would you mind if I pottered a bit? he'd enquired, the evening after he'd moved in, and George had said not at all. Will I find tools in the shed? he'd asked, and George had realised that pottering meant more than just hanging around out there.

You want to do some gardening?

If that's OK. I won't change anything, just tidy it up a bit.

He was asking permission to tidy the garden. In the weeks

since his mother's departure, George had gone out the back only to use the clothes line, pretending not to see the grass that needed cutting, or how sprawling the shrubs were, or how merrily the weeds roamed through the beds that should have been home to flowers.

And now here was Jack, asking if it would be OK to make it better.

Do whatever you want, George told him. Knock yourself out.

Really? You'd be happy for me to make changes?

Absolutely.

My father's a landscape gardener: I grew up with it. I love gardening – it's mindfulness and exercise rolled into one.

Sweat and drudgery was how George would have put it, but he wasn't going to argue.

What about the planters out the front? Jack had asked. Could I overhaul them, put down some new stuff?

The planters his mother had charged George with looking after. The ones he still walked past without seeing, every single day.

That would be great. Keep track of what you spend and I'll reimburse. Tell you what – how about you look after the garden, and I clean the house? Would that work?

That would absolutely work.

In the space of a couple of hours Jack had mown the lawn and cleared the flowerbeds of weeds, and pulled out the dead occupants of the front planters. It's a start, he'd said. I'll have a think about the rest.

Over the days that followed he'd spent all his free time out there, regardless of the weather. He'd pruned some of the shrubs and dug up others. They've outlived their usefulness, he'd told

George. I'm doing them a kindness. He'd begun arriving home from work with various things in pots that he said hadn't cost him a cent. Donations from clients' gardens, he'd called them. They mightn't all grow, but I'll give them a go.

He knew what was what in the world of flora; that much became clear. He identified each new arrival for George. Antirrhinums, or snapdragons, he said. My grandmother's favourites. Campanula – that'll spread, so I'll keep an eye on it. Marigolds, for the pops of orange. Rudbeckia, also called black-eyed Susan – they'll grow tall, so I'll put them in at the back. Lavender – I'm going to plant this close to the washing line, so the clothes will pick up the scent. Nemesia, small pretty flowers. Virginia creeper, to climb up the back wall.

George had promptly forgotten every one of the names. He'd watched as Jack eased plants from pots into the waiting ground, replacing barrenness with growth, taming the mess, watering everything in well.

Wait till it starts to bloom, George. Wait till that creeper makes its way up the wall – and just wait till you see it in the autumn. Spectacular.

Little by little, he was putting a new order on things. Bit by bit, he was nudging the garden into a different shape – and despite his previous disinterest, George found himself looking forward to seeing what the next weeks and months would bring.

This is the first garden I've worked on, Jack had told him. Patrick and I lived in his apartment; I moved in there six weeks after meeting him. I was eighteen, just out of school, and he was ten years older. My parents were appalled. I'd only come out to them a while before, and they were still getting their heads around it.

They'd met when he was eighteen, and he'd already told George that they'd been together a long time. He must be older than George's guess of early twenties.

After Patrick died they wanted me to go back home, but I didn't. I went to stay with a dear friend in her apartment, who gave me the space to mend. I was still living there when I saw your ad, and I thought I should move on. I felt she'd done enough.

He wasn't mended though, not yet. The naked devastation on his face when he spoke about his dead partner was plain to see.

Well, I'm glad you answered the ad, George had told him. You were definitely the best of a bad lot – and he'd embellished his description of the others, just to distract.

Jack was an accomplished cook. He produced a dinner most weekday evenings, insisting that George share, saying there was no sense in both of them cooking. In addition to curries, George had eaten homemade pizza and fajitas, and a chicken dish with a sauce that had tempted him to lick his plate, and a vegetable crumble that was far tastier than its humble name suggested.

He'd confessed to his new tenant that he couldn't reciprocate, his culinary expertise sadly lacking. I should have got my mother to teach me but I was lazy, and happy to let her cook. I can open a can of beans or fry a sausage, and I can rise to an omelette, and that's about it.

No worries, George. You have a live-in cook now.

How about I cover the cost of the ingredients then? I can do a weekly shop if you give me a list. Another deal had been struck, and on five nights out of seven George ate well, and washed up afterwards.

All things considered, the new order was working out nicely.

During the week they breakfasted separately, on different work schedules. Weekend breakfasts could go any way, depending on who was around and who was up, and this morning George had taken charge. 'Come and get it,' he called, and the music stopped.

'These eggs,' Jack said, forking up a mouthful. For someone so slight, he could eat. 'They're amazing. Where do you get them?'

George explained about the barter agreement between his mother and her hairdressing client.

'Eggs for cuts – love it. But I thought your mother had given up work.'

'She has, but she organised for me to keep getting the eggs before she left.'

'Ah, the Irish mammy.'

'Alice delivers them,' Suzi put in. 'I met her last time I was here.'

Jack tipped his head. 'And who might Alice be?'

Suzi shrugged. 'She just said she was the egg delivery person.'

'Interesting. I'd like a full description of her, to see how observant you are.'

Suzi thought, eyes on the ceiling. 'Not tall. Short hair.'

'Colour of hair?'

'Kind of blonde.'

'Any other distinguishing features?'

She thought some more. 'Glasses.'

'And would you say she was pretty?'

She pursed her mouth, considering. 'Kind of. She was friendly.'

'Good. Friendly beats pretty any day. So what have you planned for today?'

'We're going to see Gran – aren't we, George?'

'We sure are.'

Their first visit since the wedding. They were going to lunch – John is cooking, she'd said, so that would be interesting – and afterwards, weather permitting, a walk in a nearby park.

'I'm going to a party tonight,' Jack told them. 'It's a pal's birthday. We're having dinner and cake in an Italian restaurant.'

George had yet to meet any of Jack's friends, but they'd been mentioned. Charles who worked in the library, pharmacist Jane who'd taken him in after Patrick's death, fellow carers whose names George had forgotten, and others. He regularly disappeared at weekends to spend time with them.

Feel free to have people around here anytime you want, George had said, but so far it hadn't happened. Maybe the house wasn't cool enough, built in the last century, with just one bathroom and no downstairs loo. Maybe Jack was ashamed to let his friends see where he was living.

Bet none of them had their own personal egg delivery service though.

His mother wore a leopard print dress he'd never seen. He couldn't remember the last time she'd worn anything but jeans, apart from on her wedding day. Maybe she'd bought this one for the honeymoon. 'About time you came to see me,' she said, reaching up to kiss his cheek before stepping back to regard him critically. 'You need a haircut, George Murphy.'

'Well, I would, but my hairdresser has absconded.'

It didn't get the smile he expected. She turned instead to exclaim at how tall Suzi was getting as John approached. Three years retired from his bank manager job, still dressed in a suit. Neat moustache, beak of a nose, smile that caused his eyebrows to shoot up.

'You'll have a drink, George,' he said. 'You'll have something,' and George asked for water. No drinking and driving, not since the death of a school friend at the age of nineteen from just that.

Lunch was fish cakes. 'John's speciality,' George's mother told them, and he protested mildly, saying he had lots of specialities, and she smiled and patted his hand and said of course he did. They looked to be comfortable in one another's company, George thought – but was she a bit distracted?

'I hope you're practising the piano,' she said to Suzi – she'd always taken pride in her granddaughter's musical flair – and Suzi told her she was. 'I'm getting a keyboard for my birthday,' she added.

This was news to George. 'You are?'

'Yeah, from Mum and Rob.'

It stung. It shouldn't have, but it did. He had no idea how much keyboards cost, but he was fairly sure they were a damn sight more expensive than the fifty-euro Penneys voucher he'd given her for the past two years. It was what she wanted, what she'd asked for when he'd enquired on her tenth birthday – but now it seemed horribly small in comparison.

'That's a big present,' George's mother replied. 'Not that the size of a present means anything – it's the thought that's important. But you know that, don't you?' Saying it casually, almost throwing it away. Maybe she'd seen something in George's face.

She'd met Rob at an end-of-term concert at Suzi's school last year. Introductions had been unavoidable, so George had made them. The four of them had tossed about the usual polite nothings until a bell had summoned them to seats.

George had waited for a reaction from her afterwards, but none had come. Such reticence was uncharacteristic, and he'd wondered if it had been out of consideration for him. Even if he and Claire were history, his mother still mightn't be sure how he'd feel about his ex being in another relationship. Claire had been involved with other men over the years, of course, and his mother had been aware of them through Suzi, but Rob was the first to be introduced to her.

Similarly, when George had told her at Christmas that Claire and Suzi were moving in with Rob, she'd said little. Holding her tongue, maybe sensing that George mightn't appreciate a discussion – and in truth, the news *had* unsettled him. The first man to live fulltime with her, the first man to occupy the space he'd once occupied. He knew it was unreasonable, and yet it sat uneasily within him. Maybe you never really let go of your first love, particularly when you'd created a child together.

A keyboard, though. For the rest of the meal it bothered him, despite his attempts to let it go. He wondered whose idea it had been, Rob's or Claire's, and whether it had been designed to make him feel inadequate, or if that was accidental. Let it go, he told himself, but it niggled.

After lunch they put on jackets, the May day being dry but chilly, and set off for the park, which featured a duck pond. Despite the nip in the air there was an ice-cream van parked just inside the gates.

'Who's for a cone?' John asked, and with Suzi the only taker, George and his mother walked ahead to the pond, and found a bench there.

'I hope you're still getting the eggs from Kate,' she said.

'I am. Someone called Alice delivers them.'

His mother shook her head. 'Don't know who that is. How's the new tenant settling in?'

'Very well. He and Suzi have really hit it off.' He told her of the musical exchanges.

'How old is he, did you say?'

He hadn't said. 'Twenty-eight. I was surprised when he told me – he looks younger.'

She digested this in silence.

'He's doing a bit of gardening too.'

'Is he? What kind of gardening?'

It suddenly occurred to him that maybe she wouldn't want anything changed from his father's time. 'Just tidying it up really. He mowed the lawn, and did some weeding, and planted a few new small things, climbers against the walls, stuff like that – oh, and he refilled the front planters too. They were ready for a change.'

Silence.

'You'll have to come and see it.'

'I will.'

More silence.

'Is everything alright?' he asked. 'You seem a bit quiet.'

She gave a little shake. 'Everything's fine, George. I'm just getting used to the new way of things, that's all.'

He looked at the pond, where a little boy was squatting by the edge, his attention focused on the scatter of ducks that bobbed on the water. A man hovered nearby, presumably his father.

Or maybe not his father, or not his birth one. Who knew any more, with relationships so fluid now, uncouplings and new unions so commonplace?

His mother gave a sigh, ran her hands along the thighs of the jeans she'd changed into for the walk. 'Did you ever try that Pilates class you were talking about?'

'I did, the other night. Not for me.'

He'd been the only male. That in itself hadn't bothered him – work had taught him not to mind being the minority gender – but despite his regular runs and workouts and weekly soccer, the unfamiliar stretches and twists and gut-clenches of the class had left him feeling like a wrung-out sponge. He'd hurried away afterwards, avoiding the eye of the female instructor with the Eastern European accent who'd manipulated him none too gently a couple of times during the class into even more impossible positions. Never again.

'Don't let the keyboard bother you,' she said.

He opened his mouth.

'You needn't mind telling me it doesn't.'

He closed his mouth.

'I'm assuming there's no piano in Rob's house.'

'No.'

'So Suzi gets no chance to practise at home.'

At home. He shook his head.

'George, are you afraid a keyboard will make Suzi like Rob more than you?'

He forced a laugh. 'Of course not.' But he was, wasn't he? He was horribly, shamefully afraid of that. 'It's over the top,' he said. 'That's all. It's setting the bar too high.'

'Look, if they want to get her a keyboard, let them. It will benefit her – that's all that matters. Suzi's too smart to let something like that turn her head.'

She was right. She was always right, or nearly always. He needed to get away from the keyboard. 'Are you sure there's nothing bothering you?'

She took her time answering. He thought she mightn't, and then she did. 'It's nothing, it's just … I miss work, George. I miss having something to do. I miss feeling *useful*.'

He saw Suzi and John approaching. Suzi was licking an enormous cone. 'What does John do with his time?'

'He plays golf. He keeps saying I should join him.'

'You're not tempted?'

'Not in the slightest. I couldn't hit one of those little balls if my life depended on it.'

Neither of his parents had ever played, although they'd had lots of friends who did.

The other two were drawing closer. He watched Suzi indicating the pond, and John making some comment that brought a smile to her face. She was such a happy kid.

'What about a book club? Have you found any here?' She'd belonged to one for years back home, five or six of them in it. They'd gone on midweek breaks around Ireland three or four times a year, claiming the over-sixties packages even before any of them had turned that age.

'Haven't looked,' she said shortly, and with no time for more, the topic was dropped, and they didn't get a chance to revisit it.

'I'll ring you tomorrow night,' he said, hugging her goodbye later. 'And come and see us soon, both of you.'

'We will. Mind yourself, George.'

On the way home, while Suzi listened to music on her headphones, his thoughts stayed with his mother. For close on forty years she'd cut hair, first in other people's salons, then in her own. During his early school years George had had a minder who picked him up in the afternoons and kept him in her house until one of his parents collected him.

When he was older, he'd made his own way to the salon after the school day ended, and done his homework on a card table she'd set up for him in a small back room, surrounded by boxes of her supplies and fragrant bundles of laundered towels. Snatches of talk and bursts of laughter would drift through to him, along with wafts of shampoo and hairspray. His little nook was warm and pleasant; he had no objection to it.

His mother had always been sociable, ready to try anything new. Now she sounded defeated, and anchorless. It wasn't like her. It worried him. He didn't think John was to blame, but who could tell?

'George.'

He shot Suzi a look. She'd slipped off her headphones. 'Yes?'

'You have your serious face on.'

'Have I?'

'Yeah. You're chewing your lip. You always do that when you're trying to figure something out.'

'Actually, I'm wondering how to help Gran. I think she's a bit bored, with no job any more.'

'Why doesn't she go back to work then?'

'Well, her old salon is gone – and anyway, it's too far from John's house. And they're probably much more expensive to rent in Galway.'

'But she doesn't need a salon. Not a proper one, I mean. Not like she had in our town.'

He overtook a car that was pulling a trailer full of mattresses. 'What other kind could she have?'

'Couldn't she use one of the rooms in John's house? It's big enough.'

It *was* big enough. It was detached, and located in a mature suburb. They'd eaten lunch in the kitchen, where presumably she and John always ate, but there were also two sizeable reception rooms on the ground floor, with a conservatory tacked on to one of them.

It was an idea worth considering. Would John be OK with her converting part of his house, their house, into a salon? Would the neighbours be happy with a business operating from a private house in their locality? Would his mother want to take on the challenge of finding a new customer base?

Maybe, maybe and maybe. It might not be feasible, but it was certainly something to run by her in tomorrow night's phone call. 'Suzi, have I ever told you that you're pretty smart for an eleven-year-old?'

'An almost twelve-year-old,' she pointed out. Her birthday was in early June, just a couple of weeks away. The thought of it reminded him of the keyboard.

'What present do you want from me?'

'Penneys voucher.' She didn't even think about it. 'Please,' she added.

'Sure? Nothing else you'd prefer?'

'No.'

His mother was right. Money meant nothing to her – but now his fifty-euro offering seemed puny. He'd hike it up a bit, but how high should he go? He decided to ask the advice of his colleague Barb, whose daughter Helena was in his class.

The following morning he woke to the smell of coffee. He opened an eye to see Suzi placing a mug on his locker. 'Hello.'

'Jack said to bring you this.'

He yawned. 'Excellent service.' Jack hadn't been home from the birthday dinner by the time George was going to bed, but evidently it hadn't stopped him from an early rise. 'What's the weather like?'

'Good. Jack says we should have breakfast in the garden. He's frying sausages.'

'Is he now. Will you pull the curtains?' Outside the window he saw the perfect blue sky that never failed to remind him of his father's last day on earth. 'I'll be down in ten.'

Jack had brought three kitchen chairs outside. He and Suzi had plates on their laps, and cups on the ground beside them. 'Hope you don't mind, George – it was too nice to stay indoors.'

'Not at all. Hang on' – and he brought out the low table from the sitting room, and they set things on it, and Jack made fresh toast and filled a plate with sausages for George. And George listened to the buzz of a bee that was bumbling about, and he looked across the coffee table and saw the contentment in his daughter's face, and it was all he needed to see.

'How was the birthday party?' he asked Jack.

'Fabulous. I'm pretty sure we cleaned the place out of prosecco. Food was great – have you been? Borelli's, near the station.'

'No, but it's owned by Kate, the woman who gives us the eggs.'

'I thought her name was Alice.'

'Alice just delivers them. Kate owns the hens, and the restaurant. It's close to where Mam had her salon – that was how they got to know one another.'

'Did you take photos of the party?' Suzi asked, and in reply Jack pulled out his phone. He tapped and scrolled and handed it to her. 'The cake,' he said.

She frowned. 'That's not a cake, it's a box.'

'No, it's a cake that looks like a box.'

'No way!'

'Yes way. Gerald, the birthday boy, makes hats, the most wonderful hats you've ever seen, so we got a very clever baker to make him a hatbox cake.'

'Wow. Is that a real ribbon around it?'

'No – we ate that too.'

'That is *so* cool.'

'It really is. Tell you what – when you're all grown-up and you need a hat, I'll bring you to Gerald, and you'll get your very own hatbox to keep it in, with a ribbon and everything. Just remember *not* to eat it.'

While his daughter giggled, George wondered exactly how much a designer hat cost. No need to worry about it just yet.

'And this one,' Jack went on, reaching over Suzi's shoulder to scroll to another snap. 'The cake with candles on.'

'Cool—' Suzi broke off. 'Hey – I think that's Alice.'

'Alice? Alice the egg lady?'

'Yes, I'm nearly sure it's her. Look, George.' She offered him the phone, and he saw two figures carrying a cake between them that was alight with candles.

'Which one's Alice?'

'That one.' Suzi pointed, and he tried to make out her features, but in the candle glow all he could be sure of was glasses and pale hair, and a petite frame.

'Weird,' Jack said, taking back the phone, peering at the image. 'Spooky that we were just talking about her. Look at this, Suzi – I made a video of Gerald trying to blow out his candles. See how rubbish he is.'

And Alice was forgotten, and Sunday passed, and at five George packed up his daughter and returned her to her mother as usual.

Rob's house was bigger and fancier than George's. Podiatrists clearly earned more than teachers, unless Rob had family money behind him. Or maybe he dealt drugs on the side, slipped a packet of coke in with the fungal-nail prescription.

'We have news,' Claire said, leaning against the doorpost after Suzi had gone upstairs with her things. No sign of Rob.

'Oh yes?'

She held out her left hand. 'We got engaged.'

He should have expected it. After two years he shouldn't have been surprised, but he was. 'Wow. That's … Wow.'

The ring was unremarkable. A gold band, a modest diamond. He'd seen better. He'd have given her a fancier one, even on his teacher's salary.

'You're OK with it, right?' she asked.

'Of course I am. Why wouldn't I be? I'm happy for you. Congratulations.'

His first love, his only proper love, engaged to someone else. Going to promise, at some time in the future, to stay with someone else for the rest of her life, to love someone else and forget about all her exes.

Suzi would gain a stepfather. She didn't need a stepfather. Nobody needed a father *and* a stepfather. Talk about overkill. 'So when's the wedding?'

She moved the hand with the ring, making the stone flash. 'Oh, not for ages. We haven't thought about it.'

She and George had thought about it, in their mad early days. They'd laughed about running off to Gretna Green. They'd laughed, but they'd considered it – well, he had anyway – and then their plans had changed. Had been changed.

I'm pregnant, she'd said, after dinner one evening – and for a second he'd felt a rush of fright, and then he'd seen the answering fright in her face and he'd held out his arms, and Gretna Green had faded away as they'd focused on the new turn of events.

Just as well they hadn't flitted off to Scotland, with future heartbreak biding its time, waiting to undo him.

'Suzi tells me you're getting her a keyboard for her birthday,' he said. He hadn't meant to bring it up, but somehow it was said.

'Yes. Rob's idea. Is there a problem?'

He heard his mother asking if he was afraid it would make Suzi like Rob more than him. It will benefit her, she'd said. That's all that matters, she'd said. He shook his head. 'No problem at all, she'll be delighted. See you Friday week.'

Later, he made the promised phone call to his mother. 'Good to see you yesterday,' he said. 'Thanks for lunch.'

'Thank you for coming. John enjoyed having you both. Suzi has completely won him over.'

'That's good … We were talking about you on the way home.'

'Were you?'

'Yes. I was a bit worried. You seemed ... not yourself. Anyway, we decided that you needed to go back to work. Suzi thinks you should open a salon in John's house.'

She laughed. 'Isn't she funny.'

'Well, you said you missed work, so we were trying to figure out the easiest way for you to go back to it. I don't think you'd care to work for anyone else.'

'I most certainly would not.'

'And rent on commercial properties is probably sky high in Galway.'

'I would imagine it is.'

'So would that be an option, converting a room in the house?'

'Oh, I wouldn't think so. No, I doubt John would want me doing that.'

'You could run it by him though. You could do it part-time, just mornings, or a couple of days a week.'

'I don't think so,' she repeated, so he let it drop.

'There's news,' he said. 'Claire's engaged.'

'*Is* she? When are they getting married?'

'No date set.'

A beat passed. 'I hope it didn't upset you, hearing that.'

'Of course it didn't.'

'There's no "of course" about it, George. I know things have been over between you for a long time, but now she's moving on, and you ...' She let it trail off. She might as well have said it aloud: she's moving on and you're moving nowhere. You're stuck fast.

'I'm fine about it.'

'Well, that's good. I wonder how Suzi will feel.'

It hadn't occurred to him to wonder that. 'She'll be fine too. It shouldn't make much difference to her.'

'George, you make it sound like she's changing bedrooms. Her mother's getting married. Rob will become her stepfather. It'll be a lot for her to handle. I think you should broach the subject at least.'

'Let's wait and see,' he said. 'If she brings it up, we can have the chat. Like I say, there are no wedding plans, so there's plenty of time.'

That night he didn't sleep well. Dissatisfaction settled like sludge inside him, causing him to shift and twitch in an effort to dislodge it. He needed to move on. He was comfortable with the way things were, but that was the problem, wasn't it? He needed change to happen – no, he needed to make it happen, or he'd be rattling around this house in his eighties, waiting for Suzi to make time to visit him with her husband and children.

Towards dawn he fell into a fitful sleep, and had a muddled dream about burnt fishcakes and Claire in tears, and he woke with a start at the sound of the radio clicking on, bringing him into another working week.

At break time he sought out Barb in the staffroom. 'I'm looking for advice,' he said, and told her about Suzi's upcoming birthday.

'What did you give last year?'

'A Penneys voucher.'

'How much?'

'Fifty.'

'Go to sixty,' she said.

'Not more? I was thinking of eighty.'

She shook her head. 'George, she's going to be twelve. There are a lot of birthdays ahead before she's earning her own money. Don't give yourself a future headache by overcompensating now.'

'I wouldn't look on it as overcompensating though.'

She gave him the kind of smile women were good at. He was familiar with it. 'George, every separated father has a tendency to overcompensate. That's just the way it is, and it's sweet, but you need to rein it in, or she'll ruin you financially. Anyway, sixty euro will give her loads of mileage in Penneys.'

'Fair enough.'

Barb turned to the others around the table. 'Did anyone see this week's Happy Talk?

Immediately there was a chorus of replies.

'Loved it.'

'The little girl who collects litter on her walks with her mum!'

'Oh, wasn't she adorable!'

George was lost. 'What are you all on about?'

'It's a good news column,' Sheila told him, 'in the local paper. It's been there for the past few weeks.'

'I love the idea of it,' Vicky said. 'It cheers me up no end' – and again, the chorus started.

'Me too – I smile my way through it.'

'Sets me up for the day.'

'They bring tears to my eyes, some of those stories.'

The bell rang then, and they finished teas and coffees and went out to claim their classes from the yard, where Dermot was on supervision duty.

'About time, Mr Murphy,' he said loudly as George approached. George ignored him and brought his gang in for the painting competition he'd promised them after break. It was one of the activities he always planned at this time of the year, to liven up their last few weeks in the school.

Happy Talk. For the rest of the day the song swam around annoyingly in his head. Nice idea though, a column dedicated to good news. He didn't normally bother with the local paper, but on the way home he picked up a copy, thinking it might be a good thing for Suzi to read.

He found it on page twelve. 'Accounts of everyday joy by Alice O'Mahony'. Funny, he didn't think he'd ever come across anyone called Alice, and now he knew of two. He skimmed through the page over coffee.

It made him smile.

Alice

'ALICE O'MAHONY,' SHE SAID. 'I'M HERE TO COLLECT my new glasses.'

'Yes, indeed. Take a seat and I'll let William know.'

The thing to do, she'd decided, was to act as if nothing at all had happened. No accident at the traffic lights, no subsequent offer of coffee or lunch from her that he hadn't accepted. Just behave as if they'd met for the first time when she'd arrived for her eye test. Be cool and detached. He'd surely be happy with that – he must want to put it behind him as much as she did.

'Alice.'

Same formal smile, hair a bit shorter. The cut hadn't managed to banish the rogue lock, still jumping out from his right temple. White shirt as pristine as she remembered. Did he bleach them or have them dry-cleaned?

'Hello!' she said brightly. A little too brightly. 'Looking forward to my new specs!' God, the false excitement – he must hear it. So much for cool and detached.

The polite smile stayed put. Impossible to know what he was

thinking. 'Come this way,' he said, and led her to the rear of the reception area where a small table was set up against a wall, with facing chairs. Good: at least it wasn't the little room again.

They sat. He slid open a drawer on his side and lifted out a tissue-wrapped bundle. She didn't remember the frames being quite so green. His sister had said the colour suited her skin tone: hopefully she was right.

'Good choice of frame,' he said, polishing the lenses with a little cloth before handing them over. His nails were impeccable, far more looked after than hers. 'Try them on. See how they feel.'

A waft of his scent drifted across the table to her, more appealing than the headier, spicier fragrances favoured by some men. Chris had worn a light Calvin Klein cologne that she'd liked too.

The thought of him brought the usual stomach lurch. Every few days he rang, the calls leaving her conflicted. Loving the sound of his voice, but unable to shake the suspicion – no, the knowledge – that they were doing something wrong. He seemed to feel no such conflict, telling her he missed her, sharing work anecdotes, asking how her day was going. Harmless, she told herself – but it wasn't harmless.

'So what do you think?'

She pushed away her thoughts and studied her reflection in the little mirror on the table. Her hair could do with a cut. Her lipstick had all but worn off. 'They're fine,' she said. 'They feel fine.'

'Good. May I?' He reached across and lifted and lowered the glasses slightly, his index fingers briefly touching the sides of her head. 'Alright around the ears? Not too tight?'

'No.'

Difficult to know where to fix her gaze with him so close. He withdrew his hands and produced a laminated sheet from the drawer – again a familiar prop to her, a series of sentences decreasing in font size as they descended the page – and invited her to read from it.

Her voice sounded too loud. Twice she stumbled over words that shouldn't have been an issue. She was nervous, still dwelling, despite her resolve not to, on their traumatic introduction.

If he was aware of her discomfiture, he hid it. 'Good,' he said when she'd finished. 'Everything seems fine. Let me find you a case – or would you prefer a soft pouch?'

Pouch, she told him, and he stood and opened a drawer in a nearby cabinet and extracted a grey pouch. She thanked him and slipped in the glasses she'd worn to the shop.

'Here,' he said, producing a second. 'For the others.' She didn't need it, her old case was at home, but she thanked him and stowed it, wanting only to take her leave of him, now that their business was concluded.

'Get in touch if you have any problems,' he said, 'if they pinch anywhere, or feel a bit loose. Sometimes it takes a few days for things like that to become apparent, and it's easy to sort them out.'

'I will,' she said, extending her hand. 'Goodbye, and thanks again.' She was glad he was being so professional. And really, she wouldn't need another test for a couple of years. Of course she'd come back here for it; silly to think she couldn't.

'Can I – would you let me buy you lunch?'

He stammered it out, his composure slipping for the first time. They were still shaking hands. She regarded him in astonishment, the question taking her completely off guard.

'I was rude,' he went on, releasing her hand to push his own glasses further up on his nose. 'The night of the accident – and again when you were here before.'

'No, honestly —' Oh God, he felt obliged. He felt he needed to make up for his rudeness.

'I was,' he insisted. 'I shouldn't have been so angry when it happened. You must have been shaken.'

'Well, yes, I did get a fright – but look, there's really no need —'

'I'd like to. If you wouldn't mind. I mean, if you'd like it.'

Oh, why on earth had she felt obliged to confess to being the driver? Why hadn't she simply left him in ignorance? 'Well, I … I mean, sure, if you really —' She broke off. 'But you don't have to.'

He smiled. 'So you keep telling me. But let's just do it, if only to make me feel better. Are you free today?'

She gave in. She'd get it over with. 'Er, yes. I'm free.' What on earth would they talk about?

He named a place. 'Do you know it?'

'Yes.' It wasn't far away. Walking past it earlier, she'd admired the frontage. Bay trees in wooden tubs flanking the door, quirky font spelling out the name in pottery blue on cream, a border of flowers etched into the window glass.

'Meet you there at one?'

It was noon. She had an hour to regret this. 'Lovely. See you then.'

On her way home her phone rang, and she saw Chris's name.

'Hello,' she said, as brightly as she could.

'Alice,' he replied, and her name on his tongue worked its usual magic. 'How are things?'

They talked. By now he knew she'd moved back home. She'd

told him of the apartment, and the work in the restaurant, and Happy Talk. 'I'm going to lunch with a friend,' she said now.

'Good. Must be nice for you, looking up old pals.'

'… Yes.' Let him think that.

'I wish you were still here. I'm sorry you're not.'

Your fault, she said silently. His fault her life had veered off course, hers that she was still allowing him to be part of it.

'Do you miss me?' he asked, and she said she was too busy to miss him, and he laughed then because he knew she was lying. This was how they were now, she trying to sound as if she didn't care, he knowing she did.

When she got home she collected eggs distractedly, her mind seesawing between the call and the upcoming lunch. She tapped on Kate's back door, needing to tell someone about the optician. She'd have to come clean on his identity: so be it.

Kate was charmed when she heard the story. 'You were fated to meet,' she said. 'This was meant to be. And I love your glasses.'

'Kate, this really *wasn't* meant to be. I'm not in the least interested in him, and neither is he in me, I'm sure. He only asked me because he felt bad about being cross on the night.'

But Kate was having none of it. 'Think about it: what were the chances you'd meet him again? You knock him down on the very day you get the phone call from that other fellow's wife – and a few weeks later you walk into his shop. I'm telling you, Alice, it's Fate at work. You might feel it's a bit soon after that cheater – I don't – but you needn't rush into anything. At the very least, you'll have a nice lunch.'

No help at all. Sorry she'd spoken, Alice returned to the apartment and quickly tried on half a dozen outfits before returning to the one she'd worn to pick up her glasses. Changing her clothes might give him the wrong idea.

She parked half a block from the café, her stomach flipping. Half an hour, forty-five minutes at the most – just long enough to eat and make her escape. An early departure, she was sure, would suit him every bit as much.

He was there, sitting just inside the window. He waved; she waved back, arranging her face into a smile. Over soon, she told herself, opening the door. Home by a quarter to two.

It wasn't over soon. She wasn't home by a quarter to two.

'Tell me about yourself,' he said, when she'd taken a seat, so she gave him a nutshell resumé. When she mentioned her Italian mother, he told her about the gap year he'd taken after leaving school. 'I had plans to work my way around the world, but I started in Italy, and ended up staying there.'

'Were you with friends?'

'No, I was on my own. None of my friends wanted a year out – they were all set on starting college. I didn't mind, I'm happy on my own.'

'Did you get to Puglia?'

'I did.' He named a town. 'I picked grapes there for a month.'

'That's where my mother is from. I know it well.' She listed bars and restaurants, some of which he recalled. He tried out his Italian; she pretended not to notice the mistakes. Little by little, she felt her nervousness melting away.

'Do you go there often?' he asked.

'A few times a year, and I always go for Christmas. I haven't booked anything at the moment, but my parents are coming soon for a week, so I'll organise a return visit before they leave.'

She told him about the Italian restaurant her grandfather had opened on his arrival in Ireland, and that his former daughter-in-law now ran: he'd eaten there a couple of times. She mentioned Happy Talk: he'd read it, not realising Alice was responsible.

'I never noticed the name,' he said. 'It's a great idea, a bit of positivity. My sister says all her teaching colleagues love it.' He smiled. 'She'll be very impressed when she hears who I've had lunch with.'

'I met her – at least, I met one of your sisters.' Trying to recall the name. No memory of what she looked like, apart from dark hair.

'I've only got one, Barb. It's just the two of us in the family. Where did you meet?'

She recounted their interaction at his shop while she was choosing frames. 'She encouraged me to buy these ones.'

'She chose well.'

'Tell me more about you,' she said, and he spoke of his parents – teacher mother, architect father – who lived in Waterford, where he and Barb had grown up.

'She got a job here after college – she's six years older than me, and a teacher like Mum – and she married a local man and settled down. I worked in an optician's in Waterford for a few years after graduating, but when I decided last year that I wanted to open my own shop, I knew I'd have to move to somewhere with lower rates and rents, and not so much competition. Barb suggested I try here – there's only one other optician in the town, you probably know him, and he's close to retirement – and the rest is history.'

'So you haven't been here that long?'

'No – just since the end of February, when the deal for the shop went through. I stayed with Barb and her family for a few weeks while I got things ready. I opened at the beginning of April.'

Alice had knocked him down in mid-March, when he must have been up to his eyes in preparations. Hadn't Val said something about him damaging an ankle, about the opening being delayed? Nice of him not to make a mention of that.

'I had to get the place painted and kitted out, and I needed to furnish the upstairs before I could move in.'

I, he said. I stayed with Barb. I had to get the place painted. No mention of a wife, or a partner. His fingers were bare of rings. 'So you live above the shop?'

'I do. It's handy. I'm never late for work.'

He didn't smile often, so when it came it was welcome. 'And you've settled into the town?'

'I have. Barb's been a great help. She spread the word about the business, and introduced me to lots of people. And I meet people through work as well, of course.'

The minutes slipped by, with very few silences. After the food – tuna melt for him, seafood salad for her – they ordered coffees, and waved away the dessert menu. When he finally said he'd have to get back to work, Alice checked her watch and was amazed to see that it was almost half past two. Where had the time gone? Against all expectations, she'd enjoyed his company.

'Thank you,' she said, when he paid the bill, refusing her offer to split it.

'We might do it again sometime,' he replied, replacing his wallet. Not quite meeting her eye as he got to his feet.

Do it again. Uncertainties rushed in. Whether he should be or not, Chris was still in her life. The last thing she needed was to get involved with another man.

But this man wasn't Chris. This man, she was reasonably sure, didn't have a wife tucked away somewhere. He didn't strike her as the deceitful type. He wouldn't hide a wife and children, wouldn't pretend they didn't exist. He was perfectly nice to talk to, intelligent and interesting.

Would it be deceit in its own way, to let things progress without telling him about Chris?

She couldn't say she was attracted to him. She felt no flick of interest, no perking up of her heart like she'd experienced on meeting Chris for the first time, but he might grow on her. He might distract her from Chris. He might be just what she needed. She should at least give him a chance. As Kate said, they didn't have to rush into anything.

'You have my number,' she said, and they left it at that.

And of course Kate asked how lunch had gone, later in the restaurant.

'It went fine,' Alice told her, lighting the candles on another birthday cake. Nowhere near as spectacular as the hatbox one the previous weekend which had petrified her, so convinced she'd been that she and Claudia would drop it on their way to the table. 'We had a nice time.'

'Have you made another date?'

'No.'

Claudia appeared just then to bring out the cake, so no more was said.

The following morning, Alice packed her gym clothes and collected George's eggs from the kitchen counter. After her

Pilates class she'd lined up a Happy Talk interview with the mother of a special needs boy whose vandalised scooter had been replaced, a few days after she'd reported the incident on social media. *The new one was delivered to the house anonymously,* her email to Alice had read. *We're so grateful to whoever was responsible.*

The column was still the brightest spot in her days. The interviews, whether in person or over the phone, were invariably cheerful, everyone delighted to be featuring in the paper, eager to share their good news stories. Mike was an ideal working partner, punctual and professional, well able to put the camera-shy at their ease.

Best of all, the column was going down well, already bringing lots of positive feedback to the email account: *The stories give me such a lift ... it's the first page I turn to every week ... puts a smile on my face, a welcome change from the bad news ... a real tonic, I'd buy the paper just for this ... I always read them out to my children - they're determined to feature at some stage ... I hope it's going to be a permanent thing.*

You're a hit, Val had said. Well done. Alice loved the idea that something she produced was bringing pleasure to people. *Accounts of everyday joy.* Such a change from her years in the dental clinic – nobody looked forward to going to the dentist. The thought of a filling or a root-canal treatment never put a smile on anyone's face.

She parked outside the gym and made her way across the road to George's house. She'd been glad to see new seedlings in the planters a few weeks ago: someone must have had a word with George. They were growing steadily, looking healthy and green in their damp compost beds.

As she approached the front door it opened, and out he came.

'Oh, hello,' he said, with a wide smile. 'You must be Alice.'

'Yes. Good to meet you.' He was younger than she'd expected. Slim, boyish. He must have been a very young dad indeed.

'We've actually met already,' he said. 'Sort of. You were working in Borelli's when I was at a birthday party last weekend. You helped bring out the cake.'

'Not the hatbox cake?'

'Exactly – I was part of that rowdy crowd. Suzi identified you when I showed her a snap of you with the cake.'

Ten or twelve of them in the group, mostly males. Plenty of prosecco being sunk. Not that they'd been troublesome, just happy, and having fun – from the way they'd been hotly debating the merits of their *Strictly Come Dancing* favourites as she and Claudia had approached with the cake, she'd guessed they weren't straight. The cake, of course, mimicking a hatbox, had been another clue.

It had never crossed her mind that George might be gay. 'Is Suzi on breakfast duty again?'

'No, she's with her mum today.'

'Oh … She doesn't live here all the time?'

'No, just every other weekend. She's a delight, isn't she?'

'Yes, lovely girl.'

Nice to hear a father praise his child, and not in a boastful way. He carried a large white jug, from which he now poured water into the planters. 'They drink like fishes at this stage,' he said. 'I felt like having words with George when I moved in, the last lot were so neglected. He doesn't even own a watering can, if you can believe it.'

'Oh,' she said. 'You're not George.'

His eyes widened. 'Sorry – you thought I was George? You haven't met him?'

'No, Suzi's the only one I've met so far.'

'Well, you've just missed him – he's gone for a run. I moved in a few weeks ago. I'm Jack.' His smile widened. 'I'm the cook and gardener, he's the house cleaner and shopper. It's the perfect relationship.'

'Sounds like it.' She handed him the eggs. So George was now in a gay relationship, having presumably been involved with Suzi's mother before. 'Well, I'd better go, or I'll be late for my Pilates.'

'See you. I like your glasses, by the way. Very cool.'

'Thanks.'

Before crossing the street she checked the paths in both directions, and saw no sign of a runner. She wondered what his mother thought of his new living arrangements – or what she would think of them, if she wasn't already aware.

On Monday afternoon, her phone rang.

'I know it's short notice,' Val said, 'but would you like to come to dinner with Kate tonight? I thought you might like to see my house.'

The two friends, Alice had learnt, had a standing arrangement for Monday night meals, alternating between their houses. The one who travels stays over, Kate had told her, so she can have a few drinks and not worry. This was Alice's first time to be invited to Val's.

'Thanks, I'd love it. See you later.' She'd drive and drink water, and Kate could come home with her. She texted Kate to tell her as much. I'll sit in with you, Kate replied, but I'll still stay over – Val and I will be nattering till the small hours. The walk home will do me good in the morning.

'You look pretty,' she told Alice when she turned up at the apartment. 'I haven't seen that dress before.'

'I don't often wear it,' Alice replied, thinking of the night in the Greek restaurant, and the photo on her phone she'd deleted, and afterwards regretted. The blue dress had remained unworn since the days of Chris, but for some reason she'd felt it was time to take it out again. 'You look nice too. That tunic's lovely.'

'This?' Kate brushed at something on the shoulder. 'Ancient. And my hair's a mess for want of a cut – but I got a text from my old hairdresser today to say she'll be back in business soon.'

Alice slipped on her jacket, took her car keys from the counter. 'Isn't she George's mother?'

'She is. Evelyn.'

'I thought she moved away.'

'She did, but only as far as Galway: the drive will be worth it.'

'Has she opened a new salon?'

'No, just refurbished a room in her house. I told her to put me at the top of the queue.'

As they left the apartment, a woman came hurrying across the road towards them, crossed arms wrapping her cardigan tightly about her. 'Kate, I was just coming to see you.'

'Hello, Marian – this is my niece, Alice. Everything alright?'

The woman gave a distracted nod in Alice's direction before turning back to Kate. 'You mightn't have heard, Mr Costello is dead.'

'Ah, is he?'

'His carer found him this lunchtime. I saw the ambulance pulling up as I was heading back to work, and I went in.'

'End of an era. Poor thing, he didn't have much of a life.'

'The son will probably get the house,' Marian said. 'And no sign of him in years.'

'I imagine he will,' Kate replied, opening her car door. Flicking a lightning look at Alice, who recognised it, and opened hers.

'I just hope he puts it up for sale, and doesn't leave it to rot.'

'Yes, indeed. Well, we need to get going or we'll be late for our booking. Thanks for letting me know, Marian. I hope the poor man rests in peace.'

They got in. Alice started the engine as the woman turned into the next driveway. 'She misses nothing,' Kate said, buckling her seatbelt. 'She's thrilled to be doing the rounds now, spreading the news. I can just see her, annoying the paramedics with questions while they were trying to sort out the old man. Hope he's happier now.'

Alice thought of the carer, entering the house to silence. Opening doors, calling maybe, before he'd found him. She tried to imagine making that discovery. Pressing fingers to a cold wrist or neck, feeling for a pulse that wasn't there. Looking into eyes, if they were still open, that didn't look back. Slowly coming to the realisation that someone who'd been alive, someone who'd breathed and spoken and eaten, was simply gone. Age wouldn't come into it, she thought. At any age, unexpected death, the discovery of it, must be awful, just awful.

They reached the end of the road. 'So where does Val live?'

'She's behind Boland Street. I'll direct you when we get closer.'

Alice turned left for the town centre. 'You've been friends a long time.'

'Certainly have. We met when we had babies a day apart. I had Paolo, and Val had a daughter, Leonie.'

'Val has a daughter?'

'Not any more. She died at sixteen weeks, cot death.'

'Oh God, terrible.'

'It was. Val was on her own: the father had bolted when he heard she was pregnant.'

'And she hasn't met anyone since then?'

'She's met someone,' Kate replied. 'She has someone.'

She didn't elaborate, and Alice didn't want to sound like she was prying. 'Any sign of Paolo coming?'

Kate rubbed at a mark on the windscreen. 'Not till the autumn, I'd say. The busy season's just starting.'

He hadn't been to Ireland since Christmas. Alice had arranged to meet him at Dublin airport to give him a present for Kate before she'd flown the other way to be with her parents for the holiday. And now it was almost June, and he'd had all those months before things got busy in the *trattoria*, but he hadn't come back once. He was twenty-six, old enough to realise that his mother needed to see her only son more often.

'You won't feel it till your folks are here.' Kate's voice broke into her thoughts.

'I won't.' End of next week they were arriving, flying into Shannon on Friday and staying in Kate's house for two nights before travelling on to Limerick, where Alice's sisters lived.

Alice had been the surprise, arriving nine years after Sarah, the second-born of her two sisters. With just over a year between them, the older girls were a tight unit long before Alice's arrival, and all through her growing up years she'd been aware of the distance that existed between her and them. Not deliberate, no exclusion intended, just the way it was.

Both girls had left home while Alice was still in school, Sarah following Jean to college in Galway. They'd gone from there to jobs in Limerick, where they'd both settled. Sarah, a nurse, was married now with two children; social worker Jean shared her house with a couple of dogs and a cat.

In adulthood the age gap was less obvious, but Alice still felt they treated her differently. Kindly and warmly, but differently. More like aunts, it sometimes felt, than sisters. She'd never caught up.

A few raindrops spattered on the windscreen, unexpected on a bright day. Kate slid up her window. 'Go left at the traffic lights, and first left again. I'd better not mention the optician tonight, with his sister living next door to Val.'

Alice had forgotten that. 'There's nothing to mention.'

'He hasn't been in touch?'

'No.'

Ten days of silence since their lunch. Surprising, after he'd given the impression that he'd like to see her again – or maybe that had just been politeness. It was something you said, wasn't it? Must do it again sometime, like all her old friends promising to meet up.

Probably for the best, given the Chris complication – but contrarily, she was a little put out. Hadn't she been interesting enough for him?

'This is our turn.'

Val's house was located on a little side street, a few blocks behind one of the main thoroughfares. Even though she'd grown up in the town, Alice didn't think she'd ever been on this particular street. It comprised a dozen or so narrow two-storey cottages on either side, whose front doors opened directly onto the path. Val's property, halfway down, featured a window box of purple and red flowers just coming into bloom on the single downstairs sill. They put Alice in mind of the twin planters in front of George's house.

She wondered which of the neighbouring properties belonged to William's sister. A teacher, he'd said, like their mother. Barb, presumably short for Barbara.

'There you are,' Val said, all in lavender this evening. She seemed to favour fabrics that draped, that rippled like liquid when she moved. 'Enter,' she said, stepping back.

The interior was a surprise. The entire ground floor was open plan, affording a wonderful airy feel to the place. No hall: they stepped directly into a seating area with an old wooden floor and a fireplace, around which red armchairs were grouped. Like the rest of the place, the walls were painted cream. A flat-screen television was centred above a wooden mantle shelf; an abstract painting on the adjoining wall picked up the red in the chairs. Cosy, Alice thought, although no fire burned.

Val led them through a tiled kitchen with stainless steel hardware and cabinets painted lemon, and a table set for three, and a trailing wall plant next to a reclining female nude in a thin black frame. The kind of art that looked so easy – just a few lines, daubs of paint – but was probably far from it. Whatever was cooking smelt good.

'Grab those glasses,' Val told Alice, taking wine from the fridge. 'I thought we'd sit outside till dinner's ready; that rain seems to have changed its mind.'

Leading on from the kitchen was a little conservatory, still light-filled this early in the evening. It held just a single rocking chair behind which a floor lamp was positioned, and low unpainted wooden shelves filled with books, and the occasional potted plant. A papier-mâché hen, the match of

Kate's Bertha but coloured differently, perched on its thin legs by the rocker.

A small paved courtyard beyond the conservatory held a brick barbecue and a pair of wooden benches silvered with age that were set against whitewashed walls, and more plants in earthenware pots grouped on either side of a wrought iron gate in the old stone wall at the rear.

There was a woman seated on one of the benches. She lifted a hand and waved at their approach. Alice remembered the face then. Same shape as her brother's, a similarity about the mouths, but her smile was wider.

'I bumped into Barb earlier,' Val said. 'She's joining us for a drink.'

'Hello there,' Barb said. 'Hope nobody minds me crashing your get-together. I'll be gone by dinnertime, promise.'

Introductions were made. 'We've met,' Alice told her, and she said yes, of course, at William's, and she admired the new glasses. 'I said she should get those frames,' she told the others. 'Wasn't I right?'

Had he told her of his lunch with Alice? She made no reference to it now, so probably not.

Val lit a citronella candle and placed it on the rim of the barbecue. 'I should have fired that thing up – didn't think the day was going to be as good as it is. Barb's husband is king of the barbecues around here.'

Barb laughed. 'He really is. I must get him to dust it down for the summer.'

Val produced little bowls of olives and nuts. They sat chatting as tiny flying things darted about in the mild early-summer air, and distant high-pitched cries of children at play drifted about, along with the scent of lately-cut grass. Val rose to check on the meal, returning with a fresh bottle of wine. 'Ten minutes,' she announced.

Alice watched her moving about. She'd been a mother for just sixteen weeks. A long time ago, but the heartbreak, the sorrow of a lost child must surely never grow old for a parent. Alice couldn't imagine that pain. It was literally unimaginable.

She's met someone, Kate had said. She has someone. It didn't look like he lived here.

At length, Val announced that dinner was ready, and Barb departed. 'See you around, Alice,' she said as she left, and Alice thought, Another throwaway remark.

They began with a leafy salad, into which Val tossed a tangy orange dressing. They followed it with a creamy mushroom stroganoff, served on a bed of wild rice. Afterwards Val produced a rough wooden board, half the length of the table, on which she had set out various cheeses, figs, chutneys and crackers.

And the talk, over two and a half hours, never flagged.

'I hope Barb's brother didn't fleece you, Alice,' Val remarked. 'I passed the shop the other day, thought it looked pricey.'

'No, not bad – cheaper than Dublin.'

'I should hope so. How was he?'

'He was fine.' And then, because suddenly it felt mean to be keeping it from Val, she added, 'Actually, we've been out to lunch.'

Val's eyebrows lifted. 'Have you really? Whose idea was that?'

Alice hesitated. 'It's complicated,' she said. Might as well tell all – Val didn't come across as a gossip. She sketched out the sequence of events, from the phone call that had brought her and Chris to an abrupt end to the collision with William on his bike, and her subsequent realisation in his shop that here was the cyclist she'd almost killed.

'Interesting,' Val said when Alice fell silent. 'Some men want to have their cake and eat it – you were unlucky to fall into the path of one of them. Was that why you left Dublin?'

'Pretty much,' Alice admitted. 'I know it sounds pathetic.'

'It sounds understandable, if you had real feelings for him. And then to encounter the optician so soon afterwards.'

'Literally the same day.'

'Yes. So what's he like?'

'He's nice. I was afraid the lunch might be awkward – he's not very chatty – but it was fine.'

'So you enjoyed it.'

'I have to say I did. I'm not really attracted to him though.'

'And if he phones again?'

'Oh, I don't expect him to. It's been over a week.'

They switched topics. Kate spoke of her plan to introduce tasting menus at the restaurant, and Alice told them of the lone man who'd shown up for a recent Pilates class. 'I'm guessing it was his first. I think he found it a bit of a challenge. He scooted away the minute we'd finished, and he hasn't reappeared.'

Val talked about her father's upcoming eighty-fifth birthday. 'He's in a nursing home,' she told Alice. 'He hasn't recognised me for the past five years, but he's still physically strong, so I'll take him for a little walk around the grounds if the day is dry, and we'll eat sausage rolls – he loves those. And after that I'll light a candle on a bun and get him to blow it out. He'll call me by his sister's name – she's been dead thirty years – and I won't correct him,' which struck Alice as both sweet and sad.

She made her excuses soon after the cheeseboard had been taken away, declining Val's offer of coffee. It wasn't late but she fancied a glass of wine, and maybe a little silence after all the conversation – and the two old friends, she knew, wouldn't miss her.

The streets were quiet. Within ten minutes she was home. She pulled into the driveway behind Kate's car and got out. By now darkness had fallen, light spilling from the neighbouring houses. She looked across the road at the bungalow and saw that someone – the carer maybe – had left a light on in the hall.

She'd never met the man who'd lived there, and what she'd heard hadn't painted a very good picture of him, but still his death unsettled her. Maybe because he'd died alone while his neighbours went about their business, unaware that a life was ending close by.

Inside she logged on to one of the job sites and did her usual search – and finally found a receptionist job on offer. It was in a hotel, in a town about twenty miles away. She bookmarked it: tomorrow she'd apply.

Her phone pinged with a text. She rummaged in her bag for it, thinking it might be Chris. Sometimes he texted around this time to say goodnight.

It wasn't Chris. Are you free for lunch on Wednesday? William asked, and Alice waited until she'd taken off her jacket and shoes, and poured a glass of wine and curled up on the couch with it, before replying that she was.

Might as well give it a try. She had nothing to lose.

George

'MR MURPHY?'

He turned to see Deirdre Daly's mother hurrying up the corridor behind him, her shoes slip-slapping on the tiles. She must have left the younger children with Deirdre in the yard. 'Can I have a word?'

'Of course.'

He couldn't have said he knew her well. She wasn't given to small talk, far from it. At the parent–teacher meeting in February she'd listened silently as George had done his best to play up Deirdre's strengths – artistic ability, helpfulness, punctuality – and make as little as he could of her academic shortcomings.

Any questions? he'd asked at the end, and she'd shaken her head and thanked him and left. The husband hadn't shown up for the meeting – par for the course, the other teachers told George, didn't come near the school if he could help it. George had never laid eyes on the man, although four of his six children attended the school.

She followed him into the empty classroom, his class having just gone home. He invited her to take his seat.

'I'm fine,' she said. Unsmiling, the same solemn expression on her face that she generally wore, an edge of wariness to it. Waiting, George thought, for the world to deal its next blow. Not chatty like a lot of his other parents, not in the least. He knew nothing about her that he didn't need to know.

She remained just inside the door, feet planted wide, hands pushing into the pockets of her green raincoat. Dark hair gathered into its usual tight ponytail. Tall, five foot seven or eight. One of his younger parents, late twenties he put her at. A faded prettiness, six children in quick succession having taken its toll, but still the large brown eyes, still the full lips.

He leant against his desk and waited.

'My sister had this idea,' she said. 'I thought I'd better run it by you first.'

'OK.' He folded his arms.

'You know how Deirdre won first prize in your painting competition?'

'I do. Well deserved.'

He'd announced the results in class the day before, making a bit of a ceremony of it. Three main prizes he'd come up with – a family day ticket to the local aqua centre from a pal on the council, a book token he'd been given at Christmas that he'd forgotten about, and a voucher he'd wangled from the manager of the pizza place he and Suzi often visited.

Deirdre's painting, as he'd anticipated, was far and away the best. He'd given them the theme of animals, and Deirdre had painted a rearing horse, the body presented with such accuracy, the proportions and perspective so true, that nobody could argue with her getting the top prize of the aqua-centre pass. 'She's marvellous,' he said. 'A real artist.'

Her mother's face softened slightly. 'We had a special tea to celebrate,' she said, the faintest of smiles passing over her face. A rare glimpse into home life.

Did she have a job? Hardly, with two children yet to start school. He rarely saw her without them in tow. The elusive husband, he could gather from staffroom talk, was also a bit of a layabout. He imagined money wasn't plentiful. He guessed she had to shop carefully. A special tea, anything involving more than the bare necessities, would probably take some ingenuity.

'My sister wants to email the paper,' she said. 'You know the page with the good news stuff?'

Happy Talk, she must mean. 'I've read it.'

'So is it OK if she writes in about Dee getting the prize?'

'Of course it is.'

In most subjects Deirdre hovered around the bottom five in the class – and George, who had been teaching long enough to tell the lazy from the genuine strugglers, knew it wasn't lack of interest that held her back. All through primary school she'd had difficulties, getting learning support along the way, scraping by in everything but art. From her early schooldays, teachers had remarked on her drawing and painting. It was the one place she shone – and now her mother wanted to ensure that her first-born shone as brightly as she could.

'I think it's a great idea,' he said. 'It would be really good to see it in the paper.'

'And we could give your name?'

'Certainly you could.'

'Thanks.'

He should have been smarter. He should have slipped a fifty-euro note into the envelope with the family day ticket. They'd have assumed it was part of the prize; they'd never have known it hadn't come from the council.

He could still do it. He could wait till tomorrow and ring the mother. He could say the council had been in touch: they'd forgotten to include the money part of the prize.

But even as the thought occurred, he dismissed it. She might see through him, might see the handout for what it was, and be humiliated. He couldn't risk it.

'I'll be off so,' she said. She turned abruptly and was gone. He listened to the slap of her shoes growing fainter, and was glad at least that they'd have the day out.

He'd got into the habit of picking up the local paper, and saving page twelve for Suzi to read when she came. He understood the appeal of the column: you couldn't read those stories and not feel uplifted – and seeing their good experiences in print must give the contributors a thrill as well.

He wondered if Deirdre's story would be chosen for inclusion. The page must get lots of submissions: how many of them never made it into print? He imagined Mrs Daly's disappointment if Deirdre's moment of glory was passed over.

He'd do what he could to help. When he got home he climbed the stairs, causing a dark heap on the landing to streak away at his approach, and disappear through the open door of Jack's room.

'Hello to you too,' he said. He took his laptop from his room and brought it downstairs. In the kitchen he made coffee and opened page twelve of last week's paper and tapped out an email to the address given.

Hello there,

I'm a sixth class teacher. I organised an end of year art competition in my class lately, and a girl called Deirdre Daly won first prize. Her mother called in today to say that her sister, Deirdre's aunt, is planning to send in the story for your consideration. I'm getting in touch to ask that you please include it. The family situation is complicated, but Deirdre has an amazing artistic talent. I know it's only a class competition and nothing dramatic, but she'd get a real kick from seeing her name in the paper, and her mother would too.

I hope I'm not being too forward. It's not something I normally do, but I'd really appreciate it.

Thanks,

G. Murphy

He read it through, and clicked *Send* before he could change his mind. It couldn't hurt, and it might help. He was going through his other emails when he heard the front door opening.

'Jack?' he called, and got a 'Yup' in response. More subdued than normal, the breeziness gone out of him since he'd discovered the body of one of his clients the week before.

He was in the sitting room, he'd told George that evening. He'd fallen between the couch and a china cabinet. He was all huddled up like a child … I know he could be difficult, but I hate the thought that he died alone, without anybody to hold his hand or say a prayer – or just to be with him, you know?

And then there was the matter of the cat.

There's no one to look after it. I couldn't leave it, George. If you don't want it in the house maybe it could stay in the shed, just till the weekend, and then I'll take it to the animal welfare.

Where is it now? George had asked.

In the car, Jack had told him – and what could George say but bring it in? So in had come a hissing, wriggling bundle that had leapt from the towel Jack had wrapped it in, narrowly missing a collision with George before darting from the kitchen and squeezing under the hallstand where it had remained for the next several hours, growling if either of them approached.

In the few days since then, after Jack had eventually managed to coax it out and transport it to his room, it had spent most of its time under his bed, emerging only to eat or use the litter tray that Jack had also brought from the bungalow. This was the first time George had seen it on the landing, which he supposed was progress. It was a pathetic creature, gaunt and fierce and with half its tail missing. The only sounds it seemed capable of producing were hisses or growls.

Still, it was only short-term. A bit longer than originally intended – Jack had suggested they hang on to it till Suzi saw it, so it had got a reprieve till this coming weekend, although George recognised the potential danger of this move.

Jack appeared, carrying a hatbox striped in blue and white. 'Am I interrupting school work?'

'No, just doing a bit of emailing. Kettle's boiled. Did you buy a hat?'

'Not quite.' He advanced into the room and set the box on the table. 'Something for the birthday girl,' he said, lifting the lid and taking out a potted plant in which a cluster of tiny white and purple flowers were growing. 'I thought she might get a kick out of the packaging. I stole it from Gerald.'

'Good of you to get her a present. I hope you didn't feel obliged.'

'Not in the least. It's nemesia: I planted some down by the shed. I showed it to you, but you've probably forgotten.'

'I have, yes.'

'Well, Suzi admired it when she saw it. She can plant this one where she wants, or leave it in the pot.'

She was due tomorrow, three days after her birthday. They were having a belated celebratory lunch for her on Sunday, attended by her grandmother and step-grandfather. George had been invited to Rob's house for the official party on Tuesday; thankfully, he'd had a dental appointment, so he'd dropped in on his way to the dentist and presented her with her Penneys gift voucher. She'd made no mention of the keyboard, and neither had he.

'Might make a weekend for the chairs,' Jack said, looking out.

'It might.'

He'd arrived home the previous Saturday with two wooden garden chairs that he'd spotted in a skip on his way home from lunch with friends. All they need is a clean, he'd said. They're perfectly solid – so he and George had hosed and scrubbed, and now the chairs stood on the little patio, awaiting sitters. And maybe a coat of paint, if anyone had the inclination.

Suzi might fancy it. He could let her choose the colour.

While Jack made coffee, George opened an email from his mother. *We're both looking forward to Sunday*, he read. *Can't believe my granddaughter is twelve already.*

'George, can I ask you something?'

He glanced up. Jack had got the sides of his head newly shaven the day before, making his face look leaner. 'What?'

'When was the last time you went on a date?'

The question took George by surprise. 'Er ... can't recall.'

He'd told Jack about Claire. He'd felt it was unavoidable, with Suzi coming and going. He'd left it at the bare bones – the unplanned pregnancy, the relationship breakdown.

'Roughly how long has it been?'

George shrugged. 'It's been a while. Look—'

'A while as in months?'

It was longer than months. It was a lot longer than months. His mother had given up trying to encourage him to put himself about more. She might even have given up asking the saint for a daughter-in-law. 'Jack, I'm not really comfortable talking about this. I'm fine as I am.'

Jack nodded. 'Of course you are. There's comfort in being alone. I get it. It's safe.' He fell silent again, and George returned to his mother's email. *Well, thanks to you and Suzi, I'm officially back at work since yesterday.* He was delighted she'd decided after all to ask John about converting a room. *Kate from Borelli's was my first customer, she was telling me all her news. Her niece has—*

'Have you ever considered online dating though?'

He looked up again. 'What?'

'Online dating. Ever thought about it?'

He gave an emphatic shake of his head. 'Definitely not. Not for me.'

'But you haven't tried it?'

'I don't have to. I know I'd be rubbish at it.'

Silence.

George returned to the email. *Her niece has moved back from Dublin and is—*

'My sister used to think that. She was dead against online dating too.'

George sighed. 'Jack, you're wasting your—'

'We persuaded her to give it a go, Patrick and myself. She'd been burnt in her early twenties – her boyfriend of three years did the dirty on her, and she couldn't face going back on the scene, so we made her our project. We did all the legwork, signed her up on a site, even vetted the guys, and picked out a few likely ones.'

Since the conversation didn't look like it was going away, George closed his laptop and did his best to appear interested in the online-dating story of a woman he'd never met, and probably never would.

'Ask me how we got her to go along with it.'

He couldn't care less. 'How?'

'Bribery. Patrick's family own a house in Tenerife, and we used to get it for two weeks every summer. We told her she could have one of our weeks with a couple of her buddies if she went on six first dates.'

'And?'

'She actually went on three first dates. The third was with Kev, and she stuck with him. She ended up bringing *him* to Tenerife. They're married now. They've got two girls – I think I might have mentioned them.'

'You did. They live in England.'

'That's right. Kev's from Manchester.' He moved from the window to the door. 'That's the thing, George. You get your share of weirdos online, everyone knows that – but most people on those sites are just looking for someone they can connect with.'

George made no response. Online dating wasn't for him, he was sure of that – but this was the first time he'd seen a spark of the old Jack since Monday, and he didn't want to cause it to disappear again.

'Life's short, George,' Jack said, opening the door. 'I've had too much evidence of that. Just think about it while I check on Puss.'

George didn't want to think about it. Granted, the online thing might be easier than trying to chat someone up in a pub or wherever – at least with online you could take your time with what you wrote, tweak it until it came out right, but eventually you had to meet them. The face-to-face had to happen at some stage, and it was not something he shone at.

Did he have to shine though? His shyness, his social clumsiness, hadn't mattered with Claire. It hadn't put her off. He remembered the happiness of the early days with her, the excitement at the thought of seeing her, the bliss of being with her. The delight they'd brought to one another simply by being together.

And the small things they'd done for each other, just because they wanted to. The multitude of oranges she'd squeezed by hand into a jug, one time he had a cold. (He hadn't had the heart to tell her that the juice didn't agree with him, and had spent the following week scratching furtively at his new hives.)

The farmer's market across town that he'd driven to every Thursday after school to get the smoked cheese from the stall she liked. The out-of-print book by his favourite author that she'd searched for online, and eventually found. His late-night trips for whatever she suddenly craved – wine gums, salted peanuts, chips, raw cubes of lime jelly – when she was pregnant.

But in the end she'd walked away – and afterwards, after he'd patched his heart back together and learnt how to live without her, George had wondered what he would have done if he'd known they wouldn't last. Would he have shied away at the start, before they'd become entangled? Impossible question, with Suzi such a blaze of joy in his life – but if there'd never been a Suzi, if it had just been him and Claire, would he have chosen to avoid the heartbreak if he'd seen it coming?

He didn't think so. He'd have wanted the happiness, the enrichment she'd brought to his life. He'd have welcomed it, even if he'd somehow known that it was only short term, even if he'd sensed the hurt that lay ahead. And just because they hadn't lasted, and he hadn't managed to make another meaningful connection since Claire, didn't mean he never would.

So what was he doing about it? Bugger all, really. He went with the soccer lads for a drink after their game on Wednesdays, and he normally met up with a couple of others on a Friday or Saturday night that Suzi wasn't around … but the rest were all married, or well settled in relationships, and while they might give the females in the vicinity a glance or two when they went out, the evenings were more about the chat among themselves than the flirt.

They'd try to fix George up, every now and again. A female would be mentioned, usually a friend of one of the wives. They'd suggest organising a blind date, which he always turned down. Or he'd be asked to dinner, or to a barbecue, and there she would be, the one they'd picked out for him. And sometimes he was interested enough to find the courage to ask for her phone number, and sometimes his question got the right answer – but nothing lasted. Nothing he started lasted.

And here he was, working steadily towards his thirty-fifth birthday in September, and in all those years he'd fallen truly in love only once. And by now his friends, like his mother, had all but given up trying to sort him out, maybe thinking he was happy with his single status, and who could blame them?

He returned to his mother's email.

Kate from Borelli's was my first customer, she was telling me all her news. Her niece has moved back from Dublin and is living with her for the time being. She's helping out in the restaurant, and doing something for the local paper too. She's the one who delivers your eggs. I think you mentioned her. Can't remember her name. She must be nice, being related to Kate.

He smiled. Still trying. Hadn't quite given up. He imagined how thrilled his mother would be if he found someone new. Much as he shrank from it, maybe it *was* time to consider the online option. He didn't have to commit to anything, didn't have to meet anyone he didn't want to.

He could have a look. He could dip a toe in, lurk around a bit, see if anything caught his fancy. There really was nothing to lose.

He tapped out a reply to his mother, telling her yes, it was great that she was back at work and no, he hadn't yet met the niece, whose name was Alice, although Suzi and Jack both had. *I'd say she's avoiding me*, he wrote. *She must have heard I'm desperate for a woman, and she might be afraid I wouldn't be able to control myself if I saw her.* He imagined his mother chuckling at that, but tutting as well.

We're looking forward to seeing you and John on Sunday – Jack will be here so you can meet him. Jack had offered to cook for the occasion, which meant the food would be good.

I've agreed to let a cat stay here temporarily, he wrote. *It belonged to an old man who died, a client of my tenant's, and there was nobody to look after it. It stays in his room, I hardly see it. Very timid.* Timid was one way of putting it; feral was another.

Over dinner, he asked Jack, as casually as he could, what website his sister had used. Jack spooned more apple sauce onto his pork chop. 'You're going to give it a try?'

'I'll think about it. That's all I'm saying.'

Jack named the site. 'Want me to show it to you after dinner, help you find your way around?'

'No need, I can do it myself. I'll give a shout if I want help – and to be honest, I'd prefer if you didn't ask me about it.'

'I've already wiped all knowledge of this conversation from my mind. So tell me about your day at school.' George turned with relief to his conversation with Mrs Daly, and his subsequent email to the Happy Talk page, and Jack promised to cross his fingers.

After the meal he washed up. He put away the dishes and swept and mopped the floor, listening to the piano music that floated out from the sitting room. When he'd finished in the kitchen he brought his laptop upstairs, earning himself another hiss as he stopped to peer through Jack's still-open door at the cat that was hunched now beneath the bed. 'You're welcome,' he said. 'No thanks needed for the accommodation. Happy to help.'

In his room he went into the website and pottered about cautiously, ignoring the *Sign up now!* messages that flashed on the screen every few minutes. He investigated a few profiles, male and female, until he figured out how it all worked. He found nothing too complicated, nothing too intimidating.

Without signing up he could make no contact with anyone, even if he wanted to. He clicked out of the site. He'd think about it, sleep on it for a few nights.

The following day he called to Rob's after school to collect Suzi.

'How are things?' Claire asked.

'Fine. You?'

'Good. Won't feel it now till you're on holidays.'

Since he'd begun teaching sixth class, he'd had mixed feelings about the end of the school year. His charges were moving on, leaving the relative safety of primary school, going from being top dogs to starting again on the bottom rung of a new ladder. He couldn't protect them: all he could do was wave them off, and hope he'd offered enough encouragement for them to survive and bloom.

Your best is always good enough – he'd drilled it into them from their first day in his class. They raised their eyes to Heaven, he reminded them of it so much, but he wanted it embedded in their brains, imprinted onto their minds' eyes.

'Birthday party go well?' he asked.

'Yeah, the usual.'

Her top was the shade of green, jade he thought it was called, that matched her eyes exactly. There was a tiny dark dot at the outer corner of her left eye. Mascara, he supposed. Out of nowhere came a long-ago memory of her sweeping her lashes with a mascara brush, mouth stretched into an elongated *o*. He would mimic this expression, making her laugh and bat him away.

She turned. 'Suzi,' she called, 'George is waiting,' and their daughter came flying downstairs, the little blue rucksack she always brought with her bumping along behind.

On the way home he told her about the garden chairs Jack had found. 'I was thinking it would be nice to paint them. You can choose the colour if you like.'

'One blue and one green,' she said immediately.

'You don't want to think about it? You don't want to see them first?'

'No. I like blue and green together.'

So they stopped at the paint shop, and she selected a grass green and a dark blue that he thought would look well side by side. 'We'll need brushes,' he said, and asked advice from a staff member, who told him, when he heard what the job was, that they also needed primer and white spirit.

'Oil-based primer is best for outdoor use,' he said. 'The oil seals the grains of the wood and prevents the paint from bubbling due to water damage. And you should really sand the chairs before you start, to get a nice smooth surface.'

'Fair enough,' George said, handing over more cash than he'd anticipated. Still, the chairs had cost nothing, and she'd get a kick out of transforming them.

When they got to the house he told her there was a cat inside.

Her eyes widened. 'What? You got a cat?'

'Not exactly.' He explained where the animal had come from, and told her it wasn't friendly. 'It's not staying either,' he said as they approached the front door. 'Jack is taking it to the animal welfare tomorrow. We thought you might like to see it before it went.'

'A cat!' She hopped impatiently as he unlocked the door and raced straight up the stairs.

'It's not friendly,' he called again. 'Don't get too close, it'll scratch you.'

He got no response. He left her to it and went to make his usual coffee. When he eventually investigated, he found her lying on her belly outside Jack's door, murmuring softly. 'It's under the bed,' she whispered. George could hear no hissing or growling, which in itself was miraculous. Maybe it was just men the cat hated – or certain men. He retreated silently.

'It's just scared,' Jack said, when she finally gave up and came down for dinner. 'It's not used to this house, and maybe it was never around people much.'

'Has it got a name?'

'I don't think so. I never heard Mr Costello calling it anything.'

'Is it a he or a she?'

'A he.'

She turned to George. 'Can we keep him for a little while? Please. He's got nobody else, and he's scared. Please, George. I just want to try and get him to like me. Just for the weekend.'

Such an anti-social animal, he knew, hadn't a hope of being rehomed. He wondered what became of the ones nobody wanted. He looked at the pleading face of his daughter, and the slightly less pleading face of Jack, and he knew he had no choice in this.

'Just for the weekend then,' he said, and Suzi threw herself into his arms and told him he was the best dad in the world, which might or might not have been accurate, but which he was happy to go along with.

As soon as dinner was over she disappeared again, and spent the rest of the evening communing with the cat – which she told George, just before bedtime, she'd named Oscar. 'Because of my old Oscar,' she explained, and George abruptly remembered the little soft blue rabbit – huge eyes, ridiculously long ears – that had gone everywhere with her until she'd outgrown it.

They woke the next morning to sunshine, and the chairs got sanded and primed, in between Suzi's several trips to the landing, where her efforts to soften Oscar continued. Just before lunch, she came downstairs in great excitement. 'He let me rub him, just a tiny bit!' she told George. 'I think he was trying to purr!'

Just for the weekend my foot: that cat knew a good thing when he saw it. George decided to accept his fate.

In the afternoon they applied a first coat of paint to both chairs. It was agreed that cushions would be needed, and should be bright yellow, so George was charged with finding them.

Later, after Jack had gone out to meet friends, and as he and Suzi accompanied a takeaway dinner with what felt to George like their hundredth viewing of *Up*, he found himself imagining, as the familiar events unfolded on the screen, as he drew another slice from the pizza, pinching off the strings of melted cheese, how it might be if there were three of them on the couch instead of two. How it might be, after Suzi had gone to bed, to have someone to share a bottle of wine and get cosy with.

Next day, his mother and John arrived for the birthday lunch. Jack was introduced – and right from the start, he and George's mother found common ground.

'Garrihy,' she said. 'Our dentist was called Garrihy when I was growing up in Limerick city.'

'Denis, in Pery Square,' Jack replied. 'My grandfather.'

'No – was he really? Is he still with us?'

'He is. He's retired a long time, in his late eighties now, but still in pretty good shape.'

'I'm glad to hear it. He'll hardly remember me, but tell him Evelyn O'Shaughnessy says hello – and she still has all her own teeth.'

Jack laughed. 'I will. He'll be pleased to hear that.'

'There's a new cat here,' Suzi announced. 'I've named him Oscar. He's all black.'

'Oh yes – George told me about him. Where is he?'

'Upstairs, in Jack's room. He's really shy, but I'm trying to make friends with him.'

'That's nice.' Her gaze roamed the kitchen, no doubt looking for changes since she'd left. She caught sight of the garden outside, and her expression changed. 'Oh,' she said. 'Well,' she said, 'look at that.'

George waited. She'd remarked on the front planters when she'd arrived. She'd complimented him on how well they were looking – but this was different. This wasn't just refilling two planters.

The silence stretched. George realised he was holding his breath, and let it out. Finally, she turned. 'This is all your doing?' she asked Jack, and he told her he'd had help from his trusty assistant, Suzi.

'Would you like us to walk you through it?' he enquired, and she said yes, that would be lovely, and the three of them headed out, John staying behind to help set the table, and George could see through the window that she approved of Jack's changes, and he relaxed.

Lunch went well, with everyone in good spirits. After the lemon tart that followed the chicken korma main course, Suzi was presented with the book token from her grandmother that had replaced the books she'd been given every year until she'd turned eight. When it came to presents, George thought, originality didn't run in the family – but he and Claire, both readers, had worked separately to plant a love of reading in their daughter, so a book token was always a welcome gift.

'My turn,' Jack said, and produced the hatbox, which he'd hidden with the saucepans under the sink. 'A happy birthday from me.'

Suzi regarded the box. 'Is it a hat?'

'Open it and see' – so she lifted off the lid and peered in at the contents.

'Nemesia!' She reached in and lifted out the pot, and dipped her face to the tiny flowers. 'Thanks,' she said. 'I might plant it in Rob's garden, George, since we have some here already.'

Was she asking his permission? Did she feel she needed it? 'Sure,' he said, 'whatever you want,' and imagined the little flowers pushing roots into Rob's garden, and quelled the childish hope that the podiatrist's soil would prove too inhospitable for them to thrive.

After lunch John offered to do the washing up, and Suzi disappeared to check on Oscar, and Jack left to meet up with friends.

'Why don't you two take yourselves out to the garden?' John suggested to George and his mother, so they refreshed their coffee cups and went to sit on the new chairs, with cushions borrowed from the couch until proper ones could be sourced.

'So you're happy to be working again.'

'I am, very happy. What was I thinking, giving it up just like that? How did I imagine I wouldn't miss it? John has been so sweet – really, he couldn't have made it easier – and most of my old customers have said they're coming back.'

'That's good. Sounds like you'll be busy.'

He sipped his coffee. She sipped hers. He followed a butterfly flitting about. There'd definitely been more of them in the garden than he remembered from previous years. News of the recent plantings must have got around.

Next door's cat bounded suddenly onto the dividing wall and fixed them with his steady gaze. George wondered how the two cats would get on, when and if they came face to face. A matter of time, presumably. He'd cross that bridge when he came to it.

His mother set her empty cup on the ground by her chair. 'You could do with a table out here.'

'I could. I'll tell Jack to keep an eye on the skips.'

She sat back, crossed her ankles. 'He tells me he plays the piano.'

'He does, he's good. He and Suzi are trading tunes.'

'Did she get that keyboard?'

'I presume she did.'

'Has she said anything about the wedding?'

'Not yet.'

Since Claire had told him of the engagement he'd found it straying into his thoughts. He couldn't shake an obscure sense of … what? Disappointment, deflation, at the notion of her walking up the aisle to another man. Wanting what he couldn't have: so typical of the human condition. Once the deed was done he'd get over it.

That evening, after the visitors had left, and Suzi had been returned to Claire and Rob, he got an email.

Hi there,
Alice here from Happy Talk. Thanks for your message. Deirdre's
aunt did email me about the art prize, and I'm happy to include
it in next week's column. It was thoughtful of you as her teacher
to canvass on her behalf – any chance I could get a quote from
you, maybe about how proud you are of her, or something along
those lines? We could have a quick chat, I'll put my number at
the end – or you can just email back if you'd prefer. And have you
returned the painting to Deirdre? I've chosen it to be the main
item, so we'll be looking for a snap of it.
Thanks,
Alice

He was happy it was going to be included, photos too, but he hadn't reckoned on having to give a quote. He imagined Dermot reading it aloud in the staffroom, making a right laugh of it.

Bugger Dermot. He clicked *Reply* and a new message box opened.

Hi Alice,
Thanks for your response, and I'm grateful that you're going to
include Deirdre's good news story. I returned the painting, so
hopefully she still has it. Here's my quote:

He stopped, thought.

Deirdre is a great little artist. She deserved to win the prize.

Great little artist. He frowned, and pressed *delete*.

Deirdre was a worthy winner of the art competition, and I'm very proud of her.

He imagined the mileage Dermot would get out of 'worthy winner'. *Delete.*

Deirdre is a lovely girl, and a very promising artist. I'm proud of her, as I am of all my students.

He read it through three times. He signed the email George Murphy and sent it off. Two minutes later, he had a response.

Thank you, George. Have a happy week. Alice

He imagined Deirdre having her photo taken with the winning painting. He pictured her mother clipping the page out of the paper. As he was closing the laptop, his phone rang.

'I planted the nemesia,' Suzi said. 'Tell Jack. It's just under my bedroom window.'

'Excellent.'

Pause. 'George.'

'Yes, love?'

'I think you should look for a new girlfriend.'

He laughed. 'What's brought this on?'

'Well, it's just with Mum getting married, I think you should have someone too.'

Here it came. 'How do you feel about that? About Mum and Rob getting married?'

'Fine. I'm going to be bridesmaid. Mum says I can choose my dress.'

So simple life was for her. He thought maybe he should dig a little. 'And Rob will become your stepdad.'

'I know. He says nobody will believe he's old enough to have a daughter my age.'

He felt a dart of anger. The man was twenty-eight: of course he could have fathered a child at sixteen. Idiot. 'Stepdaughter,' he said. 'Not daughter.'

'I *know*, George. So will you look for a girlfriend?'

He thought again of the dating website, and all the possible girlfriends it might contain, waiting to be found. He thought of Claire, who was still hanging around stubbornly in his system, and whom he needed to evict. 'I'll keep an eye out, I promise. Goodnight, love. Sleep tight, don't let the bedbugs bite.'

'Goodnight, George.'

He hung up. He eyed his laptop. Should he sign up, start the hunt for someone new?

Not tonight. Maybe tomorrow.

Alice

THE SECOND TIME THEY MET, THEY HAD LUNCH IN the same café. The third time, a few days later, they went to the cinema in the evening, and got bags of chips afterwards, and he kissed her cheek as he dropped her at the gate of Kate's house. The fourth time, a Sunday, he drove her to a beach that was forty minutes away, and a light drizzle fell as they walked by the shore, and he reached for her hand in the middle of a sentence and held it lightly, fingers laced through hers, till they got back to the car.

They had yet to have a proper kiss. She'd jokingly kissed him on both cheeks as they'd parted after the trip to the beach – Italian style, she'd said – and now that was what they did, on meeting and parting. Maybe he thought that was all she wanted.

Maybe it *was* all she wanted – for now.

But she did enjoy his company. He wasn't a chatterbox, far from it – sometimes their silences stretched till it felt a bit awkward, and sometimes it seemed like she was prising conversation from him – but when he did talk, he was worth listening to. He was educated and intelligent, and not afraid to express an opinion, and balanced in his judgement of things.

He was a gentleman. He was considerate, treated her well, listened when she spoke. He was punctual. His table manners were impeccable, and he smelt good, and he dressed well.

They didn't agree on everything. He had an aversion to gyms, preferring to be out on his bike. Like her, he was a reader, but he favoured biographies and memoirs over novels. He was a dog man; she preferred cats. Their musical tastes differed too: she loved jazz and rock and pop, and a little classical; he leant more towards country and folk.

Differences were good, though. Differences were interesting. If there was anything, any tiny thing, she would change, it would be to make him slightly less … earnest. He did have a sense of humour – he loved slapstick, and stand-up comics with deadpan deliveries – but she didn't think he'd ever have her in fits of laughter like Chris could so easily. Then again, wasn't a kind and decent man more important than one who could make her laugh?

She was torn. The more she got to know him, the more conflicted she felt about staying in touch with Chris. Every few days her ex called, and her heart continued to jump when she saw his name on the screen. They were just phone calls, she told herself. Just chats on the phone.

Only they weren't just phone calls – or soon they wouldn't be.

Meet me, he'd said. One night, that's all I ask. We can meet halfway, I'll book a hotel – and she'd said no, she'd kept saying no until he'd worn her down, and in the end, smothering an outraged inner voice, she'd agreed. And since then, she'd been trying to justify it to herself.

What if his marriage really was over, like he said, and he was only staying for the sake of his children? What if Alice truly was the one he wanted? Maybe face-to-face, with several hours together, she could convince him that the children of a loveless marriage would fare better if their parents lived apart.

They were meeting tonight, six hours from now. He'd booked them a room at a hotel in the midlands. We'll have dinner, he'd said, or we could order room service, whatever you want, and Alice had felt a mix of excited and apprehensive and guilty. Thank goodness she had a Happy Talk interview lined up, to take her mind somewhere else for a while.

After she'd fed the hens and tidied the apartment she went to meet Deirdre Daly, the girl who'd won first prize in her class's art competition. She might not have included it in the column, let alone made it the main item, if it hadn't been for the email the girl's teacher had sent, which had struck her as a lovely thing to do. G. Murphy he'd signed it. Alice hadn't known he was male until the G had become George in his second message. She was featuring the item as much for him as for his student.

She was meeting the girl and her mother at the park gates. Not at home, the mother had said on the phone. My husband works nights, and he needs his sleep. A complicated family situation, the teacher had called it: that could be code for anything.

The day was mild with an overcast sky, but so far there was no sign of rain. Two females stood by the park gates.

'Mrs Daly?'

The woman gave a nod, and a tight smile that didn't last. 'Thanks for doing this,' she said. She looked too young to be the mother of a girl in sixth class. She was tall, half a dozen inches taller than Alice, and slender. Long legs in navy jeans, checked shirt, hair caught in a ponytail. Attractive, with dark eyes and a full, wide mouth, but beneath the eyes were shadows, and there was an air, Alice thought, of weariness about her, and something guarded too in her demeanour. Maybe she was shy.

'No problem: I'm always happy to hear the good news. I'm Alice,' turning to the girl, 'and you must be Deirdre.'

She nodded. She wore jeans too, and a faded blue T-shirt, and runners that were clean, but old and scuffed. She looked about the same age as George's daughter Suzi. In one nail-bitten hand she held a rolled-up page.

'Show her,' the mother said, and the girl handed it over. Alice unrolled it, expecting to see a childish drawing, prepared to be fulsome in her praise – but it wasn't childish.

'Wow,' she said quietly.

The rearing horse was perfectly in proportion, the colours of its chestnut coat beautifully blended. 'This is amazing,' she told Deirdre. 'I'm not a bit surprised it won the competition,' and the girl gave the same small quick smile as her mother.

'Nobody in the family has it only her, and I've five others.'

Six children. Little wonder she looked spent.

'Hi there.'

It was Mike, with his camera. They found a suitable spot and Alice stood by while he took snaps, Deirdre awkward and stiff throughout the process, despite Mike's cheery words of encouragement. After he left, Alice led mother and daughter to a bench.

'OK if I record our chat?' she asked the mother.

A new alertness, mild alarm in her face. 'Who gets to hear it?'

The first person to question this. 'Just me, and I'll delete it the minute I've written up the piece.'

'... OK.'

Alice set her phone to record, and positioned it on the bench between them. 'Tell me about your family,' she said to Deirdre. 'How many brothers and sisters do you have?'

The girl shifted a little. 'I got three brothers and two sisters.'

'And you're the eldest?'

A nod.

'I bet you're a great help to your mum.'

'She is,' the mother put in, and the girl threw her a quick smile.

'So how did it make you feel, winning the prize?'

Another shrug. She shuffled her feet, tucked her hands under her thighs. 'Happy,' she managed finally.

'It's a nice prize, isn't it? Have you been to the aqua centre before?'

'No.'

'Me neither, but I've heard great things about it. I'm sure you'll all have a lovely time.'

Silence. This was new. Normally people were delighted to talk about what had prompted them to write to Alice, but finding a few hundred words here might be a challenge. She cast about for another angle. 'Do you paint a lot, Deirdre?'

'Only at school.' Her top teeth grabbing at her bottom lip directly afterwards, a look darted again in her mother's direction. 'We don't have paints at home,' she mumbled.

No paints at home. A mother who looked as if someone had sucked the happiness out of her, and a father who might or might not work at night, and sleep during the day. Alice steered the conversation back to safer ground. 'I'm guessing art is your favourite subject.'

'Yeah.'

'Does your teacher often have competitions like this?'

A change occurred at the mention of him. A small ease in her posture, the first proper smile Alice had seen. 'Yeah, sometimes. It's not always art, sometimes he does quizzes. He's nice. He doesn't give out if you get low marks.'

Alice simply nodded at this, experience having taught her that silence could be more effective at drawing people out.

'He's funny. He dresses up for history. And he brings in a surprise every Monday for a raffle.'

'Like what?'

Another shrug. 'A pen, or an apple, or a badge. Anything. He doesn't tell us what it is until someone wins it.'

'Did you ever win it?'

Another smile. 'Yeah, I won a hair slide. I gave it to my sister when she broke hers. And we have a tree in the class.'

'A tree? Not a real tree?'

'No, just a mock one, on the wall. It's the kindness tree.'

'Really? I've never heard of that. How does it work?'

'When you do something kind you write it on a leaf – well, just a paper leaf – and Mr Murphy sticks it to the tree. And when one branch is full of leaves, he lets us off homework.'

'Good idea.'

It was. Instilling a kindness habit in them, the incentive of no homework to encourage them. And the raffles, and the quizzes, and dressing up for history. He sounded like an interesting teacher.

The mother cut in. 'She has to go now and get the kids.'

Alice looked at her in surprise. 'Oh – so soon? I was hoping to hear more.' She'd be lucky to get a couple of sentences out of what she had.

'I can tell you more. Go on,' she said to her daughter, 'I'll see you at home,' and the girl took her painting and walked away. Alice did her best to swallow her annoyance. So many others would have loved this moment of glory, and been more appreciative – but having chosen to feature this story, and Mike having taken the snaps, she must make the best of it.

She attempted a bright smile. 'So what more can you tell me?'

The woman didn't return her smile. 'I'm sorry,' she said. 'My sister has the kids, but she has three of her own too, so I don't like to land her with mine for too long.'

She did sound sorry. Alice instantly felt ashamed. She had no idea what lives they led, what challenges they faced. She would do her best by them.

The mother met Alice's gaze as she planted her hands on the bench. 'Let me tell you about Dee,' she said. 'She's not clever, not with books. She never gets high marks and she never will, but she does try. She's a worker. Drawing and painting is the only thing she's good at. Always was, from the time she started school. Even before it. She'd find a biro and I'd give her old envelopes, or I'd cut up empty boxes and things.'

She halted, drew a breath. Glanced at Alice's phone, still recording. 'Look, don't put this in the paper, but it isn't easy at home. I got pregnant on Dee while I was still at school. I was seventeen, and I wanted to be a model.' A half smile, half grimace. 'He stuck by me, we got married, and I was glad at the time. He had work then – well, casual work, on building sites, but it didn't last.'

As she spoke, the fingers of one hand began to drum on the bench. 'He's a drinker,' she said, 'and a gambler. He doesn't work nights, I made that up. He's been on the dole for years. It was all I could think of to say when you rang. I couldn't have you calling to the house. He wouldn't like it.'

Her voice was low, her words rushed now. Maybe she needed to say it, to get it out of her.

'I never see a cent of his dole. He says I have the children's allowance, but that's not enough, so I clean offices in the evening. Dee has to mind the small ones – and try to keep them quiet too, if he's around. He's hard on them. He doesn't hit them, but he has no time for them. He won't let me get paints for Dee, says it's a waste of money. It's tough on her, all of it, but she never complains. She's a great girl.'

She stopped again. 'Don't mention this either, but I got her a job for the summer. One of the managers where I clean is friendly with the manager at the new cinema, she had a word. Dee will be cleaning in between the films. It'll bring in a bit more money.'

A job, at her age.

'Sorry. I don't know why I'm telling you all this.' She looked down at her drumming fingers, and stilled them. 'You can say she's helpful at home, that I'd be lost without her. She's like another mum to the younger ones.'

'I will. And your sister will give me a quote too.'

'And maybe Mr Murphy might say something? You could call the school.'

'I could.' She didn't know he'd emailed Alice, already given his quote.

'He's really good with her. He gets her to make posters

anytime they need them, like for a cake sale or that. He makes her feel worthwhile, you know? At the parent–teacher meeting, he didn't go on about how rubbish she is at maths or Irish or all that, he just talked about the good bits, how she helps out, and is never late. And the art, of course. Said he never saw a child so talented.'

Another pause. A smile. 'He has a sign over the classroom door, you can't miss it. It says, "Your best is always good enough." The first time I saw it, I knew if Dee learnt nothing else in his class, that message would be enough for her.'

She folded her hands in her lap, one thumb stroking the other. 'I want her to *shine*,' she said urgently. 'She wasn't born into an easy life, but she deserves to shine. She could be a famous painter or – I don't know – something really important in art.' She gave the same grimace Alice had seen before. 'You probably think I'm living in Cloud Cuckoo Land.'

'Not at all.' Alice wished she could do more than write a few hundred words. 'She's extremely talented.'

'What chance does she have, though?' the mother demanded, and Alice remained silent. Better to say nothing than to give false reassurances – because the odds did seem to be stacked against the girl.

She moved to safer ground. 'When do you think you'll use the prize?'

The woman shrugged. 'I was thinking this Sunday. They could all do with a treat.'

Sunday. Alice made a silent note, an idea forming.

'Have you enough to write about? I should get going.'

'I have.' She'd find enough. 'You didn't tell me your name,' she said, getting up.

'Louise.'

They walked together to the gates. 'The piece will be in this weekend's paper,' Alice said. 'I hope you like it. I know everyone will be amazed when they see the painting.'

To her surprise, Alice saw the woman's eyes redden and brim. She gave a quick toss to her head, thumbed away tears before they could fall. 'Thank you,' she said. 'I really mean it. You don't know how thankful I am.' And before Alice could respond, she wheeled and strode away, and vanished around a corner.

Walking home, Alice tried to imagine living with a man whose only skill, by the sound of it, was fathering children. She pictured him drawing the dole, getting his money every week and bringing it straight to the pub, or to the bookie's. Not a thought for the wife who had to work late into the evening, had to scrimp and save to feed his children.

She deserves to shine. At least Deirdre had one parent who wanted the best for her.

Back at the apartment she checked again for a response to her recent job application, and again found nothing. Disheartening to get no reply at all, not even a negative one – but if there was one job, there would be more. How innocent she'd been, thinking receptionist jobs were ten a penny, there for the taking.

She transferred the conversation from her phone to a file, and saved it in her Happy Talk folder. She fed the hens and collected a few new eggs, and deposited them at Kate's as usual. Going to stay the night with a friend, she'd told her aunt. It wasn't a lie exactly.

She checked her watch. It was time.

She showered and changed, recalling the last time she'd got herself ready to meet him. She remembered sitting in Liz and

Emmet's house, weekend case at her feet, still hoping that the phone call hadn't been from his wife, still praying that a wife didn't exist.

She made up her face and dried her hair, pushing away the guilt. She wasn't perfect, she was human, and she missed him – and tonight she was determined to get at the truth of how he felt about her, and about his marriage.

She put on the blue dress. She added a silver neck chain that Tina had given her for her last birthday – and then took it off again. Tina wouldn't approve. Nobody would approve of what she was about to do, however she tried to justify it.

At six she sat into the car. Fifty-five minutes, Google Maps had told her, but traffic might be heavy. She set an audio book to play over the sound system, thinking to distract herself. On her arrival at the hotel fifty-eight minutes later she turned it off, with no clue as to what had been playing. Every word had drifted in one ear and flown out the other.

His car wasn't in the car park. See you in the lobby, he'd said. She touched up her lipstick and sprayed more scent, and went in. Seven o'clock exactly. A scatter of people about. She sat facing the door, stomach churning, palms damp.

Five past seven. A few minutes didn't matter, not when they had the whole night.

Ten past seven. Traffic would be heavy coming out of Dublin at this time.

A quarter past seven. She checked her phone for a text, and found none. Prickles of fear in her scalp. He was coming, of course he was. He was just delayed. A work thing, a family thing.

Twenty past seven. She felt in need of a loo. She rose and

located one. She returned to her post, sweeping about the lobby in case he'd arrived, but he hadn't.

Twenty-five past seven. She checked her phone again. She decided to text him, unable to bear any more waiting.

She scrolled to his name and selected him. *Blocked by this contact* flashed onto the screen. What? She exited the list of names and went in again, and again the message appeared. She turned off her phone and turned it on again, and still it refused to allow her access to him.

No.

Heart hammering, she retrieved their text conversation, still there. Can't wait to see you xxx his last message read, sent just this morning. She pressed *Reply. Blocked by this contact.*

She lowered her phone and sat without moving as people who weren't him came into the hotel and walked past her. Eventually, some time later, she deleted the texts, and removed his name from her contacts. Months too late – and he'd never know unless he decided to fool her a third time, and unblocked her.

Was he laughing right now at how he'd treated her? Was he boasting to friends about the woman who was desperate for him? She couldn't bear it. She stowed her phone and got stiffly to her feet. She left the hotel and returned to her car and drove home.

And for the entire journey, she beat herself up. For fifty-eight minutes, she was merciless.

How could she have been so stupid, so gullible? How could she have trusted someone who'd shown himself to be the least trustworthy person she knew? How could she have set out knowingly to deceive a woman she'd never met – and gone on to deceive William too, after she'd started seeing him? How could she think so little of herself as to allow Chris back into her life? She was filled with shame.

She thought of the people who would be appalled if they knew what she'd been planning. Kate. Tina. Val. Liz. Emmet. Dearbhla. Everyone she'd told about how cruelly he'd used her. She imagined their shock, their disbelief, if they somehow got to hear that she'd arranged to meet her married ex, that she'd intended to spend a night with him.

She got home and let herself in. She took off her shoes and her blue dress. She drank a glass of wine too quickly. She put her phone on mute and went to bed, and slept soundly despite her turmoil, or maybe because of it. Maybe he'd exhausted her, physically as well as emotionally.

On waking, the events of the previous night came rushing back, and she felt a fresh wave of shame, but also a sense of loss. Not for him, not now that she'd finally seen him for who he was, but for the man she'd thought she'd found.

Nonsense.

She pushed back the duvet. She needed to put this mess behind her and move on. She needed to appreciate what she had, and not mourn someone who'd never existed.

She rang William, ten minutes before the shop opened. 'Would you like to come to dinner on Saturday?'

'Won't your folks be here?'

'They will. I thought you might like to meet them.'

'Love to,' he said immediately. 'What should I bring?'

'A bottle of red. I'm doing beef. Come around seven.'

'Great, thanks. Any response to the job application?'

He never failed to ask. 'Nothing.'

Over the following days she kept busy. She tried out a circuit training class at the gym. She spring-cleaned the apartment. She washed the blue dress and donated it to a charity shop. She and William went to the cinema, where he bought her an overpriced box of Maltesers, which she loved.

She wrote her Happy Talk column. For the main item, she padded out what information she had. She wrote of a caring girl who was like a second mother to her younger brothers and sisters, a girl who worked hard in class, an artist of surprising talent for one so young. She spoke of a teacher who was proud of her, and an aunt who praised her for her kindness and reliability.

She rang the school and spoke not to Mr Murphy but to the principal, who told her that Deirdre hadn't missed a day in all her eight years at the school, and had never once been in trouble in that time either. She rang the aqua centre, and got the manager to say that they were looking forward to the family's visit.

On Friday she opened the new paper. Mike's photo showed Deirdre standing by one of the flower displays in the park, holding the winning painting. She wore a tentative smile, and wasn't looking directly at the camera, but the painting was clear, the artistry perfectly evident.

Later in the day she paid a visit to the aqua centre. She asked to see the manager, and reminded her that they'd spoken on the phone. She showed her the Happy Talk page, and the item in question.

'I think they're planning to come here on Sunday,' she told the manager. 'Will you know it's them when they show up with the day pass?'

'Yes – they'll have to sign in.'

'Good.' She took a slim box from her basket with Deirdre's name on it, and *competition winner* underlined below. 'I wonder,' she said, 'if I could leave this for them? It's just a little gift, and I'd like it to be anonymous.'

'No problem.'

Alice thanked her and left. It wasn't much, a set of half a dozen tubes of acrylic paint, and a couple of accompanying brushes. The message she'd put in with it gave little away: *Read about you in the paper, saw your beautiful art and wanted to send something to help you create more masterpieces. Congratulations, you have a real gift.*

They'd never know it had come from her. It was the only thing she could think of to do. Deirdre's father could hardly object to a gift of paints.

She drove from the aqua centre to the train station, where she had arranged to pick up her parents. Stopped at traffic lights, she glanced at the car in the next lane and saw a freckle-faced young girl who looked familiar in the passenger seat. Just before the lights changed the girl spotted her, and waved and smiled brightly, clearly recognising her.

It took until she was pulling up outside the station for Alice to realise she was Suzi, the daughter of George of the eggs. Maybe he'd been the driver.

For the first time in several weeks, she wouldn't be calling to his house in the morning. She was skipping her Saturday Pilates to have brunch with her parents, and Kate was doing the egg delivery.

'It's so good to see you, *cara*,' her mother said. 'It's been too long.' She wore a pink suit and smelt of roses, the same scent she'd used for as long as Alice could remember. She kissed Alice on both cheeks, reminding her briefly of William.

Had that been a good idea, to invite him to meet her parents after just a handful of dates? It had been a rebound, impulsive move after the disaster of the previous night, and now she wondered if she'd done the right thing, so early in their relationship. She'd make no mention of him till tomorrow; she'd slip it in casually that he would be joining them for dinner. A friend, she'd call him.

'You look well,' her father told her, hugging her. 'You've got new glasses.' He looked well too, tanned by the Italian sun, and better dressed than when he'd lived here. Tailored shirts instead of his looser ones, linen trousers replacing the denim. Italian stylishness rubbing off on him in his sixties.

They commented on the changes in the town since their last visit as she drove them to Kate's. The new road layout from the station to the town centre, the shops with different names, the relocated fire station.

Alice pointed out a little book swap outside a primary school. The books, twenty or so, were displayed in a painted wooden unit with a glass door that was affixed to the school railings, a message handwritten on the wood: *Help yourself to a book. Leave one in its place, or return when finished.* Alice had noticed it lately on a walk, and admired it.

'So how is life now?' her mother asked. 'How is it, being back in town again?'

'It's fine. I'm settling in, getting used to it.'

'It must be nice to meet your old friends again.'

'Well, we've been in touch, but they're busy with work and

families. I'm meeting new people though, at the gym and in the restaurant.'

Her mother made no reply. Did they think she'd made a mistake, coming back? It must have seemed odd to them, giving up a perfectly good job without securing a comparable one here. She felt bad not to be giving them a full explanation. Maybe some day, when she'd put real distance between her and Chris's double betrayal, she would.

She brought them first to Kate's house, to drop their bags in the room Kate had prepared for them. Let yourself in, Kate had said, giving her a key. Tell them I'll see them later.

From there they went to the apartment. Alice led them around, conscious of how small and cramped the place must seem to them.

'I remember when Kate did this,' her mother said. 'She was so hoping Paolo would stay in Ireland. Sad that he didn't – but good for you now.'

'Yes, very good. Have you seen Paolo lately?'

'Every Sunday, at lunch.'

Of course. She loved the Sunday lunches at Aldo's *trattoria*. The big family occasion, everyone assembled around the long table created by shoving a few together. The excellent food made more special with good conversation and laughter, and locally produced wine – and now her parents' wine featured on her uncle's menu too.

'You must fix a date for your trip, *cara*,' her mother said. 'Everyone looks forward to seeing you.'

'I will.'

She showed them the latest Happy Talk page, and they complimented her, and admired Deirdre's painting.

'You get paid for this?' her father enquired, and she told him she did.

'Have you been looking for work, Alice? I mean real work. Permanent fulltime work.'

'I have, but I only found one receptionist job, and I got no response to my application.'

'You don't want to impose, Alice,' her mother said. 'Kate has been very good to you, but you've been here for weeks now.'

'I know that. I *have* been looking for work. I keep an eye out all the time.'

'Maybe you need to broaden your search,' her father said. 'Consider other jobs.'

'Like what?'

'I don't know – shop work, maybe? Waitressing, or secretarial?'

'Maybe you could train up as a cook,' her mother put in. 'Or a baker, like me.'

'Maybe,' she said, trying to quell a feeling of annoyance. Kate didn't seem in any hurry to have her move on, so why should they? 'We'd better get going – our table's booked for seven.' They were eating that night in Borelli's, Kate's treat.

'There's another option,' her father said. 'We wanted to run it by you.'

Alice slipped on her jacket. 'What other option?'

She saw them exchange a glance. 'We wondered,' her mother said, 'if you'd consider moving to Italy.'

'To *Italy*?'

'We could use you in the vineyard – or you could get a different job if you preferred. Your Italian is fluent, and there's plenty of work. Well, perhaps not plenty, but enough.'

'They'll be looking for staff soon in a newly built hotel,' her father put in. 'It's just a few miles from the vineyard. We know the owners – I'm sure they'd be open to you joining them.'

They'd talked about it. They'd talked about it because they thought they needed to sort out their youngest daughter, since her life was going nowhere in Ireland. They might have discussed it with her sisters. What's to be done about Alice? they might have asked, and her sisters might have sighed and shaken their heads.

'I've met someone,' she said. Blurted it out, just like that. 'He's an optician. I met him when I went for an eye test. He's coming to dinner here tomorrow night.'

The tiniest of pauses. 'Alice, that's wonderful,' her mother exclaimed. 'An optician – how marvellous.'

A little too enthusiastic, Alice felt. A little too delighted at the prospect of William. She hoped he didn't disappoint them.

He didn't. He turned up the following night in an impeccable grey suit, teamed with the usual dazzling white shirt. He brought flowers and chocolates, and a bottle of Italian red wine that looked expensive.

He showed none of his usual reserve. He told them of his travels in Italy, and recited a children's rhyme that someone had taught him, and Alice's mother chimed in, marvelling that he'd remembered it. He asked them about their vineyard with what appeared to be genuine interest, and revealed knowledge of grape varieties that Alice hadn't known he possessed.

He wondered if Italian opticians operated in the same way as Irish ones, and Alice's mother, laughing, told him that he should come over and find out.

'Dinner is served,' Alice said, getting up.

He complimented the beef dish, and kept everyone's wine

glass topped up, which struck Alice as a little forward. 'Has she told you,' he asked her parents, midway through the meal, 'how we met?'

'When she went to have her eyes tested,' her mother replied, and he looked at Alice questioningly, so she found herself recounting the full story, not feeling she'd been given much choice.

Her mother was as thrilled as Kate had been. 'What a coincidence! How marvellous!' She didn't seem in the least concerned that her daughter might have been injured – or might have killed William.

Her father did show some concern. 'Alice, you were lucky it hadn't a worse outcome for both of you. You need to be more attentive behind the wheel' – and she wondered, as she got up to serve the raspberry roulade that Kate had provided for dessert, what they'd say if she explained precisely why she'd been inattentive that evening.

They drank coffee on the patio as the light seeped from the sky, and William found her hand in the dusk, and her mother told them of the pair of brothers who were looking after the vineyard and wine bar in their absence, and her father smoked one of his thin cigars, and the scent of it, nutty and sweet, drifted about, and an occasional sleepy cluck came from the henhouse.

'He's wonderful,' her mother said, after William had left to walk home. 'He's perfect for you, Alice.'

And there was no more talk of her moving to Italy – because clearly she was going to marry William and live happily ever after in Ireland.

George

'NO PHOTO,' HE SAID.

'George, you really need one. Profiles with no photos get far fewer hits.'

'How could anyone know that?'

'There's been research – and it stands to reason. If a person doesn't show his face, everyone is going to assume he's ashamed of it. You have nothing to be ashamed of.'

'I'm not ashamed.' The idea of his photo up there, visible to anyone on the site, made him hot with embarrassment. Who knew who might see it? What if Dermot got wind of it? 'Anyway, looks aren't important.'

'George, I know that and you know that, but online it's all anyone has to go on.'

'What about the profile?'

'Well, yes, the profile counts, of course – but when there isn't a face to go with it, people don't really invest in the profile. They lose interest.'

George was fast losing interest in online dating.

It must have shown on his face. 'Forget about the photo,' Jack said. 'You can always add one later if you – if there isn't the traffic you'd like.'

Traffic. Hits. The phraseology sounded so cold. What had possessed him to sign up – and why, after all, had he decided to enlist Jack's help with his profile? Granted, a few of his friends had gone this route, and he'd heard of at least two weddings that had resulted from online dating, but he remained far from convinced that it was for him. Still, he'd paid for three months' membership, the minimum that was offered, so he'd wait and see what return he got for his investment.

'Not a word to Suzi.' It was Sunday night. He'd just returned from dropping her back to Claire.

'Cross my heart.'

Single dad, he'd written in his profile. Might as well be up front about it. Jack had demurred, wanted him to wait till some contact was made, but George wasn't about to hide his child away in case she put anyone off. George M, he was going by. Not much of an alias, but it afforded him some level of anonymity.

He'd described himself as sporty – was he? Did kicking around a ball for a couple of hours once a week qualify as sporty? A runner, he'd put, when plodder would have been a more apt description. Likes to keep fit – well, that was sort of true. Enjoys a drink, he'd written, and then added occasional, in case the other gave the wrong impression. Non-smoker. For occupation he'd put professional, which left it safely vague.

Didn't exactly make for edge-of-the-seat reading. His life, satisfied as he was with it, could hardly be described as thrilling, or even mildly exciting. But this was a change, wasn't it? Online dating was definitely quite a bit outside his comfort zone. Aged thirty-four, he was trying out adventurous for size.

He exited the site and stowed his laptop in its drawer, his mind spooling back through the weekend. Feeling the loss of Suzi, as he always did when their time together ended.

We saw Alice, she'd reported to Jack on Friday evening. 'Well, I saw her. George was too busy driving.'

Alice the waitressing egg lady?

Yes. She was in her car.

You might see her again tomorrow, Jack had said, if you're up when she calls. And George, you might finally meet her – but George hadn't met her because she hadn't appeared.

Hello, the woman had said, when he'd opened the door. I'm Kate, standing in for Alice today.

Pleasant smile. Around his mother's age, he'd guessed. The Kate who owns the hens, I assume.

The very one. I hope you don't mind me ringing the bell – I told Alice not to, in case you have a lie-in on Saturdays, but I wanted to show my face and say hello, so I decided to take a chance. Evelyn's told me so much about you and Suzi – I feel like I know you.

Mam's often talked of you too.

She'd laughed. All good, I hope.

All good – and I'm sure she's told you I love the eggs.

She might have mentioned it.

I'd be very happy to collect them, if you'd prefer – and I'd rather pay for them too, but Mam got there first.

She did, she insisted. And it's no problem for Alice to deliver them – she normally goes to a class across the road on Saturday mornings.

They were joined the same gym. Maybe George had seen her there without realising it. And the one Saturday he was out of bed and at home when the eggs came, Alice hadn't brought them. Funny how they kept missing each other.

He was the talk of the staffroom at first break the following morning. 'You never told us you were going to be in the paper,' Barb said.

'I'm not in the paper, Deirdre is' – but she read out his quote, and Dermot of course had a smirk, which everyone ignored.

'William is seeing her,' Barb said. 'My brother William.'

'Seeing who?' Sheila asked.

'Alice, the one who writes Happy Talk. They've been dating for a while. She's lovely – isn't she, George?'

'I wouldn't know. I haven't met her.'

'So how did she get your quote?'

'Email,' he replied – and mercifully, Dermot was guffawing about something else, and didn't wonder aloud how Alice had got George's email address.

He'd shown the article to Suzi and Jack. It was well written, warm without being gushy or condescending. He'd read it out to the class, having cleared it first with Deirdre, who'd agreed, and who'd blushed with a mix of pride and shyness all the way through.

Her mother approached him that afternoon in the yard, as he released his class. 'Mr Murphy, can I have a word?' Nothing on her face to indicate what kind of a word she wanted.

'Sure.'

They stood into the corridor, Deirdre and the younger ones remaining outside. She flicked her ponytail behind a shoulder.

'We went to the aqua centre yesterday – Dee might have told you. I was going to wait until the holidays, but they all wanted to go.'

'She told me. Sounds like you had a good time.'

She nodded. 'They enjoyed it.' She shifted her weight, looked out at her children. 'There was a package,' she said.

'A package? Where?'

'At reception, with Dee's name on it.' She turned back to scrutinise him. 'A tin box, a set of paints.'

He thought of his belated idea to sneak a money element into the prize, and his decision not to risk it in case it backfired, and caused offence. 'Who was it from?'

'I don't know.' Looking steadily at him. 'There was a note, someone who read about Dee in the paper, and wanted to give her something. But there was no name on it.'

'Really?' An anonymous donation. Paints from a stranger. He had to acknowledge that it sounded slightly weird – or maybe it was just an example of someone being kind for no reason, with no agenda. Didn't that fit nicely into the whole Happy Talk thing?

'Mr Murphy, I have to ask if it was you.' Her face flushing. 'I want you to tell me if it was.'

He shook his head. 'It wasn't me, Mrs Daly.'

He wasn't sure if she believed him.

'It's just a bit ... A total stranger giving paints to Dee like that.'

Maybe it wasn't a stranger though. Maybe it was a neighbour or a friend who knew that a gift offered in person would be turned down, and who had decided to do it this way instead. Maybe it had come from Deirdre's aunt, whose idea it had been to contact the paper. Maybe she'd done better in life than her sister.

'I mean, don't get me wrong, Dee was happy to get them, but, it's just … you know.'

'I know.' He could imagine the battle she was fighting. Happy that someone had shown kindness to her daughter, ashamed that anyone felt the family needed help.

Interesting that someone else had had a similar idea to his own. And now that he thought about it, paints were a better gift than cash, in a household where money might have had to be surrendered to pay for more practical things.

That evening he logged onto the dating website and found a message waiting. His first. *Hi George! You're a man of mystery with no photo! Tell me three things about yourself that I don't already know!*

It was signed Sandra, the only bit that wasn't followed by an exclamation mark. Her profile picture showed a cheerful red-haired woman of indeterminate age. Her information told him that she was a psychiatric nurse in her thirties from County Galway who loved cats, and who enjoyed films and books and hill walking.

Three things about himself. He'd better play along. *Hi Sandra, nice to hear from you. Here are three things you don't know about me. I'm allergic to orange juice. I'm an only child. My late father was a piano tuner, and a fine pianist.*

He thought. Were they interesting enough? He deleted the last and wrote, *I tried and failed to play the piano* instead. No, too negative. *My daughter plays the piano beautifully.* Too boastful. *I play five-a-side football every week, badly.* He added a *ha ha*, then deleted it and replaced it with a smile emoji.

Was he expected to suggest a meeting now, or was it too soon? Jack could advise, but he didn't really want to keep involving Jack. He'd wait, throw the ball back to her. *What sort of films do you like? And do you own any cats?* Cat lovers, he knew, were always happy to talk about them. He decided against a mention of Oscar, not until Suzi had civilised him a bit more, in case a snap was requested.

He sent off the message and spent a few minutes flicking through some of the other female profiles. Even though he was a legitimate, paid-up member of the site it made him feel obscurely uncomfortable. He was checking them out, assessing them based on a photo (most of them had photos) and a few lines of description. It felt so soulless, so calculating. Was this what he had come to?

Still, as long as he was signed up, he should probably send out a few messages. Jack would definitely say he should. He selected a dark-haired woman from Limerick, another teacher. They'd have that in common. He drafted half a dozen messages until he finally had one he was happy with.

Hi Lorraine
I'm a teacher too, looking forward to the summer hols. I hope to do a bit of travelling around Ireland with my twelve-year-old daughter – lots of places I still haven't seen. Do you have any plans?
George

He sent it off and exited the site. He clicked into his email account and found the brief exchange he'd had with Alice of Happy Talk. He thought a thank you might be in order.

Alice,

George Murphy here, Deirdre Daly's teacher. I just want to say I appreciate you writing the piece on her – she was the star of the class today. Her mother told me that they used the pass yesterday. She also said that someone had dropped in a gift of paints anonymously for Deirdre, which I thought was kind.

I've told my class to read Happy Talk every week over the summer, and to take inspiration from it. I've also suggested that they submit any of their own experiences of kindness to you, so you might be inundated!

I love the idea of a column devoted to happy happenings. Have you ever considered writing a book for children? They're fans of the happy stuff.

George

He pressed *Send* – and as he did, his phone pinged with a text.

Hi George. There's something I need to talk to you about. Can I call by some day this week? If you happen to meet Rob, you mightn't mention it. C

Odd. The only time she called when Suzi wasn't here was to talk about Suzi. Why shouldn't Rob know about that? Presumably she'd enlighten him when she arrived.

Hi Claire. Wednesday suits, around half three? G

And a few seconds later:

Thanks. See you then.

The school was closing for the summer holidays on Wednesday at noon. George and the rest of them were going out for lunch, but it would be well over by three thirty. Maybe Claire wanted to alter their summer arrangements for Suzi – the usual loose plan was to split July and August between them, with Claire having her for July and George for August – but why should Rob not be in the loop about that?

He returned to his emails, and found a new one.

George,

No thanks needed re Deirdre: she was a worthy Happy Talk subject. Glad the family got to have their day out – and wasn't that nice that someone thought to leave Deirdre a gift? I wonder who it was.

No worries about inundation from your students – I love how you nurture the kindness habit in them. Deirdre told me about the tree on the wall, which I thought was a lovely idea – oh, and I also heard about your fixed raffle from Mrs Daly! She was full of praise for you, said you'd done wonders for Deirdre.

I'm flattered that you think I'd be capable of writing a children's book, but I think it might be a bit of a quantum leap for me. I might leave it to the proper authors!

Have a lovely week,

Alice

He clicked *Reply*: *I deny all knowledge of a fixed raffle. George*

And very quickly: *I don't believe you for a second, but your secret is safe with me. Alice* ☺

He smiled. He shut down his laptop and went out the back, where Jack was putting down new plants. He got to his feet when he saw George approaching.

'I hope you're coming to tell me it's cocktail hour,' he said, brushing soil from his knees. He wore tailored sand-coloured shorts, which made him appear more boyish than he already looked, and a navy T-shirt with a white illustration of the New York skyline on it. Even gardening, he was carefully put together. 'I could murder a Mojito.'

'Would a beer do?'

'Sounds good.'

They sat on the wooden chairs that had had their final coats of paint, and now sported the requested yellow cushions, and they popped the tabs on two cans of Polish beer. Approaching nine o'clock, the sun low in the sky, the birds gone home to bed. Next door's cat sat in his usual spot on the dividing wall, washing himself and paying them no heed. Someone was mowing a lawn. Someone else was roasting meat on a barbecue. The two scents drifted and twined pleasantly about.

George debated mentioning the online approach from Sandra the psychiatric nurse, and decided to wait a bit. Jack might make a big thing of it, and it wasn't a big thing, or even a medium-sized thing.

'So, holidays coming up,' Jack said. 'Seven weeks?'

'Eight. Till the last Wednesday in August.'

'Well for some. Any trips planned?'

'Not really, nothing definite. Suzi wants to see the *Titanic* thing in Belfast, so we'll go at some stage – and maybe take in the Giant's Causeway while we're up there. What about you? What kind of time off do you get?'

Jack swatted at something that had landed on his leg. 'I have two weeks to take,' he said. 'Preferably one in July and one in August.' Actually ...' he ran a finger around the base of his can, catching droplets that he flicked onto the grass '… Patrick's family asked if I'd like their Tenerife house for a week in July.'

'Did they? What did you say?'

He lifted a shoulder, his gaze still on the drink. 'It's very sweet of them. My first instinct was to say no.' His words slow and deliberate, a finger tracing the letters on the can. 'I didn't think I could bear going back without Patrick … but the more I thought about it – I mean, obviously it would be sad, but we had lots of happy times there …' He drifted off, lifting a hand, letting it drop.

'So you might go?'

'I *would* go,' still slow, still halting, 'but …' he glanced at George '… I was actually thinking –' He drew in a breath, rested his can on the arm of his chair. Rubbed his nose. 'Well, I don't know how you'd feel about it,' all in a rush now, 'but would you and Suzi be interested at all in joining me?'

George laughed. 'We'd love it, thanks. What dates should I book the flights?'

'George, I'm serious.'

'No, you're not. The last thing you'd want is us tagging along.'

'Why? We get on well, don't we? And you know I think the world of Suzi. I would honestly love if you both came with me. And we needn't be joined at the hip – we could do our own thing.'

He was joking. Wasn't he? He couldn't really want to spend his holiday with a young girl and her father.

Could he?

'This isn't spur of the moment, George. I've thought about it. You're probably wondering why I wouldn't ask one or two of my friends, but … they all knew Patrick, and I just think I'd prefer to go with people who'd never met him. I can't really explain that.' He drained the can, and lowered it. 'Look, no pressure, George. I just thought I'd ask, that's all.'

Suzi would jump at it. She loved any kind of trip, and she'd adore a holiday that included Jack. She'd been to France and mainland Spain with Claire and Rob, but George had never travelled outside Ireland with her – and now he was being offered a chance to do just that.

July was normally Claire's month with Suzi, but they were both flexible over the summer. He could certainly put it to her.

'Tell me more,' he said.

'Well, it's in an old fishing village in the north of the island, off the tourist trail. There are a few restaurants, not fancy at all, but the seafood is amazing. And lots of little coves for swimming, and a wildlife park not far away. The house is very quaint, like a step back in time. No TV, no WiFi, nothing flash – they deliberately left it like that. It's on three levels, but it's narrow, so there are only two bedrooms, one on each of the upper storeys. You and Suzi would have a room with twin beds – or there's a pull-out bed on the ground floor. And there's a rooftop terrace, with an amazing sea view.'

It sounded idyllic. 'And the family wouldn't mind you bringing two total strangers with you?'

'Not in the least. I'd clear it with them beforehand, but I know it wouldn't be a problem.'

'Which week have they offered?'

'The last week of July.'

Roughly a month from now. Assuming Claire would be happy to juggle dates, was there any reason not to accept this very unexpected offer? If there was, George couldn't think of it.

'We'd love it,' he said. 'I think I can safely speak for Suzi. Thanks so much for the invite. Let me run it by Claire before I can say yes for sure.'

He'd have to check that both their passports were in order. He'd say nothing to Suzi until he was certain it was happening.

He'd need to keep an eye on her in the sun, with her fair freckly Irish skin. He'd have to slather her in sunblock, and insist she wore a hat.

He'd never been to Tenerife, or to any of the Canaries. His one and only sun holiday had been a week in Majorca, the summer he was sixteen. He'd been invited along by a friend, who was reluctantly accompanying his parents. Please come, he'd said to George. I will literally die of boredom if you don't. The parents socialised with George's parents: permission had been sought, and granted.

The couple spent most of their days on sunbeds by the pool, leaving the boys to mooch around the resort, eyeing up but not daring to approach the skimpily clad females. They would sneak out again each evening after the adults had gone to bed and wander to the prom, where they tried out their terrible Spanish on grinning kiosk vendors who sold them bottles of ice-cold beer without batting an eyelid. They'd sit on the sand, swigging from their bottles and planning their futures while the sea lapped below them, dazzling with moonlight, until it was time to make their slightly meandering way home.

Remembering it now – the scent of sun cream in the air, the bliss of seawater hitting hot skin, the pleasure of eating outdoors on balmy evenings – George felt a little flip of anticipation. He'd have to buy shorts and new togs, and maybe replace his ancient sunglasses too.

'Thanks,' he said again. 'It's very generous of you.'

Jack crumpled his empty can. 'It's a win-win, George – you'd be doing me a favour too. Hope you can come. Another beer?'

That night George rummaged through drawers until he found his passport. His last trip abroad had been a whiskey-flavoured stag weekend in Edinburgh a few years back, memorable mainly for the impressive hangover that had accompanied him all the way across the Irish Sea on the homeward journey. This trip, if it happened, would be very different.

On Wednesday Claire wore a pink dress he hadn't seen before, and a grey jacket over it, with a smile that came and went. She closed her umbrella – the rain had returned that morning – and left it propped outside the front door. 'Nothing,' she said, when George offered tea or coffee. 'Maybe water.' He filled a glass, and added the slice of lemon he knew she liked.

She slipped her arms out of her jacket and dropped it on a chair. Her dress was sleeveless, its skirt falling to the middle of her calves. She sat on the edge of another chair and drummed her nails on the table until she caught herself at it, and stopped. She looked at the water glass, but didn't touch it. Her hands moved around each other, like they were seeking the right position. The diamond in her ring gave a single fierce flash as the light from the window caught it.

George dropped into the chair across from her. 'So what do you want to talk about?'

Her hands remained restless, fingers interlacing and disconnecting. 'I'm leaving Rob,' she said.

He was stunned. It was the last thing he'd expected to hear. He sat back, letting it sink in. Leaving Rob. She and the podiatrist, engaged just a few weeks ago – and now splitting up.

'Has something happened?'

He saw the raw bleakness in her expression. 'I don't love him, George. I thought I did, but I don't. Not enough to marry him.' Without warning her face crumpled, and she began to weep quietly into her cupped hands. Her elbows on the table now, the left one perilously close to the glass.

Of its own accord George's mind went back over the years to the night she'd told him the same thing, and he was aware of a creeping satisfaction that he tried to be ashamed of, and failed.

'I'm sorry it didn't work out,' was all he could come up with, and she went right on crying. Suzi, he thought. What would this do to Suzi? Presumably she'd grown attached to Rob. Why had Claire agreed to marry him, why complicate things by accepting a ring she must have known she didn't want? Hadn't she considered their daughter at all?

But he wouldn't mention Suzi. It might cause a row, which would solve nothing – and Suzi would be fine. She still had both her parents.

He waited until the crying passed. He sat there while she rummaged for a tissue in her bag, and dabbed at her wet cheeks and blew her nose. He stayed where he was when she rose to put the tissue in his bin. She didn't resume her seat but went to stand by the sink, her back to him.

He regarded the creases in the pink dress that sitting had caused, the lightly tanned calves and trim ankles, the thin straps of her sandals. He noted a small smudge of darkness an inch above her right elbow. She bruised easily.

'It's changed,' she said, her voice cloggy in the aftermath of tears. 'The garden.' She hadn't seen the place since before Jack's time. She'd dropped Suzi to the house one Friday, George's car gone in for a service, and she'd stayed for a cuppa. March, he thought, or April. His mother had still been here – she'd arrived home from the salon as Claire was leaving – so it was sometime before the March wedding. 'You're getting into gardening, George.'

'Not me,' he said. 'What will you do now?'

She turned to face him, her skin blotched from the tears, her eyes puffy, the tip of her nose red. She'd always been a messy crier. Silent, but messy. She shook her head slowly. 'Suzi and I will have to find somewhere else to live, but ...'

Her father had died when Suzi was three, lost his footing on a building site's scaffolding, plunged through an unfinished conservatory roof on his way to eternity. These days, her mother lived beside Claire's brother and his family in Wicklow, on the other side of the country. And of course the apartment was gone, the one Claire and Suzi had remained in after the split with George, until Rob had moved them into his house.

George had continued to pay half the rent on the apartment over the years, along with an agreed monthly sum for Suzi's expenses. When they'd moved in with Rob, the maintenance payment had remained unchanged – George didn't want or expect another man to support his daughter, not until the relationship with her mother was put on a more solid footing – but his rent contribution now went into a new bank account. For Suzi, whenever it was needed.

Seemed like it might be needed shortly.

Claire turned on the tap and bent to splash her face with

water. George got up and crossed to offer the towel that hung on a hook at the end of the worktop.

'Thanks.' She pressed it to her face, held it there. Her shoulders lifted slightly with her inhalations. He saw the darker roots in her hair, the indentation he remembered at the top of her right arm, a legacy from a long-ago immunisation.

She returned the towel to him and moved back to the table to lift the glass. He watched her throat constrict with her swallows. 'I just,' she said, lowering the glass, 'have a favour to ask.'

'What?'

'Could you hang on to Suzi until I can find us a new place? I don't know how long for, maybe a few weeks.'

'Of course I can.' He kicked himself that he hadn't offered. 'That's no problem. I can keep her for as long as it takes.'

'Are you sure?'

'Claire, she's my daughter,' he said, a little more sharply than he meant to. 'Of course I'm sure.'

Her eyes filled again. She dashed at them with the towel she still clutched.

'Sorry … thank you. Maybe starting this weekend?'

'Fine. Have you told her?'

'No … I thought I should have the conversation with Rob first.'

So the podiatrist didn't yet know that he was about to be dumped. 'What about you? Have you somewhere you can stay?'

She nodded. 'I have a friend who says she'll let me crash on her couch for a few weeks.' Her eyelashes were spiked with tears and tap water. 'Suzi's booked into a summer camp for a week in the middle of July. I could pick her up here in the mornings, and drop her back to you.'

'You don't need to do that. As of today, I'm on holidays.'

'Are you sure?' she repeated.

He suppressed a fresh dart of irritation: she didn't need anything to tip her into more tears. 'Yes, I'm sure.'

This was good news. He relished the prospect of having Suzi all the time. She'd be able to make great strides with Oscar – and Jack, he knew, would have no objection.

The thought of Jack reminded him. 'I was going to tell you – Suzi and I have been invited to Tenerife. My tenant has been offered a house for a week at the end of July, and he asked if we'd like to join him.' No need to mention Patrick, no need to go into all that.

She stared at him. 'Your *tenant*? He's invited you and Suzi on holidays?'

'That's right.'

Her forehead creased. 'This is the guy who gave her a plant for her birthday.'

George nodded. 'He's big into gardening. He's the one who's been working on this one.'

'He's a gardener? I thought she said he did something else.'

'He's a carer. Gardening is just an interest.'

'And now he wants to take her off to Tenerife.'

George smiled. 'Claire, he's invited both of us. What's the problem? She'd love it.'

'The problem,' she said evenly, 'is that Suzi's a twelve-year-old girl, and he's a grown man. How can you not see that, George? I was concerned when she told me you'd got a male tenant, but I told myself you wouldn't take in anyone dodgy – why are you smiling?'

'Claire, I can assure you he's not dodgy. He's one of the most genuine people you could meet, and he's been through a lot. His boyfriend died a year ago.'

'His boyfriend?' The suspicion didn't leave her face. 'He's gay? You know that for a fact?'

Another stab of annoyance, which he let out. 'Well, he told me he's gay, and I believe him.'

'I'm not trying to be smart, George. A person can say anything. They can claim to be anything.'

'Claire, Suzi has nothing to fear.'

'And you're absolutely sure of that.'

'Yes, I'm absolutely sure.'

She shrugged. 'Well then.'

'Well then you're OK with her going?'

'... I suppose so.'

'Is her passport up to date?'

'Yes.'

'I'll need the details to book flights. You might text them to me.' When she didn't respond, he said, 'Claire, Jack and his partner were together a long time. The Tenerife house belongs to the partner's family. He and Jack holidayed there every year, and now Jack has been offered a week in the house, and he'd like Suzi and me to go with him because he doesn't want to go alone. He and Suzi get on really well – she must have told you about the piano tune swaps. Believe me, there's nothing sinister going on here.'

'OK,' she said. 'OK,' she repeated, and burst without warning into a fresh bout of weeping. It used to kill him when she cried, even when he'd had nothing to do with the cause. 'Sorry.' She wept, blotting the new tears with the towel. 'I'm a mess, George.'

'You're just going through a rough time.' But she was sodden with misery. He looked out at the blooming garden, listening to the small wet sounds of her unhappiness.

Eventually she splashed her face with water again and dried it. She gave him a faint apologetic smile. 'I think I'm done.'

'More water?'

She shook her head. She caught his hand and gave it a quick squeeze. 'Thank you, George.'

'For what?'

'For putting up with me.'

'Don't be silly.'

She held onto his hand; he eased it away. He thought suddenly of the plant that Suzi had put down in Rob's garden after her birthday, and the new keyboard she'd recently been given. He wondered if she'd get to keep it, with Rob undoubtedly having paid the lion's share of the cost, if not all. He prayed the man would be magnanimous, and not take out whatever resentment he might feel on an innocent child.

At least she'd have Tenerife to look forward to, whatever the immediate future might hold.

'George, would you tell her? Would you tell Suzi about me and Rob?'

'Me?' His heart sank. 'I'd rather not, to be honest.'

'I know I shouldn't ask, but it would come better from you. I'd be too emotional – I'd blurt it out and upset her.'

He shrank from the prospect. Whether he liked it or not, Rob's house had been Suzi's main home since Christmas, and now she was going to be taken from it with no say in the matter – and Claire wanted George to be the one to break that news to her.

'I thought I'd pack up her things over the weekend and bring them here on Sunday morning.'

'Hang on – are you saying you'd bring her here without telling her she's not going back to Rob's? Wouldn't she want to say goodbye to him?'

She sighed. 'I don't know, George. She might – but once I tell Rob I'm leaving, I need to leave, and Suzi does too. Look, I can't figure everything out just now. Will you talk to her? Please. I'd really appreciate it. And you could tell her about Tenerife afterwards, to cheer her up.'

What could he say? She looked on the verge of tears again. 'OK.'

'Thank you. Will you let me know when you've done it?'

'Yes,' he said, like he always did. Yes to everything she asked. Yes to moving himself out of her life when everything in him revolted against it, yes to an unfair sharing out of their daughter, yes to all the other requests over the years. He was a yes man.

After she'd left, he opened the presents his students, or rather their parents, had given him on their children's permanent departure from his class, and from the school. Bottles of wine, a book of salad recipes, gift packs of shower gels and sponges, notebooks with pens attached, a 1,000-piece jigsaw, a mug with 'World's Best Teacher' on it, an indoor potted plant with sprawling leaves whose name meant nothing to him.

Even Deirdre Daly had given him a present. The box of Maltesers embarrassed him. *Thank you for all you did for Dee*, her mother had written on the card that accompanied it. *Louise Daly*, she'd signed it.

He left the plant and the Maltesers on the kitchen table, bundled up the rest of the gifts and brought them upstairs. In the bathroom he replaced the plastic beaker that held his and

Jack's toothbrushes with the new mug. As he was stacking the shower gels on a shelf, a text arrived. Suzi's passport details, Claire wrote, followed by the information he needed. He'd talk to Jack when he got home: they should book flights tonight – assuming there were still seats available at this late stage.

He checked the dating website and found another message from Sandra of the exclamation marks.

Hi George,
You're the only person I know who's allergic to orange juice, so that makes you very special, ha ha! I'm afraid I'm not a bit sporty so I won't be going to cheer you on when you play your football! You have been warned! I like all kinds of films, even the really gory ones! I've watched all the Lethal Weapon *ones so many times I nearly know them off by heart! I have two beautiful cats, a mother and a daughter. I'll attach a snap, and you'd better compliment them!*

Would you like to meet? We could get a bite to eat some evening at Borelli's restaurant if you're agreeable. I love that place!
Sandra xx

Attached was a photo of an enormous white cat, curled on a brown leather couch. Sprawled along the back was a slightly less enormous cat, white with patches of black. Both were asleep.

He thought she might be a little … vehement for his taste. He was reminded of the woman who'd come to look at the room for rent, having split up with her boyfriend. He recalled her asking – defiantly, it had to be said – if George would object to her having people to stay overnight, and reacting angrily when he'd demurred.

But he shouldn't judge Sandra, not without meeting her. The dinner suggestion was a little daunting – he'd imagined coffee to start – but he could hardly say he'd rather a shorter first meeting.

He thought of Suzi, arriving in two days' time for the weekend – and maybe staying for the rest of the summer. Might be best to get the dinner out of the way before that, which meant tomorrow night. Sandra would think he was eager: couldn't be helped.

Hi Sandra,

Thanks for sending the snap of your cats – they're certainly impressive. A cat has recently joined this household, but he's still too shy for me to take his snap, so you'll have to take my word for it. My daughter named him Oscar, after a toy she had when she was small. Dinner would work for me tomorrow night; my daughter's with me at the weekend, and my schedule is a little uncertain next week. How would that suit? Let me know and I can book a table at Borelli's.

George

He sent it off and changed into his five-a-side clothes. He was pulling on his T-shirt when her response came in: *Tomorrow night is perfect! See you at eight! Looking forward!*

He felt a mix of apprehension and anticipation. He looked up the restaurant website and booked a table for two. He recalled reading that she was from County Galway, but she must live close enough to the border if she was happy to travel to Borelli's. Cats, he thought. Cats and films, gory and otherwise, would hopefully get them through.

He heard the front door opening. He put away the laptop and went downstairs to tell Jack that they were going to Tenerife.

Alice

'THE MAN AT TABLE FIVE HAS BEEN STOOD UP.'

In the act of chopping tomatoes, Alice lifted her head. Claudia set her laden tray on the draining board by the sink, and Maggie began silently to scrape leftover food into the compost bin.

'How long?' Kate asked.

'A good twenty minutes – and he's nervous, keeps watching the door. Definitely a first date.'

'Poor thing.' Kate drained tagliatelle and twirled it into a bowl. 'Alice, would you top that with bolognese sauce please? Many thanks. Claudia, that's table one up.'

After the waitress had left again, Alice glanced through the glass circle on the door, which afforded a view of most of the restaurant. There he sat at table five, alone and waiting, his back to her, facing the entrance – but as she was about to turn away he got to his feet. She saw Claudia approach and speak, saw him nod a response as he pulled on a jacket. Tall, broad, light-coloured hair was all she could make out.

'Alice, I'll take those tomatoes if they're ready.'

'Sure.'

The door swung open again. 'He left. He gave up waiting. Kate, table three are ready for mains – and Alice, I need more Parmesan please.'

And just like that, he was dismissed and forgotten.

Alice had been stood up once. She was seventeen and it was June, a couple of weeks after the Leaving Cert. He'd walked her home from a Saturday night disco and kissed her goodnight at the gate. The smell of his leather jacket had been intoxicating. When he'd asked to see her again she'd said yes too quickly. They'd settled on Monday, in front of the department store everyone used as a rendezvous spot.

She'd gone through most of her wardrobe before deciding on her usual jeans, and a green shirt that wasn't warm enough for the chilly evening. She'd arrived at five past the designated hour and waited for ten excruciating minutes, avoiding eye contact with people who'd walked past, every one of them seeming to stare at her, to see all the way into her sinking heart. At a quarter past, she'd wheeled abruptly and rushed home, fighting tears all the way, feeling utterly exposed and humiliated.

And long after she was old enough to know better, she'd been stood up again in a hotel lobby – and now it was someone else's turn, in the middle of a crowded restaurant. Maybe there was a logical explanation: someone stranded without a phone, unable to contact him – or a sudden illness, or a simple lapse of memory. Maybe it wasn't as cruel as a deliberate decision not to show up.

Half an hour later, Kate sent her out with two main courses, an occasional task if the others were busy. 'Table four,' Kate told her. Alice didn't relish this part of the job, always nervous of dropping plates before they reached their destination – or worse, of somehow missing the table and tipping the contents onto the diner's lap.

A couple was seated at table four. Alice gave a bright smile. 'Hello! Who ordered the pizza?'

The woman raised her hand silently, and Alice set it down. 'So you must be the lasagne,' she went on, placing it before the man.

'That's me,' he agreed cheerfully.

'Enjoy,' Alice said, turning away.

'Alice O'Mahony,' the woman said.

Alice halted, looked at the face.

'It is you, isn't it?'

'Yes, but … '

'Don't you remember me?'

And then it came to her. 'Caroline Manning,' she said.

They hadn't known each other well, despite being in the same class all through secondary. Different interests, or different outlooks, had decreed that anything more than an acquaintance wouldn't happen. A memory surfaced of seeing Caroline in town after school once, arm in arm with a man who looked a lot older.

'I'm O'Dwyer now,' Caroline said. 'This is my husband Leonard.' He smiled and told Alice he was pleased to meet her. She didn't think she knew him. Several times since moving back home she'd passed faces in the street that prompted a little ping of recognition, but not now, not this face.

'I heard you were back.' Caroline had grown leaner. Her hair was lighter in colour, and cut in a long bob that grazed her shoulders. Her top was low-cut; stones flashed in the necklace that sat on her bare skin. 'You were in Dublin, weren't you?'

'That's right.' Alice was conscious of her own appearance, face heated from being in the kitchen, hair definitely not looking its best.

'And now you write that little happy thing in the paper.'

That little happy thing. 'I do.' Smile a little stiff now.

'Sweet. And you're also a waitress. Busy, busy.'

Alice's toes curled in their flat shoes. 'This is a stopgap,' she said quickly. 'My aunt owns this place. I'm just helping her out till I find a job here.'

'What's your field?'

Her field. 'Well, I worked in a dental clinic in Dublin, so ... '

'You're a dentist? Len's an orthodontist.'

Put her right? Say nothing?

'Where did you train?' the orthodontist asked, making Alice's decision for her.

'No, I'm not a dentist. I was the receptionist.'

'Oh. Receptionist.'

Silence. She felt judged, by both of them. 'Well, I'd better get back—'

'Are you married? Children?'

'None of the above,' she said lightly, in as cheerful a tone as she could muster. 'Still looking.' She laughed too loudly, and they chimed in politely. 'Well, I'll leave you to your food.' She turned and practically ran back to the kitchen. Caroline Manning, married to an orthodontist. Mother, probably, to perfect children with perfect teeth.

The conversation left dissatisfaction behind. *You write that little happy thing in the paper. And you're a waitress.* It nudged at her all evening, making the time crawl. It didn't help that she'd applied for two more receptionist jobs in the past week, and had yet to receive an acknowledgement from either.

The following afternoon, Alice spoke on the phone to Maura, a woman in her eighties, who was throwing a party for her husband's ninetieth birthday. *He had a fall last year that put him in hospital for nearly three weeks,* she'd told Alice in her email. *It took a lot out of him. The hospital offered to help me find a nursing home for him when he was ready to leave, but I wouldn't hear of it. We got a carer to come in every day instead, and it was the making of Tom. He's like a new man.*

'Oh, that's marvellous,' she said, when Alice told her why she was ringing. 'Wait till Tom hears he's going to be in the paper.' She spoke of the party, scheduled for the upcoming Sunday. 'It won't be anything grand, just some family, and a few of the neighbours.'

'Sounds good.'

'Yes, hopefully everyone will enjoy it.' Pause. 'There's just …' She trailed off. Alice waited, but no more came. 'Maura?'

'I'm here.' The voice softer, slower. Another pause. 'We had two children, Alice. We lost them both. Our daughter got cancer, she was just forty-eight, and our son was killed on the road a year after. We've carried on for each other, and for our grandchildren. They'll be at the party.'

The news, delivered so quietly, shocked Alice. 'I'm terribly sorry to hear that, Maura.' She marvelled at the enduring strength of the woman in the face of such heartbreak. Caring for her frail husband, making sure his birthday was celebrated in the company of those who loved him, even while both of them would surely be thinking of the ones who weren't there.

'Sorry, Alice. I was just … they're in my head a lot.'

'I can imagine.'

'I was just thinking … maybe you could make a small mention, say something like we've had our tragedies over the years, but we've survived them together, we've kept each other going. Just so they're not forgotten. I know Tom would like it.'

'Of course I will.'

'Thank you, dear. I hope you don't think I'm putting words into your mouth.'

'Not at all. It's your story, I'm just writing it up.'

'Oh – and Jack will be at the party too.'

'Jack?'

'Tom's carer. He's such a good boy. Do you know that he takes a grocery list from me twice a week and arrives the next day with the shopping? I'm quite sure that's not part of his job description. He's so good with Tom too, so kind. We'd be lost without him.'

'Could I take his number?' Alice asked. 'He might like to add his good wishes for Tom.'

A tiny pause. 'Would I get in touch with him, and pass on your number instead? Would that be alright, Alice?'

'No problem.'

Within minutes of ending their conversation, her phone rang.

'Jack Garrihy here,' he said. 'Tom's carer. Maura asked me to give you a ring.'

'Hello. Thanks for getting in touch so quickly.' She thought his voice sounded familiar, but she was reasonably sure she hadn't come into contact with any carers since moving back to town.

'Thanks for including them in your column – it'll make their day.' He told her that the couple were a delight. 'Always so positive, glass always half full. Did they tell you about their kids?'

'They did.'

'Doesn't bear thinking about – but they soldier on. Tom is one of my easiest clients, never complains, although Maura tells me he still has pain from the shoulder he dislocated when he fell. And she's a fabulous gardener – did she show you the garden?'

'I didn't visit them, I was just on the phone.'

'Oh, pity – it's magnificent. I was looking for cuttings a while back for a place I moved into. I was doing a bit of a renovation on the garden and she told me to help myself. She's a dear.'

'She said you do her shopping, and it's not part of your duties.'

'Stop, that's nothing. I'm around the supermarket in ten minutes. Besides, I never have to food shop for myself – my landlord and I have an arrangement: he shops, and I cook. Funny, he actually got a mention in one of your recent stories – he'll get a laugh when I tell him I'm in the next! Have you got enough to go on there?'

'Plenty, thank you.' After hanging up, she wondered which story his landlord had featured in, and wished she'd asked.

Monday came, cooler than of late, but with a blue sky. Alice spent the morning writing up the column, and the afternoon sanding old coats of paint from Kate's garden furniture. You really don't have to, Kate had said, I've got a handyman I can call for that – but Alice welcomed the mindless task, letting her thoughts wander as speckled sawdust drifted to the ground, gradually revealing the bare pale wood.

She'd booked her trip to Italy, using air miles her father had passed on when they were home. She was looking forward to reuniting with her extended Italian family, and making use of the musical language she loved. These days, she found herself thinking in Italian, her subconscious preparing for the immersion that was coming.

She'd also organised a surprise thank-you for Kate.

It had started with an email to her cousin Paolo, a week or so ago:

How about we switch places for a week? You come here, I go there. And before you say you can't take time off work in the middle of the high season, I'd be happy to replace you in the trattoria. You wouldn't have to work here – Kate doesn't need me in the restaurant, she's just helping me out. I know how much she'd love to see you, so I hope you and Aldo will consider it.

She'd written separately to her uncle:

Just an idea. Kate has been so good to me since I moved back to town, and I thought this could be my way of saying thank you. I know you'll be busy in the trattoria but I'm a wonderful waitress [crossing her fingers] and I'll be happy to cover Paolo's shifts. One of you would have to pay for his flights though – I'm not very well off at the moment!

She didn't know how Aldo would feel about her jumping in for a week. She also wasn't sure how her parents would take it, when they'd imagined her coming over to be with them – but Aldo would know how much it would mean to Kate to have their son for a week. She'd waited for their responses – and the following morning, they'd both come in.

I have no objection, Aldo had written. *We are certainly busy, but if you're happy to work I'll accept your offer – and I'll try to go easy on you, or my sister will kill me!*

Sounds good, Paolo had written. *I'd love a week off work, and to spend time with Mamma too* – and now his flights were sorted, and Alice had sworn everyone to secrecy, and Kate would be so happy to see her son again.

All was well in Dublin. Emails from Liz were keeping her up to date with the pregnancy: *Mornings are still iffy. I throw up anything I eat before eleven, so breakfast has moved to lunchtime. I expect you to come and see us when we're a family of three, by the way. No excuses – and if you stay the night you can babysit, and let us out on the town.*

Tina sent regular photos of her three. Both she and Liz asked about William whenever they got in touch, and Alice said so far, so good.

She'd told nobody about the night in the hotel that hadn't happened. She had decided that it would go permanently untold, even to those closest to her. Especially to those.

At six she swept away the old paint flakes and gave the seat a quick going-over with a cloth soaked in white spirit. Tomorrow morning, if it stayed dry, she'd make a start on the preservative.

She scrubbed the smell of white spirit away in the shower. She dressed and made up her face with more than her usual care. At ten to seven, precisely the time he'd promised to call, William arrived.

'You look lovely,' he told her, drawing her towards him and kissing her lightly on the mouth. She took wine from the fridge and found a bag for it, and they set off to have dinner with his sister and her family.

'Their house is small,' he told her. 'They bought it as a starter home after they got married, and never moved out. They like the location, and the people on the road. And they ended up only having one child, so ...'

He drove carefully through the town. Even out on the open road he was a cautious driver – which was no bad thing, of course. Chris had woven effortlessly through Dublin traffic, cutting down side streets, frequently changing lanes, manoeuvring skilfully into tiny parking spaces. Guards know all the tricks, he'd told her.

He'd been full of trickery, in every way. How much more dependable was William, who stopped at amber traffic lights and always used his handbrake.

Barb and her family lived in number seven, to the left of Val's house. The flowers in Val's window box had grown and spread since Alice's visit there: now they were a tumbling, overflowing mass of red and purple blooms. Val's car was gone – to Kate's, of course, on a Monday night.

Before William could ring the bell, the door was opened. 'Heard you arriving,' Barb said, reaching up to kiss her brother's cheek, giving Alice a quick hug. 'Come in, come in. No comparing this house with Val's, Alice – we've done nothing with ours.'

They followed her into a tiny square hall with coats and umbrellas hanging on tiered hooks, and narrow stairs climbing steeply upwards, and a door leading further. William found space on the hooks for their jackets, and in they went.

It was as different from Val's as it was possible to be. A small sitting room was made smaller by maroon walls and oversized leather furniture. A stove was set into the fireplace; a television perched on a little table to the left of it. Books fought for space on shelves behind the couch. It was very warm.

'Helena's dying to meet you,' Barb told Alice. 'She just loves Happy Talk, especially since one of her classmates featured in it.'

'Who?'

'Deirdre Daly. She won the art prize. Isn't she so talented? That painting was incredible.'

Small world. So Helena was also taught by George Murphy, who was denying all knowledge of a fixed raffle. That had made Alice smile.

'She'll be home in a bit – she's down the road at a pal's house, but I've warned her to be back for dinner. Is it wine you like, Alice, or a short? We have vodka and gin, and I'm pretty sure there's whiskey, although I never touch it. And I think there might be some beer – Donal likes the occasional bottle – I can check if you'd fancy it. That's assuming you take a drink, of course. We have Coke if you'd prefer, or sparkling water.'

She stopped for a breath. 'Wine would be fine, thanks,' Alice told her. 'Either colour, I'm not fussy.'

'Don't believe a word,' William put in. 'Her parents own a vineyard in Italy, so Alice is a connoisseur.'

'I'm far from a connoisseur,' she protested, laughing. 'William's joking.'

'But not about the vineyard,' he said.

Barb looked impressed. 'Seriously?' she asked Alice. 'Your folks own a *vineyard*? In Italy?'

'They live there.' William again. 'Her mother's Italian.'

He sounded like he was boasting. Was he? Alice rather liked it. He was proud of her – or proud of her connections. Either way, she found it agreeable.

'Golly, very posh,' Barb said. 'In that case, I'd better play safe and open your red, Alice – we haven't got a clue about wine. Donal picks up a box in Dunnes or Tesco whenever something's on offer, so that'll tell you. William, would you do the honours? The corkscrew's on the mantelpiece, beside the candle.'

She took a seat next to Alice. 'It's so great to be on holidays. I'm a teacher – I'm not sure if I mentioned that at Val's. I teach in Helena's school – and I just love the long summer break. I enjoy the job, don't get me wrong, but by the end of June I'm fit for nothing. I know people throw their eyes up to Heaven when they hear teachers saying that, with the short working hours and all, but they should try it for a day. Poor Donal's in retail, so no long break for him, but we're planning a week in west Cork next month, probably in Schull. We love that whole area. What's this you do again, Alice – besides Happy Talk, I mean?'

Alice told her about Borelli's. 'I'm on the lookout for a receptionist job though. I've applied for a few, but I've heard nothing.'

'Well, it's good you have the other to keep you going then. Now, let me get the starters. Donal's on duty in the kitchen, by the way: he's far better than me.'

She reappeared with a platter. 'Dates wrapped in bacon,' she announced. 'The main event will be ten minutes. Donal says hello.'

She talked on, telling Alice of the book swap Helena's class had erected on the school railings: 'Oh, you've seen it, isn't it great? Deirdre Daly did the lettering, of course.' Asking William if he'd had any thoughts on what to do for their parents' anniversary: 'It's their fortieth, Alice, so we'd better make a fuss.' Speaking of the attic conversion they were considering: 'With Helena almost a teenager, we thought she'd like more space. Her room is very small. We could look for a bigger house but we love this location, close to everywhere. When did you say you moved back here?'

'The middle of April.'

'Just a couple of weeks after William opened up. It should have been March, he probably told you, but he was knocked off his bike. Some woman drove right through a red light, and he had to delay things while he recovered. He was lucky she didn't kill him.'

Alice didn't dare look in William's direction. She was uncomfortably warm; a trickle of sweat was crawling slowly down her back. Should she confess, after he'd clearly said nothing to Barb?

Of course she should. She must. If it came out later, Barb would think her very underhand not to have mentioned it now, when the perfect opportunity was presenting itself.

She cleared her throat. She mentally crossed her fingers. 'Actually, that was me. I was the driver.'

Barb's face took on an almost comic look of astonishment – raised eyebrows, wide eyes, mouth a perfect *o*. In the stove, something collapsed with a soft thump.

Alice ploughed on, unnerved by the sudden silence. 'I was distracted, I wasn't thinking straight. I was very upset after – a bad day. I know it's no excuse, and I was completely horrified when I realised what I'd done ...' She trailed off. Would she be asked to leave?

Barb found her voice. 'I don't believe it. *You* were the driver? William, you never said.'

Before he had a chance to respond, Alice jumped in. 'I'm guessing he said nothing to protect me. He knew I'd be embarrassed.' They'd never talked about it after the first time, never made a decision to keep it from people, but that must have been his thinking, mustn't it? Oh, why had it come up now – and why had Alice felt compelled to blurt out the truth, just like she had in his shop?

Barb still looked puzzled. 'I thought you didn't exchange any contact details when it happened,' she said to William.

'We didn't. Alice did offer, but I didn't take them.'

'So let me get this straight. You had no idea, Alice, that William was the man you'd knocked down when you went for your eye test?'

'No – and I didn't recognise him right off. I did think he looked familiar, but I told myself I must be imagining it.'

'So you were the one who recognised Alice, William?'

He shook his head. 'Not at all.'

Barb looked from one to the other. 'So if neither of you remembered, how did the penny drop?'

'Well, he mentioned that he was a cyclist, and it just ... I just knew, when he said that – or I had a pretty good idea.'

'So you told him you'd run him over.'

'... Yes.'

She didn't look angry. She didn't sound angry. Alice took reassurance from this. 'He was very gracious.' She glanced at William; he looked impassively back. Was *he* angry that she'd told his sister what he hadn't?

And then, to her great relief, Barb laughed. 'Well, there's a story for your grandchildren if ever I heard it – you couldn't make it up! Wait till Donal hears.'

He appeared just then to summon them to dinner. Alice's revelation seemed to amuse more than surprise him. 'It's a funny old world,' he said, and Alice had to agree. In March she'd been gainfully employed in Dublin, and window-shopping for a going-away outfit: now, just a few months later, her life was different in every way.

As they took their seats around the kitchen table – thankfully, this room was cooler – Helena arrived, and was introduced. Over perfectly cooked lamb kebabs the subject of Happy Talk came up – and inevitably, so did Deirdre Daly.

'She wants to be an artist,' Helena told them, and Alice thought of the girl who would spend her summer picking up litter in the cinema, and of the father who couldn't or wouldn't see her talent, and she wondered how big a miracle it would take for Deirdre to realise her dream.

'What class do you teach?' she asked Barb.

'Third this year, but we move around to avoid teaching our own children – school policy. Except for George, Mr Murphy. He's taught sixth for years. He has a daughter Helena's age, but she goes to a different school. I think we're all a bit relieved that he stays in sixth – nobody else wants it, but George seems happy there.'

'Deirdre's mother had great praise for him.'

'Oh, he's a born teacher. All his students love him. You'll miss him, won't you, Helena?'

'Yeah, he's really nice.'

'Actually, I ran into him yesterday in the supermarket – I forgot to tell you, Donal. He's off to Tenerife for a week.'

'Well for some,' Donal said. 'The furthest we're going is Schull, Alice.'

'Don't mind him, Alice – he'd hate a sun holiday. He'd be bored in half an hour. I wanted to go to the Seychelles for our honeymoon – we ended up in Paris. I suppose I shouldn't complain, it was lovely. Have you been?'

'Actually, I haven't.'

'Oh, you must.' She spoke of the Louvre, and a dinner cruise they'd taken on the Seine, and having her portrait drawn by a street artist in Montmartre. 'I left it behind on the train back to the city centre – can you believe it? It was only a charcoal sketch, but still.'

She liked her, Alice decided. She was chatty and charming, and in her company the evening flew by.

'Don't be a stranger,' she said, standing on the path with Donal when William and Alice were leaving. 'We'll do it again.'

'I'll host next time,' Alice promised.

'I hope you didn't mind my saying it to her,' she said to William as they were driving away. 'About the accident, I mean. I felt I should, when she brought it up.'

'Not at all – she got a kick out of it. I hadn't said anything because I thought you might not want me to, but it's better out in the open.'

So considerate he was. So lucky she'd been to meet him. Maybe she deserved him, after Chris – despite being prepared to sleep with her ex behind his back. Maybe the gods had forgiven her for that.

Val's car was parked on the street outside Kate's house. There was a light on in the hall. Alice's apartment was in darkness.

She tried to remember if she'd washed up after lunch, or just left the dishes in the sink.

'You want to come in?' she asked.

Her first time to suggest it after a date. Ten weeks or more since they'd started going out. He'd been patient, had left the next move up to her.

'Are you sure you want me to?' He knew what she was asking.

'Yes,' she said. 'I am.'

So he came in, and he stayed the night.

George

HE COULDN'T MAKE SENSE OF IT. SHE WAS THE ONE who'd suggested the meeting, unprompted by him. Why would she do that, and then not appear?

It had occurred to him, as he'd waited for her in the restaurant, the minutes ticking by with no sign of her, that she had no way of contacting him except through the site. He hadn't thought to ask for a phone number, and she hadn't looked for his. He'd brought up the site on his phone and checked for messages, but there were none. He'd debated sending her one, but what was the point, at that late stage?

He should let it go, chalk it down to experience and move on. But what if she hadn't deliberately stood him up? What if there was a logical explanation? Maybe she was sick, or had been in an accident. Maybe she was dead. It wasn't impossible.

The half an hour he'd waited for her had seemed far longer. He'd been acutely conscious of a pair of female diners at a nearby table who were definitely talking about him, shooting glances his way every so often. And his waitress, giving him such a pitying smile every time she passed his table, telling him the coffee he'd ordered was on the house when he'd finally given up and asked for his bill.

He'd stopped at a chipper on the way home, needing food despite his distraction. He'd eaten it without pleasure in the car, still trying to understand what had happened, but unable to come up with a plausible explanation. Thankfully, Jack was out when he got home. He slunk upstairs and spent the remainder of the evening watching comedies on Netflix, checking the dating site every so often for a message that didn't arrive.

He waited till lunchtime of the following day, and when there was still no word from her, he decided to take action.

Hi Sandra,
Hope everything's OK. I was a bit concerned when you didn't show up at Borelli's last night.
George

He pressed *Send*, and a message flashed up immediately. It wasn't from Sandra.

You have been blocked from further communication with this member.

What? He stared at the screen in bewilderment. Blocked? She'd *blocked* him? What had he done, apart from turn up for a date she'd suggested? He was completely bewildered.

Jack wasn't, when George finally admitted what had happened.

'Ah Jesus, I don't believe it. You got one of those.'

'One of what?'

'One of those idiots who get their kicks from making arrangements they never intend to keep.'

'Seriously? That's a thing?'

'Afraid so, George. Shame you had to come across one on your first outing.'

'But her photo is up there for everyone to see – isn't she worried someone will call her out on it?'

'Pretty safe bet it's not her in the photo – and chances are the bio's a fantasy too. Probably changed it already, and put up a new snap.'

He spoke as if this was universal knowledge. George felt clueless. Was he that innocent, that naïve? It would appear that he was.

'Don't let it put you off, George. I'm telling you, the majority of people on the site are genuine – you were just unlucky.'

But it did put him off. It made him feel like a fool, which presumably was exactly how it was supposed to make him feel. 'If she's created a new bio, how will I know if she makes contact again?'

'Good question, but I can't answer it. You could lodge a complaint with the site managers, but she may well come back with a few made-up complaints of her own, so you might be best letting it go.'

And then it was time for George to pick up Suzi so they left it at that, and all the way to Rob's house he tried to shake the anger and annoyance she'd caused in him.

Unusually, Suzi came to the door, already armed with her rucksack. 'Mum's having a bath,' she told George, and he wondered if Claire was avoiding him. Embarrassed, maybe, after their last encounter. The notion made him sad: didn't she know she could always be herself with him?

Suzi didn't notice he was out of sorts on the way home, too busy telling him about a sleepover she'd had the previous night. As soon as they arrived she wanted to go straight up to Oscar, but instead he brought her into the sitting room and broke the news to her. Wanting to get it out of the way, regretting that he'd agreed to be the one to tell her.

'They're splitting up?' Her face filled with dismay. 'But ... they were going to get married.'

'I know, love. It's hard to understand, for me too. But people's feelings can change.'

'Why didn't Mum tell me?'

Why indeed? 'She asked me to. I think she wanted you to be away from Rob's house when you heard.' It wasn't much of a reason, but it was all he could come up with.

'Will we have to move out of Rob's?'

'Yes. You and Mum will need to find another place to live.'

'But ... what if we can't? We could be *homeless*.'

He hated the anxiety in her voice, the woebegone face she presented to him. He wanted to photograph it and send it to Claire. See, he'd say, see how you've made her feel.

'Suzi, there's no way you'll ever be homeless, I promise. This house belongs to me. Gran gave it to me when she married John, and nobody can take it away from me. There will always be a room for you here. Always.'

'And what about Mum?'

'She says she's got a friend she can stay with until she finds a new place for the two of you. She'll be having a good look around over the next while.'

'So will I be staying here?'

'You will, right here with me and Jack, for as long as you need to. That's OK, isn't it?'

'... Yeah.'

He'd told himself the doubt in her voice didn't reflect how she felt about living with him. 'You'll still be going to your summer camp. I can bring you. And you'll still see plenty of Mum too – she can call here anytime she wants, or we can meet her in town. And we can go and visit Gran as often as you like, now that we've got holidays. She'd love that.'

Her tremulous expression didn't alter. 'So when do we have to move out?'

'Well, I think you've sort of already moved.'

'What? But all my stuff is still there.'

'Mum is going to pack it up and bring it here, sometime over the weekend.' Was it right, to be presenting it as a fait accompli to her? It seemed too rushed, too much to be expecting her to process all at once.

'So I'm not going back to Rob's? You mean ever?'

'No, love. You won't be going back to Rob's.' Not unless her mother changed her mind again.

She stood up, defeated. 'Can I go and see Oscar now?'

'Hang on, there's just one more thing. One more very good thing.' He told her about Jack's invitation – and to his great relief, the news brought a tentative smile. 'Really? Are we really and truly going?'

'We really are. I've bought the plane tickets – and Jack is

cooking tortilla this evening for dinner, because he says we have to practise eating Spanish food.'

At dinner she was full of questions for Jack, who'd been briefed about the split. He told her about the many little beaches tucked under the cliffs, and the glass-bottomed boat they could take to see all the fish that swam in the clear sea, and the sunrises they could watch from the rooftop terrace if they were up early enough. And George watched her spirits lifting higher with each new item of information, and he silently blessed his tenant for the gift he'd handed them.

He rang Claire after Suzi had gone to bed. 'I told her.'

'How did she take it?'

'Much as I expected. Confused and upset and worried.'

'George,' she said wearily, 'I'm not doing it on purpose,' and he relented. This was not the time for a row.

'I told her about Tenerife. It helped.'

'Good. I can drop her things tomorrow afternoon, around five.'

Had she spoken to Rob? She didn't say, and he didn't ask. She called the following day, and she and Suzi went upstairs and stayed there while George hauled bags into the house. When Claire came down alone, face tight and pale, she declined an invitation to stay to dinner.

'I'm going to my mother's house for a couple of nights. I'll be in touch when I get back.' Hearing her sadness, watching her drive off, George felt sympathy. Like she said, she hadn't done it on purpose. Love couldn't be forced – he'd learnt that, and now Rob was learning it too.

On Sunday morning, as Suzi and George were having

blueberry pancakes for the second morning in a row, Jack marked off a little section of the lawn close to the shed, and brought her out to see it after the pancakes.

'This is going to be our wildflower patch,' he told her. 'It's too late in the year for a lot of things now, but we can still plant some wildflowers. We can go with George to the garden centre some day this week, and you can choose your favourites.' An expedition was planned for the three of them on Thursday, when Jack finished work early.

On Monday evening George changed into T-shirt and track pants, and tied the laces of his worn runners. On the landing he glanced through Suzi's open door and saw Oscar sitting on her bed. When had the change of rooms happened?

'Salutations,' he said, and the cat fixed him with a baleful look, but didn't hiss. Progress.

In the kitchen he found Suzi and Jack in the middle of a Scrabble game. 'Going for a run,' he told them. 'Back in twenty minutes.' As he left the room, the doorbell rang.

'Hi George,' Rob said. Unsmiling.

'Rob.' He wasn't sure where to go after that. Rob here, at this house?

His bemusement must have shown on his face. 'I've got the keyboard. I presume Claire told you I was bringing it over.'

'She must have forgotten.' George had forgotten too. He hadn't given the keyboard a thought.

'It's in the car.'

They walked out in silence and carried the keyboard between them into the house. They propped it with its stand against the wall in the hall.

'Thanks,' George said. 'I appreciate you letting her keep it.'

Rob looked mildly surprised. 'Of course.' He pushed his hands into his pockets. 'How is she?'

'She's OK. It was a shock to her.'

Rob gave a short nod. He seemed about to say something, but didn't.

George felt more was called for. 'I was sorry to hear, when Claire told me.'

'Yeah ... Well, tell Suzi I said hi, will you? And tell her —' He broke off, shook his head. 'Forget it. Thanks, George. See you around.'

'Rob?'

They turned. Suzi stood at the kitchen door.

'Hello, trouble,' Rob said, attempting a grin – and Suzi walked straight past her father, and Rob opened his arms. George watched his daughter embracing the man who might have become her stepfather, and he saw the genuine affection that lay between them.

'How're you doing?' Rob asked when they drew apart. 'Are you OK?' Hands resting lightly on her shoulders.

'Yeah.'

'I'm sorry,' he said, 'that this is happening,' and she made no response, and George couldn't see her face. 'But it's good that you get to spend more time with your dad, right?' Shooting a forced smile in George's direction.

'Yeah, and we're going to Tenerife with Jack.'

'Are you? That's great. Maybe give me a ring sometime, if your dad's OK with it.' Both of them now looking to George for approval.

'Fine,' he said. What else could he say?

'The nemesia,' Suzi said then. 'It's still in your garden.'

'You want me to dig it up and bring it over?'

She shook her head. 'Would you keep it? Jack says you just need to make sure it's watered, and pick off the flowers when they die.'

He smiled. 'Sure. I'll look after it. You mind yourself, Suze.'

He called her Suze. George had never heard anyone call her that.

Rob hadn't blamed Claire for the break-up, although he could have. He could have told Suzi, truthfully, that it was her mother's idea, not his, but he hadn't. Instead he'd told her he was sorry, and he'd pointed out that she'd get to spend more time with her father. George felt bad for having resented him: what had the man done but fall in love with Claire? How could George, having done the same, fault him for that?

After he'd gone, George and Jack carried the keyboard up to Suzi's room – causing the cat to vanish under the bed – and placed it, on her instruction, by the window. She switched it on and played a few distracted chords, and switched it off again.

'The plant you gave me,' she said to Jack. 'The nemesia. It's still in Rob's garden. I told him he could keep it. I hope you don't mind.'

'Course I don't mind – we have plenty here, don't we? I think it's cool that you've left a reminder of you in another garden.'

'A reminder of me,' she repeated, a smile blooming – and George had an image of Rob, newly alone in his big house, with only a small flowering plant for company, and whatever inevitable leftovers of them he would come across in the days that followed. A sock maybe, slipped between bed and wall; a forgotten slice of pizza hidden behind something on a fridge shelf; a library book under a pillow maybe, needing to be returned. Leftovers of their intertwined lives.

On Thursday afternoon George and Suzi set off for the garden centre, having arranged to meet Jack there. The day being fine, they opted to walk. On the way they passed the new cinema, opened just a few weeks earlier. A young girl in T-shirt and jeans was leaning against the wall, next to the display board that gave the film listings. Her arms were folded, a knee bent, her sneakered foot braced against the wall. Waiting for a date, maybe, although she looked too young for that – and as they drew closer, George recognised her.

'Deirdre,' he said, and she turned her head, foot dragging down the wall, arms uncrossing, hands pushing into pockets. She didn't smile on seeing him: on the contrary, she appeared hunted, or maybe defensive, as if she'd been caught doing something she shouldn't. He wondered why.

'This is my daughter Suzi,' he said, and the girls exchanged the measured look he'd caught on faces of that age on being introduced to a peer. Twelve going on teenager, moving from the openness of early childhood to the more guarded interactions that seemed to be the norm in adolescence.

'Deirdre was in my class,' he told Suzi. 'You going to see a film?' he asked, but the girl shook her head.

'I'm helping out here for the summer,' she muttered, her gaze flicking briefly back to Suzi.

Helping out? Working, she must mean. It couldn't be legal, employing a child of that age. It would have to be cash in an envelope on payday – but who was he to judge this situation, living in a mortgage-free house with his permanent, pensionable job?

The doors were pushed open from the inside just then, and people began to emerge. 'I got to go in now,' Deirdre said, and slipped away before George could respond.

'Her picture was in the paper,' Suzi said, and George agreed that it had been. They passed the bank and the launderette and the mobile-phone outlet and the first of the vape shops, and Suzi chattered and he responded, but his mind insisted on returning to his old student.

Artist, she'd said, the day he'd asked them all what career path they'd like to follow. It had been their last hour of primary school, the books put away in favour of a chat. Artist. It was the obvious direction for her to take – but if that meant some kind of course in an art college, or any kind of higher qualification, it would be a huge challenge for her. He hoped she'd encounter a good career guidance person in secondary school who might figure out a way for her to realise her dream.

'There's Jack,' Suzi said, as they approached the garden centre, and George pulled his mind back to the task in hand. Twenty minutes later they emerged with a selection of seeds – alyssum, red poppy, zinnia, cosmos – and a purple watering can that Suzi had fallen for.

Jack indicated the battered red Mini across the road. Gifted to him five years earlier, he'd told George, by the family of another deceased client. 'You want to take a lift home?'

'Sure.'

They were standing at the edge of the path, waiting for a break in the traffic, when the shout came. 'Mr Murphy!'

The voice, full of exaggerated bonhomie, was unmistakable. George turned, heart sinking. 'Dermot.'

'Fancy meeting you here!' Dermot exclaimed, looking not at George but at Suzi. 'And can this possibly be your little girl? Look how tall she's got! What's this your name is again, miss?'

'Suzi,' she said, and George heard the coolness in her voice. 'Little girl' wouldn't have gone down well.

'Suzi, of course! How could I forget?' He extended his hand in Jack's direction. 'George's teaching colleague,' he said. 'Name's Dermot Dunne.'

'George's landscape gardener,' Jack replied, in an equally hearty tone, giving Dermot's hand an enthusiastic pump. 'Name's Jack Garrihy. You have any landscaping needs, Dermot? I'm your man. We've just been doing a recce here,' waving an arm at the garden centre, 'planning for next spring.'

Landscape gardener.

'No,' Dermot replied breezily, 'no landscaping needs, thanks. My wife's the gardener in our house. She looks after the bits and bobs.' He turned his attention back to George. 'Off to Corfu next week with the troops,' he announced. 'Sun, sea, sand and whatever you're having yourself.' Two children he had, wasn't it? The girl just out of Junior Infants, the boy younger. 'How about you, George? You and Suzi going anywhere nice?'

Before George had a chance to respond, Suzi jumped in. 'We're going to Tenerife with Jack,' she stated. 'We're staying in a luxury house. It has a rooftop terrace, and it's really near the sea.'

Silence followed the ammunition she'd unwittingly handed over. Dermot's gaze roamed slowly from her to George to Jack, a knowing grin spreading across his face. George was careful to keep his expression neutral. Would Dermot remember this in September? Of course he would. Naturally he would. First question he'd ask in the staffroom was how George's holiday with his gardener had gone.

'Tenerife,' Dermot said. 'That'll be lovely. I hope the three of you' – a stress on the phrase that George, and doubtless Jack, didn't miss – 'have a wonderful time.' He laughed as he turned away, waving a hand in the air. '*Adios, amigos*,' he called, and off he went, the laughter floating back.

'I don't like him,' Suzi said.

'Come on,' Jack said, taking her arm, 'let's hit the road,' and they crossed and climbed into the car, and played I Spy all the way home.

That evening, George rang his mother. 'Suzi and I were thinking of coming to see you at the weekend,' he said. 'How would Sunday suit?' He needed to tell her of Claire's split with Rob, and they were due a visit so he might as well do it in person.

'That would be lovely. Will we put you down for lunch?'

'Only if you promise not to go to any bother.'

'Of course we'll go to bother. See you at one.'

He was settling down to watch the news, Suzi and Jack having gone upstairs to commune with Oscar, when his phone rang.

'I've arranged to see a property at ten on Saturday,' Claire said. 'I thought Suzi might like to come along. Can I drop by and collect her?'

'Of course you can. Why don't you come for breakfast, anytime after nine?'

'Oh … yes, OK, that sounds nice. Thank you.'

'And I could go with you to the viewing too, if you want another opinion.'

'That would actually be great, George. It's been so long since I've had to look for accommodation, I'm afraid I'll forget to ask vital questions. Thanks, I appreciate it. See you Saturday.'

He thought back to the last time they'd shared a meal, just the three of them. The night Claire told him it was over, with Suzi a tiny eight-month-old baby, unaware that the parents who'd conceived her in love were now saying goodbye. That was it, their last family meal. Over eleven years ago.

This wouldn't be a family meal, though. They weren't a family any more – and anyway, Jack would be there. It was nothing. It was just breakfast.

When the news was over he visited the dating site. He'd decided to cancel his membership, too wary of Sandra, or whatever her name was, attempting to make contact again, to have more fun at his expense. There was no way of knowing who she might pretend to be next time, so he wasn't taking the chance.

One new message was waiting for him.

Would he read, ignore, or delete? What did it matter who it was, now that he was leaving?

But curiosity got the better of him. He opened it.

Hi George,
Thanks for your message, and sorry it's taken me a while to reply.
To be honest, I'm not really looking to meet another teacher – I'd
rather find someone with a totally different way of life. No offence.
Hope you find someone.
Lorraine

He'd completely forgotten his message to her. At least she'd replied. He went through the cancellation process, ignoring the repeated pleas to think again (*Are you sure you want to leave?*) and the incentives to stay (*20% off your next three months!*) and the final plea to let them know where they'd gone wrong (*Just complete our brief survey*). He closed his laptop with a sense of relief. Should have followed his gut from the start – but Jack had meant well.

On Saturday, Claire was carrying an egg box when he opened the door to her. 'I met your delivery woman at the gate,' she said, and George thought it interesting that everyone apart from him had met Alice of the eggs.

Claire wore a short green dress, and flat sandals. Her toenails were painted blue, her hair shone. Small green stones flashed in her ear lobes as she removed her jacket and handed it to him. Her fingers were bare of rings: had she returned Rob's? What did a man do with an engagement ring that came back to him? Sell it on eBay, or hold on to it in case another chance to use it came along?

He brought her through to the kitchen and introduced her to Jack. 'Pleased to meet you,' she said. She hugged Suzi, and admired the bangle George had bought her during the week, and praised the newly planted wildflower section of the garden when Suzi drew her attention to it, even though there was nothing to see there yet. She exclaimed when George produced his blueberry pancakes. She ate two, and enthused about them.

She was nervous. It made him sad to see it.

They left Jack with the dishes, on his insistence. 'When one cooks, the other washes up,' he told Claire. 'We brought it into law,' and she smiled and thanked him.

'He's nice,' she said, as they followed Suzi to the car. 'You struck lucky, George,' and he told her of the other prospective tenants as she drove. 'God, sounds like you didn't have a lot of choice.'

'No. Jack was definitely the only one I could have lived with.'

'He's really great,' Suzi added from the back seat, and her parents exchanged a smile. George felt a tiny *déjà vu* twitch that he couldn't identify. Some other time they must have smiled at one another like that, a kind of that's-our-daughter smile.

They found the road. The houses were semi-detached, and built of red brick like George's, and all had another level beneath the ground floor, with steps leading up to the front door. Number eight looked identical to its neighbours, apart from having longer grass in front.

'It belongs to a cousin of someone at my pal's workplace,' Claire said, making no attempt to get out of the car. 'That's as much as I've been told. It hasn't been advertised yet. It's the basement apartment.'

They entered the garden and located a small gate in the black railings that encircled the house. They descended a series of steps and found themselves in a dim little paved area, with a door and a window set into the house wall. George wondered how much light the window could admit. A green waste bin stood slightly too close to the door, whose red paint was cracked and peeling.

Dandelion leaves sprouted from the angle between wall and ground. Grass and other bits of greenery pushed up in clumps through cracks in the paving. Not the most imposing of entrances but easily cleaned up, George thought. A few plants in pots would make it more homely. Jack would help.

Nobody spoke. Claire rattled the letterbox of the door, no bell being in evidence. It was opened surprisingly quickly to reveal a man of short stature, beaming and balding and gap-toothed, grey suit hanging a little baggily. Somewhere in the sixties, George estimated.

'Morning, morning,' he said affably. 'You found me, come on in. It was two of you looking, mother and daughter, wasn't that it?'

'That's right,' George replied. 'I'm just here to give a second opinion.'

'Right, and that's fine, that's grand. And you work,' turning to Claire, 'with my cousin Trish, isn't that right?'

'Well, my friend Ursula does. I'm Claire.'

'Yes, yes, indeed, so you're getting special treatment before I advertise. Leo is my name,' pumping her hand, 'and I'm guessing this is your daughter, ha ha!'

Suzi was introduced, and her hand shaken, and George's too when his turn came. 'Suzi's father,' Claire said, and Leo nodded enthusiastically.

'Well, now that we all know each other, let me walk you through. My flat is small, but perfectly formed, ha ha!'

It was anything but perfectly formed. It was dark and dank-smelling, with two tiny bedrooms to the rear – brown-edged stains on both bare single mattresses – and a windowless shower room between them whose ceiling was mildewed, and whose sink was cracked. Each room was brightly announced – 'Bedroom one! Bedroom two! Bathroom!' – in a voice that sounded like he was inviting applause.

They didn't applaud. They murmured acknowledgements and otherwise followed him silently onwards, through a sitting room that contained one small couch covered with a yellow sheet, and an electric heater set into the fireplace, and little else, and finally into a kitchen at the rear, perhaps the most depressing of the rooms.

Its floor was covered with faded lino. There was a single wall unit and two open shelves, and a waist-high fridge with a tiny freezer compartment at the top, and a free-standing cooker that looked like it had survived since the seventies or earlier, and a sink in the corner with a small curtained space beneath it. A worktop between sink and cooker, propped on wooden legs, no more than three feet in length, held a kettle and a toaster.

'The washing machine is upstairs,' Leo told them cheerfully, 'in my bit of the house. You'd be welcome to use it anytime, no charge, ha ha!'

'Right,' Claire said faintly.

George had tried and failed to catch her eye during the short tour of the premises. She couldn't possibly be considering this miserable apartment. Everywhere was dark, with windows trying but failing to let in anything but minimal light. Even the most optimistic of souls would have a job staying upbeat here.

'I'm cold,' Suzi said, rubbing her arms.

Leo laughed. 'Where's your jumper, young lady?' he asked, and Suzi shuffled her feet and didn't answer.

Claire hitched her bag higher. 'I think we'll leave it,' she said. 'It's a bit ... small.'

'Well, I *said* that,' the landlord replied, his beam fading. 'I *said* it was small.'

'Yes.'

'There's only the two of you,' he said, the words noticeably sharper. 'Isn't there enough room for two – especially when one is a child?'

'It's not just the size,' she replied, and he lifted his shoulders and turned his palms upwards.

'Suit yourself,' he said flatly. 'Plenty will jump at it.'

'I doubt that,' Claire retorted, before turning and marching in the direction of the front door, ushering Suzi along with her. George threw an apologetic smile at Leo and followed hastily. They pulled the door closed and practically ran up the steps and back to the car. Once inside, they all spoke.

'It was horrible,' Suzi said. 'Mum, I'm *very* glad you didn't take it.'

'That sitting room,' Claire said, shuddering as she started the car. 'I dread to think what was under the sheet on that couch. And those mattresses – and the kitchen. God almighty.'

'What a kip,' George remarked – and for some reason this made her burst out laughing, which in turn made Suzi laugh. It was good to hear Claire's merriment. 'Plenty will jump at it though,' he added in Leo's hearty voice, which caused more eruptions as they moved away.

'Imagine going upstairs to use the washing machine,' Claire said, as she slowed for a pedestrian crossing. 'I'd rather scrub clothes by hand in that shower-room sink.'

'Bet you'd still have to hang them on his line.'

'God, I probably would. I can just see him watching from his window. What am I going to say to Ursula?'

'Just tell her it didn't suit. Say you need more light, and you're addicted to baths.'

'I suppose that would do. Suzi, I was going to bring you shopping, get you a few new things for your holiday.'

'Oh yes, please!'

'George, do you want to come along, or would you prefer to be dropped home?'

'Come with us, George,' Suzi put in. 'You said you needed shorts,' so he accompanied them to the shopping centre, and within ten minutes he had found and bought two pairs of shorts and new togs. He wandered around, using up the rest of the hour they'd separated for, until he happened to spot them at a rail of clothes in a department store.

He kept his distance. He saw Claire hold up a dress, and Suzi saying something before selecting another. He liked the novelty of seeing them together, liked hearing Suzi's familiar laugh as it floated across the floor to him. He watched as they made selections and brought them to the changing rooms. He was glad for Suzi to have both parents around, albeit temporarily.

They met as arranged at a café in the centre. He queued for coffees and a milkshake, and admired their purchases when Suzi pulled them one after another from the bag. 'We got you a surprise,' she said, and held up a grey T-shirt that had a little black kitten emerging from a fake pocket.

'Wow, that's … wow.' He'd have to wear it at least once. Thankfully, it looked too small.

'It's Oscar,' Suzi said, 'as a kitten.'

'Beautiful.'

He glanced at Claire, who was struggling to keep a straight face. 'Suzi chose it,' she said. 'It was on the sale rail.' He bet it was. 'I thought it looked a bit small though.'

'Oh, I hope not,' he replied, and she lifted her coffee to hide her grin.

'Thanks for coming with me,' she said when she dropped them back, after Suzi had rushed inside to show Jack her Tenerife purchases, and she and George were alone in the car. 'That man gave me the creeps. I was really glad you were there.'

'No problem. How's where you're staying?'

She shrugged. 'It's fine, and I'm delighted to have it, but I'm hoping it's only short term. I don't want to impose on Ursula and her husband for any longer than I have to. Sorry about the T-shirt, by the way. I knew it wasn't your style but she begged. It was only three euro.'

'No worries. I might lose it in Tenerife.'

She smiled. 'I've heard Tenerife is a terrible place for losing things.'

Silence fell, an easy one. The sky was clouding over, the best of the day gone. He reached for his door handle. 'I'd better let you get off.'

'This was fun,' she said. 'We must do it again.'

'What – go and view the basement again?' he said, just to make her laugh.

She needed to laugh.

Alice

ARE THEY FOR GEORGE? THE WOMAN HAD ASKED, making Alice's heart jump because she hadn't heard her approach. I can take them, I'm going in – so Alice had surrendered the eggs and left, wondering if she'd just encountered Suzi's mother. She hadn't seen any great similarity with the girl – this woman's features were more angular, her hair straighter, her face freckle-free. Maybe Suzi took her looks from her father. Maybe George had a face full of freckles.

She'd set it aside and got on with her morning, and now it was lunchtime, and she was going to Kate's, the invitation issued the night before at the restaurant. Alice had thought it a little odd: they'd worked together last night, and would be together again this evening. Still, a free lunch was a free lunch.

'Sit,' Kate said, setting bread on the table. 'I've made vegetable croquettes.'

'Lovely.'

Over lunch they spoke of Alice's upcoming holiday, and Kate's decision to replace her ancient barbecue, and the continuing dry spell, and a film that Alice and William had seen. And then, when the food had been despatched, Kate pushed aside her plate and said, 'Alice, there's something I need to say.'

Alice swept crumbs from the table onto her plate. 'Yes?'

'I think it's time you found your feet here. It's nearly three months since you came back from Dublin, and you're no closer to getting a job – I mean, a real job.'

The words were gently spoken, but still carried a mild sting. 'I've applied for anything I've seen,' Alice replied. 'I told you about them all.'

'You did, yes.' Kate bundled plates and bowls and got to her feet. 'I think you're going to have to cast your net a little wider, Alice.'

Just like her father had said. Different words, same message.

'I said from the start that the job at Borelli's was just to tide you over.'

'Yes, I know that, and I appreciate it, Kate.' A small current of something began to thrum through her.

'And it looks like you're not going to get the job you want, or not right away, so I think you'll have to settle for something else for a while.'

Alice nodded. 'I will,' she said. 'You're right. I'll start looking this afternoon.' She made to stand, but Kate, dropping into her chair again, said, 'Hang on, Alice.'

There was more?

'I've been thinking about the apartment. I really should be getting an income from that. I should have put it up for rent when Paolo chose to live in Italy. It was crazy leaving it empty all the time, just so he'd have his own place when he came, so I've decided to do it now.'

The apartment, where Alice had finally begun to feel at home – but of course it had never been intended to be long term either. So her job and her accommodation were suddenly no longer a given. It felt like everything was shifting, everything she'd become accustomed to was being eased away from her.

And what about Italy? In less than two weeks she was supposed to be flying there. How could she go, with this new turn of events? How could she take a holiday when she needed to find work?

'Alice, stop looking so anxious. I'm not planning to make you jobless or homeless; I'm simply flagging up that time is passing, and for your own sake you need to be a little more pro-active. You can stay on in the restaurant until you sort another job, and you can move into the house with me when I let the apartment, again just until you start earning a proper salary. And whenever Paolo comes, he can stay in the house too. There's plenty of room.'

Paolo. He was arriving the day Alice left for Italy. What a mess. 'So when will you start looking for a tenant?'

'Well, I was thinking I could get Val to put an ad into next week's paper, so I could show it while you were away. If we said it was available from the beginning of August that would give you a few days to pack up when you get back from Italy. How does that sound?'

'Fine.'

It didn't sound fine, it sounded awful. Paolo would be occupying the apartment while Kate was showing it to prospective tenants. It wasn't a huge deal, but it was bound to impact on his week, and leave Kate with less time to be with him. So much for her big surprise.

'Kate,' she began, and stopped. Where to begin, what to say?

Before she could find the words, Kate spoke. 'I know I'm throwing it at you all at once – but I just feel you need a little push, delivered with love. Look on me as your pusher.'

She smiled, and Alice tried to smile back. 'I'll make a start,' she said, getting up. 'I'm sorry you had to give me a push; I should have acted sooner. I'll try to have something sorted before Italy.'

'Well, that would be great, but the main thing is you apply for more positions, anything you think you'd be suited to. See you at Borelli's this evening.'

Back in the apartment she rehashed the conversation. She was ashamed that Kate had had to prod her: she should have been more aware, should have realised all on her own that she wasn't going to get the job she wanted anytime soon.

She went online and visited the usual sites. She found ads for shop assistants and supermarket shelf stackers, bar staff and waitresses, chambermaids and call-centre operatives. All within her capacity, but none of them grabbed her. They all felt like the jobs she and Tina had taken on their arrival in Dublin. Applying for any would feel like she was taking several steps back from the dental clinic.

She hovered over nanny. Did she want to look after other people's children? Not particularly. What about crèche assistant? No – two years' childcare experience needed.

Typist? Her skills weren't good enough.

Dog walker? She was nervous of large breeds – and a few small ones too.

Librarian, PA, pastry chef, bookkeeper, bus driver, all requiring qualifications she didn't have. But she'd have to apply for something, if only to keep Kate happy.

She pulled up the application letter she'd used for the receptionist jobs. She thought of how carelessly she'd handed in her notice at the dental clinic, sure that a similar job was waiting for her at home, or would soon materialise.

A thought occurred then: should she go back to Dublin? She could contact the clinic, tell them things hadn't worked out as planned – she'd have to come up with a plausible reason. She could ask if they knew of any Dublin clinics who might hire her. Emmet and Liz would let her stay, she was sure, until she found other accommodation.

No. It would be an admission of failure. Tina wouldn't say it, but she'd think it. *I told her it was a mistake,* she'd think.

She eventually settled on nanny, chambermaid and shop assistant openings. She tinkered with the original letter, tailoring it to fit each position. She attached her CV, such as it was, and the reference from the clinic, and sent them off. Would she hear back from any? Did she care?

She wondered if she should look for accommodation. Not much point, she decided, until a job was offered. She wasn't sure how she felt about sharing Kate's house, wasn't sure how she felt about Kate in the wake of their conversation. Would this sour things between them? She hoped not.

Anxiety gnawed at her. She attempted to read, and found it impossible. She mopped a floor that didn't need it, ironed clothes she wouldn't normally bother ironing. When the time came for her shift at Borelli's she set off, feeling gloomy. Would Kate bring it up again, ask if Alice had begun looking for work?

She didn't. Nothing was said, Kate genial as ever, but time dragged, and the usual tasks felt even more tedious. 'You look tired,' Claudia remarked at one stage, which didn't help.

At the end of the evening she told Kate about the jobs she'd applied for, and Kate said she was pleased to hear it, and wished Alice well, and the matter was dropped.

She told William the following day. It was lunchtime and they were in the park, eating sandwiches she'd prepared.

'I suppose you can see where Kate is coming from,' he said. 'This is one great sandwich. How do you get them to taste so good?'

He didn't seem to realise the seriousness of her predicament. 'I pickle the cucumber and onion. Yes, of course I can see where she's coming from, but I don't want to take a job just for the sake of it. I don't suppose you need anyone at the optician's?' She was attempting a joke, trying to lighten her own mood, but he treated the remark seriously. She might have known.

'Not unless I sacked Nuala, and I wouldn't imagine she'd be too pleased to be replaced by my girlfriend.' He took another bite. 'I'm trying to define the flavours here. I think I'm getting dill, but there's something else I can't—'

'Oh, stop going on about it!' she snapped. 'We're talking about my future here, and all you can think about is what I put into a sandwich!'

He chewed and swallowed silently. Her outburst hung in the air between them. 'Sorry,' she said, not sure that she was. She shouldn't have agreed to meet: she wasn't in the mood for him.

He brushed crumbs from his shirt – white on working days, blue or grey on Sundays, grey today – and regarded her quizzically. 'So what kind of job do you think you'd like, besides receptionist?'

She shrugged. 'Some kind of office job, secretarial or something, but I'd probably need to improve my typing speed, and update my computer skills. The system in the dental clinic was old, and it's the only one I'm familiar with.'

'There are loads of online computer courses.'

She shook her head impatiently. 'I don't have time to do a course. I need to start earning as soon as possible. Maybe once I get a job I can think about upskilling, but not now.' She took another little sandwich triangle, smoked ham and egg on granary bread. She pulled a shred of ham from it. 'My parents think I should move to Italy.'

He regarded her in astonishment. 'They do? You never said.'

'I never said because I turned them down. The only reason they suggested it was because they feel sorry for me. They think I'm getting nowhere over here – job-wise, I mean.'

And they were right, weren't they? No wonder they pitied her.

She lowered her sandwich, her appetite gone. 'Sorry,' she repeated. 'I'm no company today. I'm worried about what's ahead.'

'It'll happen,' he said. 'You'll find what you want. It's out there' – and even though she knew he was trying to make her feel better, she had to resist the urge to give a sharp retort. Discontent scratched at her until she wanted to scream at it to leave her alone. It felt like a clock was ticking, every tick jabbing at her. Quick. Quick. Quick.

'I'm thinking I should have stayed in Dublin: at least I had a proper job there.' The minute it was out, she regretted it. 'I don't mean— That didn't come out the right way. I just meant I had work, that's all, not a charity handout from my aunt.'

'So why did you leave Dublin?' he asked. 'You never really said.'

She lifted a shoulder. Should she tell him the truth? Did it matter any more? No: the truth would make him pity her, and pity was the last thing she could cope with right now.

'I wanted a change, and Kate offered me the apartment and the part-time work. It made sense at the time.' She brushed breadcrumbs from her lap. 'I think I should go,' she said – and felt annoyed with him all over again for not protesting. She was impossible today.

Silently they gathered up the remains of the food. 'You won't be able to stay over when I'm living in Kate's house,' she said, as they made their way to the gates. 'I wouldn't feel comfortable.'

'That's fine. You can come to mine.'

They'd taken to spending a few nights together in the week, either in her apartment or in his rooms above the shop. His living space was as orderly as she'd expected to find it, the furniture modern and minimal, the colour palette neutral. His bed was firmer than hers, the linen as brilliantly white as his shirts. It amused her, how methodical he was at bedtime. How precisely he folded his clothes, how meticulously he brushed his teeth. In his company, she felt obliged to brush for the recommended two minutes.

'Do you mind if I don't take a lift?' she asked, when they reached the gates. 'I'd like the walk.' He kissed her cheek and told her he'd call later, and she didn't say anything in response to that.

She made her way despondently back to Kate's. When she got there she saw a large blue van parked across the road, outside the home of the man who'd died a few weeks previously. The van's rear doors were open, revealing a jumble of furniture: kitchen chairs, bedside lockers, tables, mattresses, a couch standing on its end.

A skip sat in the driveway. She saw a rolled-up carpet and newspaper bundles, and battered paint tins and saucepans, and ragged strips of paper that must have hung on the walls, and sections of rusted ironwork that might have been a gate once upon a time, or a fence. A life being packed away, all trace of him banished.

Kate and a few of the neighbours had gone to the funeral. I spoke with the son, Kate had reported. He's going to let the house for the time being, while he decides what to do with it. It looked like the work of preparing it for tenants was underway. Alice supposed it was good that it wouldn't be lying idle.

She wondered who Kate would find to rent the apartment. It would have to be a single person: it really wasn't big enough for more than one. Someone gainfully employed, who could afford to pay for where they lived.

She went inside. She sat on the couch and closed her eyes. She took a few of the deep, cleansing breaths the Pilates classes opened with, and tried to gather her racing thoughts. She'd applied yesterday for three jobs she didn't want – but there must be something out there, something besides receptionist, that she *did* want, and that she was qualified to do.

And then, out of nowhere, it came to her – and she couldn't understand why it hadn't occurred to her sooner. There *was* something she wanted, something she'd happily do every day. She picked up her phone.

Val answered on the first ring. 'Alice. Everything alright?'

'Yes, everything's fine. Hope you don't mind me calling you on a Sunday afternoon.'

'Not in the least. How can I help?'

She crossed her fingers. 'Well, there's something I'd like to ask you.'

'Fire away.'

Alice took a breath. 'I need to find a job, Val. I'm guessing Kate's filled you in on all that.'

'She has.'

Yes, she would have. 'I want to get a fulltime writing job. I love writing Happy Talk, and I'm wondering if I could make my living from writing. I want to ask you if I have any hope, with you or with anyone else.'

'Well, you *can* write. I knew you could, before you started – and in the weeks you've been writing Happy Talk, you've improved. I hope you'll be able to keep doing it when you find fulltime work. You'd make a fine journalist with a bit more general experience, but not here. I have no openings, I'm afraid. I said that the night I met you.'

'Yes.' It wasn't unexpected – Val had hardly been going to conjure up a fulltime position for her – but it was disappointing not to hear her offer even a glimmer of hope. 'So I'd have to leave town to find a job with a newspaper.'

'You would. With no journalistic experience apart from Happy Talk, nobody would offer you freelance work, and to be in with any chance of picking up a job you're really talking about Dublin, and one of the national publications – and you'd be starting at the bottom. You'd be on low wages, I mean really low wages, and you'd get the gigs nobody else wanted. Unless you stumbled on the story of the century, it would be a long, hard slog before you were earning anything like decent money, so finding accommodation you could afford would be a huge challenge.'

It didn't sound promising. On the contrary, it sounded completely dispiriting. Alice tried not to let her dejection show in her voice. 'I'll have to set my sights elsewhere so.'

'I think you might. Think about what else you love to do. Find your passion.'

'Right.' But she'd found it, or thought she had. She told Val about the jobs she'd applied for. 'None of them are really what I want.'

'But they'll do short term,' Val replied, 'till you find what you do want. So remind me – you fly to Italy when?'

'Thursday week.'

'And you'll write me up an extra column before you go?'

'Yes, no problem.'

'Good – I'd be shot if we missed a week. You've become a habit with readers. I'm sorry I can't be more helpful, Alice. I'm sorry I can't offer you a job. I'd like to, if that's any consolation.'

It wasn't. If anything, the knowledge that Val would employ her if she could made it harder to accept that writing would not in all likelihood become a career for her. 'Thanks, Val.'

'Find your passion, Alice,' she repeated. 'Let me know when you do. I have every faith in you. In the meantime, I promise to keep an ear to the ground, just in case anything interesting comes along,' and Alice had to be content with that.

Later she stood under the shower before changing for her restaurant shift, wishing for Liz and Emmet's big old cast-iron bath, wishing she could fill it with scented foamy water, and stretch out and unwind.

All going fine, Liz had said in her last email. *Bump coming on nicely. We were asked if we wanted to know the gender, but we both decided we'd prefer a surprise. Won't feel it now till September – and you will have to come up when the new arrival puts in an appearance, whether you like it or not.*

As she was getting dressed, her phone rang.

'Feeling better?' William asked, and she told him she was, and apologised again for her snappishness in the park.

'Barb's dying to see your place,' he said.

'Great.'

Her heart sank at the reminder that Barb and Donal were coming to dinner tomorrow night. She'd been looking forward to it before her conversation with Kate, but in her current humour she didn't feel like meeting anyone. Still, Barb could be depended on to keep the conversation going, and they might help take her mind off things.

And who knew – they might even have a few job ideas for her.

'Alice, can I ask you something?'

'Yes?'

'You're not considering moving to Italy, are you?'

What could she say? 'I'd rather not. I'd rather live here and holiday in Italy – but I have to be realistic and look at all my options. I can't rule it out, William.'

'What about us?'

She didn't have the energy for this conversation. 'Let's not worry about something that probably won't happen, OK? I need to get moving for Borelli's now, so I'll see you tomorrow.'

'Sleep tight,' he said. 'Mind yourself. Try not to worry.'

Try not to worry – was there any more useless piece of

advice? But he meant well, so again she found herself biting off a retort.

Later, much later, after she'd got home from the restaurant and was preparing for bed, Alice's mother rang. Her parents regularly stayed up till the small hours.

'*Mia cara*, it's not too late, is it?'

'No, Mamma, not too late. How are you? How's Papà?'

'We're well, all well. Paolo dropped around this morning. He's excited to be seeing his *mamma* soon.'

'Oh good. Kate will be thrilled too.' She wouldn't mention the ultimatum she'd been issued, and her consequent troubled mind. Time enough to fill them in when they were all together.

'And *cara*, you know we want to see as much of you as possible while you are here, so I've told Aldo not to work you too hard.'

'Don't worry, he's promised to let me off lightly.'

Her mother spoke then of the vineyard – Alice pictured the pendulous clusters of Sangiovese and Bombino Bianco grapes, the two main varietals, ripening slowly under the Italian sun – and the birth of Alice's cousin Carmela's first baby, and plans for the Christmas wedding of another cousin.

'And how is William?' her mother asked.

'Fine. He's fine.'

'You know you would be welcome to bring him. I should have said it sooner.'

The thought of inviting William to join her in Italy hadn't once crossed Alice's mind. Whatever about introducing him to her parents, she wasn't ready to offer him up for all her cousins to speculate about. 'I'm fairly certain he would have said no. The shop hasn't been open long enough for him to take holidays.'

'Next time then.'

'Yes.'

'*Ti voglio bene, carissima.*'

'Me too, Mamma. *Buona notte, a presto.*'

Kate rang while she was making toast the following morning. 'Do you need anything in Galway? I'm off to Evelyn to get my hair cut.'

'Not a thing. Are you cooking tonight, or is Val?'

'I am. I've prepped a fish dish. Want to join us?'

'Thanks, but I'm having William's sister and her husband to dinner.'

'Ah, yes, I'd forgotten. What are you serving?'

'Chicken tagine, your recipe.'

'That'll go down well. Enjoy the evening.'

'Thanks, safe trip.'

She was glad nothing seemed to have changed between them as far as Kate was concerned. She should have known her aunt wouldn't do that. She still wondered how it would be when the two of them were sharing the house. Time would tell – and maybe it wouldn't be for long, if one of the jobs materialised.

She made a few Happy Talk calls and wrote them up, and then went to meet Mike at the house of a woman who'd located her birth mother at the age of fifty-one. In the afternoon she gave the apartment a thorough clean, trying not to count the days she had left in it.

At length she began to prepare dinner, Kate's recipe on the counter beside her. As the spicy citrus tang of the dish wafted about the apartment she lowered the heat and readied the fold-up table she'd borrowed for the second time from Kate, and hurried off to change.

The three arrived together, William having opted to be the designated driver. Barb brought a scented candle – 'Hope you like sandalwood' – and a small box of handmade chocolates. 'Isn't this adorable?' she said, turning to take in the living space. 'So cosy.'

Alice laughed. 'So small, you mean. But I don't have a lot of things, so it suits me fine. You're my first proper dinner guests, apart from my parents.'

'You said your aunt lives next door?'

'Yes.' She spoke of Kate's short-lived marriage to Aldo, and her reason for converting the garage, and Paolo's subsequent decision to move to Italy.

'How sad – for your aunt, I mean. But he comes to visit her, right?'

Alice pulled out a drawer in search of the corkscrew. 'Not often enough, considering he's only three hours away on a plane – but he's due soon. In fact, he'll be staying here while I'm in Italy.'

'Well, that's good.' Barb shook her head. 'You're so lucky, with family living there – if I were you I'd be emigrated like a shot.'

'Hey,' William protested, and his sister laughed and said obviously it wasn't going to happen now, and Alice thought of the hotel job her father had practically promised her when they were here. It wouldn't hurt to check it out during her holiday.

'Did your aunt ever meet anyone else after her marriage broke up?' Barb enquired as they took their seats at the table.

'Not that I'm aware of.'

Alice had wondered about that over the years. Surely a

woman of means, the owner of a thriving restaurant, would have attracted the attention of the available men in town, even if it was only her money they were after. But no man had ever been spoken of, gold-digger or otherwise. Kate had always struck Alice as perfectly happy on her own – but was she?

Over dinner they spoke of the continuing dry spell that had farmers warning of crop failures, and a supermarket in town that had sold a winning Lotto ticket, sparking rumours about the identity of the winner. As they were nearing the end of the meal, Alice told them of the talk with Kate, and of Val's suggestion that she find her passion.

'Your passion,' Barb repeated. 'I wonder … I suppose teaching is mine – and retail's yours, Donal. And William, obviously, is passionate about helping people to see better. But what's yours, Alice? What do you really love to do?'

'I love writing Happy Talk,' Alice replied, 'but Val thinks it's highly unlikely I'd make a living from writing, and she'd know.'

'Well, what are you good at then, besides writing, and being a receptionist? What are your strengths?'

'Sandwiches,' William said immediately. 'Nobody makes a sandwich like you do.'

Alice stared at him. 'You think making sandwiches is my passion?'

'I was joking, sorry. But you *are* good at them. You're inventive. And didn't you say you worked in a sandwich shop once?'

'Well, I did, years ago, for a few weeks.'

'You know, that's not a bad idea,' Barb said slowly. 'If you enjoy making them, I mean. There's no place in town that sells sandwiches, apart from those awful pre-packaged ones in the supermarket.'

What was wrong with them? 'Barb, are you suggesting I open a sandwich shop?' It was laughable.

'No, I wasn't thinking of a shop. That would be too expensive – unless you're secretly loaded.'

'Definitely not, secretly or otherwise.'

'So what about a delivery service?'

'What – a sandwich delivery service?'

'Exactly. I'd love not to have to make my lunch every morning – and I know plenty more on the staff who'd feel the same.'

'They do it in the States,' William put in. 'And in England, I think.'

'I've seen it in films,' Donal agreed. 'They go around to workplaces delivering lunches. Sandwiches and wraps and stuff.'

'They might do it here too,' Barb said. 'In the bigger cities. Did you ever come across it in Dublin, Alice?'

'No, never.'

But she remembered scenes in films too, people dropping into offices with baskets of sandwiches and muffins. And Liz and Emmet had always praised the sandwiches she'd thrown together for a Saturday lunch.

'You'd have no expensive overheads,' Donal said. 'You'd be your own boss.'

'Seriously? You think I could earn enough to live on, just making sandwiches and delivering them?'

'How much you'd earn,' William said, 'would depend on how many you could produce in a morning.'

'And how would I find that out?'

'Time yourself, I suppose. See how many you could put together in ten minutes, and then do your sums. Once you had a rough idea of the number you could produce, multiply it by – what? Four euro each?'

'Five,' Barb said. 'People would expect to pay more for a delivered handmade sandwich.'

Five euro a sandwich. Five euro for something she could make in a couple of minutes, maybe less. This was becoming interesting, even as a hypothetical exercise. 'And how would I find out if there's any demand?'

'That's the easy bit,' Donal replied. 'Make up a leaflet, drop it into the businesses in town, see what response you get. I'd say you'd have a few takers in my workplace.' He was manager of the largest hardware shop in town. Must be twenty working there at least.

Twenty sandwiches. A hundred euro, less the cost of the ingredients.

'Your editor at the paper might help to spread the word,' William said.

'Google it,' Donal said. 'See if you can find anyone else doing it, anywhere in Ireland. If you can, get in touch and pick their brains.'

'Your aunt might be able to advise,' Barb added, 'being in the food business.'

The more they talked about it, the more Alice thought about it, the more intriguing the prospect became. It might not be her passion, but she had no objection to making sandwiches. She enjoyed thinking up new filling combinations, seeing what went together and what didn't. She could work away happily, with the radio on for company – and it would be lovely to be her own boss.

Her only outlay would be the ingredients, wouldn't it, and whatever petrol she used to deliver the finished product? And because all her deliveries would be lunchtime ones, her afternoons would be free for Happy Talk, and whatever else she might choose to do.

It was definitely worth finding out more.

They were all looking at her, all seeming to believe in this crazy new idea. 'I'll investigate it,' she told them. It couldn't hurt.

As soon as they'd left, William promising to return after he'd dropped the others home, she went straight back online, ignoring the waiting dishes, and the table that was strewn with glasses and crumpled napkins. She felt wide awake, fired up with this new idea. Could it possibly work?

She hunted for sandwich delivery businesses operating in the west of Ireland, and within minutes she found the Happy Belly Sandwich Company, based in Galway. She dashed off a quick email, saying she was thinking of setting up a similar operation, and asking if she could get in touch for information – and the following morning, after William had left for work, a response came through as she was tackling the clean-up: *Hi Alice, Short notice but we're free to chat this afternoon if you want to drop by around three – Joe*

He added an Eircode, and his phone number. She fed the code into Google Maps and found that they lived in a little village just outside Galway city, and that the journey would take her roughly forty minutes.

Thanks so much, she replied. *See you then.* She tamped down a flutter of excitement as she sent it off. Take it easy, nothing might come of this. Baby steps, one at a time. She was eager to get Kate's opinion of her new venture, or possible new venture, but she decided to wait until she'd spoken with the Galway people. It would make it more real, make her sound more committed, if she could report on a meeting.

She spent the morning going through the latest crop of Happy Talk emails, trying to decide which ones she wanted to follow up for the two columns she'd promised Val before her trip. It had become the weekly dilemma: she hated having to leave some out. Every one of them deserved column inches, but twelve hundred words could only cover so much.

After a lunch of leftovers she set out. She located her destination without difficulty, a small white van parked outside, emblazoned with the logo she recognised from the website, telling her she was at the right place. She rang the bell and made the acquaintance of Joe and his wife Winnie, who brought her in and sat her down.

And over the following two hours, and very good coffee, they talked her out of the idea.

That wasn't their intention, of course. They walked her through all the steps they'd taken when they'd set up three years previously. They explained that she'd have to register as a business, and gave her details of the food hygiene course she'd need to have under her belt. They told her of the insurance policy that was mandatory, and the regular visits she could expect from the Food Safety Authority inspector.

They advised her on the marketing material she'd have to equip herself with, and showed her their leaflets and business cards, carrier bags and stickers. They told her she'd need a logo and a memorable company name, and they gave her contact details for the graphic designer and printer they'd used.

They also gave her the email address of Joe's niece Laurie, a student computer programmer who they said would provide a basic website for half the price of anyone else, because of course Alice would have to have a website to function properly as a business – oh, and probably an accountant too, to help with her tax returns.

They showed her the checklist they worked from each morning, and brought her into their spotless roomy kitchen with its dedicated fridge for storage of sandwich ingredients. 'Do you have a decent kitchen at your disposal?' Joe asked.

Alice thought of Kate's homely, cluttered kitchen, with an old fridge generally full of restaurant leftovers, and eggs, and a tumble of egg-boxes on the worktops at any given time, and a cooker that was reliable but shabby. 'I'm not sure it would be passed by a health inspector.'

'How about a community hall? Would there be an option to use a kitchen there? It would make life easier if you had access to a place like that, already set up for food production.'

'… Maybe.'

'Six weeks,' they said, as Alice got up to leave. 'It mightn't take that long, but allow six weeks to set everything in motion. Do your homework, equip yourself with what you need, and then just go for it.'

Just go for it, they said, as if it was only a matter of deciding, when the truth was that she couldn't go for it. It simply wasn't going to happen. The cost of setting it up was way beyond the remainder of her savings.

Winnie walked out with her. 'Best of luck, Alice. I hope we haven't overwhelmed you. Give a shout if you have any questions as you go along – and let us know when you're up and running.'

'You've been great, thanks so much.'

She wondered how long it would take them to realise they weren't going to hear from her again. They might search for a new sandwich business in her town, and when they didn't find it, they'd assume she'd given up on the idea. She hoped they wouldn't resent the time they'd given her so willingly.

How could she ever have thought this was a viable proposition? She'd been swayed by the enthusiasm and encouragement of the other three last evening. She'd allowed them to convince her that the idea was worth trying. How clueless she'd been, thinking all she had to do was buy a few loaves of bread and some fillings, and make the sandwiches.

When she got home it was past six, her return journey slower with commuter traffic. She took the paraphernalia Joe and Winnie had given her from her bag and transferred everything to the kitchen bin and closed the lid. That was that. Just as well she'd said nothing to Kate.

She showered and got into pyjamas. She poured the last of the previous night's wine into a glass, and took a salmon cutlet from the fridge for dinner. She hoped William wouldn't ring: she couldn't face his earnest questions tonight. To be on the safe side, she texted, Having an early night, will catch you up tomorrow, and she got a Pleasant dreams xx in return.

In the morning she brought eggs next door, and met Kate coming out with a bag for the bin. 'Come in,' Kate said. 'I have coffee on' – and then, seized with a sudden urge to share the recent events, Alice found herself telling Kate all about them.

'I had this mad idea,' she began. 'Well, the others did, really.' She spoke of the suggestion being tossed around the dinner table, the slow coming together of the plan. She told Kate of her subsequent discovery of Joe and Winnie, and her trip to their house that had opened her eyes. 'It's too expensive,' she ended. 'It might have been fun, I think I would actually have loved it, but it's not feasible.'

'Is it just the expense?' Kate asked.

'Well, pretty much. I mean, there's tons more involved than I thought, but the big stumbling block is lack of money. I could probably handle the process if I could afford everything I needed, like a website, and an accountant, and marketing stuff.'

'So you'd do it if you had the money?'

'I would.' The more she thought about it, the more she wanted to do it. 'But it's not possible, Kate. My savings won't cover half what's needed – and even if they did, I wouldn't want to risk letting them all go. I'd need a cushion, just in case it didn't work out.'

'What about your parents?'

'What about them?'

'Why don't you ask them to finance it? They paid for your sisters to go to university, didn't they?'

'Yes …'

'And you didn't cost them a penny after you left school. I remember your mother telling me that you were pretty much self-sufficient from day one in Dublin.'

'Well, that's true …'

'They won't say no,' Kate said, 'if you ask,' and Alice knew that she was probably right. She'd never really asked them for any financial help – she couldn't see them refusing now.

'I hate the thought of looking for a handout though.'

'Call it a loan then, if it makes you feel better. Do your sums before you travel to Italy. Figure out how much you'll need to start up, then add a bit extra. Make out a business plan, so you can show them you're serious. I can help you with that. We can include a repayment schedule.'

Maybe it was possible. Kate seemed to think it was. Alice was aware of a resurgence of excitement. Maybe she could pull it off – but then she remembered the lack of a suitable kitchen, and mentioned it.

'Borelli's,' Kate said immediately. 'You can use that kitchen.'

Alice stared at her.

'It's free in the mornings, up to half eleven. You wouldn't be putting anyone out.'

'Honestly? You wouldn't mind me using it?'

'Of course I wouldn't mind. We'd have to work out the logistics, and you'd have to be gone by half eleven, and leave it spick and span after you.'

'Of course … Wow.' Kate was talking as if it was going to happen. She had faith in it, even if Alice was far from sure. 'Thank you for the offer, Kate. I seem to spend an awful lot of time thanking you.'

'It's what families are for – and I happen to think this is a very good idea, and you seem to want it. Do you? Do you want it enough to put in the work?'

Alice took a deep breath. 'I really do.'

'So you'll ask your parents?'

'I will – and if they say yes to a loan, I'll give it a go.' She caught her aunt's hand and squeezed it. 'Thanks, Kate – and thank you for the wake-up call. I needed it.'

Kate smiled. 'Happy to help. We all need a little push sometimes.'

The thought of not having to take a job she didn't want purely for the sake of getting a wage made her light-headed with relief. She reminded herself that nothing was certain yet: even if her parents provided funds, who knew what other obstacles might present themselves?

She shrugged away the thought. She wouldn't think like that. She'd assume, from this minute on, that this crazy new scheme would work. Out of nowhere, George Murphy's motto slid into her head: *Your best is always good enough.* Designed to spur his students on to try hard, to give every challenge all they had. She'd use it now to make this idea happen. Her best *would* be good enough. It would.

'There's one more thing,' Kate said. 'Totally unrelated.'

'Yes?'

'Val and I …' She stopped, and seemed to consider, and began again. 'I told you we met in the maternity hospital.'

'Yes, and Val had the baby who died.'

'That's right. We've been friends a long time. I think Leonie's death actually … cemented us, in a funny way. It was such a raw, terrible time for Val.' Pause, rubbing one hand slowly with the other as she looked somewhere beyond Alice. 'I'm not sure when I realised … that she meant more to me than just a friend. She knew right away, she said, but it took me longer.'

She shifted her gaze then to meet Alice's. 'You know what I'm saying.'

'… Yes.'

A memory stirred. Alice asking if Val had met anyone else, and Kate saying yes. *She has someone*, she'd said, and Alice had assumed she'd meant a man, but she hadn't.

'Aldo ...' Kate said, and again drifted away, and came back to him. 'I loved him, Alice, but not in the way a wife should love a husband. We should never have got married. It was my fault, my mistake. I didn't know then that I preferred women. I was slow to catch on to that.' She lifted a shoulder. 'But I don't regret my marriage – how could I regret something that gave me Paolo? I'm sorry for Aldo's sake, of course, that he married a woman who could never be a proper wife. The physical side of our relationship never worked for me, and I assumed it was something that was lacking in me. It never occurred to me that I was just with the wrong person. The wrong gender. It took Val to make me realise.'

It shouldn't have surprised Alice. She'd seen them together, and witnessed their strong friendship; she just hadn't made the next connection. And maybe it had taken Kate for Val to discover where *her* preference lay – or maybe she liked both.

'I'm telling you all this,' Kate continued, 'because on Monday nights Val and I sleep in the same room – and since you'll be staying in this house soon I thought you might appreciate some advance notice.'

'Oh ... sorry, Kate. Now I feel I'm really intruding by moving in here.'

'Not at all.'

'And Val won't mind that you told me?'

'No.'

'But ... why don't you just live together?'

Kate tilted her head. 'We like our own space. It suits us.'

A new thought occurred to Alice. 'Does Aldo know?'

'Not as far as I'm aware. Nothing happened until after he'd left. I told him, truthfully, that I didn't feel the way he did, and that it wasn't anything he'd done. I didn't want to hurt him further by telling him any more.'

'And Paolo?'

She spread her hands. 'I honestly can't say, Alice. We were discreet while he lived here – Val never stayed the night … I don't think he guessed anything. We've never discussed it. I'd have told him if he'd asked, as soon as I felt he was old enough to understand.'

Alice thought back over the years, how she'd drop in casually to Kate's house, with and without her parents, after Aldo had gone back to Italy. Never knowing, never guessing where her aunt's heart lay.

On her return to the apartment she retrieved Joe and Winnie's materials from the kitchen bin and dusted them down. Even though she mightn't get the funding, it wouldn't hurt to do some advance thinking. For starters, she could try to come up with a name. The Happy Belly Sandwich Company was cute, but a bit of a mouthful.

She stopped.

A bit of a mouthful.

She tried to see it on the top of a leaflet, on the side of a van. A Bit of a Mouthful. A familiar expression, meant to indicate something that tripped up the tongue – but taken literally, didn't it also describe a bite from a sandwich?

Make it memorable, Joe had said. They'd remember this, wouldn't they?

She texted Joe. She asked him what he thought, and he was back within minutes. We both love it – quirky **and** memorable. Raging we didn't think of it! Now get cracking on a logo.

And just like that, she had a name. A logo, though.

According to Joe, she needed a graphic designer for this. Unless, he'd said, you know someone arty who'd do it a bit cheaper. Sadly, Winnie and I didn't.

Who did she know who was able to draw? She had a think, a mental riffle through her acquaintances – and eventually, when she'd almost given up, she thought of Deirdre Daly, whose painting of a horse had won a prize.

No. Deirdre was a child. It was one thing being the best at art in sixth class, and quite another coming up with a business logo. She'd probably never even heard the word.

But she didn't need to know the word to recognise logos. They were all around, weren't they? Impossible to avoid them really. Cadbury, Kellogg's, Volkswagen. The McDonald's golden arches, the Nike swoosh. And Deirdre's painting had been really good.

Did her age really matter? Wasn't it worth a try?

Not yet though, not until Alice knew she was going ahead with the enterprise. And then she thought, But why not? Why not ask Deirdre anyway? Why not offer her something, say a hundred euro, to come up with a couple of logo designs? Even if they never saw the light of day, Alice would be helping out. A hundred euro was one Happy Talk column; she could put it to a good cause.

All the same, it was a gamble. She decided to get some advice. She hunted through her emails till she found the address she wanted.

*George, it's Alice from Happy Talk. Quick question: I need a
logo for a little business I'm thinking of starting up, and I was
wondering whether to ask Deirdre Daly to design it. I would, of
course, pay her. What do you think of that idea?*

She sent it off. What else? What other groundwork could she lay
at this stage?

She checked out an online course in food hygiene, and
made contact with Joe's insurance provider and got a quote.
She spoke with a woman at the Companies Registration Office,
and learnt what she needed to do to have A Bit of a Mouthful
officially registered as her brand name. 'I like it,' the woman
said. 'It's a name you'd remember', which Alice took as a very
good omen indeed.

She also made contact with Laurie, Joe's computer-
programming niece. She explained that she wasn't certain yet
whether her idea was going to go ahead. 'If it does, I'll be looking
for a basic website like you did for Joe and Winnie.'

'Sure. Give me a call when you know.'

And with each step, with each new advance, her confidence
increased.

George's response arrived:

*Hi Alice, I think it's a great idea. I have no doubt that Deirdre
would rise to the challenge, once she knew exactly what you were
looking for. When it comes to art, she puts her heart and soul
into it. Very kind of you to think of her, and best of luck with the
new venture – George*

That was all she needed. She rang Deirdre's mother.

'Hello?'

'Mrs Daly, Louise, it's Alice from Happy Talk. I have … a little drawing job, a paying job. Do you think Deirdre might be interested?'

'She would,' Louise said immediately. 'Anything to do with drawing she'd go for. Thank you for thinking of her.'

'Not at all. I'd love her to try it.'

'Hang on, she's here. I'll put her on.'

Pause, muffled talk.

'Hello?' Cautious.

'Deirdre, it's Alice. I'm looking for someone to draw something for me, and I thought you might like to have a go.'

'Draw what?'

'It's a bit hard to explain on the phone. Will you meet me, and I can go through it properly?'

'… OK.'

They arranged to rendezvous at the library the following morning. Alice would bring a sketch pad and some pens, and images of popular logos. She'd tell Deirdre she wanted something fun, something fresh and appealing for a sandwich delivery business. She'd hope for the best.

Later that day, Val rang. 'Kate told me about your new idea.'

'What do you think?'

'I think it sounds great, very enterprising.'

'Glad you approve. I'll need my folks to back me, but I've been making enquiries in various quarters and I'm definitely getting a little excited.'

'That's the spirit. Kate seems to think your parents will be happy to provide the funding.'

'Hope she's right.'

'In the meantime, I have another idea for you, just something to think about. I know you were disappointed when I couldn't offer you a job, or hold out much hope of a career in journalism, but what about writing a picture book for young children?'

'What? A *book*?' She laughed. 'Val, I wouldn't know where to start.' Someone else had suggested that she try writing a book for children lately – who was it?

'Well, you can laugh all you want, but I've looked it up. Picture books generally range from eight to twelve hundred words. You write twelve hundred words every week for me. Every week, Alice. Think about that.'

'But a picture book would be very different, Val. Happy Talk is real, I don't have to come up with ideas, just put a shape on things that have already happened. And I wouldn't have a clue how to write for children.'

Although maybe that wasn't quite true. She recalled the books she'd bought for her little nieces over the years, with their colourful images and funny, happy stories. She'd read them often enough when she was visiting. She might have a clue how to write for children.

And didn't she already have an illustrator – who, she was sure, would be willing to come on board?

'I suppose it's worth considering,' she said slowly. 'I will be busy though, if the sandwich business goes ahead.'

'Of course you will – but can't you give it some thought while you're away, before anything else kicks off? You could come up with a character, and a story idea, and then you could tinker away with it on your computer. Look around you for inspiration. It might have hens in it, or someone who delivers sandwiches.'

Alice smiled. 'It might. I promise to give it serious thought.'

'You do that. I'll expect a progress report when you get back.'

First Kate, now Val, giving her a push. 'I'll keep you posted.'

The following morning she met Deirdre as planned. She explained what she wanted and showed the logos she'd brought along, and the girl nodded, and seemed to understand. 'Something simple and light-hearted,' Alice told her. 'Nothing too serious. Something people will look at, and smile at, and hopefully remember.'

'OK.'

Her eyes widened when Alice took fifty euros from her wallet. 'Half now,' Alice explained, 'the other half when you have it done. I'm going away for a week on Thursday. Is your mum's phone the best way to reach you?'

'Yes.'

'I'll ring when I get home to see how you're getting on. Fair enough?'

'Yeah, thanks.'

Alice left her at a library table with the pad and pens, and wished her well, and that particular ball was rolling – and this time, she was the one doing the pushing.

The day before her departure for Italy she readied the apartment for its next occupant. She changed the sheets and made as much space as she could in the wardrobe and drawers, and emailed Paolo to let him know where to find the key. In his response, he said his father was delighted to be getting rid of him for a week, and looking forward to getting someone who would actually do some work.

That evening she stayed the night at William's. His eyebrows lifted when she admitted that a young inexperienced girl was designing her logo, and he looked a little taken aback too at the company name she'd come up with, because it was probably a bit frivolous for his liking. Being William, he was tactful. 'It's original,' he said, and Alice made do with that. He didn't have to love everything she did.

'I'll miss you,' he told her in the morning, and she promised to miss him too. 'I have a proposition for you,' he said. They were getting dressed, she with one eye on the clock.

'Oh?'

'Why don't you move in here?'

She stared at him. 'What?'

He buttoned his shirt. 'Instead of moving in with your aunt when she lets the apartment, I think you should move in with me. And if you wanted to make it permanent, we could do that too.'

Permanent. He was asking her to live with him, possibly for the rest of her life. 'William —'

'Just think about it,' he said, 'while you're in Italy. How about that? I'll leave you alone, I won't get in touch.'

She stepped into her shoes, grabbed her jacket and bag.

'Alice?'

'Yes,' she said. 'It's – sudden. It's unexpected.' Three months, was it, since they'd started going out?

'Sorry,' he said. 'It's my first time asking anyone. I don't seem to be very good at it.'

He looked so lost, so uncertain. 'It's a kind offer,' she said. 'I'll think about it, I promise.' She gave him a hurried goodbye kiss and left, her head spinning.

Move in. Live together. A lot to think about.

Back at the apartment she scattered food for the hens and flew around collecting eggs. She transferred her toiletries to the case she'd packed the day before, and stowed it in the car boot. She hugged Kate goodbye. 'See you in a week.'

They'd agreed that if she got the go-ahead from her parents, Alice would do one final week at Borelli's on her return from Italy. The ad for letting the apartment would be in tomorrow's paper. Changes were afoot, on all fronts.

'Give Paolo a big hug from his mother. Tell him not to leave it too long.'

'I will.'

If his flight landed on time he should be in town before Kate left for work at four: if not, he'd make his way to Borelli's and surprise her there. Either way, she'd be thrilled. Alice wished she could see her face when he walked in.

On the drive to the airport, Alice turned William's invitation around in her head. Moving in together … was she ready for that? Maybe it would be good for them, give them a chance to see if they would work long term. She wasn't madly in love, she knew that – but didn't love sometimes take time? And wasn't a slow steady burn a safer bet than instant fireworks?

William was a good man. He was clearly hiding nothing, no wife and children tucked away. He was solvent – and he was generous. If it took longer than it should for the sandwich business to take off, she didn't think he'd object to carrying her for a while.

She'd fantasised about living with Chris, in some universe that didn't include a sickly mother. She remembered the dormer house she'd pictured the two of them in, with old wooden floors and lots of light, and a big back garden with an apple tree they could hang a swing from.

That fantasy had never materialised – but William's invitation was very real. It might work.

As she pulled into the airport she put him from her mind and thought again about Val's picture book suggestion. She had three hours in a plane ahead of her: it might be a good chance to jot down a few initial thoughts, but she'd need paper.

After checking in for her flight she went through to the departure area and found a bookshop. Rounding an aisle in search of notebooks, she stumbled over a soft toy on the floor, and would have fallen if someone hadn't grabbed her arm to steady her.

'Gotcha,' he said.

She looked up. He towered above her, a foot taller. His hair needed cutting and combing. 'You OK?' he asked, bending to scoop up the toy and replace it on the shelf from which it must have toppled.

'I'm fine, thanks to you. Good reflexes.'

He wore a grey T-shirt with a little black cartoon kitten peeping from a false breast pocket. She couldn't help smiling. It looked ludicrous on him, and too small for his broad frame.

He caught her looking, and gave a wry grin. 'My daughter thought I'd like it,' he said.

'I'm sure she meant well.'

He laughed. She laughed.

'Safe trip,' she said.

'Thanks, you too.'

Sweet of him to wear it for his daughter's sake. She got the notebook and made her way to the departure lounge – and as she settled into a seat, it came to her.

George. It was George the teacher, wasn't it, who'd asked in one of his emails if she'd thought about writing a children's book? And she'd laughed it off, said she'd leave it to the proper authors, or something like that. But then Val had suggested it too, and now Alice was going to try to be a proper author.

Several hours later, with the germ of an idea captured within the pages of the notebook, she switched on her phone in Bari airport and found a text waiting to be read:

He's here. He tells me it was all your idea. Thank you so much, best gift you could have given me. Have a wonderful week. K xx

George

THEY SHOULDN'T HAVE LEFT IT LIKE THAT. THEY should have made their peace before parting, but they hadn't. He tried to forget it as they flew south over the Atlantic, as Suzi ate overpriced peanuts and played solitaire on her iPad, as Jack read a book three rows back – but their conversation a few days earlier in John's house refused to leave his head.

She's playing you for a fool, George. She did it before and she's doing it again.

What do you mean? Of course she's not.

You're at her beck and call is what I mean.

That's not fair. I'm just helping her out.

Helping her out? George, the woman has only to crook her finger and you go running.

Mam, you're being ridiculous. I've gone to see a few properties with her —

Isn't she able to do that on her own? She's a grown woman.

Of course she is, but what's wrong with getting a second opinion? She wants to make sure she picks the right place – and

Suzi will be living there too, so I have a vested interest in making sure it's suitable.

And you said she's been to dinner at your house.

What's wrong with that? Suzi likes it when she comes. And it's only happened twice since they moved out of Rob's – you make it sound like she's there every night.

George, how can you not see what's happening here? How can you be so blind? She's worming her way back, now that I'm out of the way.

What? What are you talking about?

Well, I presume she knows that you own the house now. I'm guessing you told her.

… I might have mentioned it, I don't remember.

Or she might have asked you.

She didn't ask me – she's not like that. I wish you wouldn't be so judgemental about her. She's the mother of your granddaughter.

You don't need to remind me of that, thank you. I'm just saying it would suit her fine to move in with you, and have no rent to pay.

For God's sake – she has no intention of moving in with me. In case you haven't noticed, we're not together any more.

She's working on you, George. It's as plain as day. She's pulling you back in. Mark my words, she has no intention of renting a place. And another thing: how do you know she was the one who ended that engagement? You only have her word for it.

And on it had gone, she coming up with more ludicrous scenarios, George protesting, while Suzi played in the garden with the little Jack Russell pup that John's daughter Sally had left in their care before she went on holidays.

Be careful, George, his mother had said on parting. That's all I'm saying. Listen to what I'm telling you – and he'd been too annoyed to do more than nod a response, and their hug had been perfunctory, and all the way home he'd prickled with irritation.

Her resentment of Claire was clouding her judgement. That much was crystal clear. She'd always read an agenda into everything Claire did, from the minute she'd heard that Suzi was on the way – but her assertion now that his ex was trying to inveigle her way back into a relationship with him just to save on rent was hurtful. She made it sound as if Claire couldn't possibly want him for any other reason.

Naturally there was still feeling between them. They had a child in common: for as long as that was true, their lives were going to be entwined. They'd loved one another once upon a time, and he was still very fond of her. He enjoyed being in her company, and he thought she felt the same – and yes, he'd resented other men in her life. He couldn't deny it.

But would he risk letting himself fall for her a second time, and possibly having his heart broken again? If she did indicate that she was willing to give it another go, would he agree?

Maybe. He couldn't rule it out. And maybe after all it wouldn't be such a risk, now that they were older, and supposedly wiser. Maybe they'd work, second time round.

His mother would be dead against it – but he couldn't let that stop him. Much as he loved her, and much as he generally valued her opinion, he couldn't allow her to dictate whom he could and couldn't love. She'd just have to accept it, if it happened.

Imagine if she knew that Claire was staying in his house while they were in Tenerife.

It was purely practical. They'd needed someone to feed Oscar, and Claire had offered. I can call by morning and evening, she'd said – but rather than drag her twice a day from the far side of town, George had suggested she move in for the week.

His suggestion, not hers. Whatever his mother might think, Claire, he was certain, didn't have her sights set on his family home. She was far more interested in the house that had belonged to Oscar's late owner.

His son's been in touch, Jack had told George a few nights ago. He found my number in his father's address book. He's letting the house, and he's asking if I can recommend anyone – since he lives abroad, he wants to be sure he gets reliable tenants. I mentioned Claire to him, and he's happy to let her have a look at it. He says he's willing to offer low rent in return for peace of mind. Will you say it to her?

It sounded promising. A bungalow in a settled area, newly painted and furnished. Absolutely I want to view it, Claire had said, so the son had already mailed a key to George's house, and on its arrival she was going to check out the place.

'George, your seatbelt. We're landing.'

He clicked his belt closed as they descended. He looked past Suzi and saw the scorched sharp-peaked volcanic landscape of Tenerife, patched with unexpected green and set against the turquoise blue of the ocean that lapped onto beaches whose sands went from yellow to black.

He regarded the back of his daughter's head as she looked out too. He saw the familiar slender slope of her neck, the tendrils that crept from the short fat plait Jack had constructed, the single freckle that sat on the curve where neck met right shoulder, the straw hat with its green band that rested on her lap, her hands curled around it, nails painted blue the previous evening by Jack.

The plane bounced as it descended. His heart gave an answering bounce, his hands clenching the arm rests, but Suzi didn't react. Twelve years old and fearless: he prayed secondary school would do nothing to change that, would instead enable her to blossom and thrive, and grow into the marvellous woman he knew she was capable of becoming.

Of course he was biased – but he was also right. She *was* marvellous. He would never understand what he'd done to deserve her.

The hot air was a shock as he stepped from the plane. He'd forgotten that intensity of heat, the instant feeling that he was wearing too many clothes after the coolness of the air-conditioned cabin. They crossed the concourse with the other passengers, pulling their small cases behind them. Hand luggage only, Jack had recommended, and George was glad of it as they walked past the crowds in the baggage reclaim area and out to the arrivals hall. Within thirty minutes they were on the road, Jack behind the wheel of their rented yellow Fiesta.

'Journey's about an hour,' he told them. 'Coast pretty much all the way' – and George, who'd surrendered the front seat to Suzi, was content to sit back and take in his new surroundings.

To his left was a rutted brown landscape that looked like a charred version of the Burren, and mountains that rose up behind, and sporadic stunted trees, and occasional petrol stations.

On his right side, visible almost all the time, was the Atlantic, shimmering in the sunshine and topped with a blue and white sky. On the horizon he could see the rise of a distant landmass: he consulted his phone and discovered it to be Gran Canaria.

Eventually, Jack announced their approach to the village where they were to stay. 'We'll have to park away from the house,' he said. 'You'll see why.'

He dropped the car into a small parking area that already held several other haphazardly positioned vehicles, most of them considerably older and dustier than the Fiesta. After the air-conditioned car, the heat hit them again when they got out. They crossed the packed-earth surface, their cases bumping along behind them, and ascended a short flight of wide steps. This led onto a paved pedestrianised street lined with various businesses. 'The main thoroughfare,' Jack said. 'This is as busy as it gets.'

It wasn't busy. There was hardly anyone around. They walked past a small supermarket with tatty yellowed advertising posters in its windows, all in Spanish, and a stand outside for newspapers with no English publications that George could see. Beyond that was a hairdresser and a tobacconist, an off-licence and a greengrocer with fruit on display outside. 'The mangoes,' Jack remarked. 'Amazing.'

George lifted an arm to wipe sweat from his forehead. The too-small T-shirt stuck damply to him: he longed for a cold shower and looser clothing. They passed a restaurant, small and unassuming, and closed. 'Siesta,' Jack said. 'Some close, some don't. Best seafood in town right there.'

Halfway along the street he directed them left onto a smaller one, also pedestrianised, that climbed fairly steeply upwards in a curve, a low step breaking the ascent every few yards. The houses, tall and narrow and white, were tightly packed together. Containers of vivid flowers were suspended from balconies. Above each unpainted wooden front door a short ledge projected, capped with red tiles.

Jack halted at a house a third of the way up, identical to its neighbours. 'Here,' he said, the key already in his hand. George and Suzi waited for him to open up, but he simply stood there while the seconds ticked by.

Finally, he turned. 'Tell you what,' he said, in a voice that was too bright. 'Why don't you two leave your cases here and get some lunch in Antonio's?' He indicated a premises directly across the street that appeared to be an eatery so tiny it hadn't even registered with George. Food images were tacked to its single ground-floor window; its door stood open. 'Antonio's' was chalked on a blackboard above the door. 'The sardines are good,' Jack said. 'I'll follow you in a bit.'

'Sure,' George replied. 'Take your time.' The shower and clothes change could wait.

'But why—' Suzi began, and George threw her a look that silenced her. They abandoned their cases and crossed the little street. Inside the café they were greeted by a smiling waitress, who led them straight through the little room to a shady patio at the rear.

'*Dos*?' she enquired, holding up two fingers, and George showed her three, and she beckoned them to a table set for four. From there they could look down on the red roofs of lower houses, and the straggle of businesses they'd just passed on the main street, and beyond that, a sea of dazzling blueness that spread as far as the horizon.

George counted six tables in total, three of which were occupied. A few heads turned at their entrance, but nobody paid them much attention. Over plates of very good sardines, which were accompanied by little potatoes with wrinkled and deliciously salted skins – 'Papas arrugadas,' the waitress told them, 'special for Canaries' – George told Suzi about Patrick.

'This is Jack's first time to come back here without him,' he said, 'so he's going to feel sad sometimes. We need to be really kind to him.'

'OK.'

Had this been a mistake? Maybe Jack was wondering the same thing. Would they have to cut the trip short, or find another place to stay? George guessed that neither option – getting last-minute return flights, or alternative accommodation in the middle of the high season – would be easy.

Jack hadn't reappeared by the time they'd finished. George's uneasiness grew. Should they go back and see how the land lay, or stay out of his way for longer? The waitress returned and told them in her broken English about desserts.

'Can I get ice-cream?' Suzi asked him.

'Sure.' He ordered coffee for himself, glad of a reason to linger. He looked out at the sea, wondering what the next few hours would bring.

'Here he comes,' Suzi murmured, and George turned to see Jack in conversation with the waitress at the entrance to the patio. He'd changed into fresh shorts and T-shirt, and his hair was damp. George saw the waitress put a hand on his arm and say something, and Jack nodding a response. Yes, she would know him, and the history.

He spotted them and came over. 'Hey,' he said, pulling out a chair, 'Gloria tells me you were dancing on the table just now, Suzi. She said to tell you it's really not allowed.'

'She did *not* say that!'

'Well, maybe I got it wrong – my Spanish isn't that good. But she definitely said somebody was dancing. Was it you, George?'

He was trying. He'd cleared the first hurdle; he'd entered the house without Patrick, gone upstairs, opened doors. Set his case, presumably, in the room that had been theirs. Acclimatising. Walking his heart through the new arrangement.

Gloria reappeared with a plate of sardines for Jack, and George's coffee and Suzi's ice-cream, and a dish of little pastries that nobody had ordered, and the news that lunch was on the house. 'Antonio say,' she declared. 'He is happy you are here, Jack, with your friends' – and as she spoke, a bearded, full-bellied man in a white apron materialised from inside the building.

'Jack,' he said, tipping his head to one side and spreading his arms. Jack rose and walked into a long and wordless hug, and when it ended, Antonio shook George and Suzi warmly by the hand, and told them he was happy to meet them. 'When you are friends for Jack,' he pronounced, 'you are friends for me and Gloria.'

And that set the tone for the week.

The house was wonderful. Old and faithful to its origins, tiled underfoot and whitewashed of wall, its rooms were small and simply furnished. The kitchen cabinets were of dark wood, and full of china and glassware. The sink was deep, with old brass taps. The worktop was marble, chipped in places. Despite the outside heat, the house's thick walls kept the interior beautifully cool.

The two bathrooms had more brass, and temperamental showers, and impressively vocal plumbing, and the larger of the two held an enormous bath that would easily have accommodated the three of them.

The beds, soft and comfortable, were draped in white lace coverlets. The windows were shuttered from within. The walls were decorated with gilt-framed oil paintings of pious-looking characters.

A spiral staircase wound upwards, all the way to the promised rooftop terrace from where they looked down at the sun rising above the Atlantic each morning as they breakfasted, and up at the stars each night before bed.

Antonio's became the lunch venue on the days they stayed in the village, and in the evenings they barbecued on the terrace or strolled to one of the local eating spots. Every other day they took a trip in the Fiesta, with Jack as their guide.

They drove around Teide National Park with its ribbons of petrified lava and volcanic deposits, and took a cable car that brought them close to the summit of Mount Teide, Spain's highest peak. They visited the characterful city of La Laguna, once the island's capital, its old town now a World Heritage site. They checked out a giant animal and marine adventure park. They swam and snorkelled, and took a trip in the promised glass-bottomed boat.

Under the Spanish sun Suzi's freckles multiplied. Despite the layer of sunblock her father insisted on each morning and afternoon, her skin reddened and then darkened slightly. She took great satisfaction in bidding *Hola* to each passing local, until Gloria taught her *Buenos días*. She would sometimes loop an arm casually through Jack's as they walked, and George knew she was looking after him, her twelve-year-old heart brimming with kindness, and he loved her for it.

And Jack did well, most of the time. They learnt to let him off when he needed to be on his own, and wait for him to return when he was ready, and that seemed to work.

Each day, photos of Oscar landed in Suzi's phone as instructed – and on the third day, he wasn't alone in the snaps. 'He's made a friend,' Claire reported, although Oscar's stare at next door's tom, who was looking down at him from the dividing wall, seemed to hold more wariness than friendliness.

In the week before they'd left for Tenerife, Suzi and Jack had finally succeeded in coaxing the cat out to the garden, where he would sit hunched as before, regarding the outside world with the same suspicion he'd displayed in the house. Now, it seemed, he'd found a new object of distrust. George could only hope that the tom, which seemed slightly more civil, would teach Oscar a few manners.

On their fifth day, Claire rang George. 'The key came this morning,' she said. 'I've been to see the house.'

'And?'

'George, it's perfect. I'm going to take it. The rent is only thirty euro a month more than that horrible basement flat, and the lease is for a year, so we'd have that security. And the neighbourhood's lovely. I emailed the owner telling him we'd really like to rent it, and he says we can move in right away.'

'That's great.'

'Isn't it? I'm so happy. Will you tell Suzi?'

'She's right here: you can tell her yourself.' He passed the phone to his daughter, and she received the news with what sounded to him like muted delight.

'Aren't you happy?' he asked, after she'd hung up.

'Yeah,' she said, dragging out the word. 'It's good that we got a place, and it's cool that it's Oscar's old house ... but I really like living with you and Jack.'

His heart swelled. Did children have any idea of the impact their words could have on parents? He slid an arm around her shoulders. 'And you know we love having you too – but so does Mum. We all want you.' They were outside the supermarket, waiting for Jack who was inside buying macadamia nuts and water for their trek.

She scratched at a mosquito bite on her knee. 'What if,' she said, 'you asked Mum if I could swap houses every week?' Shooting a glance at him. 'That would be fair, wouldn't it?'

'Every week? You mean you'd like every weekend with me and Jack instead of every second one?'

'No, I mean a full week with you and Jack, and a full week with Mum.'

Half and half. What he'd wished for since he and Claire had split up. 'Just for the rest of the holidays?'

'No, all the time.'

Why had he agreed, all those years ago, to having Suzi only every second weekend? It was paltry, it was too little – his mother had frequently pointed out how pitiable it was – but of course he knew why he'd agreed to it. He'd still been hoping for Claire to come back to him, and unwilling to go against her in any way, in case it jeopardised his chances of a reunion. By the time he'd given up hope the arrangement was set, and it was easier to let it be.

But now Suzi was the one looking for a change.

'Will you ask her, George?'

'I will,' he promised, 'as soon as we get home.'

He'd ask. He had nothing to lose. When Jack emerged from the supermarket the news was passed on, and he declared himself delighted. 'It's a good house,' he told Suzi. 'All it needed was a bit of cleaning up. You'll love it – and Oscar will love being back home again.'

That evening, as Suzi was showering before bedtime, George sent his mother a text.

Just letting you know that Claire has found a house to rent. She and Suzi will be moving in soon. Everyone's relieved. Hope all is well.

Telling her, without saying it, that she'd been wrong about Claire – but her response, ten minutes later, made no mention of that:

Good to know, thank you for telling me.

As short and polite as the rest of her texts since their row. He'd pay her a visit, the day after they got home. He'd clear the air between them, put this small disagreement into the past. Surely she'd let it go, now that Claire and Suzi were sorted with new accommodation.

All too soon it was the afternoon of their last full day, and George had come to their favourite beach ahead of the other two, who were finishing their packing. It was the last of the string of coves that lay a short distance from the village, the sea a little rougher than at the larger town beach but an altogether more scenic place, with its curved strip of dark sand, and low cliffs off to one side, and its fringe of dunes behind, through which a weather-beaten boardwalk meandered.

The usual small crowd was assembled when he arrived. Sunbathers stretched on towels, beach umbrellas studded here and there. A couple of heads bobbed in the water. Children poked at the sand with sticks and plastic spades. Above the rush of the sea conversations rose and fell, sporadic laughter erupted. Gulls wheeled and swooped overhead, sounding exactly like Irish ones.

George selected a spot and set out his towel and book. No sunbeds here, no beach bar, no showers, no hawkers – apart from the settled weather, he might be on a strand in the wilds of west Cork. He could see why Patrick's family had chosen this location for their holiday base.

A sudden new sound, a hissed word, made him turn. A couple to his left, several feet away, appeared to be arguing. The man gestured angrily as he spoke, stabbing the air with his words; the woman shook her head and threw a sharp remark back at him. The language was unfamiliar, Eastern European maybe. The man suddenly turned and caught George's eye, and fixed him with a glare. George immediately dropped his gaze. As long as no blows were being dealt, he felt justified in ignoring it.

Within minutes he felt his skin becoming uncomfortably warm. He needed to cool down. He pulled off his T-shirt and shorts and strode in his togs to the water's edge. He wasn't a good swimmer, far from it – his self-taught approximation of a breaststroke left much room for improvement, but the pleasure of getting into the water, feeling the soothing lap of it on hot skin, was immense.

A naked little boy who looked about three or four hunkered by the edge of the sea, poking a finger into the wet sand, watching the small hole he'd made fill up as the foamy water rushed in.

'Having fun?' George asked, but the boy didn't react. Black hair, skin darker than George's. Not a freckle in sight. Definitely not Irish.

George waded in as far as his chest, the sand smooth underfoot, the movement of the sea pushing and pulling against him. He ducked under, enjoying the relief of water on his head.

A sudden incoming wave knocked him off his feet as he surfaced. He tumbled under again, feeling the drag of the water before he was able to twist himself back to vertical and find air. Another wave crashed in, and another. Each time he floundered momentarily, feeling the wave pull him along with it until he was able to find his footing. When the series of waves abated, he looked out to sea and found the ferry that had caused the backwash.

He'd been swept closer to the shore: he waded back in and swam for a bit, letting the gentler waves lift and drop him. When he began to tire he trod water, searching the beach for the other two.

Something bumped suddenly against his thigh, making his heart jump. He jerked away from it – jellyfish? crab? worse? – then ducked his head under, needing to identify it. In the moving water he made out a small dark mass just below the surface, a couple of feet to his left. What the hell was it?

And then it turned, the sea turned it, and it became a child, limbs waving limply.

A child: Jesus Christ. He reached down and grabbed it, grabbed an arm, and yanked it upwards out of the water. Dark hair, tanned skin, eyes closed. It was the little boy he'd seen by the water's edge, not five minutes ago.

Another wave caught them up just then and swept George off his feet once more. He hung on tightly to the child as they were pulled along, blinded and spluttering, and trying desperately to reclaim his footing.

After a lifetime, after an eternity, he stumbled to his feet, still clutching the little boy – and only then, as he waded on trembling legs towards the shore, did he see people splashing towards him, a wailing woman, a few others, a man who whisked the child from his arms and turned quickly towards the shore with it. Immediately, George slumped to his knees in the water, overcome by what had just occurred.

A man put a hand on his shoulder, another took his elbow and guided him upwards. They both held on as George walked unsteadily from the sea, fighting a sudden stupid urge to cry. Someone handed him a towel that wasn't his; he scrubbed at his hair and face, trying to compose himself. 'Take the breaths,' a man ordered, and George obediently drew in shuddering breaths as he saw, hurrying across the sand to him, Suzi and Jack, their faces full of fear.

'What's going on?' Suzi asked – but George had turned to find the child, to see what was happening. A small crowd had gathered nearby, a metre up from the water's edge. He hurried towards it, glad of his height, able to see above heads. He watched a man pushing at the small chest, bending to put his mouth to the child's. A woman kneeling in the sand continued to wail – and George abruptly recognised her as half of the arguing couple. Was the man now attempting to revive the child the other half?

George felt a hand slip into his. 'Are you OK, George?'

Suzi. He nodded, unable to speak, still watching the drama unfold on the sand, still fighting the ridiculous urge to cry – and then, a little splutter, a little gush, a loud babyish wail – and an answering shout of relief from the woman, who gathered up the boy and cradled him and rocked him and babbled words that meant nothing to George, as the man sat back on his heels and dropped his head, and the crowd sent up a spontaneous roar of happiness, and someone clapped George on the back, and he felt then the rush of tears that refused to be stemmed, and Jack handed him a towel, his own this time, and he buried his face in it, half laughing, half crying as Suzi hugged him.

Afterwards, after George had accepted the broken-English thanks and the handshake of the man who had looked so aggressively at him before, as the three of them were setting towels on a new patch of sand, a little removed from the rest of the beachgoers, another man approached.

'Hello,' he said to George. 'Sorry to disturb' – Irish, nose peeling, phone in his hand – 'but I saw what happened just now. Well done.'

'Thanks.'

'He was one lucky boy. Can I ask, what exactly went on in the sea?'

'He bumped into me,' George said. 'He was under the water. I thought it was a crab or something.' He told the man about seeing the child earlier at the water's edge. 'He was on his own, just playing in the sand.' He wouldn't mention the arguing parents. 'I pulled him up and brought him out, that's it.'

'Amazing. I actually work for the *Indo* – Cathal Roche is my name. I'd love to write it up, if that's OK.'

A journalist. What were the odds that an Irish journalist would be on this small beach, among this small crowd, at just this time? George shook his head. 'Ah no, honestly, it's not worth writing about – it was over so quickly.'

'But you saved his life,' Suzi put in. 'You're a hero, George.'

The man smiled at her. 'Hero is right. Is he your dad?'

'Yes, and his name is George Murphy.'

'Suzi,' George began, but they both ignored him.

'Did you see what happened, Suzi?'

'No, I got here just after, with Jack.' She gestured in his direction, and Jack gave the man the thumbs-up.

George felt it had gone on long enough. 'Look, I'd honestly prefer not to make a thing of this.'

The journalist turned back to him. 'Just a few sentences, George, that's all. A happy story to cheer everyone up at home. There isn't half enough good news to write about' – and George thought of Happy Talk, devoted to good news stories.

His mother got the *Independent*. She'd love to read about him in the paper – he could just hear her bragging to everyone. 'No photo,' he said, and the man agreed, and took a few more details before thanking them and leaving.

That evening they had dinner in Antonio's, sharing plates of grilled cheese dipped into the spicy *mojo* sauce that featured on every menu they'd encountered, and fried salty *pimientos de padrón* and *churros de pescado* that reminded George of the battered cod he and Suzi would sometimes pick up on Friday nights – and without being asked, Gloria also brought a bowl of the *papas arrugadas* they'd eaten on their first visit there. 'You like,' she said, and they all agreed that they liked, and dipped the little potatoes into more *mojo* sauce.

'Our last night,' they told her, and she presented Suzi, on their departure, with a little wrapped package. 'Is aloe soap, made here in Tenerife,' she said, 'so you can remember your holiday' – and hugs were exchanged, along with promises to return.

They rose early and stripped their beds before breakfasting on the terrace, watching for the final time as the sun appeared above the horizon and began its slow ascent into the sky. Afterwards they packed up the car and locked the house and drove away, and as they passed the path that led down to the coves, George thought of the little dark-haired boy whose life had so nearly ended the day before.

He took out his phone and checked for messages, and found none. He opened a text box.

Hi Mam, en route to the airport after a great holiday. I'll give you a call when we land.

He sent it off and kept his phone out, waiting for some response, but by the time they reached the car hire drop-off point, none had come.

The airport was filled with the usual bustle, the newly arrived conspicuous by their expectant expressions and paler skin shades, the travellers queuing for the Dublin flight check-in looking sunburnt and rumpled and resigned.

Suzi sighed happily as she flopped into a chair at the departure gate between George and Jack. 'That was the best holiday *ever*. I loved everything – especially you saving that little boy's life. I can't wait to tell Mum.'

'We need to pick up a paper on the plane,' Jack said. 'It

might be in' – and there it was, right on the front page, much to George's dismay. Or maybe half dismay, and half quiet satisfaction. Just a few column inches, below and to the left of the main article, under a heading that read 'Irish Holidaymaker in Dramatic Beach Rescue'.

'Read it to me,' Suzi commanded, so George obliged, as quietly as he could.

Irish teacher George Murphy (34), on holidays this week in Tenerife with daughter Suzi and companion Jack Garrihy, yesterday came to the rescue of little Fyodor Petrov (3) from Slovakia, who had wandered away from his parents on a small local beach in the northern part of the island, and was washed into the sea by a freak wave. 'I felt something bump against my leg while I was swimming,' Murphy said. He pulled the child from beneath the water and managed to get him ashore, where he was resuscitated. Thanks to Murphy's quick action, what might have been another holiday drowning was averted.

Again he thought of his mother, and knew that this would go some way towards mending what had gone awry between them.

They landed ten minutes early. In the arrivals hall, waiting outside the toilets for Jack and Suzi, George pulled out his phone and switched it from aeroplane mode, and saw a missed call.

His mother? No: the number was unfamiliar. *You have a new voicemail*, his screen told him.

It was from John. *Please ring as soon as you get this, George.*

John, asking him to ring. John, who'd never rung him before. He felt a creeping sense of dread as he selected *Call back*.

John picked up immediately. 'George?'

'Yes. What's wrong?'

And then, as Suzi emerged from the Ladies, as people hurried past with bags and buggies and foreign tongues, as someone made an announcement about not leaving luggage unattended, as a baby began to cry somewhere to his left, all that, all the noise of the airport, all the sounds and the motion and the colours that surrounded him seemed to dim and still as he listened to John telling him what was wrong.

Alice

THE MINUTE SHE STEPPED INTO THE KITCHEN, ALICE knew something was up.

'You're home,' Kate said, her tone empty, her face drained of colour and happiness. 'That's good.' She was leaning against the sink, holding the old coffee-maker that had travelled from Italy with Aldo and his family over forty years earlier.

Alice set her gifts – olive oil, truffle oil, wine – on the worktop. 'Kate – what happened? What's wrong?'

'I got some sad news, just a few minutes ago.' Blinking rapidly, looking on the verge of tears.

'What is it?'

'Evelyn. My hairdresser. She died, Alice. Evelyn died. She collapsed early this morning, and by the time the ambulance arrived she was gone.'

'Oh Kate, I'm so sorry. You knew her a long time.'

'I did, years.' She sat, head in hands, while Alice went about making coffee. Her voice was low and muffled: Alice could barely make out the words. 'She was only sixty-six, just five years older than me. I can't get my head around the fact that she's gone. She cut my hair just a fortnight ago.'

'I remember.' Alice took mugs from the draining board, cream from the fridge. A bowl of brown sugar lumps sat in the centre of the table. For Paolo, she thought. Such a sweet tooth he had.

'She was telling me about a cruise John had booked for her birthday in October. She was so excited about it.' Kate took a shuddering breath, let it out in a whoosh. 'I can't believe it.'

'How did you hear?'

'I rang her. There was a bit about George in the paper. He saved a child from drowning in Tenerife, and I wanted to tell her I'd seen it. I knew she'd be thrilled – but her husband answered her phone. Poor man was devastated, could hardly speak.'

Alice's mind had snagged on the mention of George. She'd forgotten he was the hairdresser's son. And now his mother was dead, suddenly dead, and he was in Tenerife.

Kate shook her head slowly. 'Poor George. Evelyn worshipped the ground he walked on. He was all she had after her husband died – well, him and his daughter.'

'Suzi. I met her at the house.' Alice remembered thinking him a Mummy's boy when she heard that his mother had organised a regular delivery of eggs for him. So quick she'd been to judge, without knowing either of them. So quick to put an uncharitable spin on a simple act of kindness from mother to son. And now she was gone from him, and Suzi, that lovely friendly girl, had lost her grandmother without warning.

Water bubbled. The smell of coffee drifted about the room. Alice spotted the newspaper, tossed onto the worktop. She picked it up – and there it was, right on the front page: 'Irish Holidaymaker in Dramatic Beach Rescue'.

She began to read. She stopped, and looked at Kate. 'His name is George Murphy.'

'You knew that.'

'No, I just knew him as George. And he's a teacher.'

'Yes. He teaches in St Kevin's.'

Mr Murphy the teacher. 'He sent an email to the Happy Talk address a few weeks ago,' she told Kate. 'I didn't know it was the same George.'

'That's right, the girl with the painting. I remember that. I meant to say it to you, and forgot.'

Alice began joining pieces together. He was Mr Murphy. Barb had said that Helena's teacher had a daughter Helena's age. Suzi's father, the George whose house she called to every Saturday morning, was also the teacher who'd taken time to email Alice on behalf of his talented student. He was George Murphy, who had a kindness tree in his classroom, who drilled into his students that their best was always good enough. He was the teacher who fixed raffles so that everyone in his class won a prize. That George, and George of the eggs, were the same person.

She skimmed the brief account of the rescue. Yes, daughter Suzi, companion Jack. She imagined George's mother delighting in the fact that her son had saved a little child's life, but it sounded like she'd died without knowing.

She set aside the paper and brought the coffee pot to the table. 'Are you working today?'

Kate nodded. 'On duty at four.'

'Can you get someone to cover for you?'

'I could, but I'll be better off keeping busy.'

'I'll come in with you.'

Kate shook her head wearily. 'Alice, you don't have to do that. You're not scheduled till tomorrow.'

'I'd like to.' She was tired after a dawn start, but she'd survive. She added cream and a sugar lump to Kate's coffee before taking a seat and stirring cream into her own mug. 'Kate,' she said, 'just to let you know, my parents are giving me the money. They've sold half the vineyard, the work was getting too much for them, and they got a good price for it. They were planning to divide it between my sisters and me. It's a lot more than I was going to ask them for, far more than I need to start the business.'

'Well, that's wonderful,' Kate said. 'I'm happy for you, Alice.'

'It means you're off the hook with me. You don't have to support me any more. I'll come to Borelli's this evening, but I won't take payment for it, and we'll make it my last night. Call it a parting gift.'

Kate managed a wan smile. 'If that's the way you want to do it.'

'I do. Did you get someone for the apartment?'

'I did, a nice young man from Donegal. His work is transferring him here for a year. He'll be moving in a week from now.'

'There's something else,' Alice said, and she told Kate about William's invitation, and what she'd decided to do about it.

Back in the apartment, she opened her laptop and began a new email.

Dear George,
My aunt Kate has just told me your sad news.

She stopped. She deleted it. The typewritten words looked too impersonal – and maybe it was too soon. He'd still be in shock, and up to his eyes trying to change flights to get home. She'd get a Mass card tomorrow instead and drop it through his letterbox when she delivered the eggs on Saturday. She'd write a short note to accompany it – no, she'd write two notes, one for Suzi.

She opened her suitcase and began transferring clothes into the washing machine, her thoughts drifting back over the week she'd left behind. She'd had just three shifts at the *trattoria*, Aldo letting her off lightly, like he'd promised. The place had been busy but the rest of the staff had lightened her load when they could, and Aldo had poked his head out from the kitchen every so often to check on her too.

On Sunday she'd taken off her apron to join her relatives at the big table for lunch, and to make the acquaintance of the newest family member, plump little Federico, just three weeks old. The child's grandmother, Alice's aunt Aurelia, had nudged Alice. Your *mamma* told me there is a new man in your life. You will be the next *mamma*. Alice had imagined them all wondering what was taking her so long to settle down and become a wife and a mother.

And one evening towards the end of her week, as they sat after dinner with little glasses of amaretto, she'd told her parents about her new idea.

She'd shown them the business plan Kate had helped her to draft, and outlined the steps she'd already taken. I know it's a risk, she'd told them. I know the safer option would be to get a regular job – but I really want to give this a try. If it doesn't work out I'll find something else, and if you agree to loan me the capital I *will* pay you back, whether I make a success of it or not. It might take a while, but you'll be repaid in full.

Her father had tipped ash from his cigar into a saucer. Something had rustled in the garden beyond the open patio doors, and was gone.

You don't have to say yes or no right now. Will you think about it?

A look had passed between them – and then they'd told her about selling half the vineyard, and how they'd planned to let her and her sisters know once the funds had cleared. They'd explained what it would mean for her, and they'd applauded her enterprising spirit, and she'd gone to bed that night full of elation.

She finished unpacking and switched on the washing machine. As she was stowing her suitcase under the bed her phone rang.

'Hey, stranger,' William said. 'Welcome home. It's been a long week without you.'

'Hi William. I was going to call you earlier, but I was with Kate.' She told him of the hairdresser's death. 'I'm going to Borelli's with her this evening – she could do with having me around, she's very upset, so I won't see you as planned.'

'Sorry to hear it. So tomorrow then?'

'Yes.' She took a deep breath. He wasn't asking. He wasn't pressing her, but he must want to know. 'I'll come for dinner,' she said, 'with my luggage.'

She had decided, somewhere during the week, to take a chance on him. She had decided he was a chance worth taking.

'Does that mean what I think it means?'

'It does. I'm moving in – unless you've changed your mind.'

'Not a chance. Are you really sure it's what you want?'

'I am.'

'You've made me very happy, Alice,' he said.

'I'm glad. See you around seven.'

'Perfect.'

She ran the hoover about the place and put fresh sheets on the unmade bed, wishing she could climb into it and sleep. As she prepared for her final restaurant shift, the washing machine beeped. She hung out the clothes and returned inside to hear her phone ping with the arrival of an email. It was from her father: *Alice, funds from the sale are in, so I've lodged to your account; keep an eye out for it. We both want to wish you the very best with your business idea. Do keep us posted on developments – Dad and Mamma xx*

She checked her bank account and saw the lodgement. Not cleared for three to five business days, but landed there. Hers to spend as she wished. Hers to make sure A Bit of a Mouthful got her best shot. Not a loan, no repayment expected. *The money is there. Thank you so much, Dad. I'll put it to good use, I promise – and I'll update you when things start happening.*

Just before leaving the apartment for Borelli's, she dialled Louise Daly's number.

'Thank you,' Louise said, 'for what you're paying Dee. It's very generous.'

'Not at all. Is she there?'

'Hang on.'

'I've got two logos to show you,' Deirdre told her.

'That's brilliant.' Was there an undercurrent of excitement in the girl's voice? Certainly there was more brightness about it. 'Are you free in the morning?'

'Yeah.'

'Ten o'clock at the library?'

'OK.'

'Great – see you then.' Fingers crossed she'd like at least one. She didn't like one. She loved both.

The first was a simple line drawing of a nicely filled sandwich from which a slanted cocktail stick projected, at the top of which a little sign read *A Bit of a Mouthful*. The second featured a caricature of a man with smiling eyes and mouth agape, about to take the first bite from a sandwich he held, the image encircled by the brand name.

She'd drawn seeds in the bread. The tomato slice that poked from the first sandwich was impeccable. The man had comb marks in his hair. There was nothing Alice could fault, nothing.

'They're perfect. How did you come up with the ideas?'

Deirdre shrugged. 'I just thought about it for a while.'

She was a natural. Without a day's training in commercial drawing, or any kind of marketing expertise, she'd produced a logo – no, two logos, either of which Alice would be happy to use.

'Deirdre, you have real talent.' She opened her wallet and took out the second fifty euros. 'Thank you,' she said, handing it over. 'It hardly feels like enough.'

Deirdre looked at the note in her palm, her face going pink. 'It feels like … too much,' she said. 'I mean, it wasn't even real work, it was just drawing.'

Alice laughed. 'That's because you're so talented, it comes naturally to you. Have you heard of graphic designers?'

'No.'

'Well, this is the kind of stuff they do for a living. It's called commercial drawing, it's aimed at businesses. I'm not sure, but I imagine people usually go to art college to be a graphic designer, and you're what? Twelve?'

'Thirteen.'

'Right – and you've had no training, and you've given me two perfect logos. I'd say graphic designers had better watch out when you're a bit older.'

Deirdre smiled. She tucked the money into her pocket.

'I'll let you have samples of the logo as soon as it's printed,' Alice said. 'And you never know, I might be delivering sandwiches to your new school. You can tell everyone you made my logo – if I can ever decide which one I like more, I mean.'

They left the library. They stood on the steps.

'Graphic designer,' Alice said. 'Remember it. And if I hear of anyone else looking for a logo, I'll give them your name.'

'Thanks, Alice.'

First time she'd used her name. Alice fancied there was more of a spring in the girl's step as she moved away. If there was any justice in the world she'd make money, a good living, from her art.

Back at the apartment she laid the two logos side by side. Which was better? Which gave out the strongest message? Which would prompt more people to order a lunchtime sandwich from Alice? She took snaps of both and sent them to Liz and Tina and Joe – and all three went for the sandwich with the sign poking from it, so that was that decision made.

She rang Laurie and told her she had a name and a logo sorted. 'What happens now?'

'Now we meet. How's Sunday, about three?'

'Fine.'

'I'll text you my address.'

She spent the afternoon packing up the car, and stripping off the bed linen she'd put on only yesterday, and doing a final round of egg collection before ushering the hens into the coop for the evening. 'I'll miss you,' she told them, and they didn't take a scrap of notice.

She boxed up the usual dozen eggs for George before leaving the rest in Kate's back porch. I don't expect you to keep delivering to him once you move, Kate had said, but Alice had told her she'd continue for as long as she could. She could pick up the eggs on Friday, give her an excuse to visit Kate.

It would be strange though, not living here any more. Calling William's place her home would take some getting used to. It's soon, Kate had said. It's a big step. Just make sure it's what you want.

She did a final check of the apartment. She took the rubber duck she'd forgotten from the bathroom windowsill. She locked the door for the last time and slipped the key under the patio mat, as Kate had instructed.

Done. Moved out. It felt oddly disorienting. It would pass.

As she approached her packed car a movement caught her eye from the opposite driveway. She looked across and saw a woman attempting to haul something from a car boot. She crossed the road.

'Need a hand?'

The woman turned. 'Oh, hello – this thing is stuck.'

It appeared to be some kind of black metal frame, one end caught among a jumble of shoes. Garden furniture, Alice guessed. A base for a table, or part of a swing. A young child moving in, maybe. She pushed the shoes out of the way and managed to free it, and lifted it out.

'Thanks so much,' the woman said. 'It's the stand for my daughter's keyboard. I can take it from here – it's not heavy.'

'It's bulky though. I'll give you a hand. I'm Alice,' she added. 'I live across there – well, I did, until today. I'm actually moving out.'

'Glad I caught you then. I'm Claire.' They carried the stand between them into a hall that smelt of paint. 'It's fine here,' Claire said. 'I'm not sure where Suzi will want it.'

Suzi. She was Suzi's mum. She thought she'd seen her somewhere.

'Have we met?' Claire asked. 'You look familiar.'

'Eggs,' Alice said. 'I was bringing them to George's house a couple of weeks ago.'

'That's right. Small world.'

'Sorry about his mother.'

'Sudden,' Claire agreed.

'Suzi's a lovely girl. I've met her a couple of times. Tell her Alice says hello.' She took a step back, lifting a hand. 'It was nice to meet you. Hope you're happy here.'

'Thanks, Alice.'

So George's ex and his daughter would soon be living across the road from Kate. It seemed that the universe had decreed that he and Alice shouldn't meet, but that their lives should glance off each other's every so often.

'Good to see you,' William said, holding her close. 'I missed you.'

His embrace felt familiar. The apartment smelt of curry.

'Welcome,' he said.

'Thank you.' She drew away to pull a bottle from her bag. 'It's from the family vineyard. My mother insisted on personalising it for you.' *Per William con amore*, she'd written.

He took the wine and read the message aloud. 'That's very sweet of her. I have another bottle open, so we can save this for a special occasion. Now – what about your luggage?'

She indicated the bag she'd brought in. 'This will do for now – let's leave the rest till tomorrow. It's just clothes and books.'

He filled two glasses. '*Saluti*,' he said. 'So tell me about the holiday,' and she described her week, and showed him photos of her family, and of little Federico.

'Sounds like you had a good time. Maybe I'll join you on your next trip.'

'Sure.'

He left to put on rice. She heard him opening a press in the kitchen, lifting a saucepan lid. 'Not much happened here while you were away,' he said on his return. 'I had dinner at Barb's on Monday. Donal did a barbecue – it was a perfect day for it.'

'Val called him the barbecue king of the neighbourhood.' She paused. 'You haven't asked about my sandwich business.'

He took a seat across from her and positioned his glasses a little higher on his nose in the way he had – two hands, a lift at the outer corners. He laced his fingers together, caught a knee in them. He laughed lightly. 'Go on.'

'Well, it turns out my parents have just sold half the vineyard, so I got a lot more than I was going to ask them for. And the good news is, it's not a loan, which means I can forge ahead now.'

'Ah.' He blinked. He took off his glasses and polished them with the cloth he kept in a trouser pocket. She'd joked that he must be the only person in the world with his name printed on his polishing cloth.

'And I got a great logo from that girl I asked – wait till you see it, it's perfect. And I'm meeting—'

'It's just …' he said, their words overlapping. She stopped.

He set his glasses back in place. 'I mean, you're not seriously thinking about going ahead with that?'

She looked at him in surprise. 'Of course I am.'

'I didn't think you meant it.'

'William, you *know* I meant it.'

'It's just,' he repeated, 'I never really thought you'd want something like that. I thought you were just – keeping the joke going.'

She frowned. 'It wasn't a joke. When was it a joke?'

'Banter,' he said, 'around the dinner table. I mean, the idea of you delivering sandwiches … it's something a student would do as a holiday job, isn't it? It's not work for a woman your age. It's not … appropriate.'

'Appropriate,' she repeated. Yes, that would be a William word. He would set great store by appropriate behaviour. His entire life was appropriate.

'Have you heard back from the other jobs you applied for?'

The jobs he knew she didn't want. 'As it happens, I have. I got two responses while I was in Italy, both offering me interviews. I turned them down as soon as I got my parents' backing.'

He adjusted his shirt cuffs, made another precise little repositioning of his glasses. 'But Alice, are you seriously considering making sandwiches for a living? Can you honestly say your ambition doesn't go any higher than that? You have so much more potential.'

A sudden hiss in the kitchen just then, water boiling over

it sounded like. 'Hang on,' he said, and disappeared. While she waited for him to come back she looked around the room, familiar to her by now. The orderly bookshelves of pale grey wood, the white-framed prints on the cream walls, abstract and pastel and all the same size. The television located above the closed-up fireplace, its remote control sitting in a little bracket on the side.

A magazine rack filled with his cycling magazines, an aloe vera plant in a white ceramic pot. Alexa on a little side table, obediently playing Adele. He knew she loved Adele. He thought of everything.

The suede bag she'd dropped inside the door, crumpled and dark green, and out of step with the pale orderliness in which he lived.

'Sorry about that.' He was back. 'Dinner will be ten minutes,' he said, resuming his seat and picking up his glass. 'Hope you're hungry. The wine's Italian, by the way.'

'William,' she began carefully.

'Yes?'

'… I think I made a mistake.'

'Pardon?'

She thought about where to go next, what words to use to let him down kindly. He was the sort of man mothers wanted for their daughters. He ticked so many boxes, he would be so many women's ideal mate – but she hadn't really missed him while she was in Italy, and she didn't love him, and she was pretty sure she never would.

'I made the wrong decision,' she said.

'About the business?'

'No. About us.'

He sighed. 'Alice, I've upset you now. I just thought I should be honest. I couldn't pretend to approve of your plans.'

'No, I wouldn't want you to pretend. But … I want someone who supports me in whatever I choose. I want someone who wants me to be happy, even if it's … inappropriate.'

'Oh, now you're being dramatic. Look, if you want to be a sandwich maker, go ahead. I can't see it as a viable career, but you obviously want to give it a go, so fire away.'

She got to her feet, almost tipping her glass over. She'd had a sip, two at the most. 'Sorry,' she said. 'William, I'm sorry. I can't do this.'

He stood too. 'What are you saying?'

'I can't move in with you. I can't … be with you any more.'

'So that's it? You're giving up on us, before we even try? I say one thing you don't agree with, and that's us finished?'

She shook her head. 'It's not what you said this evening, not just that. We're not right for one another, William. I said yes to moving in because I wanted to make it work, but I see now that I was just trying to convince myself. We don't fit together like we should – I don't feel that we do.' She crossed to the door and lifted her bag.

'Please,' he said, 'please don't do this, Alice,' but she hitched the bag onto her shoulder and opened the door.

'No.' He stepped towards her. 'No. Don't go. I'm sorry I was negative about your plans.'

'William,' she said, 'I was still in touch with my ex while we were dating. I arranged to meet him at a hotel, about a month ago. He stood me up, but that's not the point. The point is, I was prepared to spend the night with him, to go back to him if he left his wife.'

It was cruel. She saw by his face what it did to him, and still she said it. 'I'm truly sorry. I don't love you. I'm sorry.' She stepped outside and closed the door quietly behind her. She descended the stairs, her steps loud in the silence.

She reached the street and glanced up. He wasn't standing at the window. She pulled the door closed and got into her car. She drove back to Kate's, knowing she'd done the right thing but feeling sad and dispirited. In every way that mattered, William was a better man than Chris, but he was just as wrong a choice for her – and even if the right man never came along, she'd rather be alone than with one she'd settled for.

Her mother would be disappointed, Barb too. She hadn't told her parents of her decision to move in with William. She'd told herself she wanted to surprise them with a fait accompli, but maybe her subconscious was urging her to say nothing, unconvinced that it would actually happen, or last long if it did.

She stopped for takeaway fish and chips. Back at the apartment she brought them around to the patio and ate them sitting on the bench that she'd sanded and painted not so long ago, trying to shake the despondency that clung to her like a wet sheet. Was William right? Was she ridiculous to consider making sandwiches for a living? Look at her, setting up a business with no real clue, spending money on a website, commissioning stationery and packaging that might never be used.

What if she got no orders at all? She could sink without a trace in her first month. Should she stop now, give up on the whole idea before too much had been invested in it? Should she contact the companies that had offered her interviews and ask them to reconsider?

She thought of her parents, wishing her well. She thought of Kate and Val, willing her to succeed. Find your passion, Val had told her. I have every faith in you, she'd said.

She thought of the perfect logo a thirteen-year-old had created for her. She thought of Barb and Donal at dinner. Had it all been just a joke to them? She didn't think so.

She pictured William, alone in his ordered apartment. Would he eat the curry he'd cooked for them? Probably: he wouldn't want to waste it. He'd package the leftovers neatly and put them in his freezer. She pictured him telling Barb that Alice had broken things off. She wondered suddenly if Barb's school would now be out of bounds for her sandwich deliveries, if Barb would tell her colleagues not to order from Alice, who'd knocked her brother off his bike and then jilted him.

Thirty-one, and on her own again, another relationship gone in just a few months. A less traumatic ending to this one, but an ending nonetheless.

Eventually she got to her feet. She brought her overnight bag inside and remade the bed. She opened her handbag and took out the Mass card she'd bought on the way back from meeting Deirdre, and the notebook she'd bought at the airport on her way to Italy. She sat at the kitchen counter and began to write. *Kate – I'm back. Long story, tell you tomorrow after Pilates. A x* She ripped the page from the notebook and left it in the porch with the eggs, and returned to the apartment.

Dear George
My aunt Kate told me of your mother's death, and I'm truly sorry. It must have been a terrible shock. Sending condolences to you and Suzi at this sad time.
Best wishes
Alice (who delivers the eggs, and writes Happy Talk)

She re-read it. Full of clichés – but that was all you had, wasn't it, when something like this happened? Often-repeated phrases, hopefully comforting in their familiarity, like the *Sorry for your troubles* mantra everyone murmured at funerals. Falling back on the tried and trusted, in the absence of anything else.

She started another page.

Hi Suzi,
Alice here, the one who brings the eggs. I just wanted to say that I'm so sorry about your gran. It's awful when we lose people we love, especially if it happens suddenly. Thinking of you and your dad, and hoping you're OK,
love Alice xx

She slipped the two notes into the Mass card. He might be at home when she called in the morning.

He wasn't, but Jack was. He emerged from the house as Alice opened the gate. He was tanned, his red-brown hair looking more coppery than she remembered, and dressed in a dark grey suit whose trouser legs tapered to black loafers. He halted on spotting her.

'Alice,' he said.

'Hi Jack.' She walked up the drive and offered him the eggs and the card. 'It's for George,' she told him.

'Thank you, very kind.' He placed them on something in the hall before pulling the door closed. 'I'm just leaving for the funeral,' he said, falling into step with her. 'George and Suzi have gone ahead.'

'Oh – that's today.' Kate would be going. 'How are they?' she asked Jack.

He opened the door of an old red Mini. 'Both devastated,' he said. 'George and his mum were close, and Suzi loved her gran. I met her once, just a few weeks ago. Nice lady.'

'I never met her, but she was my aunt's hairdresser for years. It was too bad you were away when it happened.'

'We flew home that morning. George got the news when we landed.'

'Poor thing. I have yet to meet him, but we've exchanged emails.'

Jack looked at her in mild surprise. 'On the dating website?'

She stared at him. 'What? No.' Dating website? Wasn't he with Jack?

'Sorry,' he said. 'I'm a bit all over the place. I persuaded him to sign up on a site, I was trying to play matchmaker. I didn't mean to imply anything. I hope I didn't offend.'

'No.' So they weren't a couple after all. 'George got in touch with me a while back to ask if I'd feature one of his pupils in Happy Talk. I didn't connect him to this George until I saw the piece in the paper about him saving that little boy. I didn't know he was a teacher.'

Jack was looking at her in astonishment. '*You* write Happy Talk?'

'Yes.'

'You did a piece on Tom and Maura, just a little while ago. I'm Tom's carer – we spoke on the phone.'

'That was you …' She remembered him telling her about his landlord featuring in another Happy Talk, and it was George. George was his landlord, not his partner.

'I'd better go,' he said then, so she stood on the path as he got into the car and rolled down the window. 'George will be sorry he missed you again. You should call around sometime he's here.'

'Maybe I will.'

But she wouldn't. There was no law that said she and George Murphy must meet. She watched the red Mini disappear around the corner, and wondered if it was the same car she'd noticed once or twice outside the house across from Kate, before the old man died. He might well have been a carer there too – and that could explain George's ex moving into the house left empty after the man's death. All the connections, all the strands that wove lives together.

William drifted into her head as she crossed the road to the gym. She imagined him checking his watch, waiting to open up as he brushed his teeth after breakfast. The thought of him brought just a small pang, a faint twinge of regret. Nothing like the heartbreak that Chris had caused her.

On her return to the car after her class she checked her phone and found a missed call, and a voicemail from Kate: *Alice, I'm just heading off to Evelyn's funeral. I meant to tell you yesterday but I forgot. Freya's filling in for me at work tonight, so I might see you later. I must hear what happened with you and William.*

She drove back to the apartment, the day stretching before her. She'd check the Happy Talk inbox, make a start on that – but she was barely in the door when her phone rang. She smiled when she saw Liz's name.

'Hi Liz.'

'Alice. You're home.'

'I am. I was going to give you a ring over the weekend. How are things?'

A pause then, long enough to worry about.

'Liz?'

'… Alice, we lost the baby.' The words coming out slow and heavy. 'I wanted you to know.'

'Oh, no. I don't believe it. Oh Liz, I'm so, so sorry. What happened?'

'Late miscarriage. I started bleeding –' She broke off.

'Liz. Sweetheart.'

'Will you come to see us, Alice?' Through tears. 'We'd love to see you, both of us would. Just to sit and talk.'

'Of course I will.'

'My mother's with us now, she insisted, but she's going home on Friday. Maybe you'd come on Saturday?'

'Yes. Saturday's good.'

'And you'll stay the night? Your old room is waiting for you.'

'I will, I'll stay. Mind yourself, Liz. Hug Emmet for me. I'll text when I'm setting off.'

'See you Saturday. Bye, Alice.'

Liz was thirty-four, three years older than Alice. She and Emmet had known one another since secondary school, had been each other's first and only loves. 'It took him seven years to propose,' she'd told Alice. 'We got married six months after that. We were in no hurry to have kids, but we felt the time had come to tie the knot.'

And then, after almost ten years of marriage, the time had come for a child – but it wasn't to be. Two tragedies Alice had heard about in the last couple of days, George's mother and now this. Two families left grieving.

Her phone rang again. Liz, calling back? But it wasn't Liz, it was Barb, who'd given Alice her number the night she and Donal had come to dinner.

She pressed the answer key warily. 'Hello, Barb.'

'Alice, William told me you've broken up. I'm so sorry. I was so hoping you and he would last. Break-ups are horrible – believe me, I know. Before Donal, I had plenty of them. Are you very sad?'

'Well … '

'Let's meet for coffee and cake, my treat. You need serious cheering up. What time would suit you?'

She wasn't mad at Alice. She wanted to buy her coffee and cake. 'Barb, you should know – I was the one who ended things, not William.'

'I know that. It doesn't matter. The heart goes where it wants, Alice. I love William, but if he wasn't for you, so be it. Is it awkward that I'm his sister? Would you rather not meet?' She gave a little laugh. 'Have you broken up with me too?'

'No, of course not.' Barb was bubbly and chatty, and just what Alice needed. 'I'm free now.'

'Wonderful! Will we say half an hour, in that cute little place beside the post office?'

'Perfect.'

She'd bring Barb up to speed with developments for the sandwich business. She'd show her the logos, and see which Barb would have chosen. She'd order coffee cake, or lemon drizzle. She could go shopping afterwards, spend some of the savings she no longer needed to hang on to so tightly. She might see something nice for Kate, a new scarf maybe.

And she might find a smart shirt, maybe olive green like her glasses, that she could stitch a sandwich delivery logo onto.

She took lipstick from her bag, her heart lifting.

George

HE COULDN'T THINK OF HER, IT KILLED HIM TO THINK of her, so instead he focused on his father. All through the funeral Mass, as he sat in the front pew with Suzi and Claire, and his two uncles and one aunt, he kept his gaze steadfastly away from the coffin on its stand to the left of the altar, and filled his head with memories of his father.

A tortoiseshell comb minus a few teeth sitting on the bathroom windowsill, or sometimes on the side of the sink. Piano music – Bach, Brahms, Vivaldi – floating from the sitting room on Sunday afternoons. The humming accompaniment to the buzz of the electric shaver from the bathroom. A blackened pipe-cleaner forgotten on the arm of a garden seat. Tobacco smoke, the lazy upward curl of it.

Their steps in sync as they walked to a hurling match. A spade handle jutting from the earth of a freshly turned flowerbed on certain dry Saturdays. A tomato cut into wedges and thrown on the pan with the Sunday-morning sausages and eggs. Nobody but his father liked fried tomatoes.

The slow parade of mourners after the Mass forced him back to the day, and the occasion. He listened to their murmurs – *So sorry, George, sorry for your trouble, very sorry* – as his left hand was shaken again and again, his right holding tight to Suzi's while his daughter went on sobbing, and he tried to forget, but he couldn't forget, that his last conversation with his mother had not been a happy one, and that they hadn't had a chance to fix it.

'Mr Murphy.'

Deirdre Daly's mother stood before him, in a black coat he'd never seen. 'Sorry, Mr Murphy, for your trouble.'

She took his hand and pressed it briefly. He felt the roughness of her palm as she withdrew it. The sight of her was unexpected. He didn't imagine it was easy for her to go anywhere without children. Deirdre might be outside with the younger ones. 'Mrs Daly, thank you for coming.'

'I remember losing my mother,' she replied. 'You look after yourself.' She nodded and moved on, and his hand was claimed again.

'George.'

A woman he couldn't immediately place. Sixties, dark hair, the same pitying concern on her face as all the rest. 'It's Kate,' she said, 'from Borelli's. We met, not so long ago.'

'Kate, yes, of course. Thanks for coming.' A memory flashed: sitting alone at a table in Borelli's, watching for a woman who hadn't shown up. And another: a photo of a lit cake, two waitresses holding it between them.

Her hand was warm in his. 'She was more than my hairdresser,' she said. 'We were friends, since you were a little boy. And this is poor Suzi.' She rested her free hand for an instant on the weeping girl's head. 'Evelyn loved to talk about you both. I would have gone to your father's funeral, but I was away at the time.'

His teaching colleagues appeared, one after another. Barb hugged him and told him she remembered his mother buying a Swiss roll at one of the school cake sales. Sheila and Vicky came together, both in navy. Dermot appeared, subdued for once, gripping George's hand as he told him how sorry he was. Everyone was sorry. They shuffled in their line from George across to John, widowed for the second time, who sat in the opposite pew with his sisters and children.

I'd like her to be buried with your father, John had said, late on the evening of her death, after George, after both of them, had had time to let the knowledge settle in that she was gone. I think she would have wanted that – and George had silently thought the same, so that was what was happening. And John, when his time came, would no doubt be buried with his former wife. It felt fitting to George, both of them returning to their first choices.

After the graveyard, which featured an unexpected violin rendition of his mother's favourite 'Peggy Gordon' by a friend, George sent Suzi home with Claire and went on with John to the nearby hotel, and endured the buffet lunch he didn't want with people who insisted on reminding him, simply by their presence, that he hadn't said a proper goodbye to her, that she'd died before they'd had a chance to mend the fence they'd damaged.

Driving home alone afterwards, he called to mind her wedding to John, after which he'd returned at the end of the day, alone too, to the house he'd shared with her. He remembered leaving the landing light on when he was going to bed, needing the yellow glow around the door to banish the alien feeling of the empty house.

It was different now, of course. Now he had Jack in the next room, and Suzi, still living with them while Claire readied the new accommodation. No empty house for him, but an ache in his chest that no number of housemates could relieve.

Orphaned. He rolled the word around in his mouth. Plenty younger than him deprived of both parents – but age didn't come into it. Her loss was an emotional wallop. He kept having to fill his lungs, to try to shift the heaviness that was lodged inside him.

Claire met him in the hall.

'How is she?' he asked.

'Quiet. She's in the garden with Jack. I was just leaving, actually. I can come and take her tomorrow if that suits, now that the house is ready.'

He watched her getting into her jacket. 'I wanted to talk to you about that,' he said.

'You want to hang on to her for another bit?'

He hadn't intended bringing it up. Not today, not now. He'd been planning to wait a while, to choose the right moment, to think about how to put it – and yet here it was, blurted out with no forethought. Was it grief, whipping away his usual reservations? Or was it his mother, prodding him from beyond the grave?

The thought of her, that thought, helped him to go on. 'I was wondering,' he said, 'if we could change the arrangements.'

Claire looked at him. 'What arrangements?'

'The living arrangements. Who Suzi lives with. I think it might be time to review it.'

'What do you mean?'

Say it. Say it. 'Claire, I'd like more access to our daughter. I'd like to have her with me more.'

A long pause, during which he forced himself not to look away. 'Are you mad at me?' she asked.

'What? No, why would—'

'Because I left Rob. Because I uprooted Suzi.'

A beat passed. He needed to be honest. He needed to say what was in his head. 'I'm not mad,' he said. 'I was a bit, at the start. I was puzzled when you said you were leaving, seeing as how you'd just got engaged – and I was concerned for Suzi's sake, but she's fine. We had a good time on holiday. I'm not mad,' he repeated. 'I would just like more contact with her. I feel I'm due it, since you've had most of her up to this.'

He watched her digesting the words. She nodded slowly. 'You're a good father, George,' she said.

His mother used to tell him that. She'd marvelled that he could change a nappy. Your father never changed one of yours, she'd say, not a single time – and George's father would protest that he'd never been asked, and then disappear quickly behind his newspaper.

'What were you thinking?' Claire asked now.

Go for it. 'I'd like a fifty-fifty split,' he said. 'Every second week. I think that would be fair – and I think Suzi would be happy with that too.'

'Have you spoken with her?'

'It came up during the holidays,' he admitted. 'I didn't bring it up – it just happened.'

'And it's what she wants?'

'It is. It's not that she's unhappy with you—'

She put up a hand to stop him, so he stopped. She hitched her bag onto her shoulder. 'I was afraid,' she said. 'I could see how good you were with her, how much she loved when it was time to go to you. I was afraid she'd … choose you.'

'Claire, she's not choosing me. That's not what this is. This is just … well, it's us, levelling the playing field. Giving her equal access to us, that's all. She's never once hinted that she'd rather be with me all the time. Never.'

A long pause followed this. He searched her face, but didn't know how to read it any more.

And then she spoke.

'OK.' Quietly. 'You're right, I've had it all my own way. I didn't think you minded. You never objected.'

'I did mind. I should have spoken up, long ago.' It felt good to say it.

She smiled. It wasn't much of a smile, but it was there. 'You were keeping the peace.'

'I was,' he agreed. 'I'm good at that.'

Another pause ensued, one that felt a little calmer.

'So,' she said, 'week on, week off. Will we say changeover day on Sunday, starting tomorrow?'

'That sounds fine.' Sorted, just like that. The relief he felt. 'Thanks, Claire.'

'What about the cat?' she asked then. 'Where will the cat live?'

'Well, I wouldn't mind him staying here, I'm used to him now, but I think Suzi might want to bring him back to his old house. Would that be OK with you?'

'I suppose so. Will you sort that out with her?'

'Sure. I can drop her over to you tomorrow if you like.'

'That would be good.' She reached up to open the front

door. 'Come about six and stay for dinner, if you have nothing planned. I can give you the grand tour.'

'OK, I'll do that.'

He stood at the door until she got into her car, ready to wave if she looked back, but she didn't. He went into the kitchen and looked out at Suzi and Jack sitting on the two wooden chairs, the cat sprawled on the paving stones at Suzi's feet.

They really needed to get more chairs.

As he was pulling off his black tie a white envelope on the table with his name on it caught his eye. He didn't recognise the writing. No stamp. Another Mass card, it had to be. Thrown in while they were at the funeral.

Alice O'Mahony, it was from. He read the two notes that accompanied it. He studied the signature at the bottom of the one addressed to him. *Alice (who delivers the eggs, and writes Happy Talk)*

She wrote Happy Talk. She was that Alice too. Accounts of everyday joy by Alice O'Mahony.

Suzi and Jack had both met her – and so had Claire, he remembered suddenly. A few weeks ago, when she'd called to the house for breakfast before going to see that awful basement flat. Everyone had met Alice except him. He'd emailed her about Deirdre; she'd emailed him some time later asking what he thought of her getting Deirdre to design a logo for her. She called to his house practically every Saturday morning with eggs, but they hadn't once come face to face.

He took off his suit jacket and hung it on the back of a chair, and rolled up his shirtsleeves. He added the Mass card to the bundle on the worktop and slipped Alice's note to him into his trouser pocket, and went out with Suzi's.

'For me? Who's it from?'

'Read it.' As she scanned it her eyes gleamed with tears. 'Alice,' she said, scrubbing them away.

'She called today,' Jack put in. 'I was just leaving. She brought the eggs.'

Eggs, from George's mother. He felt a thickness in his throat. He'd call to Borelli's tomorrow and sort things out with Kate. He'd keep on taking them, if she was happy to keep providing them.

Jack got to his feet. 'Take my chair,' he said. 'I'm hitting the road soon.' He was visiting his parents, staying the night with them.

When they were alone, George sat back and regarded his daughter. 'How do you feel, sweetheart?'

'OK,' she said, but she looked tired and sad. She looked wrung out, and his heart ached to see it.

'What were you and Jack talking about?'

She gave a tiny smile. 'He asked about my happiest memories of Gran.' A wobble in her voice, but she tilted her chin and held it together.

Thoughtful Jack, sensitive Jack. Knowing exactly how to distract a child from her sorrow. 'Tell me,' George said, and she spoke, not of the holidays and the birthday parties he'd expected to hear about, but of smaller things. Stories read to her when she was in bed with measles, and a green dress with red cherries on it that his mother had bought her once, although he had no memory of it.

She spoke of being brought out to tea, just the two of them. 'Gran said ladies needed time to themselves,' she said, and George could just hear his mother saying such a thing. 'We had tea and buns. The buns all had different-coloured icing on them. Gran said I could eat as many as I liked, but not to tell you or Mum.' She gave a weak little giggle, and George adopted a mock shocked face, which made her merrier – but the merriment wasn't long turning to tears, and he stroked her hand and let her cry while the cat looked unblinkingly at them.

He appeared fatter to George. Was he putting on weight? Probably. Spoilt rotten here, cat food in pouches, and treats that he gobbled, and little bottles of cat milk.

When her tears had dried, he told Suzi about his conversation with Claire, and the change in their custody arrangements.

'She said OK? She didn't mind?'

'She didn't, really. We're going to start tomorrow. I'll bring you over to the new house and stay for dinner, and you can have your first week with her, and then she'll bring you back here next Sunday.'

'OK.' She gave a bleak smile. 'Thanks, George.'

'We weren't sure about the cat,' he said. 'Which house he should stay in, I mean.'

'He'll come with me,' she replied. 'He'll be wherever I am.'

Of course he would. She'd tamed him, she owned him now. She knew it, and the cat knew it. 'Fair enough.'

That evening they ordered pizzas and watched *Shrek* and *Shrek 2*, one after the other. George was bracing himself for the third, but to his relief Suzi yawned and said she was too sleepy so he sent her to bed, Oscar padding up the stairs behind her.

Left alone, he poured himself a glass of beer and sat in the darkened sitting room, but before long a yawn came without warning, and another. He realised he was bone tired, so tired his legs felt embedded in concrete. He poured the second half of the beer down the sink and trudged upstairs.

He eyed himself in the bathroom mirror as he brushed his teeth. His hair could do with a cut: no scissors at it since his mother had moved out. Maybe he should get it shaved, like Jack did with his sides.

He pushed open the door to Suzi's room. In the light from the landing he saw her curled into a ball, the cat making another curl at the end of the bed. He tiptoed across and straightened the sheet that was slipping sideways – and something fell from it to the floor. He picked it up and tilted it towards the landing light, and found it to be Alice's note. He placed it on the locker and left the room.

The next morning, after a better night's sleep than he'd expected, he phoned John while he waited for Suzi to appear. 'Just checking in,' he said.

'Thanks, George. I'm doing alright. Sally's with me. She's going to stay a couple of weeks and work from here. How are you and Suzi?'

'We're OK.'

For a few months John had been his stepfather, and maybe still was – George was vague on how the step thing worked post mortem. But John had his own deeper ties, and now that his and George's connection had been cut, he thought they would probably drift away from each other in time.

They'd exchange Christmas cards, for a few years at least. They might meet occasionally at his mother's grave, or at other future gravesides, and remark on the time that had passed since their last meeting, and spend a few minutes in chat – but that, he felt, would be it. That would probably be the extent of it.

And wasn't that the way it went, lives intersecting for a while, connections being forged and broken, paths crossing and sometimes twining before moving apart again? Wasn't that how it worked?

No, of course it wasn't always how it worked. Lots of connections lasted. Some – his parents, John and his first wife, Jack and Patrick – ended only when death forced them to. Many relationships endured through the years. George wondered why he didn't seem to have the knack.

'Don't eat too much,' he told Suzi when she surfaced. 'I'm taking you out to lunch. We're going to a restaurant.'

'Where?' she wanted to know, and he told her about Borelli's. 'You haven't been there before,' he said. 'It's owned by the lady who gives us the eggs that Alice delivers.'

He might not get a chance to talk to Kate if she was busy, so he'd written a note just in case.

Kate
Thank you again for coming to Mam's funeral, it was good of you. I'd like to continue with the eggs if you're OK with that, and I can pick them up if it's easier. Let me know how you'd like me to pay. I owe you for yesterday's – George

He added his phone number and slipped it into an envelope. At lunchtime they headed to the restaurant. He wondered if he'd meet the same waitress as before, and if she'd remember him being stood up, but a different person showed them to a different table.

'Is Kate about?' he asked.

'No, she doesn't cover lunchtimes. She's usually in around

four' – so George handed over the envelope, and asked for it to be passed on.

'Why are you writing to her?' Suzi wanted to know, and George explained about having to make a new arrangement for the eggs.

'Gran paid for them,' he said, and he saw how the mention of her grandmother caused a dimming in her, and he wished he could spare her the sadness of all the inevitable future reminders.

They ordered antipasti to share – prosciutto, olives, cherry tomatoes, anchovies and mozzarella – served with ciabatta slices toasted and drizzled with oil. Most of the dozen or so tables were filled this Sunday lunchtime. Kate must be doing well.

Halfway through the meal, he suddenly remembered the party that Jack had attended here, and the large cake that had been carried to the table by Alice and another waitress. He'd forgotten she worked here, along with writing the Happy Talk column. She mustn't be on duty now, or Suzi would have spotted her.

The day was wet. On the way home from lunch, at Suzi's request, they made a detour to the cemetery. He held an umbrella over them as they stood in the drizzle before the freshly turned mound of earth that was topped with flowers. So many flowers she'd got.

'Do you remember Grandad?' George asked, more as a distraction than for any other reason. 'You were seven when he died.'

'I remember him.'

'What do you remember?'

'Him teaching me the piano, and playing Snakes and Ladders.

He tried to cheat, but I always caught him. And he'd give me toffees from his pocket.'

George had forgotten the toffees. Taken up one time when his father had attempted to ditch the pipe – had his doctor advised him, or was it on the urging of George's mother, who'd never approved of it? However they had come about, the toffees hadn't worked as a substitute, and the pipe-smoking had resumed – but the sweets hadn't gone away. George would come across scrunched-up wrappers on top of the piano, or on a window ledge, or sitting in the angle where the banister rail met the bottom post.

'Do you think they're together now,' Suzi asked, 'Gran and Grandad?' George heard the hope in her voice and told her he was certain of it. They went to the cinema, where she picked out a Marvel film, and he had a snooze while superheroes saved the world. On the way out he looked for Deirdre Daly, but didn't find her.

They spent the rest of the afternoon playing Scrabble, until the time came for Suzi to pack her things. Jack showed up shortly afterwards.

'How are your folks?' George asked, and he said they were the same as ever, and didn't elaborate.

'I'm bringing Suzi to Claire's in a bit. I'm staying for dinner.'

'Nice. I'm eating out too.' He turned on the cold tap, turned it off again. Opened the fridge, took nothing from it. Fiddled with the handle of the cutlery drawer. 'I have a date,' he said.

'A date.' George tried not to sound surprised.

'He's a friend of a friend. We've met a couple of times in a group, but this will be the first time it's just us.' He ran a hand through his curly top. 'I'm completely terrified, George.'

'Don't be. This is good. Where are you eating?'

'Borelli's. That was where we met, at Gerald's birthday.'

'We were there at lunchtime. Just try not to worry. Be yourself.' He heard how useless it sounded. He had nothing else. Who was he to offer advice in that area?

Footsteps thumped down the stairs just then, and Suzi appeared. 'Hi, Jack. George, we need to get Oscar into his carrier.' The carrier had come from a charity shop; this would be its first outing.

George's heart sank. He'd forgotten that the cat was travelling with them. He turned to Jack.

'Towel,' Jack said. 'It may be a job for three' – so they got a bath towel from the hotpress, and advanced on Suzi's bedroom.

At their appearance the cat immediately set up a low growling, and darted under Suzi's bed.

'Close the door,' Jack murmured. 'Suzi, call him over to you. George, stand by with the carrier.'

It took them ten minutes. At the end of it, George had sustained a single long scratch to his left cheek, the stack of comics by Suzi's bed had been demolished, and the curtains had suffered an impressive tear. The cat glowered in the carrier, half in and half out of the towel, as George hefted it from the house. He deposited it on the car's back seat and returned upstairs to dab TCP on the cut in the hope of avoiding rabies, or tetanus, or whatever disease the cat was capable of inflicting on him. If this was to be a weekly occurrence, they'd need a better strategy.

They drove across town to the bungalow, following Jack's directions. Pebbledash front, one bay window, he'd said – and there it was, separated from the road by a low wall, and a lawn that could do with cutting. Claire emerged as they were getting out of the car, wearing a lime-green apron imprinted with wine glasses over her dress. George wondered when she'd started wearing an apron.

'What happened to your face?' she asked, and in response George lifted the cat carrier from the back seat. 'Oh, no,' she said, and exchanged a quick grin with Suzi. 'Oh, poor George. You might need to go for a tetanus shot. Come on in.'

The hall was very white. White walls, bleached floorboards, white coat rack, small white-edged window. It smelt equally of new paint and fried onions. The cat, released from its prison, streaked through a door at the end of the hall with Suzi in pursuit. 'Wonder if he'll recognise the place,' Claire said. 'It must smell totally different.'

'You can let him out, since it's familiar territory.'

'Good. Has he been vaccinated, or neutered?'

'Doubt it.' The thought had never crossed George's mind.

'I'll bring him to a vet then, just to be on the safe side – if Suzi can persuade him back into that carrier. Come on, I promised you a tour.'

The house had two decent-sized bedrooms, one a double and the other a twin, both kitted out with wardrobes, dressing tables and lockers that all appeared brand new. He saw pyjamas draped over the end of Claire's bed in the double room, and his mind spooled back of its own accord to the nights he'd taken them off her.

There was a bathroom with a bath and an overhead shower, and a smallish sitting room with a fireplace and a pair of neat green couches. The kitchen, where the cat sat now on the deep windowsill, had plenty of storage and all the usual equipment, and a table in the centre with six chairs around it.

The walls throughout were chalky white, lending the place an airy, bright feel. He couldn't find fault with any of it. 'Come out to see the garden,' Claire said, opening the back door.

.It was larger than he'd been expecting. Roughly the footprint of the house, with ragged shoulder-high hedges marking it off from its neighbours, and a breezeblock wall to the rear whose coating of white paint was patchy. The lawn, like the one in front, needed a cut, and was yellowed with moss. A clothes line drooped between posts set into the grass.

There was a dilapidated wooden shed, door hanging crookedly, single window missing its glass, and a minuscule patio just outside the kitchen with cracked paving slabs from whose every gap weeds sprouted enthusiastically. Clearly, the renovations hadn't extended beyond the house.

All fixable, though. George imagined a fresh coat of paint on the wall, and a facelift to the shed. A bed for flowers dug out at the rear, another just beyond the patio. Climbers making their way up the wall like Jack had done at his place, or a row of shrubs stretching across. The patio cleaned up, the hedges clipped. Might be worth checking with the owner: he might agree to some rent relief in exchange for a garden overhaul.

'It's not a long walk to town,' Claire told them, over a dinner of homemade burgers and chips. 'Suzi, you'll be able to take the bus to your new school. The stop is about three minutes from here.'

She looked well. She'd changed her hair while they were in Tenerife. The colour was lighter, the cut bolder. She was wearing darker lipstick than normal, a shade between crimson and wine that suited her, and she'd exchanged her scent for something tangier. Maybe she was redesigning herself in the wake of her split from Rob.

Had she taken similar action when she'd finished with George? He couldn't remember.

'This is good,' Suzi said. 'The three of us together, like a real family – and we have a cat.'

George caught Claire's eye: she lifted eyebrows at him as she rose. 'Ice cream,' she said, taking a tub from the freezer, prising off its lid. 'You need to make sure the cat doesn't scratch the furniture, Suzi.'

'I will. He sleeps on my bed in George's house.'

'Does he indeed?' Claire scooped ice cream into bowls. 'I nearly forgot to tell you,' she said. 'I met the woman who lives across the road. She helped me take the keyboard stand out of the car. And guess what – you both know her.'

'Who is it?' Suzi asked.

'Her name is Alice. She brings eggs to George's house.'

'*Alice* lives across the road?'

'Actually, she doesn't any more. She was just moving out.'

'She wrote me a note,' Suzi said, 'to say sorry about Gran. We were gone to the funeral, but she met Jack and gave it to him.'

'Aw, did she, darling? That was kind.'

It *was* kind. George and Suzi were virtually strangers to her, but she'd taken the time to write two notes and slip them into a Mass card.

'She writes Happy Talk,' Suzi told Claire. 'That page in the paper that I showed you, the time the girl in George's class was in it.'

'Really? She writes that?'

George recalled the note he'd written to Kate, offering to collect the eggs in future. If she took him up on that, it would mean the end of Alice calling around on Saturday mornings.

After dinner he and Claire washed up while Suzi went off to unpack, and establish Oscar in her room.

'So you think you'll be happy here?' he asked, taking a plate from the water and slotting it into the drainer.

'I know I will. I love the house already, and it's really quiet at night – and like I say, very close to town. And Suzi could have a friend to stay over at weekends if she wanted, with the twin beds.'

He fished cutlery from the water. 'And how are things otherwise?'

She dried a knife and dropped it into the drawer, and took up another. 'How are things?' she repeated slowly. 'Things are good, George. Actually, things are very good indeed.'

Something in her voice made him look more closely at her. She returned his gaze, a small smile beginning to grow. She reached up to touch her cheek briefly with the back of a hand.

'I've met someone,' she said.

He felt a soft kind of whoosh that travelled from his chest to the floor. He found a fork in the water. He lifted it out and set it in the drainer with the rest.

She resumed drying. 'I know what you're thinking, that it's too soon after Rob. I agree. I wasn't looking, really I wasn't. It was the last thing on my mind. He's the brother of the pal I was staying with, and he called around a couple of times, and ... well, we just – sort of clicked.' She darted a look up at George.

'And before you ask, you don't have to worry about Suzi. I won't bring him here, not while she's around. Not until ... we see if it's going anywhere.'

She dropped the last spoon into the drawer and slid it closed. She draped the tea towel over the side of the worktop. 'It just feels right, George. And he's not pushing me. I've told him about Rob. He knows the situation there. He's separated, and he has a daughter a couple of years older than Suzi.'

George dipped the pan into the water. He scrubbed hard at it with the rough side of a yellow sponge.

'He's a builder. He's setting up his own construction company. He was involved in the building of the aqua centre.' She pulled off the apron she'd put on again after the meal. She laid it on the table and folded it carefully, and made a small bundle of it. 'He's funny.' She smiled, looking off into the distance. 'He can be hilarious actually.'

Silence fell. George pulled out the plug and watched the water swirling away. He rinsed the sink and dried his hands. 'Good luck,' he said. 'I hope it goes well.'

What else was there to say?

They'd been in love once. They'd made a child together and then they'd separated, and they would never be a couple again. Finally, he saw it. Finally, he understood.

She'd known that he still loved her, that it had taken a long time for him to stop loving her. She'd known, and she'd used it to get her way. She'd used it when she'd decreed that he'd only see their daughter once a fortnight.

She'd also used it whenever she'd wanted to offload Suzi at other times. He recalled a conference in Geneva that Rob was attending, a year or so ago; a weekend on a boat with other couples the previous summer; a yoga retreat in France in November, and a lot more instances over the years. Do you mind, George? she'd say. I hate to ask – but she hadn't really hated asking.

She'd used him. She was still using him. The new week-on-week-off arrangement with Suzi would suit her very well now, would leave her free to see her builder more often. George should have known, when she'd agreed to it so easily.

His mother had been right.

And he, so slow to see what he should have seen long ago, had been imagining them happy with one another again, not because he still loved her – he didn't, not in that way, not any more – but because he was lonely.

He was lonely. He was horribly, unbearably lonely. He'd been lonely for years.

'I hope you find someone, George. I'd love it if you did.'

The words sounded hollow to him. She was looking at him with a concern that didn't now feel genuine to him. But she was Suzi's mother: they would always be linked, so he must ignore what he couldn't change.

He summoned a smile. 'One of these days.'

'I really hope so.'

He said he should be going then, and she put up no protest. He went to Suzi's room to tell her goodbye. 'I'll see you in a week,' he said. 'Mum said she'll bring you over.' But the phone call would come, he thought, Saturday night or Sunday morning: Could you collect her, George? I hate to ask.

Suzi hugged him. 'I'll ring you tomorrow. Sorry about Oscar scratching your face.'

'I'll live.' He dropped a kiss on her head. 'Love you. Best girl in the world.'

He returned to the hall. He let himself out, pulling the door closed quietly behind him. Before he drove off he glanced at the house across the road, a two-storey with an extension to the side that might have been a garage, once upon a time. There were two cars in the driveway. He wondered if that was the house Alice used to live in.

Back home, he called for Jack in the hall and got no reply, and remembered the date with the friend of a friend. He took a can of beer from the fridge and brought it into the sitting room, and flicked through TV channels until he found an old episode of a sitcom he used to love. It wasn't as funny as he remembered, but it prompted the odd smile.

As the credits rolled, his phone beeped. He read the text from an unfamiliar number.

George, sorry I missed you today. I hope you're feeling OK. Please come back to Borelli's some evening soon with Suzi – I'd love to treat you both to dinner. We're closed on Mondays, and I generally take one other day off too, moveable feast so let me know when you're thinking of coming, to make sure I'm there. Of course I'll keep providing the eggs, and Alice is happy to go on delivering them. I'm paid up to the end of the month, so I'll bill you after that – Kate xx

He pressed *Reply*.

Kate, many thanks for the dinner invite, we'll take you up on it soon. And thanks for the eggs, to you and to Alice, whom I have yet to meet, would you believe? – George

He finished his beer as the light dimmed outside. He thought of his birthday in September, thirty-five looming. Last year his mother had given him a jumper that she'd got one of her hairdressing customers to knit. The shade of green didn't do a lot for him, and the sleeves stopped above his wrists, but he'd pulled it on and pretended to be on the catwalk, and his mother had laughed and told him he was a tonic. She'd roasted a chicken for dinner that night, and told him as she spooned stuffing onto his plate that John Stewart had asked her to marry him, and what would George think if she said yes.

That night, Jack not having returned by the time he was going to bed, George left the landing light on. As he waited for sleep, he decided he'd go to the school in the morning. The secretary or the caretaker would be there to let him in, and he'd sort out his classroom and ready it for the year ahead.

He normally left this task until the last Friday of the holidays, when everyone else would be there on the same mission. They'd go to lunch somewhere and trade summer stories, and groan collectively at the prospect of a new school year. But there were still three weeks to go before that happened, and with Suzi gone, he needed something to distract him from his grief, and school would do that for a few hours.

'Good,' Jack said, when George asked him the following morning how the dinner date had gone. 'Early days,' he said, spreading honey on toast. 'We went from Borelli's to the new wine bar.'

'I didn't hear you come in.'

'I got back around midnight, bit tiddly but otherwise in good order.'

'You meeting him again?'

A beat passed. 'Probably.' Jack blew on his coffee. 'He knows about Patrick. He's leaving it up to me.' He cradled his mug. 'It's strange,' he said, 'starting again. It'll take some getting used to.'

'Sure ... Claire's met someone. She told me last night.'

'Has she? That was quick.'

'Yup.'

'You OK, George?'

'Yeah, fine.'

Not one hundred per cent true. He'd woken with a headache, and the sharp pang of his bereavement – and a sense of softer gloom that had been caused, he knew, by his after-dinner conversation with Claire, and the acknowledgement of an absence within him that had nothing to do with the death of his mother.

The school was quiet at ten o'clock on a holiday Monday morning. 'Didn't expect to see you,' the secretary said, after she'd buzzed him in. She'd been at the funeral. 'How are you doing, George?'

'Doing OK,' he told her, because nobody wanted to hear about a fractured heart.

'What happened to your cheek?'

'Cat scratched me, it's grand. Got any paracetamol? Bit of a headache.'

She gave him two from the first-aid box, and filled a paper cup with water from the sink behind her. 'Can I bring you a cuppa? I was just about to make one.'

'No, I'm grand, thanks. Not long since breakfast.'

'Well, shout if you change your mind.'

The air in his classroom smelt stale. He flung open windows

and left the door ajar. He took out his iPod and found one of his running playlists. He turned it up loud and got to work.

He pulled open drawers and sorted their contents. He climbed onto a chair and took down posters, and stored the ones with life still in them. He went through his stash of whiteboard markers and binned the duds. He peeled the paper leaves carefully from the kindness tree and sat at his desk to read the kindnesses he'd recorded on them.

Mowed my neighbour's lawn ... read my brother a bedtime story ... picked up rubbish in the park ... tidied my room before Mum asked me ... gave my seat on the bus to an old man ... held the shop door open for a woman with a buggy ...

He bundled them together and slipped them into an envelope. He always saved them to read to his new crop of students, give them a few ideas for their own kindnesses. As he was stowing the envelope in his desk drawer a hand landed on his shoulder, making him jump. He looked up to find Dermot standing there, mouthing something he couldn't hear above the music in his ears.

He pulled out his earphones. 'Dermot.' He switched off the iPod.

'Didn't mean to startle you,' Dermot said, hitching a buttock onto the desk. 'I was saying hello, but you couldn't hear me. Irene told me you were in.' Subdued, for Dermot. 'You got a scratch,' he said, peering at George's face.

'Cat.'

'Right. I thought I'd be the only one in today. How sad are we, in school in the middle of the holidays?' He gave his usual bark of a laugh then, but George heard the hollowness in it.

'Sad enough,' he said.

The smile slid off his face. 'Jesus, sorry, George – I didn't think.' He actually did look sorry. 'How are things? How are you doing?'

'I'm OK. Thanks for coming to the funeral. How's everyone in your house?' He'd forgotten the wife's name.

Dermot made a face, a twist of his mouth. 'Well,' he said, tapping with the pads of his fingers on the desk, 'here's the thing, George.' Tap, tap, tap. 'I don't know how everyone is, because Greta walked out on me four days ago, and I haven't seen her or the kids since.' A lift and a drop of a shoulder.

'What?'

'Truth, George.' Another short mirthless laugh. 'Can't say I blame her – she married an awful fool.'

'I'm sorry, Dermot.' George *had* thought him a fool, so many times. He conjured up an image of Greta, full-figured and curly-haired. Fond of blusher. 'That's rough. Do you know where she's gone? Have you had any contact?'

'She's at her mother's, which is the worst place she could have picked. Mother hates me, can't stand me.' He gave another shrug. 'She'll be hanging out the bunting, now that Greta has finally found sense.' He plunged his hands into his pockets and rattled coins, or keys. 'I made the mistake of calling her "Mother" after I married Greta. "My name is Paula," she told me, real snotty, so I was warned.' He looked up at the ceiling, gave another long sigh. 'I need to see my kids, George. I'm going mad without them.'

'She has to let you see them.'

'Yeah. She says we can work something out.' He shifted his gaze back to George, his face bleak. It was like someone had sucked all the merriment out of him. Abandoned by his wife, missing his children and hated by his mother-in-law, and still he'd shown up at George's mother's funeral.

George got to his feet and lifted his jacket from the back of the chair. 'Come on,' he said. 'Let's get out of here and find a decent coffee.'

'You sure? I wouldn't want to put you out.'

'I was just finishing up.' It wouldn't kill him to pass an hour in a café. They went to the one closest to the school, and Dermot spoke of the rows that had started long before the summer, and his five-year-old son Brian, who'd been diagnosed with a heart condition in May, and the holiday in Corfu that had been meant to patch things up with Greta but hadn't. And George thought of all he had been masking with bluster and teasing and silliness.

He asked George how Tenerife had gone, and George braced himself for a crack about the landscape gardener, and it didn't come. On impulse he told Dermot about saving the child at the beach, since he seemed unaware of it, and of being approached by the journalist after. 'It was in the *Indo* on Thursday.'

Dermot shook his head. 'Didn't see it. Haven't opened a paper in the last few days – but it's every parent's nightmare, isn't it, that something will happen to their kids? I haven't had a proper night's sleep since we got the news about Brian. Well done to you though, that's something to be proud of.'

George thought he might like the new Dermot.

The rest of the week crawled by. He trudged across the road to the gym every other day, and played the usual five-a-side on Wednesday night, and jogged without pleasure in the mornings along streets he'd always known, with music pounding in his ears. Every action was an effort, every movement needing more energy than it should. He felt as if he was making his way through an ocean of thick sludge. He supposed it was grief.

He spoke with Suzi on the phone every day, and on Thursday he heard about the vet visit that had thrown up two surprises: Oscar was a she, and she was pregnant. The tom next door to George had clearly been more than just a friend.

'What did Mum say?' he asked.

'She said I could have a party after the kittens are born and invite all my friends, and see who wants to take them when they're big enough.'

Clever Claire. 'So will you change Oscar's name?'

'Well, I don't think I can, because he's used to it – I mean, she's used to it. Imagine if someone changed your name to … Gerry or something. You'd be all confused.'

He smiled. She never failed to lift him. 'That's a good point. I miss you. How many more sleeps till you're back in this house?'

'You're funny, George. Tell Jack about Oscar.'

Jack was amazed. 'He's a *she*? I don't believe it.'

'She must have had litters before – she's not exactly a spring chicken.'

'Well, I never saw kittens around the place but she could have had them somewhere else – she was always in and out. I presume you or Claire will get her spayed after this lot.'

'For sure.'

On Friday afternoon George went to a barber for a haircut – a wrench to have someone other than his mother cutting it – and afterwards he invested in two more garden chairs that he spotted on sale outside a hardware shop, now that summer was past its best. When he got home he found a note from Jack saying that his father had fallen, and had been taken to hospital with a suspected broken hip. *I'll stay with Mum tonight*, he wrote, *and check in with you tomorrow.*

He brought the new chairs around to the patio. He tested one out for half an hour with his book until hunger drove him indoors in search of food. He found leftover chickpea and spinach curry in the fridge – with Jack in the house, there were usually leftovers.

Tomorrow he would take a trip to the beach. He might give the Tenerife togs another airing, if he could brave the chilliness of the Irish Atlantic.

He thought back to his last swim, the day before they'd flown home. He felt again the gentle but shocking bump against his leg, the limp little child he'd pulled up, his panicked, clumsy return to shore. He thought of the paragraph in the paper that he'd read on the plane, imagining his mother's pleasure on seeing it, little dreaming that she never would.

He went to bed an hour earlier than normal, and slept properly for the first time in a week. He woke just before nine and pulled on his running gear before the rational part of his brain could object. Get it over with, so he had the rest of the day free for his trip to the sea.

In the bathroom he brushed his teeth, splashed his face. As he went downstairs, the doorbell rang. Not the postman on a Saturday – and too early, he thought, for parcel post. Someone with a smile and a clipboard then, looking to switch his electricity account. He ran a hand over his newly shorn head and pulled his sweatshirt straight and opened the door.

'You must be George,' she said.

Alice and George

HE WAS TALL, AND BROAD WITH IT. HAIR SHORT, THE colour of sand. Tanned – yes, Tenerife. Suzi's eyes, the same brightness in them. Dressed in a loose grey sweatshirt, well-worn, and navy tracksuit bottoms. I can't believe you still haven't met him, Kate had said. Ring the bell, for God's sake – so Alice had, because by now she was curious.

'You must be George,' she said when the door opened. 'I'm Alice. Eggs,' she added, offering them to him. Feeling a little tongue-tied, now they were face to face.

But had they met somewhere?

She was short, a foot shorter than him, and slender where he was broad. He could pick her up: she'd weigh nothing. Blonde hair, different shades of blonde, choppily cut to follow the curve of her head, not quite long enough to touch her shoulders. Glasses with green frames, full bottom lip, a small point to her chin. Dressed in a sky blue T-shirt and dark leggings and grey trainers.

Familiar, for some reason.

'Alice,' he said, taking the eggs. 'Good to finally meet you.'

'I'm so sorry about your mother.'

'Thank you. And thanks for your card. It was kind of you to put a note in for Suzi.'

'Have we met?' she asked then. 'You seem …' He watched her trying to figure it out, an eyebrow dipped, the skin of her forehead crimping – and then it came to him.

'The airport,' he said. 'Couple of weeks ago. The bookshop.' The soft toy she'd nearly tripped over. Grabbing her arm instinctively to halt her fall. The green glasses he remembered, and the petite frame.

'The bookshop,' she repeated, giving a slow nod. 'That was you.' Her gaze flicked to his head. 'Your hair is shorter.'

'Yes.'

'Your T-shirt,' she said, a rich laugh bubbling as she remembered, 'with the kitten.' A small dimple popping in her left cheek. He'd always been envious of people with dimples.

'I told Suzi it was too small. I passed it on to my tenant.'

'Jack.'

'Yes. He's going to use it for gardening.'

A brief silence fell. 'Well,' she said, beginning to turn away – and something, some impulse, some gentle little nudge from somewhere, made him say, 'Would you care to come in for a cuppa?'

A cuppa. Her Pilates class was starting in five minutes, less than five.

The world wasn't going to end if she missed it.

'I would,' she said, and he stepped back, and she followed him into the kitchen, which smelt faintly of curry.

'There's nobody here,' he told her, lifting the kettle from the hob and holding it under the tap. 'Suzi's with her mum this week, and Jack stayed with his family last night. Have a seat.'

A little ball was on the table, the kind a cat might play with. She picked it up absently and rolled it against her palm. She wished she wasn't wearing her gym clothes.

The kitten T-shirt had stretched across his chest. She remembered liking that he'd worn it for his daughter.

Funny that they'd already met.

He was nervous, and conscious of the curry smell that was hanging around after last night, and trying to figure out what had possessed him to invite her in. Maybe he should offer breakfast at this hour. 'Would you like toast? There's gooseberry jam – or I could do eggs.' Nodding at the box she'd brought that he'd deposited by the cooker.

'No eggs for me,' she replied. 'I only like them later in the day. But toast sounds good.'

'Brown OK?'

'Brown's perfect' – so he slotted two slices into the toaster and pushed down the lever as the kettle began to sing.

'So,' he said, putting out plates and mugs, 'Happy Talk.'

She dimpled again. 'Happy Talk. I didn't know that was you, I didn't know you were a teacher, and Kate never said your last name. It wasn't until I saw the piece in the paper about you saving that little boy —'

She broke off, her smile diluting. He knew she was thinking of his mother again. 'She didn't see it,' he said. 'My mother. I only agreed to it going in because I knew she'd get a kick out of it.' What was he saying? Why was he telling her this? He was sharing too much.

She didn't look as if she minded. She didn't look uncomfortable. She had Oscar's little yellow ball in her hands, rolling it between them. 'Of course she would. Any mother would have been proud to read that about her son.'

To his horror he felt the hot rush behind his eyes that heralded tears. He turned away from her and busied himself assembling butter and knives for the toast as he drew in furtive steadying breaths. 'Tea OK, or would you rather coffee?'

'Tea is fine, thanks.'

He scalded the pot and dropped in teabags, wishing he was dressed in something more decent.

He was upset. Of course he was upset. His mother dead just over a week, any mention of her bound to stir him up. She cast about for a new topic. 'I met Suzi's mum – Claire, isn't it?'

He brought plates and mugs to the table, took jam from the fridge. 'Yes, Claire. She mentioned that she'd met you.'

The toast popped as he was setting the teapot on the table. He started slightly at the sound, causing a few drops of tea to splutter out. 'Oops,' he said, pulling a sheet from a paper towel roll on the windowsill. 'You want sugar?' Putting toast on her plate. 'And we have marmalade too, if you'd prefer it to the jam. Or juice? I could make orange juice.'

He was nervous. She wondered if he was regretting his impulse to ask her in.

He was babbling. She probably regretted taking him up on his offer.

'Honestly, I'm fine,' she said. 'I have everything I need. Why don't you sit down?'

So he sat and began to butter his toast as she spooned jam onto hers. 'I love gooseberries. They're hard to find though.'

'Farmer's market,' he told her, 'across town. They always have them around this time, and jam too.'

'Kate mentioned a farmer's market. It's new since my time. I must check it out.'

'Thursday afternoons and Saturday mornings. So you're from the town?'

'Born and bred here,' she said, licking the tip of a finger. 'I moved to Dublin when I was eighteen, and came back just a few months ago.' She cut the slice into quarters. 'My folks live in Italy now – Mum's Italian. Kate is my aunt – well, she was married to my uncle. They're divorced a long time.'

She bit into the toast, brushed crumbs from around her mouth. 'Mmm,' she said, and he saw a tiny dot of butter below her bottom lip. He should have left out the kitchen roll in case she wanted a serviette. He searched for something to break the new silence.

'So you write Happy Talk, and you work in Borelli's.'

She shook her head, and swallowed before answering. 'I'm not in Borelli's any more.' She sipped tea. 'Actually, I'm in the process of starting my own business, if you don't mind.'

That smile again. That dimple again.

'I remember now,' he said. 'You were wondering if you should ask Deirdre Daly to design a logo for you.'

She'd forgotten her email to him. Another connection. 'Yes, and thanks to you I did, and she came up with two really good ones.'

'That's great. I'd love to see them sometime' – so she took out her phone and showed him the photos she'd taken. 'Which one would you prefer?' she asked, and he pointed to the one she'd already chosen.

'She's so talented, George, and she's only, what, thirteen? She told me but I forget.'

'Thirteen since the tenth of April.'

She looked at him in astonishment. 'Do you know the birthdays of all your pupils?'

He smiled. 'No: I only remember Deirdre's because my father's was the same.' And he lifted his mug abruptly and drank, and she thought, Poor George, his fresh mourning stirring up earlier losses, his heart fragile as fine crystal.

Get a grip, he told himself, his tongue scalded from too hasty a gulp of tea.

'Tell me more about this business,' he said, and she did, her voice taking on a new eagerness. He could see her coming into a workplace with her sandwiches, greeting everyone with that bright smile. He could imagine people looking forward to her arrival.

'It's quite nerve-racking,' she said. 'I'm half terrified, but I really want to try it.'

'It sounds great,' he said. 'A fun way to earn a living.'

'Seriously? You don't think it's a bit … trivial?'

'Trivial? Not in the least. Nothing trivial about food. I can help, if you like. Drop in a leaflet when you have one, and I'll put it up in the staffroom after the holidays.'

'That's so kind of you. Actually … I know Barb, your colleague. She's already offered to advertise me in the school, but thank you.'

Abruptly, he recalled Barb telling them that her brother had begun seeing the writer of Happy Talk – and evidently she had become friendly enough with Barb, presumably through the brother, to share plans with her. George digested this.

'Can I tell you something else?' she asked then, hands wrapped around her mug.

He elbowed Barb's brother aside. 'Sure.'

She paused. 'I don't know if you'll remember, but you suggested that I try writing a book for children.'

He remembered. 'It did seem like a logical progression.'

'Yes … well, my editor at the paper thought so too, and I decided to give it a go. I haven't actually written a word yet though; I'm still working on the plot.'

'I'd love to hear your idea.'

'Honestly? You're not just being nice?'

'Not in the least' – so she told him of Polly, a young girl whose superhero parents saved the world every day instead of going out to normal jobs. 'But here's the thing – Polly wants to be a superhero too, just like her parents, even though she's only eight, or maybe younger, so the granny who lives with them tells her that all superheroes must start out by doing an act of kindness every day, because kindness has the power to change the world.' She laughed. 'It sounds corny when I say it out loud.'

He loved how enthusiastic she was, the child-like fervour that had crept into her voice when she'd spoken of her new sandwich-making enterprise, and again now as she was describing this book in the making. 'It doesn't sound corny at all, it sounds like the perfect message to give to little kids. You must write this story, Alice.'

'I'll certainly give it my best shot. I was thinking Deirdre might like to illustrate it – if it ever sees the light of day, I mean, and if I have any say in that side of it.' She bit into her toast, scattering crumbs, as he thought how wonderful that would be.

She couldn't believe she'd told him about the book. She hadn't planned to tell anyone until she had it down on paper, and then she was going to ask Val, and only Val, to read it and see what she thought – and at the first opportunity, she'd blurted it out to George. He was easy to talk to, that was why – and he approved of the sandwich-making idea. He didn't think it was inappropriate for a woman her age.

He seemed to approve of the book too. You must write it, he'd said, and now she was determined. And maybe she'd ask him to read it too. He was a teacher, in tune with young minds. He should be good to advise.

She wondered what William would think of her writing a book for children.

Time passed. He made a fresh pot of tea, and another round of toast. 'What do your parents do in Italy?' he asked.

'They own a vineyard, and they operate a little wine bar. I was on my way to visit them when I met you in the airport.'

'What's the Italian for George?'

'Giorgio.'

'Giorgio,' he repeated, but it didn't sound half as good when he said it.

She told him about the hens that laid his eggs. 'I look after them. They're the closest thing to pets I ever had. They're full of character.'

He told her about Jack arriving home with Oscar. 'His owner had died, one of Jack's clients.'

'Would it be a black cat, by any chance? From the house Claire's living in now?'

'Yes.' He looked surprised.

'Kate told me about it. She knew the old man. Her house is just across the road.'

'Ah yes, I'd forgotten you used to live there.'

'Still am.'

'I thought you were moving out, the night you met Claire?'

She shook her head. Should she explain? Suddenly she wanted to. 'I was to move in with someone. A man' – giving a small laugh – 'Barb's brother, actually, but … I realised that it wasn't the right thing to do. You needn't mention it to her, George. I mean, she knows about us splitting up, but I wouldn't like her to think I'd been talking about it.'

'Of course. I'll say nothing.'

'I never saw the black cat, just heard about it. Where is it now?'

'Still with us. Jack was going to bring it to the animal welfare place, but Suzi begged me to let her keep it. It's at the other house this week; it's going to split its time between here and there.' He ran a finger down one cheek. 'You can't see it any more, but it left its mark on me last weekend when I was getting it into the carrier.'

'Oh, no. I like cats though. Is it a he or a she?'

'Funny you should ask.'

He grinned. He had such a nice grin.

He told her about his mother's wedding to John in March. 'The night before, I asked her if she had her something old, something new stuff sorted, and she said the something old was herself, and the something borrowed was me, to walk her up the aisle.'

'What were her new and blue things?'

'A new husband, and blue flowers, sort of giant daisies, in her bouquet. It came from Aldi.'

'She sounds so sweet. I wish I'd met her.'

She told him about Liz and Emmet, the couple whose house she'd shared in Dublin, and their recent loss. 'I'm driving there this afternoon,' she said. 'I'm staying the night with them.' She glanced at her watch, and was amazed to see how much time had passed. 'I need to get moving: I have a Happy Talk interview lined up before I hit the road.'

She didn't want to leave.

He didn't want her to go.

At the door she pointed across to the gym. 'I should have been at Pilates,' she said, 'instead of eating toast.'

He remembered Kate telling him Alice was a member. 'I've joined too,' he said. 'I usually just do a circuit of the machines and lift a few weights, but I tried out a Pilates class a few months back. It was not a good idea.'

'Oh, my God – I was there.' She laughed. 'I remember you.'

'I cannot believe you're laughing at me,' he said, doing his best to look offended. They'd been in the same room without realising it.

'I'm sorry,' she said. 'I'm being very cruel. You were so out of your comfort zone though,' and she went right on laughing, and he thought he might as well join in.

'Thank you for breakfast,' she said. 'I really enjoyed it.' She put out a hand, and he took it, glad that shaking hands was finally back in fashion. 'Goodbye, George. So nice to meet you – I mean properly. Officially.'

'Bye, Alice. Likewise. Don't be a stranger.'

She walked away. She reached the gate and put a hand on it, knowing he was still at the door, not having heard it close. He'd text, she thought, or maybe he'd phone her, because he had her number: she'd included it in her first email to him. He'd wait a day or two – or possibly longer, knowing she'd just broken up with someone – and then he'd be in touch. He'd suggest lunch, or maybe dinner, and she'd say yes. That was how it would play out. That was how they would start – because over the time she'd spent at his kitchen table, she'd slowly arrived at the realisation that they were going to become something important together. For some reason, she was absolutely certain of it.

'Alice.'

She turned to see him advancing down the path towards her. He wasn't going to wait after all. Like her, he wanted things to begin.

She smiled.

A year later, give or take

Happy Talk

Accounts of everyday joy by Alice O'Mahony

Editor: This week, just for a change, we are delighted to hijack the column in order to feature its usual writer Alice O'Mahony with some very happy news of her own. As you read this, Alice (32) will be honeymooning in Florence, Italy, with her new husband, local teacher George Murphy (35), the couple having tied the knot on Wednesday in the vineyard part-owned by Alice's parents in the south of Italy. Our photo shows the bride and groom with their trio of bridesmaids, George's daughter Suzi (13) and Alice's nieces Milly (10) and Flora (7), matron of honour Tina Brennan and best man Jack Garrihy. Interestingly, both best man and groom featured in separate Happy Talk stories last year, before Alice had made the acquaintance of either man. Jack, a carer, contributed to a story about a ninetieth birthday party being organised for Tom Moriarty, one of his charges, by Tom's wife Maura, and George in turn gave a quote when a talented student in his sixth class, Deirdre Daly, won an art competition with her wonderful painting of a horse. To jog readers' memories, we're reproducing the accounts that Alice wrote on each of those stories below, along with the picture that accompanied the piece on Deirdre, and a more recent snap of Maura and Tom in their beautiful garden.

In a further serendipitous twist (we promise we're not making any of this up), artistic Deirdre (14) is also the illustrator of *How to Change the World When You're Small*, Alice's debut picture book, which secured a deal last year with Allied Publishing, and which will be appearing in all good bookshops early next month. We were lucky enough to procure an advance copy, and we can confidently predict that this book delivers such a strong kindness message, along with beautiful watercolour illustrations, that it will become an essential bedtime story for all young children. 'We're so proud of our girl,' Deirdre's mother Louise told us when we contacted her, 'and so thankful to Alice for having faith in her.' Alice isn't the only one – we see great things ahead for this young artist.

In addition to being a writer of note (and currently drafting her second picture book), busy Alice was also the founder last year of A Bit of a Mouthful, the sandwich delivery enterprise that has proven such a success with local businesses that Alice is planning to expand, and will shortly be in search of one or two like-minded individuals to come on board.

Asked at the wedding how he had acquired such an accomplished wife, George told us that it was all down to his late mother. 'It's a long story,' he said, 'but she arranged for me to have eggs delivered every week, and Alice was the one who brought them. Mam's wish was that I would find a good woman – but I think even she'd be surprised that I managed to strike it so lucky with Alice.' And the bride, when asked if she had any wish of her own, replied that a room with a view in Florence would do her nicely. 'I've got everything else I wished for,' she told us. We're happy to report that she's since made contact to tell us that they are indeed enjoying a wonderful view of the city's famous Piazza della Signoria, so it looks like all of Alice's wishes have come true. She promises to be back in two weeks with a new Happy Talk column, so do keep your joyful stories coming in to us.

Alice lowered the paper that Val had posted to Italy. She was curled into the window recess, like Helena Bonham Carter in *A Room with a View*. She turned to regard her sleeping husband, the heat of Florence proving too much for him each afternoon. You don't mind? he'd asked on the first day. I just need an hour – and she'd told him no, she didn't mind, because while he slept she was content to look down at the beautiful square that had featured in so many films, and to enjoy the quiet bubbling happiness that lived within her now.

As she studied him, he opened his eyes. She watched him return slowly to consciousness, yawning and stretching. She saw the smile form when he registered her, and she loved him for the joy that was in it, the happiness in him that matched her own.

'Hello, my darling,' he said, his voice patchy from sleep.

'*Ciao, Giorgio*,' she replied, and left her window seat to kiss him, because he was irresistible.

Acknowledgements

A big thank you as ever to all who contributed to getting this book from first idea to last full stop:

All at Hachette Books Ireland, in particular Ciara Doorley and Joanna Smyth, the two I pester most often;

My invaluable and indefatigable agent Sallyanne Sweeney;

Copy-editor Hazel and proofreader Aonghus, both completely dependable;

Mags Hough, Caroline Moloney, Niamh Hough and Rachael Finucane, all of whom provided info when I came calling;

Last but absolutely not least, my parents and siblings, greatly supportive as ever.

And after the last *t* was crossed and the last *i* dotted, thanks to book bloggers for early reviews and spreading of the word, and thanks to anyone who's shared or retweeted my pre-book blather online – it hasn't gone unnoticed.

Thanks in particular to my faithful readers, without whom I would have gone belly-up years ago, and welcome to the newcomers – I hope I don't disappoint.

Roisin xx

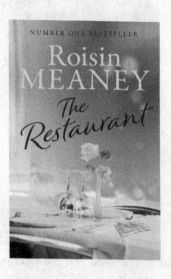

NUMBER ONE BESTSELLER

Roisin
MEANEY

The
Restaurant

When Emily's heart was broken by the love of her life, she never imagined that she would find herself, just two years later, running a small restaurant in what used to be her grandmother's tiny hat shop. The Food of Love offers diners the possibility of friendship (and maybe more) as well as a delicious meal. And even though Emily has sworn off romance forever, it doesn't stop her hoping for happiness for her regulars, like widower Bill who hides a troubling secret, single mum Heather who ran away from home as a teenager, and gentle Astrid whose past is darker than any of her friends know.

Then, out of the blue, Emily receives a letter from her ex. He's returning home to Ireland and wants to see her. Is Emily brave enough to give love a second chance – or wise enough to figure out where it's truly to be found?

Also available on ebook and audio

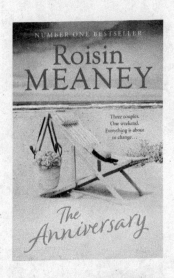

Roisin
MEANEY

Three couples.
One weekend.
Everything is about
to change…

The
Anniversary

It's the Bank Holiday weekend and the Cunningham family are escaping to their holiday home by the sea, as they've done every summer for many years.

Except that now, parents Lily and Charlie are waiting for their divorce papers to come through – and have their new partners in tow.

Their daughter Poll is there with her boyfriend and is determined to make known her feelings for Chloe, her father's new love. While her brother Thomas also has feelings for Chloe – of a very different nature …

And amid all the drama, everyone has forgotten that this weekend also happens to be Lily and Charlie's wedding anniversary.

Will any of the couples survive the weekend intact?

Also available on ebook and audio

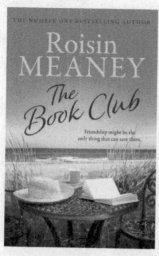

In the small seaside town of Fairweather, the local book club – a tight-knit group – is still reeling in the aftermath of a tragic accident.

Lil Noonan hasn't spoken a word since, and her grandmother Beth is worried that she plans to spend the rest of her life hidden away with only books for company. Beth, meanwhile, is trying to keep busy with the running of the local library and decides to make a fresh start by renting out her daughter's now-empty house to a newcomer in town.

Tom McLysaght tells the book club that he's eager to escape his high-flying life in London. Closer to the truth is that he's hiding a much bigger secret, one he can't escape from, no matter how hard he tries.

As the months pass and the book club continues to meet, Beth starts to open up to the idea that the future might still have some happiness to offer to her grand-daughter – and to her as well. But will they have the courage to reach for it? And will Tom trust them enough to reveal his secret?

Also available on ebook and audio